STARHEART

and other stories

David Spangler

STARHEART AND OTHER STORIES

Copyright © 2013 by David Spangler

Edited by Julia Spangler

Starheart Cover and Interior Illustration by Joshua McDonald
Leaf King and Franklin's Key Designs - Jeremy Berg
Interior Illustrations:
The Sidhe Who Came For Christmas - Joshua McDonald
Dragon's Ride - Joshua McDonald and Kaitlin Spangler

ISBN 10: 0-936878-65-7
ISBN 13: 978-0-936878-65-2

Spangler, David
Starheart and other stories / David Spangler

First Edition: December 2013

LorianPress
2204 E Grand Ave
Everett, WA 98201

Printed in the United States of America

0 9 8 7 6 5 4 3 2 1

www.lorian.org

Dedication

To Julie, John-Michael, Aidan, Kaitlin, and Maryn....
for whom these stories were originally written...

And to Story-Lovers everywhere!
May your Star-Hearts always burn brightly!

Contents

FOREWORD

Welcome to my imagination.

When I'm not writing books, articles or text for online classes about Incarnational Spirituality, I relax by writing stories. In particular, I've had a tradition for more than twenty years of writing a new story every Christmas which I give to family and friends. There is something about the dark of winter. the mystery of Christmas, the coming of a new year, and the rebirth of light with the Solstice that seems to invite wonder and magic, which I've tried to capture in my stories.

A few years ago, some of these stories were collected and published in an anthology, *The Story Tree*. This is a new collection of tales. Unlike the previous collection, only three of the stories here were written at Christmas time, and of these, only two, *The Sidhe Who Came For Christmas* and *Dragon's Ride*, relate in some way to the Holiday. The other two, *Franklin's Key* and *The Leaf King*, were originally written as birthday presents for my wife and my youngest daughter respectively.

For three years, I wrote Christmas novellas that paid homage to some of my favorite writers and fictional characters, such as Arthur Conan Doyle (Sherlock Holmes), Edgar Rice Burroughs (John Carter of Mars), and Stephen King with his masterful tales of ghosts and other creatures of the night. I sought to write in their style and in a manner that honored the imaginative worlds they created. *Dragon's Ride* is one of these stories, and my indebtedness to the Good Don, Professor J.R.R. Tolkien, will be obvious as you read it.

Starheart, the story from which this anthology takes its name, holds a special place in my own heart. For years, I've been working slowly on a novel, *Starshaman*, that is about a boy, Webster Graham, who discovers an ability to talk with the stars and in the process opens humanity to the hidden wonders of the universe. The novel has a ways to go yet, but *Starheart* is a spin off from it, a tale taking place in the same fictional universe as Webster's adventures but many years later.

In presenting these stories to you, I particularly want to acknowledge and thank my wonderful wife and partner, Julia. She has been an invaluable editor for my stories, and thanks to her excellent suggestions, they are all much better than they would have been otherwise. I also want to thank Joshua McDonald, Jeremy Berg, and my oldest daughter

Kaitlin for their wonderful work in creating covers for my Christmas stories each year. You can see their work in the interior illustrations of this collection, as well as on the cover itself.

My view of the world is that it is a wondrous and magical place, and my stories all reflect this perception in one way or another. Whether you agree with this assessment, I hope that these tales will let you live for a little while in such a universe and bring you enjoyment.

David Spangler
November, 2013

The
Leaf King

David Spangler

Mary studied the Monopoly board. "I need a ten to get safely past you, Grandpa," she said, eyeing the solid row of hotels stretching from St.Charles Place to New York Avenue from her temporarily safe perch visiting the Jail. Even the Electric Company and the Pennsylvania Railroad were owned by him. She closed her eyes and rolled the dice. "Come on," she said. She opened her eyes and scowled at the three and the five that looked back at her. "Tennessee Avenue. Drat!"

"And you owe me some rent, young lady!" her grandfather William said, holding out his hand. She had long ago learned that when she or her older brother Teddy played their grandfather, he made no allowances for the fact that they were kids, at least not since she had turned seven three years ago. "If you're IN the game," he would say, "you PLAY the game." At least he didn't gloat when he won like Teddy did.

But she wasn't out of the running yet. Her grandfather might own more properties, but she owned the big ones, Park Place and Boardwalk, plus the Yellows and Water Works. All her properties had hotels, except the Utility, of course. And his piece was currently sitting on North Carolina Avenue, only seven squares away from the biggest rent in the game.

He looked at her, grinning. "Figure I'll land on Boardwalk and you'll get your money back, don't you? Well, sorry, kiddo, but I'm going to roll double fours and land on GO. Then I'll roll a nine, buy Connecticut Avenue, and I'll have a monopoly of all the light Blues. You can concede then."

"In a pig's eye," she said. But inwardly she frowned. Her grandfather had an uncanny way of rolling just what he wanted.

The dice rattled across the table and came up two fours. Her grandfather chuckled, moved his piece to GO and took his two hundred dollars. Then, having rolled doubles, he rolled again. A five and a four. He grinned even wider as he put his piece down on top of Connecticut Avenue.

"Ah, Grandpa, you cheat!"

"When did you see me cheating?" he asked in a pained tone of voice, putting money in the bank and taking the deed to the property.

"You voodoo the dice or something!"

"Maybe I'm just lucky. Are you going to give up?"

She looked at the board. "If I roll a seven, I'll get the B & O Railroad, which will give me three railroads. If I roll a five, I'll get Indiana Avenue, which will give me two Red properties. No, I'll hang in. You haven't won yet."

"Actually, you're going to roll a three and land on Kentucky Avenue, which I own. More rent for me!"

"Grandpa, stop that!" She picked up the dice and held them, concentrating on getting the roll she wanted, not what her grandfather wanted. Suddenly, there was a prickly sensation in her arms, and she felt certain that a two and a one were precisely what she was going to roll. It was as if the dice had somehow heard her grandfather and had agreed to do what he wanted.

Oh no, you don't, she thought fiercely. *You don't listen to him. You listen to me. I want a seven.* She held her breath and rolled the dice. To her delight, it was a five and a two. "Ha!" she said, "You were wrong, and I've got another railroad!" She grinned at her grandfather across the board and was surprised to see a look of puzzlement and delight on his face.

"How did you do that?" he asked.

"Simple. I landed on the B & O square which no one owns, so I can buy it for my third Railroad."

"No, I mean, how did you roll a seven?"

"I just rolled it." She smiled at him, "And I told the dice what I wanted." *And told them not to listen to you,* she thought, but that sounded so silly, she didn't say it aloud.

"I see. Well, all right, young lady, I'm going to roll a six and a five and land on Free Parking. What's in the pot there? A couple hundred dollars?" They always played with the rule that all the fines in the game were paid into a fund that went to whoever landed on Free Parking. "But first, I'm going to put hotels on all my light blue properties."

She watched in dismay as he put the red hotels up on the three squares. Now he had three complete monopolies all in a row. It really did look bad. He was ahead for sure, which was a good reason for him not to get Free Parking as well. *Don't listen to anything he says,* she thought at the dice as she passed them over to him.

"Here comes a six and a five," he said confidently, shaking his hand and letting the dice fall out. It was a three and a two. "Well, I'll..." he said in surprise.

"Ha! Lost your dice magic, didn't you," she gloated.

He looked at her strangely. Then he smiled broadly. "Jinxed my dice, did you? Now who's cheating?"

"I'm not doing anything you weren't doing, Grandpa," she said smugly, reaching for the dice herself.

"I guess not. And that's got me wondering..."

But Mary didn't find out what her grandfather was wondering about, for at that moment her budgie Kiwi began trilling loudly from its cage against the wall where the dining room merged into the living room. Her grandfather turned to the bird and said, "And what's got you all excited?"

"Oh," Mary said. "Kiwi's hungry. He wants a treat." She paused and listened to the budgerigar's chirping. "And I think he heard Mrs. Jin, the neighbor's cat, in the bushes outside."

"Really?" asked her grandfather. "How do you know all that?"

"Oh, she and Kiwi have been talking together ever since she raised him," said another voice. They both turned as Susan Hamilton, Mary's mother, came into the dining room where they were playing. "So, how's it going, you two?" she asked.

"We're having fun, Mom." Mary said. "I'm unjinxing Grandpa's jinxed dice."

"Are you now?" Her mother looked at her daughter. "And how are you doing that?" She raised an eyebrow at her father, who shrugged.

"That," he replied, "is what we were about to explore."

"Well, it will have to wait. You said you were going to clean your room before Brian came over. He's coming in an hour or so, so you'd best get started. "

Mary frowned. "Ah, Mom, we're in the middle of a game here, and I'm winning!"

Her grandfather laughed. "Excuse me? Who's the one with the most hotels on the board?"

"And who's the one who can keep you from jinxing the dice?" she shot back.

"We'll have to see about that! But we can finish the game later. You've got your chores, and I do, too. I promised your mother I'd rake the leaves in the backyard before the game starts." He looked at his watch. "And that's only an hour from now. I'd better get started."

"Oh, you don't need to worry about that, Dad," his daughter said. Jack can do them when he gets home."

"No, no. I want to do it," he said. He got up from the dining room table and stretched. "Some physical exercise will do me good after all this sitting!"

"Well, if you'd enjoy it." Susan turned to her daughter. "As for you, little Miss Mary, let's go to your room and see what needs doing"

"All right, Mom. I'll beat you later, Grandpa!" Mary and her mother headed down the corridor towards the bedrooms.

"In a pig's eye," he called after her. Then, looking down, he picked up the dice and rolled them around thoughtfully in his hand. "Two threes," he whispered to them and dropped them onto the table. They bounced and rolled and came up two ones. They lay there like two square eyes looking at him, and he thought he heard a faint trill of laughter way off in a distance. "Hmmm," he said to himself, glancing down the corridor where his daughter and granddaughter had just disappeared. Then he went to the closet to get his wool hat, scarf and coat.

Forty-five minutes later, he removed his hat. It was cold, but the wool as well as the work was making his head sweat. He thought of leaving the hat off. He'd never been one to abide cold ears. "Keep my ears warm," he often said, "and the rest of me will be just fine." But there was no wind, and the sun was out in a cloudless sky as blue as his first son's eyes. He figured his ears would survive a minute or two in the open air.

His breath puffed out around him. Looking around, he caught his reflection in the glass of the sliding French doors that led into the kitchen from where he stood in the backyard. A man of medium height and build, slightly stooped, wrapped in a brown winter coat and red scarf looked back at him, his full white hair askew from the blue pullover hat he held in one hand while the other held a leaf rake. His scalp itched from the sweat and the wool, so he massaged it vigorously, watching his twin in the window do the same. At least, he thought, at sixty-five he still had most of his hair, unlike his son-in-law Jack who was only thirty-eight and already almost as bald as an egg. A knobby egg. Hair or no hair, though, Jack was a good husband and father, which was what counted. And he had two great children.

This reminded him of Mary and their Monopoly game. It certainly seemed, he thought, that she had communicated with the dice. That and her attunement to her bird made him wonder if she, like he, was a Listener.

His reflection disappeared along with his thoughts as the glass door slid open and his daughter stuck her head out. Red hair glinted in the sunlight. "Almost game time, Dad," she said, pointing to the watch on her wrist for emphasis. "Come on in. I've got hot chocolate heating up."

He looked at the piles of leaves scattered around him in his son-in-law's back yard and scowled. There was still a lot to do. He knew he'd started the raking too late. But if he stopped now, any wind that might come up that night would scatter all the leaves again. "Be right there!" he replied.

He jammed the wool hat back down over his head and his ears and began vigorously dragging the tines of the rake across the grass, pulling more leaves towards him. The pile was building up. He just had to move the whole thing into the corner near the fence where the wind wouldn't reach it.

Snap! The rake suddenly broke in two in his hands as he put pressure on it to move the pile. He looked at the two pieces. The wood had rotted, he realized. He could probably fix it, but by the time he did that and finished raking up the pile, it could be as late as the second quarter into the game. He didn't want to be doing the leaves all over again tomorrow, but he didn't want to miss the game either.

He looked around. No neighbors were visible. Probably all the men were inside getting ready to watch football, and as for the women... well, who knew what they were all doing. He looked at the leaves still scattered about the lawn and the place by the fence where they had to go. Then he closed his eyes and began to Listen.

William Martin was a Listener. In southeastern Ohio where he grew up, right up against the Appalachia mountains, just about the oldest mountains on this continent and filled with the mysteries that gather around age, to be a Listener meant more than just opening up your ears and paying attention to what someone else was saying. Of course, that was a good beginning. Usually we spend so much time talking to ourselves in our heads that it's a wonder we ever hear what anyone else has to say at all, much less really understand it. Learning to be silent inside your own skull is the place to start if you want to really listen.

But a Listener has to do more than that. You've heard the expression, "He reads between the lines." Well, a Listener listens between the words to what is underneath and behind what someone might be saying. And they do more than that. They listen between and behind what's already between and behind. A really good Listener listens so deep that he or she can hear the words a tree says when it shakes its branches or that a bird says when it rustles its feathers or that the earth murmurs deep down where the lava flows, or even the jokes that stars share with each other across the vast deeps of space.

A great Listener, though, can hear some of the First Words of Creation, the words that everything else comes from. Not that he could speak them. No one can speak those First Words anymore, except perhaps the Archangels and beyond. But a great Listener can still hear them, and hearing them become one with everything around him. For when you really listen to anyone or anything, you slip into them and they into you. It's like you wear their skins for a time, enough to understand them and speak their language. Listening holds the power to communicate, and the truly great Listeners can communicate with anything.

William Martin was a great Listener. In the words of his grandfather who had been a Cunning Man, someone who understands the old mysteries of the mountains and as a result is part magical himself, listening was William's Knack. And when he wanted, deep within his own mind and heart, when he listened he could speak the language of anything. Like dice. Or leaves.

He stood there, letting his Knack take him into a stillness that dropped him into oneness with the world around him. And in his mind, he particularly Listened to the leaves upon the ground. He heard their memories of growing on the tree, their delight as the wind played with them, their longing to be with others of their kind, their loneliness and resignation at lying detached upon the ground. He felt what they felt, including the deeper sense of rightness that their time was now over and that by falling, they opened the way for new life to appear on the tree that had been their home.

But mostly he listened to their longing and memories. When he felt he knew what they felt, he spoke to them of being together again, of joining their former comrades in the great pile that was forming by the fence. He asked them if they would like to move and become part of that pile. And as a feeling of assent grew, he drew on his power as a Cunning Man and gave them energy. He stirred them and had them call to the magic that is in all things. He drew magic to himself and shared it with them. Like a cook calling friends to dinner, he invited the leaves to join the pile that awaited them. "Come home," he whispered to them. "Come home."

And in each leaf, the magic gathered. In each leaf, energy rose. In each leaf, yearning joined with power and a change began. All across the lawn, the leaves began to stir and move as if a breeze were blowing on them. They trembled. Some folded in on themselves and then stretched out, advancing a few inches like a worm. Some floated up into the air as if seeking the tree from which they had come, then fluttered back down as if tired by even so short a flight. Then they rose again, and again, like salmon leaping against gravity to seek their home.

The lawn was alive with movement as leaves crawled, humped, floated, and blew towards the pile next to the fence, landing on each other, crackling over each other, floating in-between each other. Orange sparks seemed to dance between them, playing over them, drawing them together. For a moment they were like a cloud of brown and yellow butterflies clustering by the fence. Then, with a sigh, they all settled. Only a few stragglers skittered across the grass toward the huge pile that now rested against the fence.

He smiled, holding the Power for a moment. That should do it, he thought. There was one more thing to do....

"Dad?" His daughter's voice rang out from inside the house. "Game's starting!"

He started and looked guiltily at the house. Had she seen what he'd done?. He didn't know what Susan would think of him working magic where anyone could see him. But this was such a small thing. If anyone had seen, William figured that person would assume he'd seen an odd gust of wind at work.

"On my way," he called back, feeling flustered.

He looked at his watch. He'd just make it! He turned and went into the house, not noticing that in the pile by the fence, an orange light still danced and played fitfully, a small bit of magic that had not been dispelled and showed no sign of going out.

****

"Ah, Mom," Teddy pleaded, holding an Xbox and a controller, connecting wires dangling to his feet. His friend Brian and his sister Mary stood beside him, game controllers in their hands as well. "Why can't we play our game in the living room?"

"You know why," his mother replied. "Your grandfather wants to watch his football game now. Besides, there's a TV downstairs. You can play your game there."

"Mom, it's not the same," said Mary. "This game is sooo much better on the bigger screen."

"Well, you'll just have to think small for awhile. Grandpa's our guest, and he gets the TV in the living room."

Teddy looked around. "But Grandpa's not here. Hasn't the game started? Maybe he's changed his mind."

His mother chuckled. "About a football game? You know your Grandfather better than that. He's been out raking leaves, but he'll be here any minute."

As if on cue, they all heard the back door opening. "Turn on the television!" a voice boomed out. "I'm on my way soon as I get my shoes off!"

"Well," said Teddy, "I guess we play downstairs."

"I have a better idea," said his mother. "It's a beautiful day today. I'd rather you play outside than look at screens all afternoon in a dark room downstairs."

"Is that an opinion, or an order?"

"What do you think, Theodore?" She smiled innocently, but using his given name was a dead giveaway that it was no opinion.

"Ah, Mom!" Teddy looked crestfallen. "Have a heart! I've been wanting to show Brian this new game for ages...."

"Then let's compromise. An hour outside in the fresh air, then you can play your game."

Mary piped up. "Listen, if Grandpa's been raking the leaves, I bet there are big piles out there. We can make leaf forts!"

"One big pile," said their Grandfather, walking into the living room and overhearing their conversation.. "It would make a perfect leaf fort. But if you scatter the leaves, you have to rake them back up! I don't want the wind blowing them to kingdom come and back after I've raked them all afternoon!"

"All right, Grandpa. We promise!" Mary looked at her brother and his friend. "Don't we?"

Teddy shrugged at Brian, holding his Xbox mournfully to his chest. "OK, I guess."

"Well, have fun, kiddos," said their grandfather, sitting himself down in a large, overstuffed chair and picking up the remote. The TV flickered to life, showing helmeted players running onto the field. "Ah, just in time," he sighed happily.

Five minutes later, Teddy, Mary and Brian trooped outside. Mary laughed when she saw the huge pile of leaves by the fence. "Wow! Grandpa was right! That really is a large pile. C'mon!"

"Ah, leaf forts are dorky," said Teddy, and Brian nodded. "I don't like leaf piles anyway. They're all scratchy and they make my skin itch afterwards for days!"

"So what else do you want to do?" Truth to tell, Mary would have preferred to play the new game as well, but she prided herself on being adaptable. If the situation changed, then so would she.

Teddy looked at Brian and grinned. "I think we should play 'Bury the Sister!'" He lunged and caught Mary by the arms. Brian hesitated, then laughed and grabbed for Mary's feet. "Hey!" she yelled. "Let go!"

"You like that pile of leaves so much, ve're going to bury you in it!" cackled Teddy in his best evil villain voice. "Ve vill feed you to the Leaf Gods!" Hoisting her up, he began to run towards the pile, Brian struggling to keep up and hold Mary's thrashing legs at the same time.

"Put me down!" shrieked Mary, trying to twist loose of the boys' hold, but not too hard, as she was secretly enjoying the game. Usually, Teddy and his friends just ignored her. The boys lurched across the lawn, trying to carry a squirming, laughing Mary without dropping her. When they got to the leaf pile, Teddy and Brian began to swing her back and forth. "On ze count of three!" yelled Teddy. "One! Two! Three! We gife you to ze Leaf God!"

They let go of her, and Mary soared squealing into the air. She crashed into the pile. But instead of an explosion of leaves as her body struck, she disappeared into the pile as if she had been thrown into a pool of water. A few leaves floated up like airborne ripples to mark the event, then settled down as if nothing had happened. Mary had disappeared.

"Wow!" breathed Brian. "That was cool! How deep is that pile?"

Teddy stood gaping at where his sister had landed. "Ah, she's just fooling us. She's burrowed underneath and is hiding."

"I don't see any movement, Teddy. She's lying awfully still."

"Yeah, well, she's having fun with us. Come on out, Mary, or we'll come in and get you!" he yelled.

There was no answer.

"Come on, Mary," he yelled again. "We'll jump on you if you don't come out!" The only response was stillness and silence.

"This is creepy, Teddy," Brian said. "It's like she's not there at all."

"Of course, she's there!" Teddy replied, ignoring the shiver that had just run up and down his spine. "Come on, let's jump on her!" With that, he threw himself forward onto the pile of leaves, seeing out of the corner of his eye Brian following him. He landed in the scratchy, crackly leaves, and began to thrash around with his feet. Brain, lying prone atop the leaves was digging in with his hands. But after a few minutes of searching, which saw the large pile demolished and its contents scattered back onto the lawn, there was no sign of Mary.

"Where'd she go?" asked a bewildered Brian.

Teddy, who was feeling both anger and reluctant admiration at how his little sister had pulled off this disappearing trick, shrugged. "I don't know. Somehow she got past us without our seeing her. I bet she's back in the house."

"Yeah. So what do we do?"

Teddy looked around. "Well, if we don't want to catch it from my Mom, we'd better put this pile back in order. Then we're going to go in and play my new game, and little Miss Smart-Pants can just forget about playing with us for what she's put us through." As he and Brain began to work, though, the worrisome thought crossed his mind that perhaps there were Leaf Gods and he really had just sacrificed his sister to them.

****

The game was over. William Martin looked at his watch. "Jack should be coming home soon from his shift at the hospital, right? Well, let me do dinner tonight," he said. "It's the least I can offer for your hospitality." He got up from the chair. Crumbs, the remnants of their half-time snack of crackers and cheese, were all over his sweater. He brushed them carefully into his hand.

Susan got up with him. "You don't have to do that, Dad." She paused and grinned, giving him a hug. "On the other hand, yes, you do, for I love your cooking!" Her father could have been a master chef at any gourmet restaurant, but he cooked for the joy and relaxation of it. He would have hated doing it as a profession. "But I can help!"

"No, you just relax. I'm not planning anything elaborate," he said heading into the kitchen," but if you have any ground beef, I'll make us some chili. I bet the kids would love that."

"That they would. Let's check the freezer and see. I'm sure I have some."

Her father went to a drawer and pulled out an apron. "Speaking of the kids, where are they? I especially thought Mary would be back wanting to finish our Monopoly game."

"Oh, I heard them come in and go downstairs awhile ago. They're probably playing Teddy's new video game."

"That's right. I kept them from using the big TV screen as I recall."

"They'll have plenty of chances when you go back home, Dad," Susan replied, her head in the freezer as she examined wrapped packages of food. "Here it is!" She pulled out something wrapped in white inside a freezer bag that said "Ground Meat" on the outside.

"Actually, they can play upstairs while I'm here. I'd be interested in seeing what the fuss is about." He reached into a drawer and pulled out a folded apron that he proceeded to put on.

"Teddy would love to show you," Susan replied, reaching into a large stone jar and pulling out a couple of onions.

"What would I love to show Grandpa?" came a thirteen-year old voice from the doorway as Teddy walked into the kitchen.

His grandfather turned and gave him a hug. "Your new video game… upstairs on the big TV."

"Hey! Sure, Grandpa! It's really cool! You want me to set it up now?"

William grinned. "No. Right now, I'm going to cook my famous down home Applach'a Chili, so hot even the devil himself can't abide in you once you eat it."

Teddy grimaced. "Gee, I don't know. If it's *that* hot…"

His grandfather laughed. "Don't worry about it. You'll love it."

His mother looked up from chopping one of the onions. "So where's Mary? And Brian?"

Teddy reached for an apple lying in a fruit bowl on the counter. "Brian had to go home. I don't know where Mary is." He took a bite of the apple. "Haven't seen her since she did her little disappearing act."

"Disappearing act?" asked his mother. She felt the tiniest ripple of concern. It wasn't like her daughter to do disappearing acts.

"Yeah. We were playing in the leaf pile like you said. Brian and me…"

"Brian and I," corrected his mother.

"Right. Brian and I threw her in. Then we couldn't find her."

"Couldn't find her?" asked his grandfather. He arched an eyebrow, a signal to anyone who knew him that his curiosity was being engaged.

"That's right, we couldn't find her. She sank into that leaf pile like it was water or something." He took another bite of apple and began chewing.

"And then what? For heaven's sakes, Teddy, tell me the story."

"Then nothing, Mom. That's what I'm saying. Somehow she tricked us and got out of that leaf pile without our seeing her." A look of admiration passed over his face. "Man, I'd sure like to know how she did that, too!"

"You looked for her in the pile?" William asked, his cooking chores all but forgotten. Now he was beginning to feel a premonition of trouble.

"Sure. We tore it apart, Brian and me. Then we had to clean it all up again so you wouldn't be mad at us. We figured she'd come back inside, so we came in too."

"And you didn't look for her?"

Teddy look askance at his mother. "Why should we have done that? Brain and I," he emphasized the I, "had my new game to play. Besides, I was mad at her, that's for sure."

"But didn't she want to play the game with you?" asked Susan. The little ripple of concern was beginning to widen.

"Sure, Mom. But if she'd tried, I'd have told her she couldn't play with us anyway after the stunt she pulled."

Susan looked at her father. "Maybe she's in her room. I'll go check."

Teddy watched his mother leave the kitchen. "What's the big deal?" he asked. "Mary'll turn up." He took another bite of apple.

"Hmmm," hummed his grandfather. Normally he wouldn't have been concerned. He had no doubt Mary could handle herself. But he'd invoked some magic earlier. It hadn't been a lot, but anytime magic's flowing, odd things can happen. He looked at Teddy. "Have you told me everything?"

"Sure, Grandpa. What else is there?"

"I don't know, Teddy. I just have a feeling. Can you go over your story again? The three of you were playing in the leaves and....and then what? Can you remember exactly?"

Teddy threw away the apple core. He thought for a bit. "Well, actually, we hadn't started playing in the leaves yet. Mary wanted to make a leaf fort, but Brain and me...I...we wanted to do something else."

"Like play your new video game, I bet."

"Yeah, that's right. But Mary insisted, so we grabbed her and threw her into the leaf pile."

"You threw her in?"

"Yeah. Grandpa, why are you looking at me like that? What's going on?"

"That's what I'd like to know," said Susan, who had come back into the kitchen. "Far as I can tell, Mary's not in the house anywhere."

"Well, maybe she went over to Rachel's or Casey's house, Mom."

"No, she wouldn't have done that without telling me first."

William drew up a kitchen stool and sat down facing Teddy, who was rubbing his hands and glancing between the two adults. "What's the big deal? Mary's got to be around here. Where else would she be? I bet she's still hiding. Maybe she was hoping we'd try to find her and she fell asleep somewhere. Did you look under her bed?"

His grandfather waved away Teddy's words. "Teddy, tell me again what happened when you threw her into the leaf pile. You said she sank into it?"

"Yeah, like it was water or something. Or like the pile was just a cloud of leaves and she fell right through them."

His grandfather sighed and closed his eyes, trying to remember all that he had done. But it had been such a simple thing. He had asked the leaves to go to the pile, that's all.

"Dad, what is it?" His daughter's voice held a distinct note of anxiety. He waved her to be silent. He Listened to his memories. *I asked them to go to the pile*, he thought. Then he remembered. *No, I didn't. I asked them to go home. I invited them home. But still....*

With absolute clarity, he remembered. He had been holding the Power. The leaves were in the pile. He had been inviting them home. Then his daughter had called to him and he'd felt guilty. He'd jumped. In his haste to hide what he was doing he had committed the simplest of mistakes, one that no Cunning Man should ever commit. He had forgotten to thank the forces and close the magic down. He had left the Power running.

But it had been such a little bit of Power....

He reached out and gripped Teddy's arm, who jumped in surprise at the strength in that grip.

"Ow, Grandpa...!" Teddy tried to pull away.

"Dad, what are you doing...?" Susan reached for her dad's arm, alarmed.

He ignored them both. He summoned and poured a little bit of Listening magic into his grandson and into the room around him. "Teddy, this is very important. You must remember. Listen to your memory. Did you say anything when you and Brian threw Mary in the leaf pile? Anything at all?"

The room went still. They might have been suspended in time, far out in space, farther than sound could reach them. Teddy screwed up his features, remembering. Then his face cleared.

"What did you say, Theodore?"

"It was just playing, Grandpa. I pretended I was an evil villain, and Brian and me...I..."he glanced at his mother, but she was beyond paying attention to the niceties of grammar at that point, "were going to sacrifice Mary."

William's voice grew very soft and grave. "Sacrifice her!"

"Honest, Grandpa, we were just playing. Mary was laughing. We weren't going to hurt her or anything. It was part of the game. We carried Mary to the leaf pile and when I threw her in, I said 'We gife you to ze Leaf God!' It was a corny joke, honest!"

His grandfather slumped back, letting go of Teddy. He buried his face in his hands.

Susan pulled Teddy to her, putting one arm protectively around him. "For heaven's sake, Dad, you're scaring him. And me, too! What's going on? What's happened to Mary?"

Then a scowl crossed her face. Putting her son behind her, she stood in front of her father. "Dad, have you been doing your Cunning Man thing today? Have you exposed my children to your magic?"

William looked up at her, hearing the anger in her voice. He nodded. "I didn't mean to. But yes, Susan. I did. And for no purpose other than my own convenience. It's my fault entirely. I made the most elemental of mistakes."

Seeing the stricken look on her father's face, Susan felt the anger drain away. But the fear that replaced it was worse. "Tell me what happened."

"I had broken the rake, and you had called to tell me the game was starting. Rather than take the time to fix the rake and finish the raking, which would make me miss part of the game, I used my Knack to invite the leaves to move into the pile by themselves."

Teddy's eyes grew wide. "You used real magic, Grandpa?"

"Shush, Theodore." She silenced him with a gesture. "You magicked the leaves to move into a pile by themselves?"

William nodded.

"But that doesn't seem so bad. I've seen you do far more powerful things when I was growing up."

"It was only a little thing, but I made a mistake. I forgot to seal off the magic. I didn't finish what I'd begun. You called me, and I got befuddled. I didn't want you to know what I'd done. And that damn game was starting. I came into the house without properly thanking the powers and closing down the energy."

"You mean, you left the magic running? Dad, how could you?"

He hung his head. "I made a mistake, like I said. I'm no Cunning Man, but an old fool."

Teddy, hopping with excitement, thrust his body forward from behind his mother. "You mean you did real magic, Grandpa? You're like a wizard or something? Like in Dungeons and Dragons?"

"Teddy," Susan said, exasperation and fear giving her voice a sharp edge. "Be quiet. This is important! So, Dad, what does this mean? What kind of power was it?"

"Just a minor thing, Susan. Nothing that could or should have hurt Mary, or anyone. There was no sharpness in it, only flowing."

"Then what happened to Mary? Where's my daughter?" Susan's voice went up a notch.

"I only invited the leaves to go home. That was my mistake. I meant the pile of course, but I used the word *home*."

"Dad, I don't know what this means. I don't have your Knack. What does this mean?"

"It means the magic I left running in the leaf pile opened a portal to Leafhome."

"Leafhome?" said Teddy. "You mean, like another dimension, Grandpa. That's so cool!"

"Teddy!"

"Yes, Teddy, another dimension. And when Mary went through, it used up the magic that was left. That's why you and Brian didn't go through as well."

"Bummer! Mary always gets the good field trips! But Grandpa, you can use your magic and take me there, too, can't you?"

"Teddy, I'm warning you. Be quiet. This isn't one of your computer games." Susan reached out and gripped her father's arm. "Dad, where is Mary?"

Her father sighed. "Given the time of year, Leafhome will most likely be the Autumn Country."

Susan paled. "The Autumn Country! No…"

"I'm afraid so. The Country of Falling Leaves. The country of death."

Susan's grip on her father tightened, but his face showed no sign of the pain it caused. "Dad, you're a Cunning Man. One of the best. You can get her back, can't you? You must get her back right now!"

He looked helplessly at his daughter. "It's not as easy as it sounds. It's not like she just blundered in and doesn't belong there. Remember what Teddy said. 'We give you to the Leaf God.' These beings are often quite literal. The Leaf King may feel she is his."

Though his mother had asked him to be quite, Teddy couldn't help himself. "You mean there really is a Leaf God? No joke?"

William looked at him sadly. "No joke, Teddy. And you've given him your sister."

"Cool!"

****

When Mary woke up in the morning, she liked to keep her eyes closed and just feel back into her body. She would stretch under the covers and feel the warm coziness of her blankets and the mattress beneath her. Then, her eyes still closed, she liked to listen to the sounds around her, trying to identify what she heard, picturing in her mind what was happening. She called it "seeing with her ears." Then, she would open her eyes to see if she was right.

This time Mary woke and as she stretched, she immediately knew something wasn't right. Instead of a soft mattress under her and warm blankets over her, she was surrounded with sharp, dry, uncomfortable things that rustled, crinkled and snapped as she moved. And everything was quiet, except for the noise she was making. Her eyes closed, she lay absolutely still, listening. There was nothing. No bird song, no soft breeze sounds in the trees, no footsteps or voices of her family, no creaking of floors. She realized immediately she wasn't in her bed.

Where was she?

Keeping her eyes closed, she felt around. Her fingers touched what she recognized as leaves. Leaves?

Then she remembered. She was outside in the leaf pile Grandpa had raked up. Teddy and Brian had thrown her into it. But why was everything so quiet? And why did she feel as if she was waking up from a long, deep sleep? Had she hit her head and knocked herself out? Had Teddy and Brian gone for help? Had she injured her head and gone deaf?

She opened her eyes. Since she was lying on her back, the first thing she saw was blue sky without a cloud anywhere to be seen. Then she saw the bare branches of trees above her. Several trees. More trees than were in her backyard.

She sat up and gasped. Everywhere she looked, there were bare trees. Her house was nowhere to be seen. In fact, the whole neighborhood had disappeared. She was in a forest of bare trees, and all around her as far as she could see, there was a carpet of fallen leaves.

Red leaves, brown leaves, russet leaves, burgundy leaves, yellow leaves, scarlet leaves, golden leaves, orange leaves, large leaves, small leaves, piles and piles and piles of leaves.

"I'm dreaming," she said out loud. Her voice sounded faint and almost non-existent in the presence of the silence around her. So much silence. So many leaves.

Strangely she did not feel afraid. If this was a dream—and it couldn't be anything else—it didn't appear frightening. Nothing was threatening her. She was alone, but she was often alone in her dreams.

But what was she doing dreaming in the middle of the day? Maybe she had been knocked out when Teddy and Brian tossed her into the leaf pile. Maybe she was unconscious. She'd never been unconscious before, but she assumed it was like being asleep.

She thought back. She remembered the two boys carrying her across the lawn, she remembered laughing and struggling in their grip, she remembered them tossing her into the air, and then….

It had been like falling into a cloud, a brown, orange, red, and yellow cloud. It had surrounded her. After that, she remembered nothing until a moment ago when she woke up.

If I am awake, she thought, *which obviously I can't be, otherwise I'd be lying in the leaf pile, seeing Teddy and Brian laughing and the house on the other side of the yard behind them.*

Whoever heard of falling asleep like that, between one moment and the next, especially while being thrown into a leaf pile? *I must have hit my head on something. I must really be unconscious.*

She pulled herself free of the leaves and stood up. "Hello!" she shouted. "Anybody here?" There was no reply. The silence was so deep that her words seemed to fall at her feet as soon as they left her mouth. She turned around several times, but the trees and the leaves were the same in all directions.

Well, she thought, *it's a strange dream, but I might as well enjoy it and go exploring. I'll probably be waking up soon.* It didn't seem to matter what direction she went in, so she struck out, kicking and scrambling through the leaves. She quickly discovered that they were piled in different depths. Sometimes they only seemed to come up to her ankles while a few steps further on, she would find herself wading through leaves up around her thighs. She laughed as she went and began to kick the leaves about as she walked. Her mother called this *skibbling.* "Wow, Mom," she said out loud, "I wish you were in this dream with me. This place is the skibbling capital of the universe!" She began to skip, kicking great piles of leaves up into the air before her.

"Stop that...." The voice was as dry and crackly as the leaves themselves. It seemed to come from all around her.

Startled, Mary stopped. She looked around. There was no one in view. "Who are you?" she called back. "Where are you?" Her questions were met by the same silence as before.

"Show yourself!" she yelled, spinning around. Nothing happened. No one appeared. *Well, that's the way it is in dreams, isn't it?* she thought. She resumed skibbling through the leaves.

"Stop that...." The voice came again.

"Who are you?" Mary yelled, once more looking about in vain to see who was speaking to her. "I can't see you." Again, silence was the only response. She stomped her foot, and leaves rose about her. "Listen! This is my dream, and I demand to see you."

She sensed rather than saw movement behind her. She spun around. The leaves were trembling and undulating, as if they were floating on ripples of water rather than on dry land. She jumped back. For the first time, she felt a slight shiver of fear along her spine. Something under the leaves seemed to be moving towards her, the leaves crackling and snapping as it came.

She turned and ran, bounding and leaping through the leaves. *I'm not really afraid,* she told herself over the sudden pounding of her heart, *but why should I just stand there and let something I can't see under the leaves come and get me?*

As she ran and leaped, however, the leaves got deeper in front of her and pressed against her, slowing her down, as if she were running against a wave rising from an ocean. All around her, there was the increasing noise of leaves rubbing against leaves, like old men whispering, louder and louder.

She stumbled and fell forward. The leaves before her crested over her like a wave and fell upon her, partly burying her. Sputtering, she struck out, feeling their dry, brittle substance crumbling in her hands as she fought to get to her feet.

"Stop that..."came the voice again, this time from behind her. On her knees, she flopped over so she could see who or what it was.

A whirlwind of leaves was rising above her, the leaves spiraling up and around high above her head. About seven feet above her, two bright, crimson leaves with black veins running through them hung motionless in the swirl, peering down at her like bloodshot eyes.

"Who are you?" she gasped.

"Leaf." The voice of the apparition sounded ancient and hoarse.

"Leaf? That's your name?"

"Leaf," the being repeated. It seemed to bend towards her. "You must stop."

Mary stood up and brushed leaves off her jacket. "Stop what?"

"Stop being...what you are."

"What I am? What do you mean?"

"You are noisy. You disturb our silence. You disturb us with your movement. You must stop this."

Mary laughed. "You want me to stop skibbling? You don't like my skibbling?"

"Disrupting us, yes. You must stop. Sit. Be still."

"You want me to just sit down."

The whirlwind seemed to tilt towards her as if the being were nodding its assent.

"OK, I'll sit." She fell back into the leaves and crossed her legs under her. "Now what? How long should I sit here?"

"Forever."

Mary blinked in surprise. "Forever? You mean I should just here and not move at all forever?"

"Forever," Leaf repeated.

Mary laughed again. "You are the strangest dream I've ever had, but then I've never been knocked unconscious before."

The crimson leaf-eyes came together as if in a frown. "Dream? You are no dreamer. You are not here in dreambody. Dreambody would not disturb us. You are here in lifebody."

"Lifebody? What's that?"

The being was silent for a moment. "The body you live in when you do not dream. The body leaves live in before they fall to earth. The noisy body."

"Noisy body?"

"Listen."

In the silence, Mary listened. She heard her heart beating. She heard her blood flowing. She heard her breath moving in and out of her lungs. She even fancied she could hear herself thinking. Compared to the stillness around her, she realized she really was noisy.

"You mean my physical body," Mary replied. "Well, you're wrong. I was playing and was knocked unconscious, so my body is…well, asleep somewhere, only maybe it's deeper than being asleep, so you don't recognize that I'm in my…what did you call it…'dreambody.' Maybe when a person is unconscious their dreambody looks like their lifebody, and sounds like it, but I can't help that. You're still just a dream."

"No." Leaf sounded implacable.

Mary frowned. "Why do you keep saying that? This must be a dream. It can't be anything else. How could I really be here, wherever here is, talking to a bunch of leaves? Magic?"

"Yes." Leaf seemed to nod again. "Magic."

"Yeah, right," she scoffed. "You sound like Teddy. He's always playing these fantasy games and being a wizard. He would love being in this dream."

"No dream. Enough talking and making noise. Now you be quiet. Sit still."

Mary stood up. "No. I'm tired of talking with you, and I don't want to just sit. I want to go someplace different. I'm bored of this forest and all these leaves."

The whirlwind got larger, its leaves swirling faster. "No!" Leaf said. "You will sit here. You will stop disturbing the leaves. If you do not, I will cover you, and you will breathe no more. Then you will be still forever."

With that, the leaves around her rose up like a wall encircling here, higher and higher. As they trembled over her, threatening to fall, Mary knew if they did, they would bury her so deeply she might not be able to climb out. Then she really would, in Leaf's words, be still forever.

Except it was only a dream.

Wasn't it?

****

Susan's voice was grim as she spoke to her son. "Theodore, there's nothing cool about this. This is not a joke, not a fantasy, not a game. Your grandfather has a Knack, a talent for making magic. It runs in the family. He used that talent today and made a mistake. The consequence is that your sister is now in another world and may be in great danger. It's the same as if she had been kidnapped."

Teddy thought about this. "And it's my fault?" he asked. "Because of what I said?"

"No, Teddy, it's not your fault. It's mine," said his grandfather. "I used magic to draw the leaves into a pile, but I didn't make sure everything was back to normal. I left magical energy still active in the leaf pile itself. I made a stupid mistake. You were only playing when you inadvertently set the magic off." He looked at his daughter. "Which may be to our advantage. Magic is powered by intent, and Teddy had no intent to give his sister to the Leaf King. For him, it was an innocent joke. Thus, no bonds may have been created."

Susan sighed. "Thank god for that."

"But wait, Grandpa. You're saying that I may have made a bargain with this Leaf King. If so, shouldn't I have asked for something in return? I didn't ask for anything, so it wasn't really an exchange. If the Leaf King did take Mary, it has no hold on her. It's like she's on loan or something, so we can ask for her back."

William smiled. "That's very smart, Teddy. All those fantasy games your mother says you play have taught you something, haven't they? You do have a sense of how magic works. But there's nothing in the rules that says you can't just make a gift, expecting nothing in return. You're right. It may give us a bargaining chip if we need one, but we can't count on it."

"But who is this Leaf King anyway? Some kind of nature god?"

"It's a powerful nature spirit, yes, one who looks after all leaves everywhere on all the trees all over the world. It uses its magic and energy to power and care for leaves through the cycle of their lives, from an invisible potential within the tree to being a bud, a full leaf, and then the final stage, when the leaf turns into color, lets go of the tree, and falls to the ground. Then it gives its substance back to the earth, which in turn becomes food for the roots of the tree."

"A cycle of life," said Susan.

"Exactly. All the great nature spirits govern and serve these cycles that make life possible."

"That doesn't sound so bad. How is Mary in danger, Grandpa, aside from being in some other dimension?"

"That's quite enough in itself, Teddy. But in this case, this is the time of year when leaves fall, and the leaves in the pile outside are all in the dying, falling and decaying part of their cycle. So that is the part of the Leaf King's world that Mary will go to."

"The 'Autumn Country you called it?"

"Yes, Teddy. And the governing rule of that place is death."

Susan began pacing. "We've been talking long enough. Dad, we've got to do something now before it's too late."

"I know, and I've been thinking about it. The problem will be finding Mary. The realm she's in is at least as large as our own world and probably larger. Space and time are different there than they are here. The first thing I should do is go out to the leaf pile and listen to it. Perhaps it can tell me just where Mary is. I may even be able to open it and bring her back."

"Oh, Dad, wouldn't that be dangerous?"

"A little, but I've been a Cunning Man for many years. I have some experience walking between the worlds, as you know. Besides, I have allies who can help me. I think I can bring her back."

"But what if the Leaf King says no, Grandpa? What if he decides to keep her?" Teddy asked.

"Then we'll deal with that when we know." He gave Teddy's head a playful rub. "Don't worry, kiddo. We'll get Mary back."

Putting actions to their words, the three of them put on their coats and jackets and went out to the backyard. There the pile lay against the fence, looking like an ordinary collection of leaves.

"You two stay back a bit," said William, "just in case." Then he walked forward until the tips of his shoes were just touching the leaf pile. He relaxed the tension in his shoulders and started to Listen.

Deeper and deeper he went into his Listening place. He passed through layer after layer of awareness, from hearing the lives of the small creatures in the grass around him, to hearing the life within the trees and plants, to hearing the life within the earth. He turned his Listening towards the realms of spirit beyond the physical world and specifically towards Leafhome, the realm of the Leaf King whose life nourished and served all the leaves in the world.

He heard nothing.

No matter how deeply he tried to Listen, there was only silence. It was like a bubble had been thrown around the leaf pile and all the routes into Leafhome. It was like running into a wall. It was like becoming deaf.

"Fiddlesticks," he muttered.

"What is it, Dad?" asked Susan anxiously a few steps behind him, her arm around Teddy.

He came out of his Listening and turned to her. "I can't get my Knack to work. It's like there's a wall of silence between me and where I want to go. I don't understand it. I've never experienced this before, except..."

"Except what, Dad?"

"Except once...a long time ago. But that's not possible."

"What isn't possible? Tell me, for heaven's sake!" Susan stepped forward and clutched his arm. "Is it something about Mary?"

"Maybe. I don't know." He smiled at her. "It's probably nothing. Or if it is something, it's nothing we can do anything about right now."

"You're not going to tell me what it is, are you? You're going to pull your inscrutable Cunning Man thing on me, aren't you, Dad."

"Susan, if I were sure, I'd tell you. I'm not trying to conceal anything, trust me. I just don't have enough information yet. But what I do know is that something is blocking me from Listening in to where Mary is."

"So what can you do about it? Can you get past that block?"

"Maybe. But it would take time we may not have. There's a faster way. We can speed things up if we use your Knack, Susan."

"You mean, Mom's magical, too?"

"Hush, Teddy. How can I help, Dad? It's been a long time since I've done anything like this. You know I've never been much into the Cunning Man, Wise Woman scene."

"That probably won't matter. I'm a Listener, as you know, and you're a Seer. But more importantly, you're her mother. There is no bond stronger than that between a mother and her child. That bond is what we need now. If you use it to link with her, you will See where she is and that will pinpoint her for me to use my Knack to talk with her."

Susan nodded. "I'll try. I need to get my stuff," she said, and she ran ahead of them into the house.

"Gee, Grandpa, I'm sorry about Mary of course," Teddy said, barely able to contain his excitement as he and his grandfather walked back to the house, "but this is so exciting, you and Mom having magical powers. Does that mean I have magical powers, too? Do I have a Knack? I've always wanted to be a wizard."

His grandfather laughed. "I don't know, Teddy. You're at the age where Knacks begin to show up, if they're there. If you do have one, we should know in a year or two. Being part of this family, though, I wouldn't be surprised."

"Wow! Cool!"

"But Teddy," William said, as they entered the kitchen and sat down at the table, "having a Knack and the power it brings also brings responsibility. You can see what trouble can happen when magical talent is used unwisely. Even someone as skilled and experienced as I can still make a simple mistake. And the consequences can be dreadful, though I hope not in this case. We'll get Mary back, and all will be well. But let my mistake be a lesson you don't forget. There's a lot more to magic than just doing fun tricks or casting spells."

"I won't forget, Grandpa. But I wonder what my Knack will be?"

At that moment, his mother came into the kitchen as well, carrying a sketchpad and a handful of pencils. She joined her son and father at the table, and laid her sketchbook down, open to a blank page. She sat in silence for a moment. Her hands began to tremble. William reached over and put his hand on hers. "Don't strain, Susan. You can do it. Just let your Knack have room to work and go with it. Be what you see, and draw what you are. Let your Knack be your eyes."

She nodded. She took a few deep breaths, her eyes closed, her hands becoming still. Then she began to draw. Her hand moved quickly over the page, her fingers knowing exactly what to do even though her eyes were shut. As it did, a bleak, bare forest began to appear, all the trees denuded of leaves while the ground was nothing but a carpet of leaves.

"Part of The Autumn Country, for sure," her father muttered.

As she worked, the picture became more and more real, as if it wasn't just a picture at all but an actual window. They could feel the awful silence of the scene seeping into the kitchen, and with it came a sense of the ending of all things, the laying down of life, the quiet of the grave.

William, deep in his own Knack, made a gesture and uttered a couple of words. The feeling lifted and the room seemed brighter and livelier about them, but the picture stayed just as real.

"Where's Mary," asked Teddy in a subdued and quiet voice.

Without answering, his mother flipped the drawing over to a fresh blank page, her hand with the pencil moving faster than before. Once again, trees with naked branches began to take shape, with leaves around them on the ground. But this time it was like they were looking down from a height, as if they were up in one of the trees. To one side of the drawing, there was a tall spiral of leaves, and they could see it whirling. A pair of leaves inside it seemed to stand out like eyes.

"Leaf spirit," said William.

Next to the leaf spirit, they could see a tall bowl-like shape that looked like it was about to collapse inward, and in the middle of it stood Mary, a defiant look on her face. Susan gasped. The pencil snapped in her grasp.

"It wants to kill her," she whispered.

William put his hand on hers again. "Steady, Susan," he said. "Stay calm or we'll lose the contact."

He reached over and laid his hand over Susan's picture. His hand went into the paper as if the drawing had been made on a white liquid. "Mary," he said. "Mary." The paper jerked under him. Ripples seemed to flow out across the sketchpad. He pushed harder. "It's fighting me," he said to Susan and Teddy. He frowned in concentration. "Mary, remember our game. Remember the dice. The dice! Listen to..." his hand jerked up even as he said "the leaves." The picture solidified and was only paper and ink. Even its living, three-dimensional quality vanished, leaving just a sketch of Mary frozen in time as a cascade of leaves was about to bury her.

Susan sobbed. "I couldn't hold it, Dad. I couldn't hold it!" She began to shake. Next to her, Teddy, now truly frightened, began to sob quietly, holding on to his mother's arm.

William nodded, wrapping his arms around his daughter and grandson and drawing them close. He used his Knack to gather peace around them. "It's all right. It's not your fault. It pushed me away, too. We can Listen and See, but only if something wants to be heard and seen, Susan. We're not all powerful. Whatever has Mary doesn't want us to interfere." He kept his voice calm and confident, but in fact inwardly he felt shaken. He was not used to being rejected quite so strongly. Whatever the force had been, it had been powerful, more than a match for his own Power. What truly troubled him, though, was that it had not come from the leaf spirit or even from the Leaf King. Something else, something unknown, was present, and it didn't want him or his daughter involved.

Susan nestled into his embrace, clinging to her father. "But what can we do, Dad? Who's going to help Mary then?"

At that moment, a loud, raucous trilling and chirping came from the living room, filling the air with insistent bird song. Teddy raised his head in surprise.

"Kiwi?"

****

"All right, I'll sit down and be still," Mary said. *Stupid dream. What does it mean to be bossed around by a bunch of leaves? I'll be glad to wake up!*

Around her the wall of leaves bent back away from her. They no longer threatened to fall in on her, but they still enclosed her like a cage. "Hey, Leaf," she shouted. "I said I'd sit and be quiet. Take down the wall."

The leaf spirit rustled. "You may be quiet, but your body is still noisy. These leaves will protect the rest of us from the disturbance you bring."

"Hey, wait a minute. You promised."

"Promised nothing. I let you breath. Now be quiet, or I will bury you."

Mary knew she should keep her mouth shut. If Teddy were here, he'd probably make one of his horrible puns, like she should "leaf well enough alone!" But she was angry. She opened her mouth to scream her defiance, but before she could say anything else, she felt a familiar presence and heard a familiar voice. "Mary!" it said. "Mary."

It was her grandfather.

Had her grandfather come into her dream? Immediately her anger left her and she felt relief. She must be close to waking up. Teddy and Brian must have gone to get help when she was knocked out, and now her grandfather was trying to revive her. "Grandpa?" she asked. She looked around, but she couldn't see over the wall of leaves.

"Remember our game," his voice seemed to say. It was coming from all around her, just like the voice of the leaf spirit had done. "Remember the dice." Remember the dice? *What did that mean? Why would Grandpa be telling me to remember some stupid dice?*

"The dice!" said his voice, more insistently and powerfully than before.

Then the silence returned.

Mary sat down, puzzled. If Grandpa was trying to wake her up, why would he be talking about dice and their Monopoly game? *It must be still more of this dream,* she thought disgustedly. *When is it going to end?*

Still, her mother had taught her that dreams have an internal logic, even if we don't understand it when we wake up. So if she was dreaming that Grandpa wanted her to remember the dice, then that was what she would do. *Besides, sitting and remembering is a quiet thing to do, she reasoned, which would please that grumpy old Leaf.*

She remembered playing Monopoly with her grandfather and how she suspected he was jinxing the dice somehow. But then she had started to jinx them, too. How had she done that?

She thought more deeply. Her grandfather had predicted she was going to roll a three, and she had known that he was right. Why? Because the dice had listened to him. They were going to do what he said. But she realized they could listen to her, too. She could tell them what to do instead. And she had! She had rolled the seven she wanted. Then later he had told the dice to roll him an eleven and she had had them roll a five instead. She laughed at the memory.

In that moment, as if a light had switched on in her mind, she knew beyond any doubt that she was not in a dream. She knew that everything that was happening to her was real. She was not asleep. She had somehow been magically transported to this world of leaves and stillness, and equally magically, her grandfather had found a way to give her a message. It had had to be a short message, too, for some reason. He had said, "Remember the dice." Why? Because when they had been playing monopoly, she had discovered something about herself, that she had a power to listen to things and to talk to things so they would obey her, or at least listen in return. And that power was her key to undoing whatever had happened.

That was what Grandpa was telling her. He was giving her a clue to help her escape this place. The clue was to listen.

But listen to what? Surely not Leaf. She knew what it had to say, and she was sure it wouldn't want to talk anymore. Trying to engage it in conversation might just anger it more so it would bury her. And she knew if she were buried, it really would kill her. Forever, just as Leaf had said.

For a moment, she felt panicky. More than anything, she wanted her mother's arms around her. She wanted to be out of this awful place and safe again. She didn't want to be alone.

But immediately she knew that if she panicked, she would lose control and begin screaming. And Leaf would bury her.

That was no good.

She knew she would have to get herself out of this situation. And the more she thought about it, the more she was sure she could. Why else would her grandfather have given her the clue about the dice? She had a power within her, and now was the time to use it.

But again, this raised the question. Use it on what?

She looked around to see what she should or could listen to, but all she saw were leaves towering over her. Just leaves, leaves, and more…

Leaves!

Of course, she had to listen to the leaves!

She wasn't sure how to listen to the leaves, though. It wasn't like listening to a person, she knew. But there was something there to listen to, just as there had been with the dice. A spirit, perhaps. She didn't know. Further, she didn't care. She didn't know how her computer worked either, but that didn't stop her from using it and getting on to the Internet.

This would be something like that. An "*Innernet*," she thought, and chuckled. She just had to log on.

She remembered her mother doing meditation. Going into silence, she called it. That would be the place to start. After all, you couldn't listen very well if you weren't quiet yourself.

She composed herself and closed her eyes. She wasn't sure just how one went into silence, but her mother had taught her how to calm down. She imagined it was the same thing. "Just breathe slowly and deeply while you count down from ten to zero," her mother had said, "and as you count, feel yourself going down, down, down into your body, like riding an elevator down into your body and down into the earth to a place that feels strong and calm and quiet."

And that's what Mary did. As she breathed and counted, she could feel herself settling into herself. She could feel herself going down into her own depths. As she did, she became aware that something was rising to meet her. It was a presence that was still part of her, but a deeper, wiser part. It was who she was when she was open to being all of herself and not just a small part. And with it came something that felt like a geyser of light, also rising up, surrounding her, holding her, and spilling out from her. And as this feeling of light and presence spilled out, she found herself Listening to the world around her.

Not that there was much to hear in this world of silence. But she could Listen to the purposes beyond the silence. She could listen to Words of rest and peace underneath the silence. She could hear Words of new life to come from the silence. She could hear the silence not as an absence but as a fullness of promise.

And she could hear the leaves. She could hear their memories of bursting forth as buds and of opening to the sun. She could hear their memories of the caress of winds and the song of birds nesting amidst them. She could hear the energy of sunlight and the power of the leaves to turn that energy into life and food. She could hear the warmth of summer and the cool of autumn. She could hear the chlorophyll disappearing, its greenness dissolving, revealing the bright colors of the leaf itself. She could hear the sap withdrawing down the tree at winter's approach, and the call of the soil beneath. She could listen to the leaf floating from the tree, seeking the rest at the end of its cycle.

She listened to it all. As she did, she discovered the life and power of the spirit of Leaf within herself. Leaves had their unique life and power and she had hers, but ultimately both were part of the great cycle of life itself. She and leaf were kin.

Then she heard something else. She heard the delight of the leaves as she had skibbled through them. Not at first. But as they soared back into the air as she kicked her way through their piles and then floated back to earth, they began to remember their delight at feeling the breezes blowing around them and the wonder when they had let go of their tree and descended to the world of the earth. She heard their response to her laughter. There was playfulness in leaves, no less at the end than at the beginning.

She remembered her grandmother who had died after a long illness. Though her body had grown ever more frail and weak, she had not lost her gift of fun and laughter. Life had been a joy right up to when her body had said, "Enough!" and like a leaf, had let go of the tree of her soul and had fallen to the earth.

Why couldn't a leaf be decaying and dying and still be playful, still enjoy fun?

That thought filled her. She reached out to the leaves around her, refreshing their memories, reminding them of their playfulness, offering them the power of her skibbling and laughing to set them dancing again.

Just as she had asked the dice to roll a seven instead of a three, she asked the leaves to let her go, to let her run, to let her skibble in their midst.

Around her the wall of leaves collapsed. "Right on!" she shouted, and sprang to her feet, her fist pumping the air in triumph. Power surged through her. She began to kick at the leaves at her feet, then she reached down and picked up armfuls of them, throwing them into the air and laughing.

"What are you doing? Stop or I will bury you!"

In front of her, Leaf appeared again, a whirling spiral of leaves, its two crimson leaf-eyes seeming to glower at her.

"Sorry," she said, "but leaves want to have fun, too. So, leaf me alone or else." She laughed again at her witticism. *I made a pun*, she thought. *Teddy would be proud of me.*

"I warned you, noisy creature." The whirlwind leaned towards her. She could feel power emanating from it as she Listened to it, but rather than being afraid, she reached out to the leaves swirling about it and asked them to join in the fun and take Leaf dancing. Suddenly, the whirlwind spun away and up into the air as more leaves leaped up from the ground to join it and add to its momentum.

"No!" Leaf cried. "Noooooo..." It disappeared into the sky, more and more leaves rising up to chase it and join in the fun.

Mary stopped. She looked around. Everywhere little piles of leaves were gusting into the air and back again, reminding her of flying fish leaping out of the ocean. She smiled. *Well,* she thought, *they certainly listened to me!* But then she frowned as another thought crossed her mind. "The leaves are having fun, but this isn't getting me back home," she said aloud.

At that moment, she heard a trilling and chirping that filled the air. It was a sound she immediately recognized, the happy song of a budgerigar. Her budgerigar.

"Kiwi!" Mary shouted, looking about. But she couldn't see any sign of her bird, or any other bird for that matter. Still, Kiwi's song seemed to be coming from somewhere off to her left, so she began walking in that direction, skibbling and bounding through the leaves.

She didn't know how long she walked. Time didn't seem to work in the same way in this world. Though there was a blue sky and everything was light, she couldn't see any sun in the sky. She had no idea where the light was coming from. But though she never saw her bird, Kiwi's song kept her spirit up and her energy good. She had no idea where she was going, but if Kiwi were somehow guiding her, she trusted it would be a good place.

Then she came to a road. It was really just a narrow trail, but the leaves came up to either side of it and stopped as if held back by an invisible wall. At the same time, she could see that the forest ended a little ways ahead.

Excited that something was changing in her surroundings and that she seemed to be getting somewhere at last, she ran along the trail and out of the forest. There she stopped to look around.

She was in a vast undulating plain with rolling hills and shallow valleys. There were no trees. But surprisingly, there were still leaves on the ground in all directions, though not as thick a carpet as in the forest. The trail headed off in a straight line into the distance towards what looked like a smudge on the horizon.

As soon as she left the forest, Kiwi's song stopped. *He's gotten me out of the forest,* she thought. *Now I just have to follow the trail.*

In spite of all her running and leaping, she did not feel the least bit tired, which surprised her. If she really was still in her normal physical body, she should be exhausted from all her exertions, not to mention hungry and thirsty. But she felt none of those things. Obviously, something was going on that kept her charged up. It was one more mystery to add to the larger one of where she was and how she had gotten here in the first place.

So she headed down the trail at an easy loping run, her attention focused on the smudge far ahead on the horizon and on the hope that whatever it was, it would lead her home.

As she ran, the smudge began to take shape. Before long, she could see that it was a tree. A very tall tree. In fact, as she got closer, she could see it was the tallest, mightiest tree she had ever seen. She had no idea how tall it must be. Hundreds of feet, she imagined. And it was entirely without leaves. It was a huge skeleton of a tree, not dead by any means but bare, its jagged branches thrust out like skeletal arms and hands over the surrounding field. Looking up at it, she thought that all the leaves that covered the plain must have come from this one tree.

Finally, she stopped, awed and not wanting to get any closer. The closest branches were still some yards ahead, but they looked too much like grasping fingers. She had no wish to get within their reach.

She knew without any doubt that if this strange world of leaves had a ruler, this tree was it.

She sat down on the trail. She wasn't sure just what to do now, but she felt it wouldn't hurt to become still and listen.

As she began to quiet herself and count down from ten, a deep voice boomed out across the plain. It was clearly the voice of the tree.

"Welcome, Mary," it said. "You have passed your first test. You freed yourself from my servant and made it into my presence."

A test, she thought. *So that's what had been going on.* "Who are you? Why am I being tested?"

"I am the Leaf King," the voice said. "And you are being tested to see what kind of servant you will be for me."

"Servant?" Mary couldn't keep the indignation from her voice. "I'm not your servant!"

The Leaf King chuckled. "Indeed you are, human child. You see, your brother gave you to me!"

****

Teddy and his mother and grandfather ran into the living room to see what was the matter. In his cage, Kiwi was pacing up and down on a central bar, singing loudly. He seemed very agitated.

"Wow!" said Teddy. "What's up with him?"

"Dad?" Susan asked, looking at her father.

The Cunning Man raised an eyebrow at Kiwi. "What's happening with you, my feathered brother, eh?" he asked. He turned to the others. "Let's sit down and be quiet. This is no coincidence, I'm sure. I felt earlier from things Mary said about Kiwi that the two of them were bonded in some way. I think this bird is involved in whatever is happening. I'm going to Listen and see what I can discover."

The three of them sat down, William pulling a chair close to Kiwi's cage. The bird continued to sing and pace, ruffling its feathers from time to time. Susan watched as a familiar stillness came over her father's face. She had seen this from time to time as a child. At first it had frightened her, for she sensed that in some way her father had gone away when he had that look, even though his body was still here. But he always came back, and he was always reassuring.

When she had become a teenager, her own Knack had started developing. Her capacity to See had frightened her at times, for at first she Saw things she didn't want to see. Sometimes, she saw when someone was sick, even though the illness might not have appeared in the body yet. Or she saw events from people's lives, which were usually trivial but which embarrassed her nonetheless, for she felt she was spying.

Once though she had saved the life of a neighbor's son who had fallen into an old well hole and been knocked out. No one would have known to look for him there had she not insisted. She had appreciated her Knack then, though it made her neighbors nervous. However, in those days, they knew her father was a Cunning Man, so she was protected by his reputation in the small town where they lived.

Eventually, she had learned to control her talent, but she had always felt nervous around magic. When she had married Jack and become pregnant, it seemed her Knack went into the background. Perhaps that part of her spirit in which the Knack was found did not want to compete with her motherly duties. She had been grateful

She had always known that a Knack might appear in Theodore or Mary, since these talents often appeared along genetic lines. But she had been content to wait, perhaps in denial. But now, through a mistake wholly out of character with her father, magic was back in her life in a big way, threatening her daughter. What would happen now, she didn't know. In any event, her Knack had proven ineffective, perhaps because she hadn't practiced it all these years. But even her dad's powers were proving impotent, and that surprised her. She knew of no other as powerful in these things as he.

Her father's face shifted, and he shook himself. He looked at Susan and Teddy, and his expression was grim. Her heart leapt into her throat. "What is it, Dad? What did you find out?" In the background, Kiwi continued his singing and pacing. The bird was acting as if someone had put speed into his birdseed.

William sighed. "It's true. Kiwi is in touch with Mary. All I can say is that she seems to be all right, though I have no details of what's happening. All the normal channels are closed to me. There is no assistance I can give, or anyone can give except, apparently, for Kiwi."

"Kiwi? Why Kiwi, Grandpa?" asked Teddy.

"It's because of their music. All music has the power to connect the different realms of mind and heart together. It can bring us into attunement with other realms. Bird song is special that way. It can bridge the worlds. It's one of the gifts that birds bring to the earth. Because Kiwi and Mary have a bond of love, his song can reach her where she is. He is her ally, and if she is to have any other ally, it will need to come through him."

"But why can't we reach her, too, or help?" Susan asked.

"That, at least, I can tell you. Mary is in her Awakening."

Susan gasped. "What? But that can't be! It's way too soon. It didn't happen to me until I was fifteen."

"I know. It's rare for it to begin at such an early age," her father said. "But it can happen. It happened to me, in fact, though I was twelve when it started. And something similar took place. I was in the woods and discovered a trail I'd never seen before. I thought I knew every path and trail for miles around in those hills, but this was a new one. So naturally I followed it." He turned to Teddy. "Be careful with a trail when you don't know where it's going," he said.

Teddy, caught up in his grandfather's story, started. "Uh, I will..."

"No, you'll probably forget or figure you can handle anything that comes, just as I did." William smiled. "So I ran along it and found myself in another realm. I almost didn't get back, but the struggle to get back is what brought my Knack to the fore and gave me its power."

"But Dad, that didn't happen to me."

"No, your Knack developed slowly and gracefully. It's different with each person. But the rule of thumb is, the more powerful the Knack or the energy behind it, the more drastic the Awakening."

"You mean," said Teddy, "Mary's getting magic powers right now? Before I do? Man, that's a bummer!"

"Unfortunately, that's exactly what I mean. Which makes me suspect I didn't simply forget to turn off the magic but was set up by the forces that be to bring her into this crisis. Her power is awakening, and she must be tested."

"But who's testing her, Grandpa? A council of wizards?"

William laughed. "No, not everything's like you read in your fantasies. A wizard, if that's what we are, is tested by his or her own soul. It's not really a test, like you'd get at school. It's that the power awakens and you have to be able to control it and make it your own. Otherwise the Knack can control you or simply dissipate. Wizards test themselves. In a sense, the Knack arranges what it needs to come to the forefront of the person's life."

"But, Dad, Mary's too young for this to happen. She's just a little girl! My little girl! Damn this magic!"

William got up and put his arm around his daughter. "Susan, Mary may be a little girl but she's obviously a very old and powerful soul. Her Knack wouldn't be coming to the surface so soon if this weren't true. It's dangerous, yes, but we have to trust that that part of her knows what it's doing and will see her safely back home. Remember, the purpose of an Awakening is not to damage the person but to give them the strength to live with their power."

"Can we help, Grandpa? Isn't there anything we can do?"

"No, Teddy. That's why your Mom and I were blocked. It's like a butterfly emerging from a cocoon. If you help it out, it will lack the strength to fly. The person must do the work themselves."

"But what if Mary can't do it, Grandpa?"

"Then, Teddy, Mary will be trapped in that realm she's in. Or she will die."

****

Mary looked up at the skeletal tree in shock. "My brother gave me to you? No way! Teddy can be a jerk, but he wouldn't do that. He wouldn't know how to do that, even though he's always pretending he's a wizard."

The Leaf King chuckled. "Look," it said. In the air in front of Mary a picture appeared as if on an invisible television set. She saw Teddy and Brian carrying her laughing, squirming body across the lawn. "One! Two! Three! We gife you to ze Leaf God!" her brother chanted as he and Brian hurled her into the leaf pile. She watched herself hit the leaves and sink into them without a trace.

"There was magic in those leaves, Mary," said the Leaf King. "It was a portal to my realm here. And your brother threw you in and said he was giving you to me. I accepted his gift."

"Wait a minute! We were playing. We didn't know anything about you or any magic or anything like that. It doesn't count!"

"It was a proper ritual. Not quite as formal as some, I'll admit, but the essence was there. The link was made, the gift was offered. It needs no more."

"Well, it needs a lot more as far as I'm concerned! No way I'm staying here! Take me home! If anyone's to blame, it's Teddy, so take him!"

"You would give me your brother in exchange for yourself? To be with me forever?"

She started to say, "Sure, why not," but she stopped herself. She reminded herself this really was a magical place, not a dream, not a fantasy. She didn't know what would happen if she agreed. The Leaf King might really take Teddy somehow. Much as she and Teddy didn't always get along, she couldn't do that to him. He didn't even like leaf piles!

She looked up at the tree. "No. No exchanges. You take me home and you leave Teddy alone. He didn't know what he was doing."

The Leaf King laughed. "Good. Good. You are willing to take responsibility and to protect others. And you think before you speak. I am more and more pleased with you. You will make a fine servant."

Mary stamped her foot on the trail in frustration. "I'm a human being. I'm not some tree's servant."

"Ah, you think that since you're human, you're better than me, a mere tree?" The Leaf King's voice was still amiable, but she detected an edge that hadn't been there before. Was this another trick question?

"Well," she replied, thinking fast, "we're different. I don't know who's better. I can do things you can't and you can do things I can't. I'd say the world needs us both."

"I see." It seemed pleased again. "But you bring up an important point. You are a human being, and here that is a problem."

"A problem. Fine, then you'll have to let me go."

"No, you misunderstand. The problem is that you haven't fallen off yet. My servant was correct. You're very noisy as you are. You're like a bud, full of life and growth. That's not what this realm is about."

"Then send me home. I didn't want to come here in the first place."

"That may be, but few sacrifices do. The fact is that you are here and you must adapt."

"What does that mean?"

"That means you must fall so your spirit will be like the rest of my servants."

"Fall? What's that mean?"

In answer, Mary heard a rustling behind her. Turning, she saw the leaves on either side of the trail gathering together. As she watched in growing horror, the leaves came together to form a giant human figure, one that kept growing even as she watched. And before she had a chance to do or say anything, one of its hands swept down and snatched her up, clutching her in a grip made of scratchy, crackling leaves. She yelled.

"Hey! Put me down! Let me go!"

"Don't struggle, Mary. You will enjoy being part of my world. After you fall, of course."

Mary had an idea she knew now just what "fall" meant, but she hoped she was wrong. But the Leaf King's next words only confirmed what she suspected. "Look, Mary," it said. The giant leaf man turned. Ahead of her in the distance was a graveyard. It was the largest graveyard she had ever seen, stretching to the horizon and to either side for what looked like miles and miles. And it was filled with gravestones, monuments, statues, mausoleums, and tombs, some looking very ancient and others looking new and shining.

"See, Mary, that's where human beings fall and return to the earth, just like leaves. It's my job to help things return to the earth, to fulfill the cycle of life. That's what you will do. You will help me. But first you must return to the earth yourself. First you must fall from your tree."

"No," Mary screamed, wishing this really was a dream and that she'd wake up Right Now! "No, you want to kill me!"

All the time, the giant leaf man had been growing taller. Mary knew that if it dropped her, she'd certainly die from the fall. And now it was beginning to lurch towards the graveyard, lifting her up higher as it did so.

"Stop!" she yelled. "You can't do this! I don't want to be your servant! I can't be your servant!"

Her words went unanswered. The leaf man continued to grow, lifting her higher and higher even as its long steps brought the graveyard closer.

There's a way to stop this, Mary thought. *I know there is. Screaming won't help me. I have to do what I did before. It helped me with Leaf, it will help me with this giant.*

She closed her eyes and immediately began breathing slowly and counting backwards, trying desperately to ignore the movement that was bringing her steadily closer to her death. *Deep, deep,* she thought.

She felt the geyser of power and light rising up in her. Without hesitation, she sent it out into the body of the leaf man, trying to hear the leaves, trying to become one with them, to tell them to put her down and leave her alone. But nothing seemed to be happening. They wouldn't listen to her. They wouldn't open to her. All she could hear was....

She Listened.

All she could hear was bird song. Kiwi's song.

"Kiwi!" she yelled out with all her strength and all her power and inner Light. "Help me!"

The bird song swelled around her. In fact, it seemed to multiply, until it sounded as if hundreds of Kiwi's were singing. She opened her eyes.

The sky around was filled with color. Everywhere there were budgerigars, canaries, parrots, cockatiels, and other exotic birds, all singing. And there were sparrows, nightingales, mockingbirds, robins and larks joining in. In fact, there were thousands of song birds flying around the Leaf King and the giant leaf man.

"No!" said the Leaf King. The leaf man began to disintegrate under the impact of the music, the sound causing the leaves that made up his body to dance and vibrate.

"No!" said the Leaf King again. The leaf man in a last gesture threw Mary into the air. She screamed as she flew towards a large white mausoleum with statues of crying angels at the corners of its roof. She threw her arm up in front of her face, knowing it would do little to stop the impact when she hit.

Then she was surrounded with color. Hundreds of tiny claws seized her, hundreds of tiny wings beat against her, the wind of their movement fanning her and bearing her aloft. Gently she was flown away from the graveyard and over to the trail in front of the gigantic tree. There she was lowered to the ground. When she was safe, all the birds let go and rose up about her.

At the same time, the air in front of her began to stir and whirl with twinkling, sparkling lights and colors. Streamers of color shot out in all directions, waving like ribbons in the wind. In the midst of this, Mary saw a beautiful woman appear, floating in the midst of a rainbow and shining with an inner luminescence.

"You should not be here," the voice of the Leaf King boomed out, sounding more petulant than angry.

"I was summoned," the woman said, her voice clear as a silver bell. "This child proves her power by my presence. She should not be here."

"She was given to me."

"In error, as you know." The woman's light flared out.

"No, in pursuit of her power, as YOU know." All around them, leaves heaved like storm waves on an ocean.

The woman bowed. "And has she passed her test?"

"Maybe. She is still alive."

"You have yet to release her."

"What is that to you. Bird Lady?"

The beautiful woman turned to Mary and floated over to stand in front of her. She kneeled down to bring her face in line with Mary's. "Mary Williams, Woman of Power, Woman-to-Be, would you have me as an ally?" As she spoke, a budgerigar that looked just like Kiwi flew over and landed on her shoulder. It looked at Mary and trilled a few notes.

Mary wasn't sure what to say. But a power rose up in her, filling her, and from its depths, she knew. "Yes, Lady, I am honored, Thank you."

The woman smiled. The bird flew down and landed on Mary's shoulder. It immediately sidled up to her ear and gave it a little love nip. Turning, the Bird Lady gazed up at the great tree. "I deem her worthy. She listens and hears. She will serve well. I am her ally."

Hearing this, Mary began to protest that she was no one's servant, but Listening, she knew different. She wasn't a maid or anything like that, though that, she knew suddenly, could be an honorable profession. She knew that the Power that moved in her was there not for herself alone but for others, for birds, for trees, for leaves, for all the world. She felt a great peace come over her with that realization.

The Leaf King was silent for a time. Then it spoke. "But you are still mine, Mary Williams. You were given to me. Perhaps it was in error or in play, but it was a gift. What say you to that?"

Mary looked up at the great, skeletal tree, bare of leaves or of any sign of life, and she knew that was a false seeing. She Listened. She Listened deeply. And she heard life. Life within the tree. Life in its roots. Life hidden in the branches. Life in the invisible, dark places where leaf buds rest before they appear in the spring. Life in the leaf that spreads itself to capture sunlight make it part of the earth, life in the leaf when it lets go and returns to the earth so that the cycle of life may continue.

And when she had heard these things, she said to the Leaf King, and her Power spoke within her and formed her words. "I was not given to you as you now are. I cannot serve you only as you appear before me. No one can give me away except myself, and I can serve only the whole of things, not just a part. But to your wholeness, I gladly give myself, and that wholeness I will willingly serve. And I do so as your ally and partner."

She stretched forth her hand and held it out to the great tree. As she did so, light joined the two of them. On all the branches, flowers bloomed, buds began to appear, and leaves sprung forth, green and vibrant, until a great living tree stood before her.

The Leaf King laughed. "Now I congratulate you and also name you Woman of Power. I accept you and give you back to yourself. You have drawn your Power into yourself and used it wisely to pass your tests. Now it is to me to name that Power and gift you with your own destiny."

From high in the tree, a single leaf detached itself. Mary watched as it floated down unerringly in her direction until it hovered just above her. Then it landed on top of her right hand. There was a tingle, as if all the leaf were kissing her. Startled, she watched the leaf fade into her hand, leaving only a faint outline like a pale birthmark in the shape of a leaf.

"Mary, you have the Knack of Listening. But even more, you will grow into the Knack of Journeying. For you, the Tree of Worlds is open. You will be welcome to walk its branches, and they will take you to many worlds. And wherever you go, Bird and Leaf will go with you, allies and partners in service to the circle of life."

Mary could feel her Power leaving her, and she wasn't even sure what the words meant, though she supposed it was something good. She wasn't sure how to respond. She decided that since this was a Leaf King, she should curtsey. So she did. Then she looked up at the great tree and at the Bird Lady hovering nearby, and said, "Can I go home now?"

****

Kiwi had settled down after his manic burst of singing and pacing. Not knowing what else to do, William, Susan, and Teddy just sat in the gathering dark. As time passed, Susan and Teddy snuggled together on the sofa, and eventually Teddy fell asleep.

Finally William said, "I'm going into the kitchen to finish cooking the chili. Life goes on, and we need to eat. Besides, Jack will be home soon, I imagine."

Susan looked at her father. "What are we going to tell him? He knows a little about the Knacks, but not a lot."

"Let's cross that bridge when we come to it."

He got up and went out into the kitchen. As he began to assemble his ingredients, Kiwi began singing again. It was a loud, triumphant song. He could feel Power begin to rise around him. "Susan!" he called out. Then, he saw a light flash out in the backyard. Rushing to the door, he opened it and went out.

Two beings were standing in front of the leaf pile. One was a beautiful woman clad in flowing ribbons of color. A budgerigar sat on one shoulder. The other was a man of middle age clad all in leaves of varying colors. The two could have stepped out of a costume shop or a Renaissance Faire, but William knew otherwise. His Power rose up to greet them. They smiled in his direction.

Behind him he heard Susan and Teddy rushing out of the house. When they saw the two figures, they halted. He heard Teddy mutter, "Cool!"

"Susan, Teddy, may I introduce to you the Lady of Birds and the Leaf King, two of the inner world's most powerful beings."

The two nature spirits nodded at Susan and Teddy, then stepped apart. Between them was Mary, curled up and sleeping on the leaf pile. William heard Susan gasp and begin sobbing.

"We are sorry for your distress," said the Bird Lady, her voice sweet and melodious. "We return to you a new Woman of Power. She met her tests and is Awakened to who she is. But she is still a human child and will need training and help."

"She will have it aplenty, I pledge to that," William said, relief flooding his body. "Thank you."

The Lady nodded and smiled again. Then she began to fade away. The Leaf King smiled. "The bud did well," he said. "She will be a great leaf!"

"Thank you." William said.

The Leaf King, too, began to fade back into his own realm, but then he spotted Teddy. He winked at the boy. "Ah, Theodore. I'll be seeing you too before long." Then he disappeared from sight.

"Wow!" breathed Teddy. And then, as his mother and grandfather rushed forward to gather the sleeping Mary into their arms, he added, "Cool!"

The Sidhe Who
Came For Christmas

By: David Spangler

"What's this, Uncle Perry?" I asked, holding up a Christmas ornament. Like many such ornaments, it was a glass sphere containing a little scene. What made this one different was the scene within it. It was a snowy meadow from which arose a ring of standing stones. At their center was a lone evergreen. It was cleverly wrought, for the tree twinkled with light as I held it up and rotated it, as if stars were nestled in its boughs. The artist had obviously inserted small bits of some kind of reflective material into the form of the tree, but I couldn't tell what they were. The effect was delightful. But still, it was not the usual theme one found in a Christmas ornament.

My uncle looked up from the tangle of Christmas tree lights that lay on his lap. In the months since they had last been used, one or more of the bulbs had given up the ghost, causing the entire string of lights to fail. It was, I knew, an unwritten but universally accepted rule of nature that this would happen, much like losing one half of a pair of socks in the washing machine whenever you did the laundry. Now he was testing each bulb to discover which had been naughty and which had been nice. "Lovely, isn't it?" he said. "I love that ornament."

"Yes, it's beautiful," I said, setting it aside. I was organizing the ornaments on the floor while waiting for the string of lights to go up. "I've never seen anything quite like it. Usually these globes have Santas or Nativity scenes. I've never seen Stonehenge before."

My uncle chuckled. "Oh, it's not Stonehenge, my boy. Not at all. Different place altogether."

"Really? Still...I only meant...well, you don't usually associate Christmas with standing stones."

"*We* don't. But it's different for the Sidhe."

"The Shee..? Oh, yes, the characters in your Crystal Legion novels."

"Come, come, boy. Not just 'characters!' The real thing! The High Elves. The Shining Ones. The People of Peace. The Faerie Lords. But most definitely *not* the Little People. Oh, no, not little at all!" He lifted up a row of lights and glowered at them. "The culprit's got to be in this group!"

I shook my head and took another ornament out of the box where they'd all been carefully wrapped and packed. It was Santa and his bag of toys riding on a flying carpet. *Well,* I thought, *at least this one had Santa on it, but it still wasn't the usual Christmas image.* But then Uncle Perry had a reputation in the family for being different. He lived in a world that wasn't as down to earth as everyone else's. I loved him for it, but I never was as comfortable as he was in the strange borderland between the magical and the mundane that he found so ordinary. *Like talking about faerie lords and elves as if they were his next-door-neighbors.* I smiled to myself. Perhaps for him they were!

Uncle Perry was my father's older brother. His full name was Peregrine, like the falcon. He was proud of it and insisted that everyone use it, too. He refused to answer to nicknames. As children, though, my sister and I had been unable to pronounce his name, so we'd been allowed to call him "Uncle Perry." As far as I knew, we--and now my wife, Amber—were the only ones who had that privilege.

My father was an engineer in the aerospace industry. He joked once that he had grown up to be part of space while his older brother had grown up spacey. My mother's reply was that Peregrine hadn't really grown up at all. Perhaps that's why Uncle Perry became a successful writer of fantasy novels, particularly for children. A couple of critics had even called him Tolkien's successor. He certainly made a good deal more money than my father did, especially after two of his books were made into movies. Magic sells. These days, space doesn't.

"Aha! Found the little bugger!" My Uncle held up a glowing string of Christmas lights, a huge grin on his face, blue eyes twinkling beneath thick eyebrows that were startlingly black beneath his thick white hair. He'd always been thin and gangly, but now his face seemed gaunter than I remembered. It made his face, with its curved nose, look even more like the bird of prey for which he'd been named. "Now we can proceed."

He stood up and walked to the tree, carrying the lights. Then he paused and looked at me. "Maybe we should wait, Tom. Would Amber like to be here for the adornment?" Meaning, would my wife like to help with decorating the tree?

"We can save some ornaments for her, but she's doing a double shift at the hospital. I don't expect her home much before ten or eleven tonight."

"Ah. In that case, we'll string this up now so we can put the ornaments on, but we won't light the lights until your angel of mercy comes home. That way we'll all see it for the first time together. More magical that way, don't you think?"

"That will be nice, Uncle. She'll appreciate it."

As the newest nurse on the staff, and perhaps the youngest as well, Amber had no seniority. When nurses who were older and had more tenure asked for time off, it often fell to her to take over. We'd both known this would happen when we'd moved here but the relief of simply having a job outweighed the inconveniences. I didn't like it when she had to work so much, but it was better than not working at all.

Which was the situation in which I found myself. The game company I'd been working for as a computer animator had died when the game we'd all worked on had been out-muscled and out-performed in the market place by better-funded competitors. To make ends meet for the business we'd all been on "deferred salaries," which meant that none of the creative staff had been paid for the last four months before the end. Making matters worse, Amber was just finishing her training and had not yet been hired anywhere. This situation had depleted our small savings pretty quickly. Fortunately we hadn't bought a house, but landlords could be just as inflexible about wanting the rent as banks were about receiving mortgage payments. Finding ourselves out on the street and homeless was a real possibility.

Uncle Perry had come to the rescue. "I'm just rambling around alone in this big house," he'd said to me. "I know your Dad would be happy to have you, too, but he and June have a little place, so you'd be cramped. Besides, they have each other. You'd be doing me a favor by moving in with me and giving me some company. Furthermore, where you are in Portland is a lot closer to me in Seattle than moving back to Houston with your folks." This had been a tactful way for Peregrine to give us an excuse not to burden my parents who were having economic problems of their own.

As it turned out, it was the right thing to do. A new hospital had just been opened east of Seattle in the little town of Issaquah, and they were hiring nurses. I also discovered that Puget Sound was home to a number of computer game companies such as Microsoft and Amazon; even Issaquah had a successful one. I'd had some good interviews. Chances were favorable that in the new year I would find a job myself, as animators were in demand. For the first time in months, I could look at the future without feeling my stomach tighten up.

Uncle Perry had been more than generous. He'd gone out of his way to make us feel that the house was ours, too, that we weren't just guests but family, that it was our home as well as his. He'd even gone so far as to outfit a small room as a pottery studio for Amber who in her spare time liked to sit at her the potter's wheel and create things out of clay. Not that she'd had much spare time lately with her new job at the hospital.

With these thoughts rambling through my head, I joined my uncle in trimming the tree, an expression I'd always found odd since by the time we were finished, the tree looked fatter rather than thinner. I had a system. Once the lights were up, I first put on those ornaments that seemed ordinary to me. You know the kind: the round balls of a single color, the long silver icicles, the Santas and snowmen and reindeer. I thought of them as tree-filler, the "spear-carriers" of Christmas decorations. The truly beautiful or unique ornaments, the ones I thought of as the heroes of the show, I put on last, finding just the right places where they would be highlighted as they deserved.

I'd explained all this to my uncle whose method of decorating a tree was more random and improvisational, to say the least. He would start on one side, blindly pull an ornament from the box and hang it. He would move from top to bottom around the tree, not paying attention to the ornament itself while he was hanging it. Then when he was done, he would step back and see the result.

He called it "emergent decorating," and I'd seen him do it as a child when we'd visited with him over Christmas. One year when I was home from college for Christmas vacation, I teased him about it. "Uncle," I'd said, "your trees are like goulash. On the other hand, when I decorate, the tree becomes a fine gourmet meal, elegantly prepared and presented

"You've been paying too much attention to your father," he'd said, laughing. "Always the engineer. You need to allow for the serendipitous surprise, the flavor you'd never expect and couldn't have planned for!"

This year, knowing Amber and I would be with him for Christmas, I'd expected goulash as usual, but he'd surprised me and opted for gourmet. "How'd you like to decorate the tree your way, Tom?" he'd asked me a couple of days after we'd moved in to the small suite of rooms that occupied one wing of his house. "I've been working hard lately, and I'm feeling metaphysically winded, if you know what I mean." I didn't, but that wasn't unusual in talking with my uncle. "Not sure I have it in me to do all that decorating on my own. I'd love it if you'd take over." Of course, I agreed, though I suspected it was just a ruse to help Amber and me feel at home.

Which was why I'd been sorting and laying out the ornaments as I had, sifting the unique and exotic from the merely beautiful and sentimental. I was like a cook laying out his ingredients and his spices. And at the far end of this spectrum I placed what I thought of as the "Stonehenge" globe (even if Uncle had said it was "some other place"). To my mind it was so different that it required its own special place on the tree. I would hang it last, after Amber got home.

Which was why things turned out the way they did.

Amber had been overly optimistic when she'd said she'd be home by ten o'clock or so. It was closer to midnight when she came in the door. She looked exactly like you'd expect for someone who'd worked for sixteen hours and then had driven a thirty-minute commute home

"Long day," I said, giving her hug. She cuddled close and went limp for a moment in my arms. "You feel frazzled."

She gave me a wry look as she stepped back, one hand futilely trying to push back into place a lock of red hair that had fallen over her face. "I passed frazzled four hours ago," she said. "Let me just collapse somewhere."

"I have just the thing for you," said Uncle Perry, coming into the hallway. "A special brew."

"Thank you, Peregrine," she said, kicking off her shoes and letting me lead her into the living room. Although my uncle had on our wedding day extended to her the privilege of calling him "Uncle Perry," most of the time she did like everyone else and used his full name.

Amber did collapse on the sofa. I sat down, too, taking her feet in my lap and beginning to massage them. "Oh God," she said. "That feels so good! I don't think I was off my feet for more than thirty minutes the whole time I was working."

"What's your schedule like tomorrow?"

She gave me a tired grin. "Well, the good news is that I have the day off."

"Really? That's great. You'll be able to rest up." I paused for a moment. "Um, the way you said that…is there bad news, too?"

She grimaced. "Yeah. I'm on night shift tomorrow from midnight to eight o'clock the next morning." Amber hated working nights.

Uncle Perry came in carrying a mug from which steam was rising. "Try this," he said, handing it to her. "But careful. It's hot!"

I saw that the mug was half-full of a dark liquid. Amber took a careful sip. Then another. "Wow, Uncle Perry, this is…really good.

What is it?"

"Elven brew," he said. "It has some of the same properties of rejuvenation as lembas bread. Probably has some of the same ingredients."

Amber laughed. "Oh, Peregrine, you're such a kidder. OK, keep it to yourself. I don't need to know anyway. Whatever it is, it's delicious."

"Uncle, there's nothing illegal in it, is there?" Visions of marijuana tea—or worse—crossed my mind. I was pretty sure Peregrine wasn't into drugs, but then, I realized I didn't know for sure.

He looked at me seriously, his brows knitted in thought. "No...no, I don't think so. But I will admit the ingredients are hard to come by. Probably impossible now. In fact, I only have a very little bit left. But tonight it seemed appropriate."

"Honey, let me try it," I said, now curious. It smelled a bit like mint and cinnamon mixed together, but there was something else in the aroma I wasn't familiar with.

"OK," she said, "but only a sip!" I took the hot mug in my hand and sipped its contents. It was good. In fact, it was delicious, just as Amber had said. I took another sip. "Hey," she said, taking the mug back, "just one sip, I said."

I turned to Peregrine. "Wow, Uncle, this is really good stuff. Where did you get it? Whole Foods?" I was pretty sure it was some exotic herbal blend.

"Oh, no. It was a present from the Sidhe." His eyes got a faraway look. "It was some years ago now. I've made it last. Of course, you don't need to use much at a time. Just a pinch in some hot water. And the effects last for several days..."

I chuckled. I never knew with Peregrine if he was pulling my leg for his own obscure reasons or if he really believed what he was saying. Either way, it didn't matter. I could check out the tea cabinet later and see what was there. Knowing him, it wouldn't surprise me if I found a brown paper bag with "Elven Tea" written on it in both English and Elven script. I'd discovered a number such artifacts in his house over the years. They were, I was sure, props for his writing.

"Well, whatever it is, I do feel much better, thank you." She handed the mug back to Peregrine. "But you," she said, looking at me, "can keep working on my feet."

"Yes, your Ladyship," I said, putting my fingers to work digging deeply into sore places.

She closed her eyes and lay back. Peregrine left to go back into the kitchen. I could hear him puttering around in there. I realized that with his wealth, he could easily have hired servants; he could just as easily have had a much bigger house to go with the servants. But he seemed to show little interest in money or the things that it could buy. But he did enjoy giving special gifts which were undoubtedly expensive. My first memory of him was of him standing in the doorway of this house, holding out a beautifully carved and painted unicorn to me, his face lit up with a smile. My mother immediately confiscated the toy, fearing I might hurt myself on the pointed horn. I cried until she relented and gave it back. I still have it in a box in storage.

I looked around. The house, while large, was no mansion, and as far as I could see, it hadn't changed a bit in all the years I'd been coming here. The furniture was the same as it had always been. He had never married and seemed to enjoy his solitude. The day Amber and I got married, I'd asked him if he'd ever fallen in love. He'd gotten a wistful look on his face and said, "Yes, once, but she lived far away. Long distance relationships just don't work. At least, it didn't for us." And that was all he ever said.

I continued to massage Amber's feet for several minutes. I was sure that she had fallen asleep. Then Peregrine returned bearing a tray of breads and cold cuts and veggies along with bowls of soup. He set it down on the large square, glass-topped coffee table. You could see through it to the rug underneath. I remembered how this table had been my ocean as a child. My toy ships had sailed along its clear surface, while underneath were the treasures and monsters I knew were hidden on the ocean's bottom.

"That looks terrific! I'm starved!" I turned to see my wife, fully awake, grinning at Peregrine and the food he'd brought. I let go of her feet, and she swung them around onto the floor as she sat up next to me.

"Wonderful!" he said. "There's nothing quite so magical as a midnight feast." He passed us each a bowl of soup. Nothing more was said for a few minutes as we ate. Then Amber, now looking restored, saw the tree. "Oh," she said, "it looks beautiful!"

"Wait a minute," Uncle Perry said. He went over and hit a switch that turned on the lights.

"Now it really looks beautiful," Amber exclaimed.

"We saved some of the decorations for you to put on."

"You're sweet," she said, patting my hand. "I'd like to do that. But I'll save it until tomorrow if I may. I'm feeling much better, thanks to you, Uncle Perry, with your food and the mystery brew, but I know I'd better get to sleep."

"I think so, too," I said, getting up. "And tomorrow will be fine. But I have to show you something tonight." I walked over to the ornaments that were still arrayed on the floor. I reached down and picked up the Stonehenge globe. Holding it carefully, I carried it over to the table. "Look at this, Honey. Isn't it remarkable?"

I stretched out my hand with the ornament resting on my palm. "He thinks it's Stonehenge," Peregrine said, smiling and watching me, "but it's not." Amber reached up to take it from me. Our fingers touched.

I don't know what happened then. Perhaps it was static electricity. It felt more powerful. A charge shot through us both as her hand touched mine. And as it did, the ornament flared with light as if it had suddenly caught fire, though I felt no heat from it. I pulled my hand back in reaction, and as I did so, the globe fell out of my fingers. Amber, as startled as I, was pulling her hand back towards herself, so she wasn't able to grab it. For one heart-stopping moment we watched the ornament tumble and fall.

It shattered on the glass table.

Time stopped for all of us. I saw the stone ring lying broken amidst glass shards of the ornament on the table below me. My eyes turned to Peregrine. His eyes were wide, his smile frozen in a rictus of shock. My heart sank.

Peregrine rose to his feet. "Oh dear, oh dear!" he exclaimed, staring at the remains of the ornament on the table.

"What happened?" said Amber, also rising, clutching her hand as if it had been burned.

"Oh, I'm so sorry, Uncle Perry! I'm so sorry!" I said. We were all speaking at once.

Peregrine leaned forward, his fingers touching the pieces of the ornament. He moaned, almost a sob. I reached out and gripped his shoulder. "Peregrine, I don't know what happened. But I am so, so sorry."

He looked at me, and I was startled to see his eyes filling with tears. "No. No, Tom. It wasn't your fault. It was mine. I wasn't thinking."

"No, Uncle Perry. I'm the one who dropped it. "

He shook his head. "You don't understand. No reason you should, of course. No reason at all."

"What are you two talking about?" Amber's voice seemed to come from far away. "What just happened? Did the ornament explode? I think my hand got burned."

We both looked at her, but it was Peregrine who immediately responded. "Oh, I'm sorry, my dear. Let me see it." She held out her hand, and I could see that it looked red as if it had been sunburned. Peregrine took her hand between both of his and held it for a moment.

A look of surprise came over Amber's face. "Oh!" she said.

Peregrine withdrew his hands. It might have been my imagination or a trick of the light, but his hands now seemed red to me. "How does your hand feel now?" he asked.

She looked at him in wonder. "It feels fine." And from where I stood, I could see that the redness that had been there was all gone. "What did you do? Did you just heal my hand?"

"Not really. I'd prefer to say your hand healed itself. I just helped it along." He rubbed his hands vigorously against his trousers.

Amber reached across to touch him. "Thank you, Uncle Perry. I don't know what you did, but it helped." She looked down at the table and at the remains of the Christmas ornament. "I'm sorry about the ornament. I'll buy you another one tomorrow."

Peregrine gave a sad smile. "Thank you, my dear, but I'm afraid that won't be possible."

"Sure it is, Uncle," I said, following Amber's lead. "I'll bet I can find another one just like it on the internet. You can find anything on the web. In fact, I would be surprised if eBay didn't have one."

"I'd be very surprised indeed if it did," he replied. "It was one of a kind." He reached down and began gathering the pieces into his hands. "It was a gift, you see...."

I don't know why, but in that moment I had an intuitive flash. I don't get them very often, but now and again something will come to me, and I'll just know that it's true. Right then I knew that the ornament had been a gift from the woman my uncle had told me about on the day of our wedding, a memento of his lost love. I'd felt guilty before, but now it felt like a lead weight in my gut. "Oh, Uncle," I said, "was it..." I hesitated. "Was it from her...?"

He stopped what he was doing and looked at me curiously. "Her? Oh. Why, yes… How did you know?"

"Her?" Amber asked. I'd never told her what Peregrine had shared with me that day. I gave her my "I'll-tell-you-later-when-we're-alone" look, but she'd already made the connection. There was nothing at all wrong with her intuition.

"It was a love gift," she said, reaching out and taking one of Peregrine's hands. "That's why it was one of a kind."

"I'm afraid so, my dear."

"But she must have bought it someplace. I still think I can find another one," I persisted.

Peregrine didn't answer me this time. He just looked at me sadly, then hung his head. Amber got up and gave him a hug. "I can't tell you how sorry I am, Uncle Peregrine." She stepped back, then, still holding his arm, she pulled him towards the sofa. "You need to sit down. You look like you're in shock to me. Trust me, I'm a nurse. I know these things." She pushed him down.

"Yes, maybe I'd better sit down," he said. He dropped the pieces of the ornament he'd been picking up back on the table and sat back, his eyes closed. I felt helpless to do anything.

Not Amber, though. Like she said, she was a nurse and used to emergencies. "You need something warm and soothing to drink. Say, what about that tea you made me? It helped me, that's for sure."

Peregrine looked up at her. "I don't think that would be a good idea. I'm afraid it's what caused this to happen." He gestured at the coffee table.

"What? I don't understand," Amber said, sitting down herself now in one of the chairs next to the sofa.

Peregrine sighed. "It's hard to explain. A matter of sympathies and resonance and all that…"

"What do you mean, Uncle Perry," I asked, sitting down next to him. I was afraid he was about to go off into one of his fairy stories, and I was right.

"Elven tea, Elven ornament. You drank the one and held the other. There was a reaction when the two came together, a flare-up of energy…."

"But why didn't something happen when I went to pick it up."

"You only had a sip or two. Amber drank most of it. Put Sidhe energy into her blood. When her fingers touched yours, it closed a circuit. It released the energy in the ornament which you were holding."

Amber gave me a puzzled look. She wasn't as familiar as I with my uncle's flights of fantasy or whatever they were. "You're not making sense, Uncle," I said. "I don't understand what you're talking about.

He looked at me, a wan smile crossing his face. "I know you don't, nephew. You're too much like your father. Everything has to be solid and real." He reached out and rapped the table with his knuckles. "Sometimes, too solid..."

"But Uncle," I persisted. "Your story doesn't make sense. I was the one holding the ornament. Why wasn't my hand burnt or whatever it was that happened to Amber?"

"I'm trying to tell you. It's because Amber drank the tea. She was the sensitized one, not you. The energy flowed into her." He shook his head. "I should have known. I gave her the tea. I should have known what would happen if she touched an Elven talisman. My fault. I just didn't think..."

He looked over at Amber, who by now had an expression of real concern on her face. I knew that she was thinking thoughts of 911 and ambulances and men with white coats. Peregrine must have seen that, too, for he chuckled softly. "I'm not mad, my dear. Honestly, it all makes perfect sense, but you have to understand the world in a different way than you're used to."

"I'm trying to understand, Uncle."

"I know. I know. But it's all too new to you. It will take time. Take Tom here." He patted my hand again. "He's known me all his life and he still doesn't really understand." He sighed. "I don't think this is a good time to talk about it. We're all too tired and frankly, I've had a shock. I think I'd like to go to bed. We can talk more in the morning."

"I think that's an excellent idea," said Amber, getting to her feet. "We could all use some sleep. I know I could." She reached out and took Peregrine's hands. "Come on, Peregrine. Let me help you up. Tom and I will take you upstairs to bed." She gave a tug, and he rose from the couch.

"I'll clean this up," I said, pointing to the broken pieces on the coffee table.

Peregrine held up his hand as if to stop me. "No. I'll do it, Tom, in the morning. It's broken, but it still has energy. It can't just be thrown away. Just leave it. I'll take care of it."

He turned and headed toward the stairs, Amber right beside him. I heard him say to her, "Really, my dear. I'm all right. I'm not some doddering old fool, you know."

"Never said you were, Peregrine," she replied. "But you've had a shock and I'm a nurse, and that means I know best. So shut up and let me get you upstairs!" I had to laugh silently to myself. After two years of marriage, I was familiar with her no-nonsense tone of voice. Apparently, in spite of the events of the evening, Uncle Perry found it amusing as well, for I heard him chuckle, too, but he didn't say anything. He just went along with Amber as they headed up the stairs. Smart man.

I checked the doors to make sure everything was locked, then I headed towards the stairs myself, turning out the lights, including the ones on the Christmas tree, as I went. As I climbed up towards the bedrooms on the second floor, something caught my eye, a gleam of light in the darkness of the room below. Looking back, I saw a small, dim light where I knew the coffee table was. With a thrill down my back, I realized that the broken ornament was lying there glowing.

"Curiouser and curiouser," I said to myself. I thought for a moment of going back down to investigate. But I felt drained by the night's events. I didn't want to deal with it anymore. Determined to put all thoughts of elves and Sidhe and the Faerie worlds out of my mind, I turned away from the living room and headed up to bed.

Amber and I slept late the next morning. It was after nine o'clock when we arose. I felt pretty good, but Amber...Amber bounded out of bed, claiming she was bursting with energy. She dressed quickly and headed downstairs to make breakfast. I lay in bed awhile longer, filled with a pleasant lassitude. I felt as if I were slowly returning from some great distance, though I had no memory of any dreams.

Sidhe.

The word popped unbidden into my thoughts, and as I wondered at it, I remembered the events of the night before. In an instant, my languor vanished. Worried about my uncle, I arose and quickly dressed myself. I could hear voices in the kitchen as I emerged from our bedroom. Descending the stairs, I saw that the coffee table in the living room was bare. There was no sign of the broken ornament. Uncle Perry must have cleaned it up while we were sleeping.

I entered the kitchen to find Uncle Perry at the stove making pancakes while Amber was putting together a plate of fruit slices. I saw apple peels and orange rinds lying on a cutting board, and I could smell the tang of sliced oranges.

"Hey, sleepyhead," Amber said, coming over and giving me a kiss and a careful hug because she had a sharp cutting knife in one hand. "Did you fall back asleep?"

"Almost," I said. "You're sure different this morning. You look like you're glowing with energy." And it was true. Amber was always a high energy person. She said it went with the red hair and her Irish grandparents. But this morning it was as if someone had upped the wattage. I couldn't remember when I'd seen her looking so radiant. And this after working a double shift at the hospital the day before.

"Peregrine assures me it's the effect of the Sidhe drink," she said brightly, as if she was talking about a new brand of coffee. "He says it'll last for a couple days at least, so tonight shouldn't be a problem." I remembered that she was scheduled to pull an all-nighter. Newbie nurses always got the short straws when it came to shift assignments.

"And how are you, Uncle Perry?" I asked, coming over to where he was flipping pancakes onto a serving platter.

"I'm fine, Tom," he said, giving me a smile. But I thought I could see sadness in his eyes.

I squeezed his arm. "I'm still sorry for what happened last night."

"Tut, tut, boy. Don't trouble your heart anymore. What's done is done. Let's move on." He lifted the platter. "If we don't, the pancakes will get cold! Your lovely wife has made a most tempting fruit and nut compote to put on top of them."

We gathered around the table for breakfast. "Uncle Perry's been telling me about the Sidhe. Funny my grandparents never mentioned them," Amber said, pouring coffee for each of us.

"Not everyone likes to talk about them," Peregrine said, "not even the Irish, who should know the most. And of course," he added, glancing in my direction, "some people simply find it hard to believe even if they've grown up hearing about them." I squirmed and busied myself spreading butter on my pancakes.

"Peregrine says the Sidhe are like whales," Amber said.

His black eyebrows went up in surprise. "My dear Amber, I said no such thing!"

"Ah, but you did, Uncle. You said they were a part of humanity that decided to return to the inner realms rather than go deeper into matter. The whales did that, too, you know. They were land mammals that went back to the sea that we all came from." She grinned triumphantly.

"Well, when you put it that way..." Peregrine acquiesced. Then he laughed. "I'd never made the connection with whales before, but you're quite right. The Sidhe returned to the Shining Realms, we went forward into the worlds of physicality. The great Split." He chuckled again. "I'll have to remember that for a future novel. Thank you, my dear!"

After that, the conversation drifted to other matters. We began to make plans for Christmas which was only a week away. We talked no more of elves, the Sidhe, or the ornament that I had seen glowing in the dark as it lay broken in pieces.

The days passed as Christmas approached. I had another interview with a game company which seemed to go well, but I knew no one was going to make any decisions until after the holidays. Still, I was very hopeful. Amber and I went shopping when she had free time. As Uncle Perry had predicted, the extra energy she was feeling did wear off gradually as the days went by, but Amber's natural exuberance was such that I couldn't really tell the difference.

One event stood out for us that week that seemed magical. Amber had come home after her all-night shift to inform Peregrine and me that she'd been assigned the night-shift on Christmas Eve. That's always been a special time for me, and I'd been looking forward to spending it with Amber. Her having to work that night definitely put a damper on my Christmas spirit.

I knew Peregrine was planning a special party for the evening of Christmas Eve. It was apparently an annual tradition among a select group of his friends, all writers and artists. They called themselves the "Inklings, Too," though why they'd chosen that name, I had no idea. When he heard that Amber wouldn't be able to be there, he protested. "Oh no," he said, "this mustn't be! It isn't right. Amber must be there. Leave it to me."

Nothing more was said, but three days before Christmas, Amber came home from the hospital and happily announced that she didn't have to work on Christmas Eve after all. Apparently an older nurse named Hazel had been expecting her only son home for Christmas. Something had delayed him, and now he wouldn't be home until New Year's Day.

"The good news," Amber had said, "is that he's got a new job here, so he's moving back from wherever he's been. Hazel is delighted. 'I'd much rather have him home for good than just here for Christmas,' she told me. And then she offered to take my shift on Christmas Eve. 'You need to be home with your family,' she said. 'I might as well be working here as sitting at home alone on Christmas Eve.' Isn't that wonderful?" Then she had turned to Peregrine who had been standing nearby, beaming. "Did you have something to do with this?"

"Me?" he'd said. "My dear, you give me way too much power. I'm merely a humble scribbler, a teller of tales, a..."

She'd interrupted him with a hug. "Never mind, you old wizard. I don't know how you did it, but thank you, thank you!" With that he had beamed even more.

It was that day that I determined I had to replace Peregrine's broken ornament. I'm not sure why I felt so strongly about it. I was sorry to have dropped it, of course, but in the end, it was only one of many beautiful ornaments that Uncle Perry owned. He'd said for us to move on, and by all appearances that was exactly what he'd done.

But I couldn't. Every time I looked at the Christmas tree lit up and glowing in the living room, I felt a twinge of guilt. At times I felt sadness in the house that hadn't been there before. No, I think maybe that's too strong a description. It was more like a feeling of wistfulness. Now and again, I could feel it lurking in shadowed corners as if something precious had been lost and now couldn't find its way back home. And there were moments when an expression on Uncle Perry's face would reflect that wistfulness.

I had no doubt that he had pulled some strings to change Amber's work schedule. Even my father, ever the hard-headed skeptic, said that Peregrine had *connections*, though he would never define for me just what they might be. But I felt that myself. The man seemed like a sweet, absent-minded writer, but I knew there was a mystery about him. At times he seemed cloaked in an indefinable power. But then, maybe all writers are like that.

In any event, after Amber's news, my resolve to do something special for my uncle deepened, and the thing I most wanted to do was replace his Stonehenge ornament.

So I began searching the Internet. As Uncle Perry had warned me, though, I found nothing. I found plenty of beautiful and exotic ornaments for sale but none with standing stones in them. So, I thought to myself, *doesn't anyone think druids might like to celebrate Christmas, too? Or the Solstice? Or whatever you might celebrate with standing stones and ornaments?*

I even went so far as to call a local artist who advertised himself as a glass-blower and was selling home-made ornaments. When I explained what had happened and what I needed, he didn't laugh at me outright, but when he told me what it would cost and the time it would take, I knew it wasn't going to happen, at least not this Christmas. He must have heard the disappointment in my voice, though, for he said, "Wait a minute. Do you still have the ornament that broke?"

"I think so. My uncle put it away, but I think I can get it."

"Well, if all it needs is a new glass globe around it, maybe I can manage that in time. But I won't know until I see it. And the price will depend on how large it is."

"Oh," I assured him, "it's not very large. Suppose I bring it round to your studio, maybe even today if I can?"

He agreed and gave me an address in North Seattle, not far from where we were living. I hung up the phone, hope flaring up within me; I was sure Amber would agree to cover the cost with me from her new salary, the only income we had at the moment aside from my nearly exhausted savings.

Now all I had to do was find what was left of the ornament. It was possible, of course, that Uncle Perry had simply thrown it out. It's probably what I would have done. But I remembered the odd remark he'd made that night, something about the ornament having a special energy and that he couldn't just throw it away. This meant that he had put the pieces somewhere. But where?

The simplest thing would be to ask him, and I would if it came to that. But if possible, I wanted to do this secretly and surprise him on Christmas morning. I could just imagine the look on his face if he unwrapped a present and there was his Stonehenge ornament inside. *Even if it isn't Stonehenge,* I corrected myself.

As luck would have it, Uncle Perry wasn't at home that morning. He'd said he had some errands to run and a lunch date with friends of his. So I figured I had three hours or so to hunt for the ornament. But where? *Where would I put broken pieces of ornaments,* I wondered.

I began to look in obvious places at first. I rummaged through kitchen drawers and through cupboards and closets, of which there were many around the house. When none of these places proved successful, I began to think desperate thoughts. The house had two wings. One wing had the kitchen and dining room with our bedroom above them. In the middle was the living room with its stairway. The other wing had my uncle's study and work space, with his bedroom on the second floor as well. I kept out of those rooms, not wanting to violate his private space. But now I realized that my hope of finding the ornament in some other part of the house was foolish. Of course he would have stashed it in his own rooms. And the most logical places would be his office and study.

I had been in Uncle Perry's study before but always with him there. It was a spacious room, with bookcases covering two of the walls, a fireplace on the third, and a large picture window on the fourth wall looking out on a stand of evergreens that dominated the yard to the side of his house. It had three large, comfortable chairs and two sofas. Sometimes, Uncle Perry had told me once, when he was working on a book and didn't want to take time to go upstairs to bed, he would cat nap on one of the sofas, then get up and keep writing. It was also the place where his special group, the Inklings, Too, held their monthly meetings and shared their latest creative projects with each other.

However, this wasn't where Uncle Perry actually did his writing. That was in a smaller room he called his "sanctum sanctorum." I had never been in it. As far as I knew, he never let anyone in it. It was, he had told me once, where he and his muse wrestled stories into being.

Feeling as if I were breaking a trust but reminding myself it was for a good purpose, I went into Uncle Perry's study. There weren't many places in there for something to be hidden away. There was a small liquor cabinet by the fireplace—Uncle Perry drank very sparingly but I imagined that some of his artist friends enjoyed their libations—but a quick search didn't turn up any broken pieces of glass or small standing stones. I hadn't expected it to. I knew in my heart of hearts that there was only one place my uncle would have put the ornament, and that was in his writing room, his inner sanctum.

I got up from the liquor cabinet and crossed over to the door that led to this private room. I felt a bad feeling about what I was about to do, and again I convinced myself I was doing it out of love for my uncle and a desire to give him a good Christmas. I reached out for the doorknob... and the room suddenly darkened.

I froze, my heart racing. Then I realized the light had dimmed because of cloud cover passing over the sun, which had made a temporary appearance that morning. I sighed in relief. I'm not sure what I was expecting, but I realized I was feeling a bit spooked. All of Uncle Perry's talk about the Sidhe—indeed, all of the strangeness around my sweet but mysterious uncle—was getting to me. My feelings of guilt over what I was about to do weren't helping any, either.

Settling my nerves with a few deep breaths and reminding myself that it was just an office, not the Temple of Doom, I reached out again for the doorknob.

"Tom?"

This time I didn't freeze. I jumped. The unexpected sound of my uncle's voice shot through me like a lightning strike, and I was halfway to the ceiling before I turned around. My uncle was standing in the door to his study, an overcoat over his arm and a battered old fedora in one hand. His black eyebrows were raised in an expression of surprise and questioning.

"Tom, were you going into my office?"

I could feel my face flushing with embarrassment. "Um...er...well..." I stammered.

Uncle Perry came all the way into his study, laying his coat and hat on a chair. "Are you all right, Tom? You seem flustered?"

I couldn't believe he wasn't getting angry. He'd caught me red-handed about to enter his sanctum sanctorum, and all he wanted to know was if I was all right?

He took me by the arm and led me to a sofa where he sat me down. He then went to the liquor cabinet. "I think you need a drink, nephew. Maybe I do, too." He took out a bottle of an amber liquid and poured two half glasses. I watched him, my heart still pounding, wondering when the axe was going to fall. He came back over and sat beside me, handing me one of the glasses. His blue eyes regarding me mildly, he took a sip. "Ah," he said. "Glastonbury mead. Best in the world!" He smacked his lips. "Come on, Tom. Drink up. You're pale as a sheet."

"I...I didn't expect you back so soon..." was all I could say. Then I took a swallow of the mead. It was sweet, like honey. I felt its warmth spreading through me.

"Obviously," he said. "My lunch was canceled." His calmness unnerved me. It was far worse than if he'd been angry. "Were you just exploring or were you looking for something? There's nothing hidden in there, you know. It's just an office. I don't make a habit of inviting people into it, mainly because it's so messy. I feel embarrassed about it. But I'm a pile person, you know. Piles of papers everywhere. Wonder I can even walk through to reach my computer! Can't file worth a damn, but I know what each pile contains. You're certainly welcome if you want to see it."

"I...I...oh, damn it, Uncle, I was trying to find the broken Christmas ornament."

"The ornament? Why, I threw that out a couple of days ago."

"What! You threw it out? But...but you said you couldn't throw it out, something about Elven energies..." I took a bigger swallow of mead. Normally, I don't like sweet drinks but in that moment, it tasted very good indeed. I guess I needed it.

"That's right, Tom. I had to discharge the energy from it; otherwise it could have cause mischief. But once I did that..." he shrugged. "I had no reason to keep it. It was from a part of my life that is long gone. Yes, I was sorry to see it broken, but I'm not a sentimental fool. I learned a long time ago it's best to let go of things when you have no other options."

"But...but..." I took another swallow. I saw my hope of replacing the ornament totally disappear. Deciding it didn't matter now, I told Uncle Perry what I'd been trying to do. When I was done, he patted my hand in an affectionate way. "Nephew, it means a lot to me that you wanted to do this. It really does. But you couldn't have repaired that ornament. It was much more than what it appeared to be, you see. It was a portal, a gateway. No human craft could have restored it."

"A...a portal? To where?"

"Why, to the world of the Sidhe, of course. The Faery Realm."

"You've been there? To that..that other world?"

"Many times when I was younger." He got a faraway look in his eyes. "That was where I met her."

"The woman you loved?"

"Yes. I mentioned her to you, didn't I?" He sipped his mead. "We had even talked of being married."

"Married? To a faery?" Even for my uncle, this was beginning to sound way too far out. I could just imagine what my father would say to all this. I took another swallow of mead myself.

"It's not as unusual as it sounds, Tom. It's happened many times in the past. We *are* of the same genetic stock, after all. In fact, I have good reason to believe that one of *our* ancestors married a Sidhe." He poked me in the ribs with a long finger. "That means you have Faery blood in you, Tom. You. Me. Even your hard-headed scientist of a father. Ha! Tell that to him one day. I guarantee he won't want to know."

Knowing Dad, I could guarantee it, too.

"I didn't set out to enter the Faery realm," he continued. "It happened by accident, I guess you could say. Right in this house and at this time of year, too."

"Christmas?"

"Yes. A magical time for both worlds, theirs and ours. They told me it was the Christmas tree that did it."

"The Christmas tree?" What next, I wondered. *Santa and flying reindeer?* I started to take another drink and realized my glass was empty. I thrust it out towards my uncle and said, "More, please."

He poured me another half-glass. "Best drink this more slowly, Tom. It's more potent than it seems," he said. I lifted the glass to him in the gesture of a toast and then took a little sip. It was tasting better all the time. "Christmas tree…" I said.

"Ah, yes. Well, trees are pretty magical in themselves, and they are especially loved by the Sidhe. Putting a living tree up in your house is also very magical. Ask any child at Christmas. And this house sits on a power point…"

"Power point…?"

"Never mind. It's too complicated to explain. Think of a place where our world and that of the Sidhe come very close together. Anyway, somehow, that tree in this house on Christmas Eve…well, you see, what else could have happened?" He spread his hands wide.

"What else, of course," I agreed. "Um…what happened?"

"A portal opened. One minute I was in the living room looking at the tree—I remember I was trying to work out in my mind the details of a story I was working on—and then the next minute I was standing… there…" His voice trailed off as the memory of what had happened came over him.

"There…?" I prompted.

He refocused on me. "Sorry," he said. "It was the world of the Sidhe. I was standing just outside a ring of stones. And in the center was a glowing tree, all white and covered with snow."

"Like in the ornament?"

"Yes. And she was, there, too. I don't know who was more surprised at what had happened, her or me. But it seemed...well, it seemed absolutely right." He sighed and rubbed his eyes. I was sure he was wiping back a tear or two. "I'm telling this badly, and I'm a storyteller. It must be the mead. You must think I've gone completely round the bend."

I didn't. I found myself believing him. It must have been the mead, indeed.

"Anyway, she fashioned the ornament for me. All I had to do was hold it and think of her, and I would be back at that stone circle in her world. Or she would appear here, in this house."

When he said that, the full import of what had happened when the ornament broke hit me. "Now you can't see her anymore, right? The portal is broken so you can't go into her world anymore." I'd cut him off from the woman he loved. The guilt returned even more. This time I drank all the contents of the glass in one swallow.

Uncle Perry must have sensed what I was thinking, for he took my hand and held it. I don't know what he did, but I could feel the emotion subsiding and a curious peace come over me. "Tom, listen to me and believe what I say. I haven't used that portal for years. The fact is, I've been afraid to." He let go of my hands and sighed. "I was a coward, Tom. I could feel myself being drawn deeper and deeper into her world. It's so beautiful there, and my faery blood called out to it. But I love this world, too. I couldn't forsake one for the other. But I was like an addict. I was going over there every chance I had. It was like a drug for me. I knew I had to stop."

"She couldn't stay here?"

"Maybe. She might have. It's been known to happen. But I couldn't ask it of her. A Faery in this world, the way it is now? This is becoming a mean place, Tom. The Sidhe are the People of Peace. I couldn't ask her to live in a world where people find war... entertaining. And I...I just couldn't give up my work here. I felt with my stories I might make a difference, remind people of a nobler vision, of what human beings could be if we just made a little more effort." He sighed again. "I sound like a fool. I guess I am one."

Now it was my turn to comfort him. "You're no fool, Uncle Perry. Your stories really do inspire. But, what happened to her? Did you ever go back?"

"We said goodbye," he said. "I assume she lives on—they're practically immortal, you know—and hopefully has found another love. But I haven't been back there for years. I could have gone. But like I said, I was afraid. And now…now I never will."

There was something I had to know. "Uncle, you're not mad at me? Finding me in here, sneaking around?"

"You weren't sneaking, Nephew. You were on a holy quest. A mission of love! No, I'm not mad. Funny, I don't get mad much these days. Of course, that might be because I don't pay attention to the news! But when I saw you there, I knew there had to be a perfectly good explanation. I trust you, Tom. That's all there is to it."

There wasn't anything I could add to that. Besides, by then we were both feeling the effects of the mead. So we decided that naps were in order and that we'd talk some more later. But we didn't. It seemed there was nothing more to say on this subject, though I had a million questions about the world of the Sidhe. I might have asked them, but Christmas festivities were upon us and there was just too much to do.

Christmas Eve came and with it the Inklings, Too. I'd since learned that the original Inklings had been a small group of writers in Oxford, England, that had included Tolkien and C. S. Lewis. They had gathered regularly in a pub, the *Eagle and Child*—which, Peregrine had told me, they'd nicknamed the "Bird and Baby"—and read each other pieces of the stories they were working on. Now I understood where his group had gotten their name, but they used his house as their "pub."

Amber played hostess. She had dressed in a flowing dark green gown with a red sash and a crown of holly on her red hair. She was gorgeous and obviously the hit of the evening. Uncle Perry looked so proud I thought he would bust. I knew just what he felt.

There were three men and two women in the group, and they proved a witty and lively lot. The mead had made a reappearance and I think something that might have been elderberry wine was uncorked as well, and it all flowed freely. There were light sandwiches and chocolate goodies of all kinds. Music was played, songs were sung, stories were told, and I don't think I've ever heard so many puns in one place at one time. It was, as Peregrine said, a punnery of writers.

And then at midnight, we gathered around the Christmas tree and exchanged gifts that wouldn't be unwrapped until the sun came up in the morning. This was followed by kisses and hugs and wishes for a bright and blessed New Year, after which they all departed. It was as magical an evening as I've ever spent.

Amber and I sent Uncle Perry off to bed when everyone was gone, and we cleaned up. The dishes done, I found myself strangely energized, in spite of everything I'd drunk. Amber, however, was nearly asleep on her feet. So I sent her off to bed and said I'd be joining her in a bit.

I went into the living room. The tree lights were still on, creating a colorful glow throughout the otherwise darkened room. I went to a closet where I had hidden my Christmas presents and played Santa, arranging them under the tree. Then I sank into a chair, just enjoying the twinkling lights and the ornaments. After all the creative and joyful energy that had filled it earlier in the night, the room seemed to hum. Or maybe it was just my head that was buzzing. I don't know. I just know that I felt better than I'd felt in a long time, more powerful somehow, more together and whole. Even seeing the tree didn't fill me with guilt over the ornament that had been broken. I was in a state of grace. Perhaps it was just the spirit of Christmas.

I don't know how long I sat there, my head empty of thoughts, my heart at peace, just enjoying the lights on the tree and the sense of the silent earth outside. There was an expectancy that I'd come to associate with Christmas anyway. I'd certainly felt it as a child, but then it had been for presents. Now it was for something else. Maybe it had always been for something else, something magical, something remembered but just out of reach....

Right now, it felt so close, I could touch it. What it felt like was love. I looked at the tree and thought of all the Christmas trees I'd seen growing up, each one special, each one adding its magic to our house. How I loved them. I looked around at the shadowed room, and I thought of the times I'd come here to visit Uncle Perry. I loved this house, too. And my uncle. I had always loved him, now more than ever that he was giving Amber and me a new start, saving us from disaster. In spite of the story he'd told me, I still wanted to find a way to replace what I'd broken, perhaps to give him a new chance at finding love himself.

I looked at the tree, and it seemed to wink and glow at me as if it were reading my thoughts, agreeing with me. We were in a conspiracy together, a Christmas conspiracy. I imagined its branches reaching out into some other world, some other place, touching the tree that had been in the center of the standing stones, opening a portal.

"Please help me," I whispered, not sure to whom I was addressing my desire. Was it to the tree? To the Sidhe? I didn't know. But I felt the love and I believed anything was possible, even if I didn't have a magic ornament to help me out. "If you really do exist, if a gateway really can open between the worlds," I said, "then let it do so now."

Of course, nothing happened. *So much for magic portals.*

I decided it was time to follow Amber's example and go to bed. I got up from the chair and went over to turn out the Christmas tree lights. I paused. *No,* I thought. *Let them stay lit this night, this special night. Let the tree shine in all its glory. Someone will feel the magic.*

I turned and headed towards the stairs.

"Are you leaving?"

The voice, soft and melodic, stopped me in my tracks. I felt a thrill go through me. I turned around. There was no one there. *Great,* I thought. *Now I'm hearing things.* But it seemed to me that the Christmas tree looked different. There was a glow about it that I didn't think had been there before. Was something on fire? I walked over to check and make sure that all was well...

...and stepped into snow. I stared in bewilderment down at my feet, not quite grasping or accepting what had just happened. Then I looked around. The house was gone. I was standing in a snow-filled meadow. Off to my right, I could see a forest, dark under the stars. And in front of me was a ring of standing stones, covered with snow and lit from the center by a small tree that was glowing as afire with white flames.

It was not identical to the stone circle that had been in my uncle's Christmas ornament. These megaliths had no lintels on top of them. But otherwise, it was the same scene. Only this time it was life-size. And I was in it.

"Omigod, omigod...Oh My God!" I exclaimed. I had actually opened a portal into the land of the Sidhe. Both fear and excitement warred within me. I wasn't sure whether to shout for joy or run away....but where would I run? How did I get back home? The panic began to win out.

"Don't be afraid!" The voice came again. Turning my head, I saw a young man come out from behind one of the standing stones. "If you're afraid, you will break the link that brings us together this magical evening." He appeared about my age with long, black hair framing a narrow face that looked familiar to me. He was dressed in green trousers tucked into leather boots that rose to just under his knees, with a tunic of a lighter green. Around his waist was a silver belt. His head was bare in spite of the cold. I couldn't help but see that he had pointed ears poking through his hair.

I stared at him. I couldn't help it. It was like a character from *Lord of the Rings* had stepped out of the book and was standing before me. "You…you're an elf! You're one of the Sidhe!"

The figure smiled. "You are as perceptive as you are magical, mortal. I am indeed one of the People. My name is Perenor."

"Um…thank you. I…I guess I didn't think it would work. I still don't know what happened."

"You asked…and you were heard."

"By you?"

"Partly by me. Mostly by forces much older than me." He gestured at the megaliths behind him. "There are mysteries in stones and trees that even we do not fully understand."

The reality of what had transpired struck me hard then, and I could feel my legs going wobbly. I looked around for someplace to sit down before I fell down. Magically, an easy chair exactly like the one I'd been sitting in back in Uncle Perry's living room appeared beside me. Elven magic? Gratefully, I sat down. I gazed up at the Sidhe. "Thank you. I needed to sit down."

Another chair appeared, exactly like my own, and the Sidhe sat down in it across from me. "I did nothing. You made it happen. In this place, our thoughts take form and substance when needed."

"Really? That's convenient. I suppose. Depending on what you're thinking…." I was rambling, and I knew it. But you disappear from one world with no warning and appear in another and see how calm and collected you can be! I wondered if this was what Uncle Perry had felt when it had first happened to him.

"No," said Perenor, apparently reading my thoughts. "He was already standing in his magic. You have not yet taken that step. Perhaps after this, you will." He smiled. "We knew your uncle well at one time. We called him Star Strider because he could walk the star paths with us."

That struck a chord of memory. Uncle Perry had written about the star paths in one of his novels, and there had been a hero named Star Strider as well. Was it possible that his stories hadn't been fiction after all? Were they real adventures he had had loosely disguised as fiction?

"What has happened to him? He has not been amongst us for many years of your time. One of us loved him greatly. I do not know her well, but I think she still misses him deeply."

I shifted in my chair. In spite of the snow everywhere, I felt surprisingly warm and comfortable. Perhaps because I was wishing it so? "I'm still not sure how I came here, but that is why I came, to seek your help." And I told him the story of the ornament—what Uncle Perry had called the Elven talisman—and how it had come to be broken. Then I told him what he had told me about the love he had felt for the woman of the Sidhe and why he had stopped coming into their land. When I finished, he sat for a time with his eyes closed without saying anything, apparently lost in thought. Or perhaps he was communicating with others of his kind. I had no way of knowing. If ever someone was out of their depth, it was me at that moment.

Finally he opened his eyes. "That is a sad tale, and one filled with misunderstanding, I think. But help may be possible."

"Really? That would be wonderful! Thank you!"

"Do not thank me, mortal. I am at best only one who was passing by and felt your call. There was so much love behind it, I could not ignore it. Nor, apparently, could Others." I could feel the word being capitalized as he said it. "But I am not the one who can help you. That must come from those who guard the boundaries. "

"Can I meet with them?"

He nodded. "But first, let me show you something."

He stood up and reaching over, took my hands and pulled me up, too. That was when I fully realized how tall he was. I'm six feet one in my stocking feet, and Perenor was at least two inches taller. I could see why my uncle said the Sidhe weren't the same as the "Little People."

"Walk with me," he said. He took a step forward, and I did, too, right behind him...

...and we weren't in the snowy meadow anymore. We were on a normal city street. In fact, I recognized it as the street in front of my uncle's house.

Some years ago a group of houses in a cul-de-sac near my uncle's home had banded together to decorate all their homes in a unified way with Christmas lights and various lawn ornaments and displays. In so doing, they created a small wonderland of their own. Traffic increased along the street as more and more people drove by to see the display.

This had triggered a kind of ornamentation race as other homes along the street caught the fever. The local neighborhood became like an ostentation of peacocks, each house trying to outdo the other in the colorfulness of its Christmas display. As a result, traffic increased even more as driving through the neighborhood to see and enjoy the lights became a regular Holiday outing for many in Seattle.

Now Perenor and I stood on this street. On either side of us stretched a row of homes blazing colorfully in the night. Many of the trees and bushes were decorated with lights as well. It was ostentatious, but it was glorious as well.

"I heard your call because I was near. This is a magic time of year for us, too. We are drawn to you because of this," and he waved his hand at the displays of lights.

"You come to see our Christmas lights?" I asked, astonished and not quite believing my ears.

He laughed. "No. Your lights in themselves mean nothing to us. We come because you light the lights."

"I don't understand."

The elf waved his hand at this display. "For this one time in your year, you try to see the world as it really is, aglow with Light. You think you are decorating, but in fact you are remembering."

"Remembering?"

"Yes. This!" He made a sweeping gesture, and all the Christmas lights disappeared. For a moment, the street was dark, just as it was most of the year except for the streetlights overhead. Then everything burst into light. Every house, every tree, every bush, in fact, *everything*—even the road itself—was emitting a colorful nimbus that included hues I had never seen before.

"Wow!" I said.

"This is the world we see, a world of light, a world of color, everything radiant with its own inner qualities. A world of beauty, glowing with joy."

"Wow!" I repeated.

"Your outer eyes no longer see this world, but you remember it. You remember it from when we were one people. You remember it from your dreams and your visions. You remember the light of your own souls. And once a year, you try to recreate it. You try to live once more in a world of light as we do. Christmas is your celebration of light, but we celebrate the Light as well, the Light that makes us one."

He gestured again, and we were back in front of the megaliths. The two easy chairs were nowhere to be seen. I guess it was a case of out of mind, out of sight.

"This is why we come close to your world at Christmas time. For then you are remembering a world we shared together, a world of light and joy and love. We draw near to share that remembrance. For we can forget as well. We can forget that we were once one people. But if enough of us remember, in our world as well as yours, we can be one again. That is a goal worth pursuing. Do you understand?"

"I think so."

"This is what Star Strider knew. He remembered the ancient oneness of your people and mine. He remembered that part of us is human and part of you is Sidhe. This was—and is—the source of his magic. This was—and may be again—the source of his love for one of us, and her love for him. The talisman was simply a crystallization into form of that remembrance, a token of the oneness that each of us carries within us."

"So how can I replace what was lost? How can I bring him back his talisman?"

Perenor shook his head. "You cannot," he said. "You are not he. Even if you had his magic, you do not remember as he does or in the way he does. All you can do is remember for yourself, in your way. All you can do is try to create a talisman from yourself."

"And if I do that, will it work for him?"

"I don't know. I believe so; for once made the talisman is a bridge that should help anyone to cross. But I cannot say for sure. There is magic here that...."

"...belongs to Others," I finished his sentence for him. "The Guardians."

He nodded again.

"So where do I find these Guardians?"

"You already have." He pointed to the ring of standing stones with the tree glowing in their midst. "They are there, amidst the powers of stone and tree, planet and life, that which holds and that which grows."

I looked at the megaliths towering above me. They were nothing if not daunting. But then according to Perenor they had already helped me come here. Presumably they would be willing to help me again. "All right," I said. "What do I do?"

"You have but to walk into their midst and remember. Remember the oneness I spoke about. Remember the Light that unites. Remember the world we once knew together and may yet know again."

"That's it? Just walk in-between the stones and remember? And then what?" At the look on Perenor's face, I added, "Never mind. I know. It's above your pay grade."

He seemed to know what I meant, for he smiled and gave me a little bow. "The blessings of Light to you, mortal. May your quest be fruitful." And without so much as a goodbye, he was gone. *Probably,* I thought, *to look at more Christmas lights.*

I was alone in a snowy meadow with a primeval forest on one side of me and a megalithic stone circle on the other and a suggestion to walk into that circle and remember. Remember what, exactly? That Sidhe and human beings are the same? Really?

"If this is magic, it's not what I expected," I said out loud. I didn't expect anyone to answer, and no one did. But talking to myself helped because in that moment I felt more alone than I've ever felt in my entire life. So I said, "Might as well do it. Sooner started, sooner finished. In for a penny, in for a pound."

Nothing changed. The megaliths still towered above me. The tree still glowed whitely. The forest still lowered darkly on the horizon. And no one else came to give me any more instructions.

So I walked into the stone circle.

At first I could tell no difference standing inside the circle from standing outside except that the stones exerted a greater physical presence when they were on every side of me. The tree itself, aside from the fact that it was glowing, seemed a perfectly ordinary fir tree, slightly taller than me but not as tall as the stones. I walked over and touched it. The branch trembled, and snow fell off onto the ground. Otherwise, nothing.

"Hi, guys," I said.

Nothing.

I'm sure Peregrine would have known just what to say and do in this situation. Actually, he already had because he'd gotten one of the talismans. At least, until I broke it.

I walked over and patted one of the stones. It felt cold and hard. Like a stone should in the winter. "I'd like to go home now," I said to it. "I guess for you that's just a stone's throw away..."

Amber can always tell when I get under stress or when I'm frightened.

I start to get silly. And I was feeling silly right then. Perenor had said for me to remember the oneness of Sidhe and human, but all I could think of were jokes and puns and stupid idioms. Somehow, I didn't think the tree and the standing stones would be my best audience. At least my friends would laugh politely. I wasn't sure what a multi-ton megalith might do. I mean, when I get going, I can come up with some real groaners.

I didn't want to take the chance.

So I stood in the middle of the circle and began to take deep breaths, calming myself. Maybe, as Perenor had said, I hadn't "stepped into my magic yet," whatever that might mean, but I could at least pretend. *Think wizard,* I told myself. I looked around the circle. *I am the Lord of the Ring,* I thought. Then I remembered that that had been Sauron and he'd been the Dark Lord. So I dropped that thought. I didn't want to give a wrong impression.

OK, I'm still feeling silly. Let's start over. Remember the oneness of Sidhe and Humans. But what popped into my mind was a picture of Amber sitting at breakfast a few days ago saying, "The Sidhe are whales." I laughed out loud. All I could picture was a humpback whale with long pointed ears breaching the water.

I'm getting hysterical! I thought, catching a breath in between helpless laughter. *My God, I'm going to be trapped here forever!* But try as I might, I couldn't get the image of elven whales out of my mind.

Something clicked. I guess my subconscious had been working on the problem all along. Whales. Human beings. We weren't the same, and yet we were. We were both mammals. We had a common ancestor, though now we lived in different worlds. We both breathed air. We both gave birth to children and nursed them. We both made songs. We both had language.

My problem was that I thought of the Sidhe as supernatural beings, legends and myths born of fantasy and imagination. If they existed at all—and I was now prepared to admit to myself they did—they were magical creatures woven from light and shadow while we were creatures of matter and flesh. What could we have in common? How could we be one? But then, at first glance, what did whales and humans have in common?

So the Sidhe lived in invisible realms and we lived in a physical world. Did it matter? Whales lived in water and we lived on land, yet we were both mammals. We had a connection that transcended environment.

Maybe it didn't matter where one lived. Maybe it only mattered what one was.

"Remember the Light," Perenor had said. I thought of all the lights we lit at Christmas: lights on trees, lights on houses, lights up and down streets, lighting candles. "You're trying to remember the Light within the world. You're trying to remember the world you knew when we were one." He had showed me a glimpse of that world, and it had been beautiful, far more than anything we could achieve with mere bulbs and wires and electricity. My heart had swelled and ached when I saw it.

Perenor had said the Sidhe came close at this time of year to remember with us the ancient world of Light we had once known together; sharing in our remembrance, he'd said, helped them remember, too—not the Light, for they always saw that, but that we had seen it together; that we had once been one.

Looking at the stones and the tree, though, I realized that wasn't all there was to it. They came to us for another reason, too, one Perenor hadn't mentioned. Perhaps he hadn't known. *They come to see the Light as we see it. They come to see a Light they cannot see in their world.*

The thought was a crazy one. What did it mean? But deep down, I knew what it meant. It was the reason we had split in the first place, the reason some of our ancestors had gone into matter while others had stayed behind, becoming the Sidhe. It was why some mammals had stayed on land while others returned to the sea, because the land offered something the sea couldn't.

"We see the Light as form and matter," I said aloud. "We see it as substance. We see Light in a way you can't. You see the Light within matter, but we can see the Light as matter. And that matters. It matters!" I fairly screamed the words to the stones around me, and I laughed with the joy of it.

I thought of the easy chair that had materialized for me when I'd thought of it. It had seemed like magic to me, but it had been normal to Perenor. He lived in a world that was so fluid and plastic that mere thought could shape substance and bring something into being instantly. I knew for sure that didn't happen in my world! But I thought of Amber sitting at her potter's wheel, her hands deep into the clay spinning before her, molding and creating through her touch, getting herself dirty as she shaped the wet matter under her fingers. *We turn our thoughts into creations, too,* I thought. It just takes us longer. And in the process, we come to know matter, what it is and what it can do. We know Light as matter, just as the Sidhe know Light as...what? Energy? Thought? *As something else, certainly.*

But both kinds of knowing are important.

As I said, I'm not very intuitive normally, but when I *do* get an intuitive hit, I know I'm right. And I knew it this time. We weren't the Sidhe who'd gone astray, anymore than they were the humans who'd faltered before an opportunity to go forward. We were two sides of a single mind seeing the world in a wider way, a more complete way. We were like eyes, each transmitting information that together made a whole picture.

But the eyes have forgotten they're part of a single body, I thought. *They've forgotten how to see together.*

Except at Christmas. At Christmas, the eyes draw close and there's a chance the world can be seen in its wholeness.

I don't need to remember that the Sidhe and Humans were once one, I thought. *We're still one, but we're also different. That's what I need to remember. I need to remember why we split in the first place so that something greater than either of us could see in a wider, deeper way. I need to remember how we can see together. That we can see together, as partners, as eyes in that larger body, whatever it is.*

Thinking this, I also realized what the Boundary was. It wasn't really a wall to keep someone out or the two worlds separate. It was the state of forgetting that kept us apart. And the Guardians weren't guards as such but witnesses to the act of remembering that could draw the worlds together again.

PING!

The sound echoed around the stone circle. Something had happened. I looked around. At first, everything seemed the same. Nothing was different. But then I saw it. Hanging from a ranch of the tree.

A Christmas ornament.

Bingo! I thought.

I walked over and looked at it. It was a glass globe, and in it was the very stone circle in which I was standing, with a glowing white tree at its center. I had remembered. It had worked.

I reached for the ornament.

And I began to shake.

Rather something was shaking me. Hard. I groaned. The shaking increased. A familiar voice was speaking in my ear. "C'mon, sleepyhead.

Don't spend Christmas Eve night dozing in a chair. Come to bed." It was Amber.

"What...?" I said, my mind still filled with images of standing stones and a glowing white tree. "Where...?"

"In the living room, that's where. Come on. You fell asleep in the chair, silly. Come on to bed."

I let her pull me to my feet. I felt wholly disoriented. The living room seemed dark and strange. Seeing I was upright, Amber went over to the tree. "I woke up and found you missing. I figured you'd fallen asleep downstairs, and I was right. Here, let's turn these lights off."

I put out my hand to stop her. "No. No, let's leave them on. It'll be OK. Let the lights...let the lights stay on through the night."

She looked at me, then grinned. "OK. Lighting the way for Santa Claus, right? Well, if he's going to come, we'd better get to bed." And she pulled me towards the stairs. I followed her, wondering. *The Sidhe. The standing stones. The ornament on the tree. Had it all just been a dream?*

But then I felt something in my pocket. Pulling it out, I saw it was a Christmas ornament, a white tree glowing inside it, surrounded by snow covered standing stones. I smiled to myself. *It really happened. It really, really happened!* Realizing this, the world suddenly felt *right*, as if a missing piece had been found and had slipped into place. I felt as if I'd received the best gift I'd ever had.

We all slept late on Christmas morning. When we finally got up, it was to a rainy morning and a house that felt like it had settled into a deep peace during the night. The first thing I did was find a little box and wrap up the ornament. *This will blow Uncle Perry's socks off!* I thought. I grinned. *I guess I stepped into my magic, all right!*

I did the breakfast honors, preparing my signature omelet of cheese, apple slices, sausage, and onion. Then we cleaned up. Only then did we go into the living room to open our presents. When we were done, I brought out my little package and handed it to my uncle. "What's this," he said.

"Oh, a little something I found. Open it!"

He pulled the bow off and carefully removed off the paper. The box lay in his hand. He lifted off the lid. I saw his eyes grow large and his eyebrows shoot up his forehead. It was very satisfying. He reached in and pulled the ornament from the box, holding it up so Amber and I, sitting together on the sofa, could see it.

"Oh, good, Tom, you did find another one," Amber said, clapping her hands in delight next to me. I hadn't told her what had happened last night.

Peregrine looked at me with both wonder and suspicion in his eyes. "Good Lord!" he said. "I...I'm speechless... Tom, where did you get this?"

I shrugged. "It's like I said, Uncle Perry. You can find anything on the Internet."

"I doubt that very much, but I won't belabor the point right now. But I think you and I need to have a talk very soon, Nephew."

"Anytime, Uncle. But for now, why don't you just hang it on the tree. That's what it's for."

"And so I shall," he said, getting up and going over to the tree. He took down a red globe, one of those ornaments I considered "filler," removed the hook from it and attached it to the new ornament. Then, carefully, he reached out and hung it on a branch of the tree.

A deep, resonant hum sounded through the room. Startled, Peregrine stepped back. At the same time, light erupted from the ornament, filling the Christmas tree.

"Tom, the tree's on fire," shouted Amber, gripping my arm and rising to her feet.

"No, it's not!" I said, pulling her back down onto the sofa. "It's all right!"

It seemed as if the room became larger somehow, not in size but in dimension, becoming more spacious. The Christmas tree stayed where it was, its lights twinkling as before, but spreading out behind it on either side were other fir trees, tall, dark, and majestic, as if our little tree had become part of a vast forest. I realized the house was half in one world and half in another.

Waves of light began to descend like luminous veils from the tops of these trees down onto the floor, spreading out into the living room behind us. And then shining figures, both men and women, descended down the light as if they were walking down a staircase. If I didn't know better, I'd have thought they were angels, for they were dressed in white and light swirled around them. But I knew who they were.

I put my arm around Amber and pulled her close, whispering in her ear, "It's OK, darling. They're the Sidhe." I was concerned that she might be frightened. God knows I would have been if I hadn't had my experience last night. But she seemed to be taking it in stride. Must have been her Irish background. Not taking her eyes off the descending figures, she squeezed my hand and said, "I know who they are, silly. Remember? Peregrine told me about them." She giggled with delight. "They're whales visiting us from the deep oceans!"

They were beautiful as they passed down the tree. Smiling at us, they glided by, spreading out into the room, forming a circle around us. I had never seen men more handsome nor women more gorgeous. How could they be otherwise? Their bodies were shaped by the thought of beauty itself and had never known the stresses of living in matter. Yet, for all their loveliness, they were ethereal. I knew deeply and thoroughly that they posed no competition to Amber for me, nor, I felt, for me with her. After all, they were whales and we were humans. I gave her a loving squeeze to prove the point, and she squeezed me back.

Looking over at my uncle, I could see that he was in shock. He had collapsed back into the chair in which he'd been sitting while opening presents, his mouth open in astonishment. For the first time, I appreciated what the term "slack-jawed" really meant. I was momentarily afraid he might have a heart attack. But his face took on a radiance of wonder and excitement, and I knew all was well.

It seemed like they just kept coming, and I thought I recognized Perenor in their midst, but I wasn't sure. The silly side of me said in my mind, *Who can tell them apart? All Sidhe look alike....beautiful.* But I kept my mouth shut.

The flow stopped. I had no idea how many Sidhe had come through the portal. The room was full. Then they began to sing. It was like a Christmas carol, a paean to love and to the light and to both ancient memories and new possibilities. When it was over, one of the Sidhe women stepped forward and said to all of us, "Thank you for remembering. Thank you for the possibility of new vision, for two eyes seeing together." She smiled at me and stepped back.

Uncle Perry looked over at me and mouthed the words, "What did you *do*, Nephew?"

I grinned back. "I remembered!" I said.

Then the Sidhe began to disappear. They didn't go back up the tree. They simply faded out one by one until only one was left. A woman who came forward and stood in front of Peregrine.

"I've missed you," she said.

Peregrine was on his feet in an instant, but then didn't seem to know what to do with his hands. I could see he wanted to touch her, even hug her, but he was uncertain what to do. So he dropped his hands to his sides and said simply, "I've missed you, too, Mirander."

I noticed that tears were running down his cheeks. Glancing at Amber, I saw that her eyes were welling up as well. "It's *her*, isn't it," she whispered to me. I nodded.

If Uncle Perry was shy, the Sidhe woman was not. She gathered him up in an embrace and kissed him. Drawing back, she said, "Star Strider, my love. There was no reason for us to be apart. Or if there was, it matters not now."

"But, Mirandir....." He stepped back from her. I could feel him steeling himself to send her away once again. "Nothing has changed. I cannot live in your world, and you cannot live in mine."

She snorted. "Nonsense! You're a silly old fool. Everything has changed. You feared the power of my world because you were young and still discovering your human self. But now you have sovereignty and wisdom. You know who you are. You have found your own power. My realm cannot take that from you. And as for being here...don't you think I know what your world is like? Do you think I fear it? I do not. It cannot harm me, all the more because we will be together."

"What are you saying?"

"What do you think I'm saying? We can be together again."

"But...look at you. You're still young...and I'm...I'm just what you said, an *old* fool."

She laughed. "Peregrine, my love, I am six hundred years old. In my world, I'm a teenager, a callow youth. My good judgment is suspect because I'm so young. Why else would I give myself to a mortal, eh? You are hardly too old for me! Besides, I have ways of making you young again!" And I swear I saw Uncle Perry blush.

"I think she's got you," I ventured. "It sounds good to me, Uncle. I can't see how you can argue with her."

Peregrine looked at Amber and me, a helpless look on his face. But then, as the reality of the situation sank in, he began to smile, and the smile grew until it seemed his face would split. "I guess I have no choice," he said.

"Good," said Mirandir. "Then come with me now. We're having a celebration, and I would like you there as my consort!"

My uncle bowed to her and then took her arm. I swear he suddenly looked ten years younger. "Star Strider is yours to command, my Lady. Lead on!"

Mirandir smiled, and I swear the room got brighter. They disappeared, and with their departure, the room was back to its usual size and shape, with only one tree in it, happily twinkling with Christmas lights.

"Wow!" said Amber. Now tears the streaming down her cheeks, and I admit my own throat felt a bit tight.

Three days later, we discovered an envelope and a package on the kitchen table as Amber and I came down to fix breakfast. Opening the envelope, I found it held legal documents signing over the deed of the house to us and giving me power of attorney over all my Uncle's affairs and access to his bank account. With it was a note in his handwriting.

"Read it," Amber said.

"Dear Nephew," I read. "The house is yours, and everything in it. I won't be needing it. You're my legal representative now. Use the money to pay taxes, upkeep, etc. Take a couple of vacations, too! Just finished visiting the Golden Mountains of El'Rangor. Beautiful. Must work them into a story someday. Off to the Bahamas next. Mirandir sends her love. See you next Christmas! Or come visit us. You can now, you know. Oh, in the package is a fresh supply of Lembas Tea for when Amber works late shifts. But please...Don't drink it while trimming the tree! Love, Peregrine Star Strider."

"How sweet!" said Amber. "Just like Uncle Perry. But what did he mean about visiting him? How can we do that?"

I sat back, smiling, thinking of a stone circle with a tree in it. "Oh, I think I can remember," I said.

DRAGON'S RIDE

An epic Christmas tale by
David Spangler

BOOK THE FIRST
THE FELLOWSHIP

I stood in the doorway of the Boar and Board, the warmth of the large common room before me contrasting sharply with the icy cold wind at my back. I glanced around. Bristle, the innkeeper nodded as my glance swept over him, and one of the serving maids grinned and lowered her eyelid in a suggestive wink.

No one else paid any attention to me as I stepped into the large common room and let the oaken door close behind me. This was good. I could see it was a quiet night in the tavern, which was not unusual for fifth night. Oh, there was the usual roughhousing in one of the corners, but as far as I could tell no knives had been drawn and I didn't see any fresh blood stains. All in all, a mellow evening.

I made for my customary table in the darkest corner, the better to see and not be seen. Stealth is as much a part of me as blood and bone, which is why I'm a Ranger. Someone had been sitting there, but the innkeeper must have made a signal to him, for he got up and moved. It's the arrangement we have. Anyone can sit in this corner unless I come in, then it's mine, no questions asked. I paid for it in blood when I escorted the innkeeper's daughter and her dowry to some lout of a husband who lived in Bran's Ford on the other side of Blackthistle Forest. Twelve brigands died trying to intercept us, and I ended up in bed for a week nursing a sword wound in my leg, but dowry and bride made it safely to their destination. Ever since, Bristle has made this corner and its table mine out of gratitude. Should anyone contest my right to it, the innkeeper persuades him otherwise with a wicked blackjack and the threat that he'll never be served in the Boar and Board again.

I swept my cloak back from my legs and sat down, laying my sword on the table in full view—a sign to all comers that I preferred to sit alone. I'd no sooner settled myself than a mug of ale was placed in front of me by the serving maid. Once again her eyelid closed in a slow, suggestive way, but this time she raised her free hand and gave her eye a vigorous rub. "Damn sawdust in here," she growled, her voice low and husky. "Keeps getting in my eye."

"I thought you were winking at me," I said.

She laughed. "Darling, if I were winking at you, you wouldn't just be sitting there." She grinned at me again and left me alone. Barmaids are good at reading their customer's moods.

I sat there drinking my ale, watching the other customers. There were a lot of memories for me in this tavern. It had been the starting point for many a quest, and there were many times I'd laid abed upstairs waiting for wounds to heal after some of those adventures had gone bad. Even the successful quests could leave you half-dead if you weren't careful. Delving into ancient dungeons or raiding cursed tombs could reward you with treasure but you were just as likely to find something nasty and undead with long teeth and claws crawling about waiting to suck on your marrow.

Still all in all, I had little to complain about. My leathers had blood stains front and back and down the arms, but I was still basically in one piece and healthy enough to be thinking about my future. I had gold in the King's Bank, and hidden elsewhere as well—several elsewheres, in fact—just in case; I'm never sure whether to trust bankers. If I was a settling man, I could buy some land, find a wife, and start a homestead. But that's not me. I'm a Ranger through and through. I range, I don't settle. And the one woman I love…well, it's my curse she's an Elven princess and not likely to take up a wandering life with me.

The crash of the front door being flung open and a gust of cold air blowing into the tavern broke me out of my reverie, which was good as I was starting to indulge in way too much thinking. My hand automatically went to my sword lying beside me, but then I saw that it was just Fro the Halfling who had come in. His entrance wasn't meant to be forceful or belligerent. He just never quite understood his own strength, and at nearly 8 feet in height he had a lot of strength to be ignorant of. His kind grew big, usually half again the size of an average man, which was why they were called "Halflings." An equally appropriate name would have been Halfwit, as they were not the smartest people in the Kingdom, but no one ever called them that to their face. They were sensitive about their intellectual capabilities and were known to protest with their fists if these were called into question. Still, if you were on a quest and wanted a tower of strength for smashing open a dungeon door or demolishing a horde of ravening beasties, a Halfling like Fro was just the ticket. In fact, he and I had paired up more than once, and I admit I had a soft place in my heart for him.

But not tonight. Tonight I just wanted to drink my ale, eat some stew and be left alone. So I pulled the hood of my cloak up over my head and leaned back more into the shadows, willing myself to be invisible. Fro stood in the doorway looking about, then clumped over towards a bench by one of the long common tables. I could see the other drinkers and diners on the bench scrambling to get up, but their legs were tangled under the table and they were too late. As was his wont, Fro sat on the end of the bench because his legs were too long and large to fit under the table. This, of course, launched the other diners up over his head as the other end of the bunch shot up in the air like a catapult. Seeing Fro come in, people have been known to take bets as to how far some hapless diner might be flung across the room when the Halfling sat down. Tonight the score would have been impressive. If anything, I think Fro had put on weight.

As diners picked themselves up—or were carried off unconscious— Fro looked around apologetically. No matter how many times this happened, he never seemed to grasp the mechanics of it or why people tumbled through the air when he sat down. I think he suspected magic was at work. As I say, Halflings are not the sharpest swords in the armory.

I turned back to my table as Bristle brought me a meal of boar stew and hot bread. I thanked him and dove in with a will. I had walked many miles this day, and I was ravenous.

I suddenly felt the weight of a hand on my shoulder. Someone had come up beside me without my noticing while I was eating, and believe me, that's hard to do. Damn near impossible in fact. But when I looked up to see who it was, I understood. It was Pintoglas, the elf. No one moves as quietly and stealthily as an elf, not even a Ranger, not even on our best days. I tell myself it's because they're partly magical creatures.

"Greetings, Ari," he said, in his impossibly beautiful voice. "May I join you?"

I hesitated. Like I said, I wanted to be left alone. But Pintoglas was an exception. He was one of the few elves ever to leave the Brightbark Woods and walk the roads of the Kingdom. He claimed to be an elven prince, and this might even be true; what was true beyond question was that he was a steadfast companion in a fight, an exceptional archer—even among the elves, who claimed to have invented and perfected the bow long before humans appeared on the scene—and a friend. Even more important, he was an amazing drinking companion with a legendary capacity for downing pints of ale one after the other and never showing any effect. Which was why everyone called him "Pintoglas," that and the fact that his real elven name was unpronounceable by any human being who was not thoroughly sloshed himself.

I nodded. "Greetings to you, my friend. I'd be happy to have you join me."

He smiled and dragged over a chair from a nearby table. "You lie well, Ari, but I accept. I have need of different company than I have."

"Different company...?" Then I noticed the elf was not alone. Tall and stately as he was, I hadn't noticed the short, stocky form behind him. It was Grinli, the dwarf. Dwarves and elves are notoriously ill-tempered towards each other and usually cannot abide each other's presence. But over the years and many quests, Pintoglas and Grinli had formed a relationship. No one would call it a friendship. It was more like a habit of association.

"I, too, wished to be alone tonight to contemplate the approach of Year's Turn Night, but this one..." he shrugged his shoulder in the direction of the dwarf, "persists in accompanying me wherever I go. So I thought if there were three of us, it might be the same as being alone."

This to my mind was a good example of elven logic.

Grinli's deep, rough voice, like boulders grinding together, broke in. "Hello, Ari. The fact is this elf cannot be trusted to be alone. You know how elves get at this time of year, all morose with the loss of sunlight. I am afraid he will do away with himself. Not that I would mind one less elf, you understand, but he owes me money..."

"I asked him for two coppers to buy a pint of ale, and that was three months ago..." If an impossibly beautiful and melodic voice can sound exasperated, the elf's did. "I long ago offered to buy him a pint in return, but he insists I pay him back in coin and with interest."

"A loan's a loan, and interest is part of it. So of course, I have to see he remains healthy as he frequents these human dives where the Stone One alone knows what could happen, what with cutpurses and the like." He fingered the edge of his battleaxe and glanced menacingly around him. The closest diners looked away and sank lower in their seats as if they could disappear. There might be cutpurses here tonight, but we all knew none of them were at all likely to rob an elf, much less a dwarf with his axe. Unless they were drunk out of their minds, of course.

I knew both were just making excuses to cover up the fact that they now genuinely enjoyed each other's company and were embarrassed by the fact. I might have made a joke about it, but neither elves nor dwarves are known for their sense of humor. Actually, elves—so I'm told—can be very funny indeed, but their humor is so convoluted that only another elf can understand it, and the punch line can take centuries to sink in. As for dwarves...well, let's say that in all the years I've known Grinli, I've never seen him smile, never mind laugh. Which, of course, is why I call him Grinli. He may not have a sense of humor, but I do. Besides, humans can't pronounce dwarven names either.

"All right, come and sit with me. I'd hoped for a quiet evening alone, but I see I have no chance of that now. Besides, it's good to see the two of you. It's been, what? Seven months since we went down the Snakeroot River to that liche's tomb?"

"Don't remind me," said Grinli, as he pulled up a chair as well. When he sat, his forehead was level with the table top. "All that water! The Stone One never intended for dwarves and boats to go together."

"Still," Pintoglas said, "we did rid the land of an ancient evil. And we did find those three chests..."

"Which were empty," snorted Grinli. "Water and then no treasure."

"Not empty at all," said Pintoglas. "They were filled with scrolls."

"Which no one could read and no one wanted. A chest with no gold or jewels is empty."

"Scrolls no one could read yet," Pintoglas said. "I'm working on it." He reached inside his blouse and pulled out a rolled up parchment. Carefully he partly unrolled it onto the table. "You see those markings? I'm sure they are Old Elvish, but of a dialect unknown to me. I think it describes a magical spell." Did I say that every elf thinks he's a scholar and loremaster? A few of them actually are.

"More likely it's some accountant's ledger," said the dwarf. "Where's that serving wench? I want some ale." He waved his hand in the air, but it wasn't much higher than the table itself. It's hard for a dwarf to get service as most people think no one's sitting at their tables. I caught the serving maid's eye—the eyelid was still drooping up and down—and pointed to my mug, raising three fingers. She nodded.

"Aye," echoed Pintoglas, studying the scroll. "Translating is truly thirsty work."

The feel of cold air drew my attention back to the front door of the tavern. A newcomer stood there on the threshold, obviously hesitating whether to enter or not. It was a slight figure, completely wrapped from head to foot in a hooded cloak, its face hidden in the cowl's shadow. I could see from where I sat that the fabric of the cloak was expensive, not the kind of thing one normally saw at the Boar and Board. "Uh oh," I muttered.

Grinli looked at me. "What is it?"

I nodded to the doorway. "This could be trouble." The dwarf tried to see across the room but he was too low down. The farthest he could see was into my lap. "Well, for the Stone One's sake, what is it?"

"Some noblewoman, I think, slumming it. Such a thing never turns out well. There will be screaming and swords will be drawn and blood will be shed...."

Pintoglas looked up from his scroll, glanced at the door, then went back to his attempts at translation. "'Tis no maid," he said. "It's a young man, a wizard in fact."

Did I say that elven eyesight is phenomenal and that they can sense the presence of magic?

"A wizard?" Grinli shivered. "I can't abide wizards. They bring trouble the way a dog brings fleas."

"I'm not so fond of them myself," I said. Some of the worst, most dangerous, most wound-full quests I had been on had been instigated by wizards.

I turned my head away so as not to attract the wizard's attention, but I watched him out of the corner of my eye. He was obviously looking for someone, and a feeling at the pit of my stomach said it probably was me. I don't like to brag, but as the only Ranger in the vicinity, I did have a reputation that attracted quest-seekers like gold attracts kings. Sure enough, he closed the door behind him and headed in our direction.

"He's headed this way," I whispered. "Ignore him."

"You can't ignore wizards," Pintoglas said. All too true. They can see you if you're invisible and they can blast you with a fireball if you cross them or don't pay attention to them. The gods must have been in a foul mood when they created wizards.

The hooded figure came up and stood by our table. I could tell by then that it was indeed a young man, and this was confirmed, if confirmation were needed, when he reached up and threw back his hood. Flaxen hair that was so light as to almost be white framed a round, innocent face. Although it can be very hard to tell a wizard's age, this one looked way too boyish to be anything but a boy.

He stuck out his hand in greeting to me. "You are Ari, the Ranger," he said. It was not a question. He looked at my companions. "And you are Grinologhtrogthogklantisburr, the dwarven warrior, and Pintologoloramolioral, the elven prince and scholar." Their names rolled off his tongue as if he'd been speaking Dwarven and Elvish all his life. I was impressed in spite of myself. Damn wizards.

Pintoglas half bowed to our visitor while Grinli scowled to cover up looking impressed that the stranger could actually pronounce his name. "And you are, gracious sir?"

"Ah, I am…I am…"he stuttered, and I realized to my surprise that he was nervous and shy in our presence. I'd never met a shy wizard before. This made *me* nervous.

He cleared his throat and bowed. "I am Rondol, assistant Wizard to Sandovon the White."

"Ah, the Royal Wizard," Pintoglas said. "Then I am honored to meet one who is assistant to so august a wielder of magic."

I swear the boy shuffled his feet under his cloak. "Well, really…the truth is…you see, I am only a very junior assistant, one of several. I doubt Master Sandovon even knows my name. He is somewhat forgetful about his assistant's names. But…" and here he drew himself up. "forgettable or not, I am still a wizard and fully…well…highly…um…sufficiently capable in the Magical Arts. And if all goes according to my vision, Master Sandovon and even the whole kingdom will benefit from what I do."

Uh oh, I thought, an ambitious wizardling, a sure recipe for disaster.

"And how will you accomplish this?" Grinli's gravelly voice rose from near the table's top.

Rondol looked down. "Well, that will depend on the success of my quest. And that, in turn, depends on the three of you."

It's hard to dissuade a wizard who has made up his mind, but I thought it was worth a try. This one seemed young enough and uncertain enough that a dramatic refusal just might work. I slammed my fist down hard on the table, making my sword bounce slightly into the air. Everyone else jumped in surprise as well. Well, everyone except Pintoglas. Nothing startles an elf.

"Damn it," I said. "All I wanted was a quiet evening, eating some of Bristle's goodly stew, drinking some ale, and being by myself, or..." I added, glancing at Pintoglas and Grinli, "with bosom companions. And now you come with a quest. Do you know how many people come to me with quests? Why, if I had a gold piece...no, even a lowly copper—for all the times people come to me to take them on quests, I could retire and never quest again." The fact that I was already rich enough to never have to quest again was a point I thought better to keep to myself.

"I...I apologize, Sir Ranger. I would not have intruded except... well...I've had a vision."

I groaned and laid my head down between my hands. I can be dramatic when I want to be, and I thought I might just drive this lowly junior assistant wizard away with a show of pique. "Not another wizard with a vision! That's even worse. Not even a treasure map or an ancient scroll to start the quest but a vision? Gods preserve me."

I thought my boon companions might pick up on the hint and affect being similarly outraged at being bothered, thus driving this wizardling away to find some other victim for his imaginings. But Pintoglas had, like Grinli, obviously been impressed by someone who could pronounce his name, not to mention addressing him as "prince and scholar," and this inclined him to be gracious instead. "And what," he asked, "was this vision and the quest it inspired? It must have been of some importance to have brought you to this lowly dive in search of hardened adventurers like ourselves."

"Hardened *expensive* adventurers, I might add," Grinli's voice rumbled up from below.

"I hardly know where to begin," he said, and I groaned again, more loudly but with my face still buried in my hands. "The vision is hard to describe. But the thrust of it is simple enough. We need to capture a dragon"

I lifted my head in shock. "Are you crazy?" I said, no longer posing but sincerely astonished. "No one captures dragons. No one even kills dragons. If you try, dragons kill *you*."

Rondol gave me a I-know-that-but-it-makes-no-difference look and was about to say something when Pintoglas interrupted. "Young Wizard, Ari is correct. Dragons are the most magical and powerful of creatures on this earth. In all the memory of my people—and be assured that is a very long memory—no dragon has ever been captured. They are subject to no one's will but their own—or if there is a higher will over theirs, I know not what it might be and I would not want to meet the being who wields it. I fear this quest of yours is impossible, however magnificent the vision that inspired it."

Rondol knelt down so that he was eye level with Grinli, an act of respect that made me grudgingly acknowledge this wizard knew something about the people he was dealing with. "And what do you say, Sir Dwarf? It is widely and well known that the People of the Earth have a long history of dealing with dragons and have acquired wisdom therefrom. Do *you* say it is impossible?"

I could see Grinli puff up with pride at being so acknowledged and honored, and I was afraid for a moment that he was going to encourage the young wizard in his fantasy. But after a moment's silence, the dwarf shook his head. "I fear so. You are right in saying that we have a long history with the dragons, but as the elf said, in all our memory, no one has captured a dragon. Oh, we have slain some, always at great cost but leaving many tales and songs of bravery and cunning. But to capture a dragon...nay, this is not possible."

"Not that it matters," I said, taking a sip of ale. "No one knows where the dragons are now anyway. No one's seen any for years. If they had, I'd have heard about it on my travels. It's the kind of news that people can't resist telling rangers."

Rondol stood up and shrugged. "That is not a problem. Wizards have always known where they are; we keep the knowledge secret because of the very danger you describe. Nevertheless, I must now use this knowledge to seek out and capture a dragon for the good of the Kingdom. I have no other road before me. And I do not believe it as hopeless as you all say it is. Dragons are, as you say, magical creatures, and what lives by magic can be controlled by magic."

"That may be true theoretically," Pintoglas said, "but it would take a most puissant magic indeed. I think even the great Royal Wizard, Sandovon, would be stretched to his limits."

"And I am not in Sandovon's class. I know what you're thinking, Sir Elf. And you are right. But what if there were an artifact that could bind a dragon's will?"

"I know of no such artifact," I said.

"Nor I," said Pintoglas.

"Nor....well....actually..."

"Yes, Grinli?" I said.

The dwarf harrumphed a couple of times. "There was a dwarven wizard once who claimed to have made such a thing. As you know, wizards are very rare among my people and are looked upon with some suspicion. Give us good honest stone and a good honest axe and good honest tools. We have no use for magic. But this mage was unusual, both as a wizard and as a dwarf. He is known as Longrim the Insane, and I think he truly was mad. But in his madness, he possessed an uncanny skill, some say born of darker arts, and from them he claimed to have fashioned a magic ring that could control the dragon folk. I cannot say if it is true or not. To my knowledge he never put his ring to the test." He shrugged. "Longrim lived nearly a thousand years ago, so it may all be just legend."

"What if I told you it is true? What if I told you such a ring exists? What if I told you I know where it is? Would you be interested?"

Grinli stood up on his chair so he could be eye level with Rondol, which was, I knew, a great act of respect on *his* part. "Such a thing would be priceless. I would be very interested."

"Then join with me on my quest, for there is such a ring and I *do* know where it is."

For a moment, none of us could think of anything to say. I had had no idea that such a magical ring existed, but if it did and a dragon could be controlled, the possibilities boggled the mind.

"How have you come by this knowledge, wizard," Pintoglas asked. "Was the revelation of this artifact and its whereabouts the subject of your vision?"

Rondol shook his head. "No. I discovered the nature of this ring and its whereabouts before I had the vision, but I have no doubt they are related. I think both were sent to me by the gods to save the Kingdom."

"Look here," I said. "You keep speaking of saving the Kingdom. But I have traveled the length and breadth of this land, and I know of no danger that threatens us, at least not of a nature that could bring down the Kingdom itself."

The wizard sighed. "I am telling all this badly. You are right, there is no danger right now on our horizon. But one is coming. For those of us versed in reading the signs that the future sends, it is plain. You know of the Unbodied One?"

I looked at my companions. "By legend only. He was a mage-king who entered into a pact with the Dark Lords in return for power. At one time he sought to conquer the land but was defeated by an alliance of men, elves and dwarves. But that was two thousand years ago or more."

"Two thousand, three hundred, and forty-two years, to be exact. It was a near thing for he had made himself almost a god in his power," Pintoglas picked up the story. "But in the end he was defeated."

"By a dragon," Grinli added. "Summoned by my ancestors."

"Summoned by the wizards of all of our peoples," said Pintoglas, a bit nettled by Grinli claiming the glory for his kind, "but yes," he added grudgingly, "with the power focused through the dwarves and your connections to dragonkind."

"It was not a dragon as such," Rondol said, "but the dragonpower, given by the dragons and channeled through a council of wizards. And it did not slay the mage-king for his power placed him beyond death. But it *did* destroy his body and his connection to the world. He remains alive but in a nether realm, neither here nor there, hence his name, the Unbodied One."

"But he is powerless, right?" Grinli asked. "If he has no body, no way into this world, then he cannot wreak harm here."

It was my turn to remember talk I had heard and some dark things I had witnessed on my recent trips throughout the land, particularly in the far north. "I'm not so sure. There are happenings in the land that suggest he may be finding a way back. I have heard rumors of minions of the Unbodied One gathering in small enclaves in the north and dark magics being performed. But," I added, looking at Rondol, "you would know more about this than I."

"It's true. The Unbodied One *is* seeking a way back, and there are places where the veil between our world and the nether realm that holds him are growing thin. His will seeps through and finds those he can control. Though there is no danger yet, if the threshold keeps growing thinner, there will come a time when he breaks through with the help of his servants on this side. Then we will all be in peril."

"But if you know this, can you not prevent it?"

"Master Sandovon and other wizards of his class are working on it, but it is hard, for the magics that are tearing at the fabric between the worlds are subtle and difficult to pinpoint or counter. It is not a direct assault—that we could deal with—but a slow abrasion, a weakening here, a weakening there, each one so slight as to go unnoticed. But cumulatively they are shredding the boundaries, and one day they *will* fall and we will not be able to prevent it."

"The dragons stopped him once. They can do so again." Grinli said this with the definiteness only a dwarf can manage, as if solid stone itself had spoken and would not be budged.

Rondol sighed. "Perhaps. But we cannot count on it. There are fewer dragons now, and those who remain take little interest in the world. They might abandon us to our fate when the time comes, for even if the Dark Lords take control, the dragons cannot be harmed."

"Is that why you want to capture a dragon, to make it fight the Unbodied One?"

"No! At least not directly. At the moment there is nothing to fight that would demand such power. If my plan works, then there would be no fight, as the Unbodied One would be unable to break through. It would be consigned to the nether world forever or until it fades away into non-existence. "

There was silence for a time as we all thought about this. I signaled the serving maid to bring us all another round of ales, with a new glass for Rondol, and she winked back. That was some sawdust. Then I said, "You are very ambitious for a junior apprenticed wizard."

He nodded. "But it's not a personal ambition, Sir Ranger. I hope to make you see that."

"That may be," I said. "But you still haven't told us what your vision was or about the magic ring that will let you accomplish all these wonders."

"I cannot tell you my vision. But the time will come when I can show it to you, and you will experience it for yourself. But as you have all three pointed out, without a way to capture and compel a dragon, there is no point in going further, for the vision depends on it. So the first step is to gain the Ring of Longrim. Will you help me that far at least? Then, if we are successful with that goal, we can discuss my vision and the capture of a dragon."

Grinli raised his glass of ale. "To find the Ring of Longrim is a worthy quest for any dwarf. I would dishonor my ancestors to refuse. You have my axe at your side."

"And my bow," said Pintoglas, not to be outdone. "It would be an honor for me, too, as a scholar and prince of my people to be part of locating such an artifact. I will join you as well."

All three looked at me. I sighed. So much for a quiet evening alone. "Make it three of us, then. My sword is at your service."

"Excellent!" said Rondol, clapping his hands together and seeming more like a boy than ever. "Excellent! It will be an excellent quest. And you, Sir Ranger, will be my questmaster. Now all we need is a special ringbearer."

"A ringbearer?" I asked. "You mean someone to carry the ring when we find it? Why, is it cursed or something?"

"Not exactly," Rondol said. He looked at Grinli. "Perhaps you should explain, Sir Dwarf."

I looked down at Grinli who, for the first time in my experience, seemed almost on the verge of grinning. "Well, it's very heavy."

"Very heavy," I repeated.

"Yes. Oh, I bet you thought it was a finger ring, something a wizard wore on his hand?"

"Well, the thought had crossed my mind."

"No, no. It's a magical ring that is put on the talon of a dragon's claw. It's cunningly wrought from metal and stone and is very large and heavy."

"Large and heavy," I repeated again, somewhat aghast at what I was hearing. The damn thing had to be put on the dragon's claw? I imagined the three of us—wizards never get their hands dirty or do any real work in my experience—lugging some giant stone ring up to a dragon's pinkie while the beast himself laughed and prepared to toast us for its dinner. This plan was as suicidal as trying to capture the beast in the first place.

"Yes. It would take two men to carry it, or at least a man and a half. Of course, a dwarf could carry it with no problem, but not if he's wielding his battle axe as well."

"We need someone strong enough to carry the ring while the rest of us keep the dragon occupied or fight it if we must," Rondol said.

A large heavy stone ring. Who would carry such a thing? I idly glanced around the Boar and Board while my thoughts raced, and then I grinned. "Rondol, I think I know just the person to be your Ringbearer." And I raised my glass to Fro the Halfling.

****

The following day we were on the road. I had to admit that Rondol had done a good job organizing everything, something new in my experience in dealing with wizards. Usually they just said, "Let us go questing" and left it to me to get the horses, assemble the gear, find hirelings if we needed them, buy food, pack everything up, and get us going. In this case, we simply met in front of the Wizard's Court in the early morning and everything was there ready for us. I was impressed and told Rondol so. He smiled shyly. "I have had things prepared for some time now. I didn't know who would go with me, but I knew someone would. Then I received word that you had come back into town, and I hoped things would turn out as they had. The only thing I could not find in time was a horse for Fro."

I laughed. "He wouldn't use one. There are few horses strong enough to carry a Halfling, and if it could, it would be slower than a Halfling anyway. Fro can easily trot as fast as a horse. He'll have no trouble keeping up. You could even put a pack on him, and it wouldn't slow him down."

"You make him sound like an ogre."

"Well, people have wondered if Halflings and Ogre's are distant cousins, but Ogres are even larger and uglier. Actually, an ogre would be a good ringbearer if Longrim's Ring is anywhere near the size you and Grinli say it is. If you could find an ogre and get it to help, that is. They're as rare and obstinate these days as dragons. At least they don't breath fire."

Rondol gracefully swung himself into his saddle. I was pleased to see. Apparently he knew how to ride, which would be a blessing on the trail. "No, we couldn't use an ogre. The ring is a magical artifact, so the person who carries it needs to be pure of heart."

"Well, that describes Fro, sure enough. He doesn't have a nasty bone in his body." I didn't have the heart to tell Rondol that I'd known plenty of wizards with magical artifacts whose hearts were far from pure. Best leave him his illusions awhile longer.

I mounted the horse indicated to me, immediately feeling a rapport with the grey mare. Normally, I travel on foot. It's hard to be stealthy on a horse, though I've ridden my share. Like any ranger, I have a natural affinity for animals of all kinds. It's come in handy on more than one occasion.

Rondol had been secretive about our destination, saying only that he would fill us in once we had left the city. Now, taking the lead, he led us through the streets towards the Northern gate. I would have preferred going in some other direction. As I said, strange things were going on in the north. It wasn't exactly dangerous, but it wasn't a safe stroll in the King's Park either. In fact, on my last trip into the Gloomwoods in the northernmost province, I had come across a collection of webs spun between the tree trunks. A deer was caught in one of them, wrapped in a cocoon and dried like a mummy, its life juices sucked from it. I left that area quickly and never saw the spider that'd been responsible, but it must have been at least the size of a dog.

We proceeded single file through the city. Rondol went first, followed by Pintoglas. Once we hit the trail, the elf with his superior senses would likely take point. . I was in the middle where I could easily take command should anything happen. Grinli was behind me, followed by two pack horses and then Fro, the Halfling, who loped along happily, humming some mindless melody to himself.

When I'd approached him at the Boar and Board last night, he'd been all too willing to join. "Me, a ringbearer," he had said, "and a magic ring at that." Then he had held up a hand the size of a ham as if imagining how the ring would look on his finger. I hadn't had the heart to tell him that the ring in question was most likely larger than his hand itself and he would probably carry it strapped to his back like a shield. I'd let Rondol break that disappointing news to him. Wizards, after all, have protective magical force fields around them for moments like that.

We passed through the North Gate with no fanfare or obvious notice from the guardsmen and headed up the King's Road toward Granchit's Town about three leagues to the north. Halfway there, Rondol led us off the Road towards a small copse of trees. Once under the sheltering branches and out of sight of anyone passing, he indicated for us to form into a circle. I wondered why he was so concerned about secrecy.

"We are now beginning a sacred quest," he said. His voice was matter of fact and a bit soft so we all had to lean forward in our saddles to hear him (except for Fro, of course, who just leaned forward, except when he was momentarily distracted by a butterfly that flittered by). "I think it not too strong to say that the fate of the Kingdom rests with us. Not today, and maybe not tomorrow, but for the future to come and the children who will be born into it."

"I like children," Fro commented. His voice was high-pitched and almost feminine which was always a surprise to people who first met him.

"That's nice, Fro," I said and gave him an encouraging smile. Like I said, not the sharpest arrow in the quiver.

"We come together, five brave adventurers—I dare to include myself in your number—to face whatever dangers and trials await us to find the lost Ring of Longrim…"

"I'm going to be the Ringbearer," Fro announced happily, and then paused as the butterfly alighted on the tip of his nose.

"…and use it to fulfill our mission," Rondol continued as if nothing had happened. "This means that there is a special bond between us now, a mystical union…"

My mind wandered off. Rondol might not be as arrogant and full of himself as most wizards I'd met, but he shared one common trait with them: they all liked to talk. Endlessly. At the drop of a pointed hat. Usually just saying the obvious. But I had to give the kid this one. This was obviously a special moment for him, and he really was stepping out on a quest that would most likely see him dead in some forgotten tomb or roasted for a dragon's dinner. I respected courage, and I could see he had it even if it came wrapped in platitudes and pomposities. But I noticed that Pintoglas and Grinly were listening intently and seemingly with interest and even Fro had stopped following the butterfly with his eyes and was staring hard at the wizard. I wondered if I'd missed something.

"Thus, I bless us in our endeavor with a wizard's blessing and in the name of Sandovon the White. Blessings on our Fellowship!"

I felt a tingle of energy course down my spine and I was pulled upright in my saddle. He really was using magic. Was he casting a spell on us? But if he was, it was a good one, for we all looked at each other with a new sense of our companionship, knowing that whatever we might face in the days ahead, we could depend on each other to the death.

"The Fellowship," Fro said wonderingly. His chest swelled. "Has a nice ring to it!"

BOOK THE SECOND
THE RING

The first night we slept in the foothills of the Moisty Mountains, so called because it drizzled incessantly around them and one could never quite get dry. A bit of Rondol's magic kept the rain off us, but did nothing for the cold. We kept a fire burning all night and slept close to it. We each took turn keeping watch and drew lots to determine the order in which we would do so. As it turned out, I drew the early morning hours, and Rondol's turn came after mine. When my two hours had passed, I woke the young wizard. He came immediately awake and made his way over to the campfire to take his shift. But I was not yet ready for sleep and I thought this might be a chance to have some questions answered. So I sat up next to him as he placed more wood on the fire.

"Rondol," I said, "there's much you haven't told us about this mission, not least where we're going to find Longrim's Ring. I am willing to trust you up to a point, but I am accustomed to knowing where I'm headed so I can make plans in advance."

"I understand, Sir Ranger. And believe me, I will inform you all on the morrow before we leave this camp."

"But why all the secrecy? Are there enemies you haven't told us about? If so, ignorance on our part could prove fatal. Forewarned is forearmed, you know."

"No, no, nothing of the sort. It's just...well, some things have to be secret or the mystery is spoiled and the magic is lost. Though it may not seem so just now, I am weaving a most complex and powerful spell. The fewer that know about it, the better."

"This spell...is it dangerous? I mean..."

"You mean, am I skillful enough to control it so it won't blow up in our faces?"

I nodded. "Something like that."

He chuckled softly. "It's not that kind of spell, but it's very powerful nonetheless. There is no danger in it, but if it lost its mystery, it would lose its power."

I shook my head. "You wizards always speak in riddles."

"I know. It's a required course in the school," and he chuckled again so I didn't know if he was being serious or not. "No matter. You will know and understand in time, Sir Ranger, and you will see that it is a good spell indeed, one that can only bring happiness and never harm. But it is necessary that no one knows it's happening, and in the city, the very air has eyes and ears for things of magic. I have had to be very discrete."

I thought about what he had said, and while it made a certain sense, I still was no closer to understanding it than before. But then, not understanding is not unusual when dealing with wizards. Sensing I would get no more information on this subject, I bid him goodnight and headed toward my pack.

"Good night, Sir Ranger," he said.

I turned back to him. "Oh, that's another thing. Would you please stop 'sirring' us all the time? And stop calling Pintoglas and Grinli by their real names. It hurts my head. Just call me Ari and call the others the same as I."

"You want me to call them 'Ari,' too?"

"What? No! I meant…." Then I saw his shy grin and realized he was teasing me. Oh great, I thought, a wizard with a sense of humor. But I had to grin back. Gods around, I was actually beginning to like this junior apprentice mage.

"Thank you," he said. "I appreciate being welcomed into the informality of your companionship."

"Yes. Well, just remember. It's 'Pintoglas' and 'Grinli' and 'Ari' from here on out."

"I'll remember."

Another thought struck me. I had to ask. "What is your color?"

"I beg your pardon?"

"You know. Sandovon is the White. And other mages I've met all have some color that ranks them. Balthazor the Gray, Suliman the Green, and so on. What's your color?"

He paused, and for a moment I was afraid he would say he had none, which would mean he was a rank beginner as a mage. But then he said, "Off White."

"Off White? You're 'Rondol the Off White'?"

"I know it sounds strange," he said in a rush. "It's just that I'm no longer a Gray but I haven't quite completed my graduation to become a White. I'm in-between a Gray and a White. If our quest goes well, then I shall become a full White."

"But wouldn't you still be a Gray, then?"

"Oh, no, Sir...er, Ari. I couldn't be a Gray and be an assistant to Sandovon. I have to have authority over the other Grays." He leaned close and whispered. "Office politics, if you know what I mean."

Actually, I did. It was the first thing he'd said that made sense to me. I clapped him on the back. "All right, then, Rondol the Off White. I'm off to sleep. Tomorrow you'll tell us where we're going and we'll do our best to see you can take off the 'Off.'"

"Splendid. Good night, then, Ari."

We arose early, wakened by the sounds of the forest birds and other creatures waking up as well. As we sat around the campfire eating breakfast, Rondol turned to Pintoglas and Grinli and said, "Last night Ari told me to call you 'Pintoglas and Grinli' as he does." Both the elf and the dwarf turned to glare at me, and I overheard Grinli mutter, "Just because *he* can't pronounce our names....." But then Pintoglas nodded and said, "It's quite all right, Rondol. It keeps everything informal between us as befits quest companions. Please feel free to call me what you will."

Fro piped up. "You can call me 'Fro,'" he said.

We all looked at him. "We already do," I said.

"Well, then," he replied. "That's good, because we're a Fellowship."

"Indeed we are, Fro! Indeed we are," Rondol responded, clapping his hands together. "And now that we are far from the prying eyes and ears of the city, it's time for me to tell you the story of Longrim's Ring and where we'll find it."

He paused, starring into the flickering flames of the fire. "It's not a long story actually. I was deep in the archives trying to find a particularly rare scroll for Sandovon. You've never been in the archives..." he paused as a thought struck him and he glanced over at me. "Er...Have you?" I shook my head. "Never had that pleasure," I assured him. There are some places even a stealthy ranger prefers not to go, and anyway, dusty, moldy old scrolls make me sneeze.

"No, of course not," he continued. "Anyway, take it from me, it's a shambles down there. There are piles of scrolls and stacks of books that haven't been sorted in centuries, just lying around. Personally, I think the Whites leave them that way as a trial for their assistants. If you can find anything in that jumble, then you're ready for the most difficult of spells."

He poked at the fire with a stick he picked up from the ground beside him, and sparks flew up as a log shifted. "I was failing to find the particular scroll I needed and was scrambling over a pile of books when I slipped. I put my hand out to steady myself and grabbed something that gave way beneath my weight. A whole pile of scrolls came tumbling down on top of me and something hard struck me on the back. I thought for a moment I was going to be buried and crushed, but I was able to work my way free. And when I did, I found lying amidst the scattered scrolls the thing that had struck me."

"Oooo," said Fro, excitedly. "What was it?"

"It was a stone canister of the kind used to carry and protect scrolls and it was covered with dwarven pictograms."

"Dwarven ones, you say?" Grinli asked.

"Aye, and ancient, too. I have made a study of these things. I recognized the carvings as being a form of Dwargarnish, the Old Tongue."

"But no one has used Dwargarnish for hundreds of years..."

"For eight hundred years, Grinli, since the end of the civil wars that brought the current Dwarven dynasty into power. But it *was* used at the time of Longrim. Anyway, I didn't think much of it at first. There are a great many older things in the archives, and there was nothing about this canister that made it stand out as something special. But I saw the seal was cracked and torn; obviously at one time the canister had been opened. Wizards are nothing if not curious..." I snorted, but everyone ignored me, caught up as they were in Rondol's story. "So I looked inside," he went on. Then he paused dramatically.

"Was something in it?" Fro asked.

"Indeed, Fro, something was in it. An old scroll was inside, and I was astonished to see it was made of *basalite*."

"*Basalite!*" Grinli exclaimed. "But no one's made scrolls of *basalite* since Congraght the Crafter was slain in those very civil wars you mentioned. He was the only one who knew the process, so the secret of their manufacture died with him."

"What is this *basalite*?" asked Fro, sparing me the indignity of asking the same question myself. Rangers are supposed to be a fount of knowledge, but I'd missed this tidbit of lore.

It was Pintoglas who answered, making sure we all recognized his scholarship. "*Basalite* is a parchment made of stone. It is very pliable as if it had been made from plant fiber so you can roll a sheet of it to make a scroll but it's very durable like the stone it's made from. Congraght's great-grandfather discovered how to make it and passed the information as secret lore to his descendants. When the Crafter was slain at the Battle of Four Mountains, a Bridge and a Tunnel, that secret was lost, as Grinli said."

"You can imagine, then, my excitement at this discovery. This scroll had to be at least eight hundred years old, and probably much older. And when I unrolled it, I discovered I was right. It was nine hundred and seventy-eight years old."

"You could tell that from the look and feel of the *basalite*?" I asked, astounded.

"No, it had the date written on it in Dwargarnish."

"Ah, the date....of course. And you could read it?"

"Ancient languages and history are specialties of mine, Ari. And that's not all. It was signed by Longrim the Mage himself." He stood up and brushed leaves and dirt off his robe. "Well, I won't tell you all I went through to decipher it. It's one thing to read a language and something else again to figure out a puzzle and a riddle written in it. But when I was done, I knew that the Ring of Longrim was real, for he describes it in some detail, and I knew where it was hidden."

"So," I said, standing up as well, "where is that?" Wizards can be so exasperating at times. Most times. Well, actually, all the time.

"It's in Gol Durnish." And when he spoke those awful, fateful words, the whole forest went silent around us.

****

Think of the most evil place, a place of frightful magic and dark pacts made with darker gods. Think of a place once filled with debauchery and degradation, a place of torment and suffering for many to create pleasure for a few. A place dedicated to horror. Then imagine that this place is destroyed in a great war, reduced to ruin. But now it's haunted. Ghosts and ghouls and the undead stalk its paths and hallways. Monsters from your worst nightmares have taken up residence there, and to spend even one night in its eldritch premises is to have your soul blasted forever, assuming you live through it.

There are places like that. I've even visited a couple.

Gol Durnish is not one of them.

Oh, it wanted to be. It tried hard to get an evil reputation. It was the citadel of Taurak the Unmerciful, an insane mage-king (and have you ever noticed how often "insane" and "mage-king" seem to go together in our histories?). He fancied himself an evil overlord, an heir to the Unbodied One. He hired mercenaries, employed renegade wizards, tortured a few peasants to invoke some demons, and set out to conquer everything in sight. Unfortunately for Taurak, what was in sight was the Kingdom, and he was no warlord. I think the Almost Shadow War lasted three days before he was captured and hung as a traitor, and Gol Durnish was reduced to ruin. An unhaunted one, at that. Not enough drama or pathos or mana to keep any self-respecting ghost or demon hanging about. It had the aura of a loser, and who wants to haunt that?

It should have ended there. Gol Durnish would have faded into history, forgotten by all save a few scholars like Rondol and Pintoglas. Except for one thing. Withney the Bard. He was a second-rate teller of tales who one day had a stroke of genius. He realized that people wanted to be scared. They wanted safe danger, something that would give them the thrill of being threatened without actually being in harm's way. And what better place to provide those thrills than the ruined citadel of a wannabe evil overlord?

Withney gathered some investors, invited merchants to sell wares, hired a few hedge wizards to create some scary but safe magical effects, and retold the legend of Gol Durnish, turning it into a bastion of evil but one open to anyone with the courage (and the coins) to explore it.

Of course, it became a big hit, and Withney began making gold hand over fist. People have been flocking from around the Kingdom to come and walk its tainted halls, while assistant bards regale them with ever more elaborate tales of the evil overlord Taurak who sought to conquer the world and, in their telling, nearly succeeded. Lines of donkeys roped together carry people on rides through specially constructed parts of the citadel where "evil still lingers, waiting to snare the unaware," according to the parchment advertisements Withney had posted on trees all around the kingdom. He even invoked a few ghosts to stalk the halls. I've been told that some of them in the dungeons scream horrifically as if they're being tortured, which, considering they have to do three shows a day and four on Seven-Day, they probably are.

"Can I go on the rides?" Fro asked excitedly when he heard where we were going.

****

"How did Longrim's Ring come to be in a place like Gol Durnish?" I asked Rondol as we rode along the King's Road. It was not a long journey ahead of us. We would be at the place by sundown.

"Actually, according to the scroll, it's always been there. Long before Gol Durnish became a citadel, it was a Dwarven outpost, a place where the Dwarves and the humans of the expanding Kingdom could meet and conduct business. Apparently, there was some kind of plot against the Dwarven king, and Longrim feared the plotters might try to use his ring to force the dragons to take their side. So he brought it here, far from the Dwarven court, to keep it safe. In all likelihood, that plot was the beginning of the rift that led to the civil wars centuries later. I don't know, but it's quite possible that in the continuing intrigue and conflict, Longrim was never able to retrieve his ring, so it stayed where he had hidden it."

"In Gol Durnish."

"In what later became Gol Durnish."

I chuckled. "Ironic, isn't it, that Taurak was sitting on top of something that could have given him all the power he wanted, and he never knew it."

"Assuming he could have lifted it and found a dragon to put it on."

"Yes, well, there is that, isn't there?" I didn't need to mention that that was exactly what he wanted us to do.

"So, wizard," asked Grinli as we stopped along the road at midday to rest the horses and have a meal, "What's the plan? Do we just buy a ticket and go into Gol Durnish to find Longrim's Ring?"

"Oh, no. No one must know what we're about."

"Besides, imagine the furor it would cause if people saw a ranger, an elf, a dwarf, a wizard, and a Halfling hauling a great ring of stone out of the place." I let irony fill my voice.

"They'd probably think it was part of the show," Pintoglas said.

"Not a chance I want to take. So we must go in after midnight when the customers have all gone home and the merchants have closed their stalls."

"This is good," said Grinli. "Saves paying the admission fees."

"Does this mean no rides?" Fro asked.

Rondol leaned over and patted the Halfling's hand. "I'm sorry, Fro. I'm afraid so. Not this time. But after all this is over, I'll bring you back to Gol Durnish and treat you to all the rides you want." Fro smiled happily at this and went back to eating his side of beef.

"Do you know where the ring is once we gain entrance to the place?"

Rondol hesitated. "Um...no. I mean, hundreds of years have passed since it was hidden there. Things have changed a great deal since it was a Dwarven outpost."

I looked at Rondol. "In other words, you have no idea where it is. Why, it might not even be in Gol Durnish at all!"

"Oh, I'm sure it's there. Why would it be moved? And who would move it?"

"You don't know where it is," I repeated.

"No, I don't. We'll have to search for it. But I have no doubt we'll find it."

I sighed and got to my feet. "Wizards," I said, and mounted my horse.

That night we camped less than a mile from Gol Durnish. A narrow arm from the great forest snaked down into a little valley and there among the trees where I was sure no one would see us, we made camp. After a quick meal we all lay down to rest until it was time to make our way into Withney's "Haunted Citadel of the Evil Overlord." I was tired after a day's riding and fell quickly asleep.It seemed only a minute had passed when in fact something did awaken me. I lay there quietly, probing the darkness around me with my senses, but all I heard were the nighttime forest noises. What had called me back from slumber? As usual, my fingers found my sword lying next to me, and my hand closed around its hilt.

I heard a sound. It was soft, and at first I mistook it for a breeze in the trees. Then I realized it was a voice. Turning over quietly, I looked in the direction it came from. A faint light was shining in the trees maybe twenty yards away or so. I got to my feet and crept closer to see what was going on. Did danger threaten us?

Coming up behind a tree, I looked around its trunk and saw Rondol standing in a little clearing. It was his turn to stand watch, but he was obviously doing something else. In his hand he held a crystal sphere from which the faint light was emanating. And standing in front of him was a figure who was also radiating light. It was a short, rotund man with a great white beard and thick, long white hair. On his head he wore a holly wreath and he was dressed in a red suit trimmed with white fur. He seemed insubstantial, like a ghost, for I could faintly discern the shapes of the trees through his red-garbed body. He was a spirit, then, but what kind? And why had Rondol invoked it? What was he keeping from us? Was this the source of his vision?

Though my hearing is nearly as keen as an elf's, I could not make out what they were saying. I could hear the murmur of the words, but the sound might as well have been the babbling of a brook for all the sense it made. The spirit was speaking in a language I had never heard.

The figure suddenly disappeared, and the light in the crystal sphere began to dim until it gave just enough light for Rondol to see his way back to camp. I turned and made my own way back. I thought of confronting him, but knowing wizards, he would have some convoluted explanation that in the end would make my brain hurt but wouldn't tell me anything. Better to let him think his nocturnal visitation had gone unwitnessed so he wouldn't be on his guard. I would keep a close eye on him from now on. No, let me correct that… a *closer* eye.

Needless to say, I didn't go back to sleep, but apparently Rondol did. An hour or so later, he awoke again and got to his feet. Seeing he was coming over to me, I got up, too. "I'm awake," I said.

"Good. Then let's rouse the others. It's time we entered Gol Durnish and found the Ring of Longrim."

We decided to keep the horses in the camp and make our way by foot to the ancient citadel. We traveled light for stealth and speed, though I noticed Rondol carried with him a strange arrangement of ropes that he strapped around his waist.

As we made our way through the woods, Pintoglas strode next to me, his bow at ready as always when we might be making our way into danger. Not that I could imagine what danger might await us in Gol Durnish, other than a sleepy nightwatchman hired by the merchants to protect their wares through the night.

"I saw our wizard had a visitor last night," the elf said softly so only

I could hear. "I saw you watching him, too."

"You did not. I was like a shadow."

"To another human, perhaps," he chuckled, "but to me, you were loud and noisy."

"Was not!"

Pintoglas grinned. "Like a mammoth stumbling over its own feet. 'Tis a wonder the whole forest was not alarmed, much less the wizard and his ghostly visitor."

"I fail to see how you can say this, being as blind and deaf as you are."

It was an old game we played. He knew I was proud of my skills for stealth and secrecy, and I knew that nothing escaped an elf's senses.

Then seriously, he said, "'Tis a strange game our wizard is playing. I knew not the spirit he'd invoked nor could I make out its words. I thought to challenge him, but I observed you merely watching and then retreating, so I followed your lead, Ari. Do you know what is happening?"

I shook my head. "No," I whispered. "But let's give him the lead and see what unfolds. In the meantime, keep your bow stringed and I will keep my blade sharp and loose at my side."

Have I said I don't trust wizards?

As we approached Gol Durnish itself, I began to feel uneasy, as if unseen eyes were watching me. I felt a shiver go down my back, and the cold hand of fear began to twitch its fingers in my gut. Rondol stopped and beckoned us all closer. "There are spells here," he whispered, "designed to create a mild apprehension. Just ignore them. They help foster the illusion of danger for the visitors."

Rondol might be able to ignore them; after all, he was a mage. But the feelings gave me the creeps, and I could see that Pintoglas and Grinli fared little better. Fro, on the other hand, had a blissful look on his face. "This is fun!" he said. I signaled him to be quiet, and he made a sign of clamping his hand over his mouth. But his eyes still sparkled. Gol Durnish was made for people like him.

Gol Durnish was actually a small village laid out in concentric circles. The outermost ring was filled with merchant's stalls, and if we were to run into guards, it would be here. Then came the old moat and the outer walls. Beyond them were the village itself, now in artful ruins. Most of the buildings had been created by Withney's artisans to enhance the haunted, ruined appearance.

At the center of it all was the citadel itself. This was a true ruin, though it had parts—the "rides" that Fro had hoped to take—that had been developed and installed by the bard and his helpers. At its core was the Keep. According to Rondol, within the Keep at its lowest levels were the ancient remains of the Dwarven outpost. If Longrim's Ring were here, that is where we would most likely find it.

As we moved through the merchant's circle, we did see the occasional watchman, but our stealth assisted I'm sure in Fro's case by Rondol's magic prevented them from seeing us. And truthfully, to my eye they were a bit slothful and inattentive. Three of them found a dice game more compelling than keeping watch over their masters' wares.

Gaining entrance into the village was simple enough. There was no water in the depression that had once been a moat, and the outer walls were breached in several places. We basically just walked in through one of these holes. The village, though, was another matter. The streets were deliberately twisty and winding, and the sense of being watched by some evil presences that wanted nothing more than to slowly strip the flesh from our bones was stronger than ever. I shook my head to clear it. People paid money for this?

"Parts of the village are for employees only," Rondol whispered. "The spells are particularly strong here to frighten away anyone who doesn't work here."

"Like us," Grinli muttered.

"Just keep thinking of the money you've saved not paying admission, and you'll be all right, dwarf," Pintoglas whispered back.

We moved on towards the citadel, swallowing our fear. I knew it was all illusion, but I kept my hand firmly on the hilt of my sword nonetheless. Fro, on the other hand, was hopping about with excitement, trying to look everywhere at once, taking it all in. Halflings are all just big kids, I thought.

We left the side streets and approached the citadel directly. This made the fear lessen as we left the areas we weren't supposed to be in anyway; on the other hand, as we entered the citadel through its smashed entrance, the fear increased again, which I guess it was supposed to do.

We entered the main hallway, and as we did, a transparent figure dressed in ancient armor appeared before us, its head under its arms. "Halt," it said. The lips of the head moved but the sepulchral voice came from the space above its shoulders where the head should have been. It was one of the haunts Withney had hired.

"Begone, spirit!" Rondol said, making a gesture with his hand. "Delay us not for we are on a sacred mission."

"Really?" said the haunt, putting its head back on his shoulders where it settled into place. "A real quest?"

"Yes," I said, stepping forward. "A real quest. So begone as the wizard commanded."

"Wow," it said. "I always wanted to go on a quest. Oh, by the way," it pointed an armored hand at Rondol. "You can't banish me because I belong here. I am an official employee, which," it said pointedly, "I can see that you're not. So you can't just brush me off, you know."

Rondol looked back at the rest of us. "It has a point. It was brought here by magic and to banish it, I would have to undo that original spell. Too much time and trouble. We must simply ignore it."

"You can't ignore me. You must take me with you on your quest, or I'll alert every other ghost in this place and we'll make your time here miserable, just see if we won't! And stop calling me 'it.' I'm a human being, you know, or at least I was once. Name's Harold. Glad ta meetcha!"

Rondol sighed. "All right, then, come with us, spirit, but see you don't interfere with what we must do."

Harold bounded up and down, his head jiggling on his shoulders, a broad grin on his face. "Oh yes! Oh yes! My first quest! Where are we going, what are we going to kill, what evil are we going to overcome? Oh, this is splendid!" Watching him go giddy with excitement, I wondered if Harold had been related to a Halfling.

"We're looking for a powerful magic ring," Fro said, much to Rondol's distress. I know the wizard wanted to keep our mission secret.

Harold stopped bouncing and even dimmed a bit. "A magic ring? Really? Here?" He looked a bit crestfallen. "Gee, I don't know, fellows. I've been here for a very long time, and I never heard of any magic ring hereabouts. And now that I'm a ghost, I think I'd know if such a thing were here. You hear things and know things after you're dead, you know?"

"But you don't know for sure, do you?" I asked.

"No, but...."

"Then don't get in our way. Join our quest if you wish but keep a positive attitude."

"Besides, Harold," Pintoglas said, "even if we fail to find the ring, you can still say you were on a quest."

The ghost brightened again. "Say, that's right! A quest doesn't have to succeed to be a proper quest. Indeed, a tragic quest has drama, pathos, the sorrow of might-have-beens, everything a ghost would want! Let us go forth then, my companions, and fail nobly!"

"Let me guess," I sighed. "You were a bard when you were alive."

"No, but I've had lessons since. After all, in this place, I'm one of the performers."

"Enough talk," Rondol said. "Time is short and passing swiftly. We must enter the keep and find the Dwarven ruins before the night runs out."

"Dwarven ruins? Say, I *do* know about those," Harold said. "Can I guide you? Can I?" He bobbed about some more.

"Wait a minute," I said. "How do you know about the Dwarven ruins?"

"Well, it's like I said. You learn things after you die. But in this case, he told me about them."

"He?" asked Rondol.

"The Dwarven fellow."

We all looked at Grinli. "I didn't know you had been here before," Pintoglas commented.

"I haven't," the dwarf protested. "He means some other dwarf."

"Yes, I don't mean this fellow. I mean the ghost, like me. Well, he's not exactly like me. He's not a performer or anything. He actually haunts this old pile of rocks. He's been here forever, I think. He never comes out when the guests are here. That's what we call the customers, you know. 'The Guests.' Kinda classy, doncha' think?"

"Harold," Rondol said, "can you lead us to this dwarven ghost? You see, the ring we seek was crafted by a dwarven mage. This ghost might know where it is."

"Really? I don't know....he's not the talkative type. Morose, I'd say. Never smiles, even when I do my juggling act. That always gets a rise from the guests. Would you like to see it?" Harold began tossing his head back and forth from one hand to the other. Fro clapped delightedly.

"Harold, stop. Stop!" Rondol held forth his hand, and I could see the magic flickering along his fingers. "If you are part of our Fellowship, you need to listen to me now. You can help us. You can make this quest a success."

"Me?"

"Yes, but only if you settle down and pay attention. This dwarven ghost may be able to help us. You can help us by taking us to him. Now."

"Well....sure. Have you seen enough of my juggling act? It gets better..."

"We've seen enough," Pintoglas interjected quickly. "Lead on, Sir Ghost."

"Sir Ghost! I like that! Better than Harold. Well, it *could* be Sir Harold....That would be nice, too...." Muttering to himself, the ghost turned and led us deeper into the citadel towards the ancient keep that was at its center. Along the way we passed an alcove whose floor was covered with straw. Along the wall was a line of stone hoops. Harold must have noticed it, too, for he said, "That's where they hitch the donkeys during the day. They use them for the rides, you know."

"I wanted to go on the rides," said Fro, "but the wizard says I must wait for another time."

"Really? Gee, that's too bad. They're great rides. You should see the ghosts they've hired for in there," he waved vaguely in the direction of the alcove-stable and the hallways beyond. "If you think I'm scary, you should see them."

"I'd like to," said Fro sadly. "Maybe you could call them out?"

"Nah. They don't hang around like I do. Strictly nine-to-nine haunts. Come closing time and they go home."

I was about to ask Harold where 'home' was, then realized I didn't want to know.

We walked on for about ten minutes, winding through narrow old passages until the ghost stopped in front of a wall. "This here's a secret passage. Not many know about it, mostly just the ghosts. There are lots of secret passages in this old place, and we hang out in them when we're not performing. Even ghosts need some rest now and then."

Pintoglas and I both looked the wall over, but neither of us could see any evidence of a hidden door or entranceway. We looked at each other and shrugged. "OK, we give up," I said. "How do you open this?"

"Oh, you can't open it. There's no door there, just a wall. Were you looking for a door? Ha Ha! That's funny. I didn't mean *you* could get into the secret passage here, only that I can. See." Harold faded into the wall and disappeared, then reappeared again. If he'd had a real neck,

I'd have throttled it.

"Then why did you lead us here, Harold?" Rondol asked patiently. "You know that we can't pass through walls as you can."

"Because this is where the dwarven ghost hangs out. The old ruin is just below us. Wait a minute and I'll see if I can roust the old fellow out." Harold disappeared back into the wall.

"I like him," said Fro. "Can he be part of our Fellowship, too?"

"We only take live people," I growled.

Fro shrugged. "That's too bad. He's a good fellow."

Time passed. I don't know how long. Probably no more than fifteen minutes, but standing in a drafty, musty old corridor in the dark makes time seem to go a lot slower than normal. Especially when you're being crowded by an eight-foot Halfling.

But then Harold reappeared, and with him came a dim blob of light which had only the vaguest suggestion of a dwarven form about it. Obviously, this ghost had been here a very long time indeed and was fading away. Harold must have told him something about us as he immediately drifted over to Grinli and began to talk. His voice sounded like it was coming up from a deep well, all hollow and echoing. I couldn't understand anything the ghost was saying.

Grinli looked at us in despair. "He's speaking Dwargarnish. I recognize a few words here and there, but I don't speak the Old Tongue myself. I don't know what he's saying!"

"I do," said Rondol. "I said I was a loremaster when it came to old languages." He sat down so he'd be closer to the ghost's level and began to speak. Soon the two were chatting back and forth like two old friends. I even saw the ghost's form becoming more clear and distinct. Finally, Rondol got up.

"Well?" asked Grinli. "What did he say? Who is he? Does he know about the Ring?"

"I daresay he does," replied Rondol. "As it turns out, this is Longrim the Mage himself."

"Longrim?" Grinli exclaimed. "The real Longrim? The one who made the Ring in the first place?"

"The very one. Apparently he brought the Ring here himself and hid it but was followed and killed by some of the conspirators when he wouldn't tell them where to find it."

"Can he tell us where it is?" I asked. "The conspiracy is long since done with. We're not out to overthrow his king."

Rondol shook his head. "I have explained our need, but he can't help us. Oh, he's been very nice about it. He assures me he would help if he could, but the fact is, he doesn't know where the Ring is now."

"But he hid it," Grinli said. "Has he forgotten where?"

"No. He says that human beings came and took it away. He couldn't follow them to see what they did with it, for he is bound to the ruins below us. If he strays far, he begins to fade away."

"When did this happen?" asked Pentoglas. Rondol turned and spoke to the dwarf. I could see him shrug as he answered.

"He doesn't know, does he?" I said.

"Time is different for a ghost, as you might imagine," Rondol said. "He can't be sure. But he says it was after he met Harold."

"*After* he met Harold?" I turned to the other ghost. "Harold, how long have you been here?"

"Oh, not long. Well, maybe ten years or so. It is hard to say. We don't have time the way you do. But I was one of the first ghosts the bards hired."

I thought. "That means it's only been a few years since the ring was moved. It may still be around here."

"But why was it moved?" asked Grinli. "It has no value to the uninitiated. Unless he knew what he was looking for, no human would recognize it as a magic ring. Maybe someone else read the same scroll you did, Wizard, and came here first?"

Rondol shook his head. "I don't see how that could be possible."

Suddenly I knew exactly where Longrim's Ring was. I turned and headed back down the passageway. "Follow me," I called back. "I know where it is." I least I thought I did. We would know in a few moments.

We burst out of the keep, and I ran down the hallways of the citadel itself. Harold bobbed along beside me, his head wobbling, clapping his hands and shrieking, "Make way for the questors! Make way for the questors! Oh, this is *so* exciting!" I don't know who he was shooing away, for I didn't see anything, but I didn't care. If his caterwauling kept any other spook from getting in my way, I was grateful.

Finally we came to the area where the rides began. I slowed down and walked over to the alcove with its straw floor where the donkeys spent their days. "I think it's one of these," I said to Rondol who came running up behind me. I pointed to the row of seven stone circles each sitting atop a stone pedestal.

"The hitching posts for the donkeys?"

"Makes sense, doesn't it? They probably needed an extra and found the Ring in the rubble of the ruins. It would have been perfect."

"But which one is it?" asked Grinli, looking at the posts with the rings on top.

Rondol and Pintoglas both stretched forth their hands at the same time and then both pointed to the same stone circle, the third in the row from the left. "It's that one," they said in unison. Nice to be able to sense magic.

"You found it!" exclaimed Grinli, rushing over and throwing his arms around the ring. "The lost Ring of Longrim!" Then he scowled. "Used as a hitching post! Someone should be flayed!"

"A perfect hiding place, though, you have to admit," Pintoglas said. "Who would have suspected? I walked right by these and never gave them a thought."

"There really was a magic ring here all the time? And we found it?" asked Harold. "That stone ring is a magic ring?"

"That stone ring is the magic ring?" asked Fro at the same time, looking at it and then looking at his fingers. I think the truth was starting to make its tortuous journey through to his mind.

"Yes, that's it," I said. "Our quest has been successful. At least this part of it."

"We've done it? Really? A successful quest?" Harold couldn't believe it. He spun around and bobbed up and down, throwing his head in the air in celebration. "My first quest, and it was successful! This is the most wonderful night of my death!"

While Harold was carrying on, I saw Rondol unwrapping the rope around his middle and taking it over to Fro. The two of them talked, and I saw the Halfling brighten up. Then I saw Fro putting on the ropes and realized it has a harness. He then walked over to the ring, and knelt down while Grinli hoisted the ring and slipped it into the harness so it rested against Fro's back, which, I saw, was padded for protection. He stood up. Rondol checked him over. "How does it feel?" he asked. Fro grinned. "Fine. No sweat. I'm the Ringbearer now, right?"

"There could be no better, my friend," Rondol said. Then he turned. "And now we must be off," he said to all of us. "Time is pressing."

"The quest is continuing?" Harold asked me as we began to move out of the citadel. I had to tell him the truth.

"Yes," I said. "Now we go to face a dragon."

"A...a dragon?" If a ghost could get paler, Harold paled.

"Yes. Are you with us?"

"Hmm...well, yes, I am, in spirit, so to speak, if you get my pun. Ha Ha! But, really, a dragon?"

I could see him looking for a graceful way to stay home.

"You helped us here, you know," I told him. "We couldn't have found the ring without you. You made this quest successful."

"I did, didn't I? You couldn't have done it without me."

"No. You've done your bit for the cause. So if now you feel obligated to stay here...for the guests, you know..."

"Oh, the guests...of course. Yes." He drew himself up and settled his head firmly in place. "I *am* sorry, Ranger. But though my heart would carry me with you to face the many challenges I'm sure will rise to confront you and to stand at last with my companions before the fiery breath of a Great Wyrm, I do have responsibilities here. No one else can juggle their head, you see, and I wasn't even beheaded. It's all pure skill."

"I understand, Harold. You have to stay. Gol Durnish needs you. It needs you even more than we do."

The ghost sighed. "I fear you are right. Then this is farewell. Unless of course, you come back. Oh, *do* come back. Please. Let me know how it all turned out, will you? Even if you're a ghost, burned to a crisp or eaten by the dragon." He paused. "Say, that *would* be an interesting way to go, much better than how *I* died..."

"If I can, I will," I said, fingers crossed behind my back and hoping that the dead couldn't see through one's body. With a final wave, I hurried on my way to join my companions.

We made our way out of Gol Durnish and back to our camp without incident, Fro trotting along with Longrim's Ring on his back as if it weighed nothing. No doubt about it. Halflings make the best Ringbearers.

BOOK THE THIRD
THE QUEST

In the morning we gathered once again around Rondol to hear about the next step of our quest. "My companions," he began, "this is truly an auspicious moment. Only two days ago, I came to you with a dream that I feared was beyond accomplishment. But now, thanks to your courage and perseverance..."

"And Harold," Fro said.

"What?" asked Rondol, losing his train of thought.

"And Harold. 'Thanks to our courage and perseverance and Harold.' That's what you *should* say. I liked how he juggled his head. He would have been a good member of our Fellowship. I mean, he helped us a lot. Didn't he?" Fro looked around at the rest of us. I shrugged. Personally, I think I would have found the ring without the ghost. Finding lost things is a Ranger's specialty.

Rondol sighed. "Of course he did." He rubbed his fingers over his eyes. "Where was I?"

"Courage and perseverance..." Fro said helpfully.

"Ah. Yes. Ahem....thanks to your courage and perseverance *and Harold*," he nodded at Fro, who grinned happily, "we now have the means to complete our quest. The dream is no longer impossible..."

"Yes, it is," I muttered to myself under my breath, thinking of the dragon we had yet to face. Rondol heard me and stopped again in mid-sentence.

Glaring at me, he said. "Please. I'm trying to give an appreciative, inspiring speech here to rally our spirits for the next part of our quest. Would you mind not interrupting?"

"Oooo, I love inspiring speeches!" the Halfling announced, clapping his hands.

"Oh, for the gods' sake!" Rondol threw his hands up in the air and rolled his eyes.

"I'm sorry," I said. "But really, Rondol, we don't need inspiring speeches. I know how much you wizards love to declaim and pontificate, but what we truly need now are information and plans. What about this vision of yours? You still haven't told us what it is. And where is the dragon we need to capture? That seems an important bit of information.

And when we find it, how are we going to get it to lie still while we put that hulking great stone hoop around its claw?"

"Those are good questions," Fro said, nodding sagely. "I've been thinking about them myself." We all looked at the Halfing in surprise. *Thinking* and *Halfling* aren't usually found in the same context. "What?" he said, looking back at us. "Why are you looking at me?"

"If you'd had a bit more patience, Ari, I was going to get to all that," Rondol said. "All I wanted was to make sure everyone appreciated just how much we had already accomplished."

"Fine," I said. "Thank you. Consider that we appreciate it. Can we get down to the meat of things here?"

"Oh, are we having meat for breakfast?" Fro asked, looking about.

"We've already had breakfast, Fro," Pintoglas reminded him.

"I meant second breakfast," the Halfling replied.

A burst of colored sparks in the air above us and the sight of streamers of power shooting out of Rondol's hands did wonders to refocus our attention.

Satisfied, Rondol said, "Ari, let me address your last question first."

"Why?" asked Fro.

"Why what?"

"Why the last question first? Isn't that going backward? Why are we going backward?"

I reached over and patted Fro on the shoulder. "It's all right, Fro. Wizards move in mysterious ways. Best not to question them."

"Ahh, yes..." he said, nodding. "Magic, isn't it?"

"If you are both quite finished, let me set a rule here," Rondol said. "If anyone has anything to say, please raise your hand and wait to be called on."

"Stupid rule," said Grinli, "but if you say so."

"I say so, or else we'll never get on with this quest. Now, as to putting the ring on the dragon..."

We waited.

"Ahem...well, you see...I don't know that part. I know why we're doing this and how to find the dragon, but after that...well, *you're* the adventurers. You're the ones who are supposed to figure that part out. That's why I hired you."

Grinli's hand shot up. "Yes, Grinli?"

"You *hired* us? We're getting *paid*? No one said anything about getting paid."

Fro's hand shot up as well. Rondol sighed. "Yes, Fro?"

"Well, that's why I thought we should have brought Harold with us. You see, he could juggle his head for the dragon. The dragon would be so surprised and delighted—I know I was when I saw Harold do that—that it wouldn't pay attention to us putting the ring on his claw."

I swear even the birds stopped their morning song for a moment. I know I was speechless. Fro had actually come up with a plan, and while I'm sure it wouldn't have worked, it had a tactical logic to it that I didn't think the Halfling was capable of. My opinion of my giant companion went up a notch.

"That's....that's good thinking, Fro," Rondol said, evidently as surprised as the rest of us. "In fact," he said enthusiastically. "That's what I mean! That's the kind of thinking I'm looking for from each of you. Positive problem solving. Well-done, Fro!"

Fro beamed. "Are we going back for Harold now?"

"Harold told me he couldn't come with us anyway," I interjected swiftly, just in case the wizard was actually contemplating recruiting the ghost. "Too many responsibilities at Gol Durnish."

"That's too bad," said Fro, crestfallen.

"Never mind. I just know you'll all figure it out when the time comes," Rondol said.

"And now, Wizard," Pintoglas said. "Tell us your vision. I think the time has come for that."

"Very well. I agree." He reached into his robe and pulled out the crystal sphere I'd seen him holding in the forest the night before. Was he going to invoke the red-suited spirit I'd seen as well?

"This is a *talimir*. It's a magical artifact that allows wizards to see things we couldn't see with our naked eyes. We use them to see things that are far away or that are very small. But everything we see is part of this world." He lifted the small sphere up, and it sparkled in the dawn's light. "This one, however, is different. It conjures up scenes from another world."

"I've seen *talimiri* before," Pintoglas said. "My father's wizard had one. He would occasionally let me see things through it. But I didn't know they could see into other worlds."

"They can't. This is very unusual. It may not even be a *talimir*, though it looks and works like one."

"How did you come by it?" the elf asked.

"That is a story in itself, but one I feel," he said, glancing in my direction, "I should save for another time." I nodded in agreement. Wizards will cloak stories within stories within stories if you give them half a chance. It can be confusing as hell. Boring, too. "Let me just say that it was given to me by a stranger, an old man I met while hunting herbs in the forest. He said I would know what to do with it. Then he disappeared. I think he was a forest spirit, maybe even a forest god."

See, even in not telling the story, a wizard manages to tell a story.

"Anyway, I took it back to my chambers and studied it. As I did so, a strange thing occurred. Normally, when you use one of the *talimiri*, you see your visions within it. But this one projected a vision into the air around me. This is not unheard of, but it is not common, either."

"And what did you see, Wizard?" asked Grinli.

He held the *talimir* up in front of us. "It's best you see for yourself."

I had also seen a wizard use a *talimir* before, and usually they make a production of it with grand hand flourishes and incantations. Given half a chance, wizards will make a production of anything. But Rondol simply held the *talimir* out where we could see it, and it began to glow and glow and....

****

I was standing in a rocky meadow, the land deeply covered in winter snow. Near me I could see the dark shapes of trees. It could have been the Gloomwoods far in the northernmost province of the Kingdom, but it felt different. Rangers have a good sense of the land and the spirits that abide in it. This forest had none of the dark murkiness that the Gloomwoods possesses. It felt healthy and vital and life-giving. Yet it felt unfamiliar as well, as if I had seen a friend who up close turned out to be a stranger.

Above me the sky was filled with stars, and though I looked, I could see none of the usual constellations or sky-marks. Only the moon was familiar though upon inspection even its face looked subtly different. *Another world*, I thought.

I felt energy gathering around me. I could feel it throbbing in the land beneath my feet. I could feel it in the rocks and boulders. I could feel it in the nearby forest. But in spite of the presence of such power, I felt completely at peace as if I were being held close in my mother's lap.

The land, the stones, even the trees began to glow as if candles burned within them. As I watched, power rushed out from them and into the ground before me. The snow stirred and spiraled into the air. It whirled in spirals like one of the sand devils I have seen in the desert lands to the south. The land about me was breathing light and power into this dancinging snow before me, yet the air was perfectly still.

It was earth magic of a most powerful kind.

I should be wary, I thought. *This much magic, this much power, is a frightening thing.* But I felt wholly at peace. I knew instinctively that whatever was happening would not harm me. In fact, I wasn't even sure if I was really here to be harmed. Though I looked and felt solid, this might only be an illusion of the *talimir*.

Thinking of that, I looked around to see if my companions were with me. But I was alone. No doubt they were having a similar vision as I, if vision it was, but the magic of the *talimir* made it seem that it was personal to each of us.

When I looked back, the swirling snow had changed. It had thickened and lengthened, and I could see shapes taking form within it. Energies of stone and earth and tree were gathering and bringing something into being. As I watched, it became a carriage, an open sleigh such as the men in the far north use, and hitched to it was a team of deer. But they were larger and more muscular than the deer I knew, and they had large antlers. Their harnesses seemed made of bright red leather, and attached to them were tiny bells that jingled with clear, sweet notes as the animals pranced in their places. But where was the driver of this conveyance? Was it here for me?

My question was answered when I sensed movement behind me. Turning, I saw forming out of a smaller whirl of power flowing from the land around me the figure I had seen Rondol talking to in the forest the previous night. Clad in a fur-trimmed red suit with black boots, a full white beard down to his stomach and a green wreath around his head, he seemed the personification of mirth and jollity. I couldn't help but smile as I looked upon him.

I have on occasion met earth spirits in my travels, large and small beings that live in wells and springs, forests and mountains. They are normally shy of humans, even with Rangers. But now and then they will appear, and when it's a Great One, there is always the sense of being in the presence of immense power held leashed. I had somewhat of that sense standing before this being, and there was a quality about him that he shared with the spirits of the land whom I had met. But he was more than that, much more, I felt. I am no Wizard, so I could not put my finger on the difference. I just knew I was in the presence of awesome power but one wrapped in caring and joy. I was caught between wanting to dance with him and kneel before him.

As it happened, he let me do neither. He smiled and nodded at me, but said not a word. He went over and vaulted into the sleigh, taking up the reins. Looking back, he said something in a language I could not understand but which I felt as a blessing. Then he flicked the reins, and the deer surged forward....forward and upward as they and the sleigh they pulled and the driver within it launched into the air and flew into the night sky. And why not? How else might a spirit travel save by flying?

Then it seemed I was drawn up with them, as if caught in the wind of their passing. I have never flown. I have seen wizards do so, but Rangers are men of the land and prefer our feet to stay on the good earth. Yet I feared not as the ground fell away beneath me. It felt only natural that I should go with this spirit wherever he was traveling, and if I needed to fly to do so, then so be it.

At this point the vision changed as if many miles and many hours were thrown together into one cauldron of impressions. I saw the spirit and his sleigh flying over strange and wondrous cities, whose buildings seemed to rise impossibly high into the air, and over small hamlets and villages not so different from those in my world. Everywhere he went, he laughed and threw sparkling streamers and balls of light onto the houses and buildings, which glowed in response. Sometimes he would land on the roofs and disembark, disappearing down chimneys. Other times he simply landed and threw out his magic and then flew on.

Everywhere he went, he left behind laughter and merriment. Love and generosity followed him on his journey. The children in particular seemed to feel his presence, their eyes lighting up with wonder as he paused above their homes and then flew on. This was powerful magic indeed, and though we have great gods and goddesses of Light, I knew of no spirit in my world that could or would do such things.

I know not how long I was caught up in this nighttime journey. Time and space seemed meaningless. But I became aware after a time that I was sitting back in the forest clearing where we had made our camp. Rondol stood there as he had been before, holding out the *talimir*. I felt as if I was awakening from a vivid dream.

We all looked at each other, and I could see that the others were as affected as I by what we had just experienced. Even Grinli, grizzled old dwarf and hardened warrior that he is, seemed softer. Pintoglas was enraptured. Fro had tears running down his cheeks. I had never seen a Halfling weep before.

Finally, we took a collective breath. "That was amazing," I said.

"What world was that?" asked Pintoglas. "Those cities....they were remarkable. They must be a people possessed of powerful sorceries."

"Actually," said Rondol, putting the *talimir* back in his robe and sitting down, "from what I have learned — and it is very little, I admit — they do not seem to have any magic at all, or at least they do not recognize and summon it like we do. I saw no one who passed for a wizard. Perhaps they had it once and lost it. Their cities are the result of a mechanical knowledge which has given them great power as artificers. But they seem to yearn for magic. They dream of it and tell stories about it. They look for it in their lives. And that is why the Ride is important."

"The Ride?"

"That's what I call it, Ari. What that spirit does. It rides the currents of dreams and longing and wherever it goes, peoples' lives are touched by magic, or at least the memory of it. And even that touch, small and brief though it is, makes a difference. Did you not see how people changed when they felt it? That is powerful magic indeed."

"I agree that it was powerful. But what has this to do with us? If this is the vision that is sending us to risk our lives facing a dragon, its meaning is distressingly obscure."

"You speak for me as well, Ranger," said Grinli. "When you spoke, Wizard, of the Kingdom in danger from the Unbodied One, I thought your vision was of some enemy that threatened us, someone — or something — that could feel the bite of my good axe." He lifted and shook his battleaxe for emphasis. "But in this vision, I found no enemy, only a blithe spirit that seemed to bring good, not evil. So I, too, am confused."

Rondol frowned. "When I first had had this vision and saw the Ride, I was confused as well. What meaning was there in this for me or for the Kingdom? I confess I did not know. Yet, I felt there was something of great importance here. I believe a god sent me this *talimir* to tell me what to do to face the threat of the Unbodied One, however far away — or near — in the future that threat may be. There is a message here."

"Mayhap, but it's an unclear one."

Rondol shrugged. "I can only share what I think. It is the Ride. The Ride is the message. We need such a Ride in our world as well."

"But why? We have magic aplenty. Sometimes I think we have too much, though I doubt you would agree. We have no need for such a being or such a Ride, joyous as it was."

"I think you are wrong, Ari. But we shall have to discuss this later. We have had enough words for now. Now we have another ride to take, and a swift one at that. If I am right and such a magical Ride is needed, then it must happen, as it does in that other world, at Year's Turn Night, for that is when the veils between this world and realm of spirits is thinnest. That is when the spirit is strongest."

"But...but that's only four nights from now," protested Grinli. "Surely you don't mean we must find and capture a dragon by then?" Dwarves like to move slowly and deliberately. There actually is no word for fast in the dwarven language.

"Nevertheless, that is what we must do."

"And you know where we must ride, Wizard?" I said.

"I do. We must make all haste to the Bitterstone Mountains, for that is where the dragon we seek is lairing."

"The Bitterstone Mountains? Wizard, it will take us two days of hard riding just to reach them, and that's by passing through the Gloomwoods."

"Then we had best get started. Time waits for no being, be he man, dwarf, Halfling, or elf."

"I bet it doesn't wait for our Fellowship or the Ring, either," said Fro, and he reached down to put his harness on his back.

****

Our ride that first day was uneventful. However, the further we pressed northward, the more uneasy we all felt. At times we rode (or ran, in Fro's case) into areas where the land seemed oppressed by some unseen force as if a weight of gloom pressed down upon the very stones around us. Even the sky seemed more grey at such times. The world seemed ready to weep but not yet able to find tears. Then we would top a rise or pass through a grove of trees, and all would be well again. The sun would shine, the land felt good, and the gloom became just a memory.

Had this only happened once, I would have put it down to imagination. When you're on a quest to face a dragon, it's only natural that gloomy thoughts might arise at some point. The possibility of imminent death can have that effect. But it happened again and again as if the land were being torn apart in some great tug-of-war between the gods of Light and Dark, leaving a countryside divided like a quilt into patchworks of hopefulness and despair.

As this pattern became more and more evident, Rondol became more and more grim and determined. Along one particularly barren stretch of road, we rode together, feeling cheered somewhat by each other's company. As our horses brushed against each other, seeming to seek comfort themselves from their own closeness, Rondol leaned towards me and said, "The land is sicker than I'd thought. I think the Unbodied One may be closer than we think. This is surely his doing or that of his minions." I nodded, not willing to put that thought into words myself lest it gain the power to shape our imaginations as we rode. But I had to admit he could be right.

Mostly we traveled single file, but later in the day, after we'd passed through one of the 'sick patches' as Rondol called them, he and I found ourselves riding next to each other again. I took advantage of the moment to ask him a question.

"Rondol, I still don't know why the need is there for this Ride as you call it, but if you're right, why not just conjure up a spirit such as we saw, give it a sleigh and send it flying across the kingdom?"

"Ari, I cannot duplicate what we saw in the vision. I tried to summon such a spirit, but I failed. It doesn't exist in our world. I *could* make a team of deer fly but not for very long and not at the speeds and over the distances we saw. It would take a great deal of magical energy to do that, and no wizard…not even, I daresay, the Council of the Whites all acting together—could manage it. That is why I need a dragon. A dragon is a magical creature, as much of the air as of earth and fire. It *could* fly like that and carry me throughout the kingdom. That is why we need to capture and control one."

"But why, Wizard? To what end?"

Before he could answer, there was a shout from Pintoglas who was pointing towards the western horizon off to our left. I rode up to where he was and looked where he was pointing. A small band of horsemen was headed our way. That they were brigands I had no doubt and that they meant to accost us was clear as well by the way they drew their swords as they rode. I reached behind me and drew my sword from its scabbard. As always when faced with action, I could feel my blood begin to sing, and the sword seemed to vibrate with eagerness in my hands. I'm a peaceful man, but if someone brings battle to me, I'm ready to respond.

At that point, Fro came running up, Longrim's Ring bouncing on his back as he jogged along. He had not seen the brigands. Lost in his own thoughts—if, indeed, he had any—he was staring unseeing at the road ahead, his legs moving in a steady rhythm. He was not breathing hard at all.

At that point, to my amusement, the brigands turned aside and began to ride away. I was sure they had finally seen Fro. No one tangles with a Halfling if they can avoid it, not if they're smarter than the Halfling. I admit I was disappointed as I slid my sword back in its scabbard. I'd been hoping for a little action to relieve the frustration I was feeling at the wizard's continued failure to reveal the purpose of this quest. I determined that we would have it out when we camped for the night.

Aside from the brigands, who really didn't count, we saw no evil beings that day. No minions of the Unbodied One accosted us. Apart from oppressive feelings here and there, now and again, the day passed uneventfully. We made good time. Nightfall found us on the outskirts of the Gloomwoods, the densest, darkest forest in the Kingdom. That is where we made our camp for the night.

After our meal, as we sat around the campfire, I could contain it no longer and confronted Rondol.

"All right, Wizard. Tell us why this Ride is so important that we should risk our lives for it. And you'd best be convincing, for the Gloomwoods are not entered lightly. We might not live even to reach the Bitterstone Mountains." I thought about the giant spiderweb I'd seen and the deer that had been ensnared. "There are things that live in these woods that no sane person would want to face. If we are to chance encountering them just to find your dragon, we need to know why."

Rondol drew a long-stemmed pipe from the interior of his robe. Wizard's robes are like that; I think you could store a house's worth of furniture and goods in them and not create any bulges anywhere nor feel the weight of what you carried. I'd often wished I had one to pack my gear in, but you have to have magic to wear them. On the other hand, if I could just figure out how to persuade a wizard to be my pack animal....

He fiddled with the pipe, obviously using it as a prop to give himself time to think. This inspired Pintoglas and Grinli to bring out their pipes as well. Finally they all got them lit and going and the aroma of sweetweed filled the air around us. I'm not a smoking man myself, but I have to admit, sweetweed smoke is a blessing to one's nose. On the other side of the campfire from me, Fro pulled out a hambone and nibbled on it, his way of keeping the smoker's company.

"Remember what you saw in the vision. The red-garbed spirit flew throughout the land, filling the air with magic and where he went, people's hearts opened to receive it and were full of happiness and generosity. His Ride created magic."

"I don't doubt that, Rondol. But what has this to do with us? We have magic aplenty. If anything, there are times I think we have too much magic, though as a wizard you may not agree with me."

"I understand it," said Fro.

"What? What do you understand, Halfling?" asked Pintoglas.

"Why the Wizard wants to do this. It's for the magic."

"What do you mean, Fro?" I asked.

"Well, there's magic and then there's magic. Do you know what I mean?"

"No."

He scratched his head, looking for the words to explain his feelings.

"Do you mean like good magic and bad magic," I prompted him.

He looked at me. "No, Ranger Ari. I mean like...um...head magic and heart magic. There's the magic that does stuff, like Wizard Rondol does; it lives in your head and makes you a wizard. But then there's the magic that lives in your heart. It makes you kind to others and makes you feel good. Like our Fellowship. You make me feel good because you accept me. Isn't that magic? It is to me!"

It was the most complex thought I'd ever heard a Halfling utter, and my estimation of these gentle giants went up another notch. At least my estimation of Fro did.

"That's it exactly!" Rondol exclaimed. "By the gods, Halfling, you have said in a few words exactly what I've been trying to formulate for the past two months." Rondol stared at Fro as if at any moment the Halfling might change into an earth god himself.

"Head magic, heart magic. It's all the same to me. I still don't understand the purpose of this. How does all this tie in to keeping the coming of the Unbodied One where he is?"

"Grinli, think about it. You felt the depression in the land today. That draws the Unbodied One the way good stone draws your people. He finds sustenance in the burdened heart. He lives on sadness and fear. When hearts are full with joy and hope, he can find no purchase. He must slip back to his nether world. But when they are empty with despair, he finds flesh to clothe his evil. He lives in the body of our hopelessness; he dies in the body of our laughter and generosity."

"Don't you see?" he continued. "The Ride creates kindness. Magic cannot do that by itself. But it can create the wonderment that opens the heart to that kindness."

Silence descended upon our little fellowship for a time. I watched the flames dance about and thought about what the wizard had said while he and Grinli and Pintoglas puffed on their pipes and Fro munched on his hambone. A thought occurred to me. I looked away from the flames to see the wizard watching me.

"You have a question, Ari?" he asked.

"Not so much a question but a thought. If the matter is as you say and our land needs something to brighten it again and bring joy and kindness to our people, why don't the gods attend to it? They have the power. They can send one or more spirits to enliven the countryside. Why is it up to us to do this thing?"

Rondol drew on is pipe and blew a smoke ring into the air. "That would be nice if the gods could do it. Unfortunately, it doesn't work that way. The gods may be loving and willing, but we have to open the doors of our hearts through our actions before their love can pour into our world. Similarly, the dark gods cannot pour their suffering into the world unless we open the door through our acts of hatred and violence. It's up to us, Ari, not the gods."

He tapped his pipe on a nearby rock, then took another puff. "As for why us, I don't know the answer to that, Ari. It might have been anyone. The *talimir* was given to me, I know not why, but I have chosen to accept its vision and use it to help our land. And I found you and your friends and you have chosen to join me in my quest. In the end, it isn't who we are that is important. It's what we do with who we are. We choose the path, and that makes us the ones the gods choose as well."

I yawned. "Well, let us hope we and they chose rightly."

******

We rose before dawn's first light, ate a cold breakfast, and started into the Gloomwoods. We had a long way to go to cross the forest and reach the foothills of the Bitterstones. I knew many trails through these woods and felt that we could do it if we kept up a steady pace, but it would be a long and difficult day. And that was without running into any of the nastier denizens that lived in the shadows under the trees.

This was not a place for horses, so we let our mounts go. There was plenty of grazing nearby and I was sure they would be fine. Who knew? They might even be nearby when—or if—we returned.

What followed was a tiring and tense slog through undergrowth and over giant tree roots. Some of the trails I remembered had disappeared—not an uncommon thing in the Gloomwoods—but there were newer trails, created by large creatures whose nature I wasn't sure I wanted to discover.

No matter how thick the forest became, the elf and I could have moved through it quickly as our woodskills are highly developed. But this was not true for Grinli or Rondol. I suppose the wizard could have used magic to open a path for us, but the Gloomwoods react badly to magic, especially if it harms the trees in any way. And don't even think about the reaction to someone wielding an axe. Fro on the other hand, simply pushed his way through like an unstoppable battering ram. I swear I saw trees moving aside as he approached. We ended up putting him in front with the rest of us following in his tracks.

After that we made steady though slow progress. Rondol was happy about that, but I was worried. We weren't moving as quickly as I'd hoped. From time to time we ran into barriers even Fro couldn't push aside or push through. I began to fear that dark would find us still in the woods. That was not a comforting thought at all.

We didn't stop for a midday meal but ate what rations we could as we kept moving. I thought Fro might grumble about this, but he was stoic and steady. He knew we were on a mission and time was important. If he had to give up second and third breakfast, lunch, post-lunch snack, and afternoon tea, he did so for the good of the Fellowship.

It became a race between us and the sun, and the sun was winning. I tried to hurry us along, but we were already moving as fast as we could, and I could see the wizard tiring. I was amazed he had kept up for so long as wizards are not known for their physical prowess, but now Rondol was showing real signs of fatigue, though he was doing his best to hide them.

Then we ran into the spiders.

At first it was just a white gleam off to the left in the distance that warned me. Peering into the gloom, I was sure what I was seeing was one of those large webs. I moved up in front of Fro and indicated we should move off to one side. I didn't want us going anywhere near that web if we could help it.

My plan would have worked if there'd been just one web. But others began to appear, more to the left, then some to the right, and finally right in front of us. As of yet, none of us had seen any of the spiders, but we all knew by the growing number of webs and their proximity that it was only a matter of time. I drew my sword in preparation.

Then I heard Fro grunt behind me. Turning, I saw that a large green and white spider had dropped down from above and had landed on top of Longrim's Ring, its fangs quivering over the back of his neck. Fro's height obviously made him the most tempting target, or the easiest to land on anyway.

Before I could say anything, though, Fro whipped his hand back, moving faster than I thought a Halfling could, grabbed a leg of the giant arachnid and hurled the creature away from him. It flew through the air and hit a tree with a resounding splat.

"Hate spiders," he said.

"Me, too, Fro," I said, raising my sword up in case more were about to drop on us. "Especially when they're bigger than a dog."

"Bigger than a pig, I think," he replied, also looking up and around. But it must have been a lone sentry, for there were no other spiders in sight.

We held a council of war, our eyes roaming the surrounding woods and webs as we spoke. "What now, Ari?" Rondol asked.

"We have to keep going. If we stop for long, darkness will fall and that could be fatal. I have no doubt the spiders can see in the dark."

"I can make light if we need it."

"Excellent. But I'd still rather be far from here as quickly as possible."

"Agreed. Besides my light cannot tell you the direction as the sun can."

"I'm not worried about that, Rondol. A ranger can always tell what direction he's moving in, and that's true for an elf as well. I'm not concerned about getting lost. I'm concerned about getting eaten. A lot of things besides the spiders come out in these woods at night."

Weapons at the ready, we pressed on, trying to keep our distance from the webs we could see, and looking up, down, and around as we moved. The need for constant attention in all directions slowed us down, too.

A rustling in the undergrowth warned me, and I stopped, my sword at the ready. A minute later, a green and black spider twice the size of my head came scurrying out of the undergrowth ahead of me. Its fangs were easily as long as my fingers, but what worried me wasn't their size but the venom that I knew they could inject.

It paused in front of me and then it *jumped*. I hadn't expected that, though I should have, and it nearly cost me my life. It leapt up right for my face, and only my fast reflexes enabled me to get my sword between me and it, skewering it and then flinging it away.

But it was only the first. Easily a dozen more came out of the undergrowth all around us, and we were quickly engaged in a fight for survival. Out of the corner of one eye, I saw Grinli's axe rising and falling as he sang his battle song, and on the other side of me, I saw Fro's fists pumping back and forth, each ham-sized hand felling any spider that it hit. I couldn't see Pintoglas, but I knew he could wield his bow and arrows as skillfully in close quarters as at long range. As for Rondol, I couldn't see him either, but I could hear the sizzle as magical bolts flew through the air. He couldn't hurl fireballs here in the Gloomwoods, but a wizard has other weapons at his disposal.

It seemed like we were fighting for a long time, for other spiders took the place of those that fell, but in fact it was probably not more than five or ten minutes. As quickly as the spiders had appeared, they disappeared, leaving more than a dozen arachnid bodies lying around us.

"Come. Let's get out of here," I yelled and pushed through the undergrowth heading north. If we could just put this spider-infested region behind us, we still had a chance to make it out of the forest before sunset.

I knew this was a lost hope as soon as we exited a particularly thick area of woods and came into a clearing. For there in the center was the largest spider I had ever seen, much larger than a horse. I had heard legends and rumors of this monster. It was Bolehs, the queen spider of the forest.

What was worse than its size was the gleam of an evil intelligence in its eyes. This was no common arachnid, even one grown to giant proportions, but a forest demon. We would have had a hard time killing it if it was alone, but it was surrounded by spiders like the ones we had just fought, only half again as large. This was it, the encounter I had most feared might happen. I had little hope we would survive it.

We moved out into the edge of the clearing, watched by dozens of black, feral eyes as we moved. We lined up shoulder to shoulder. If we died, we would do so as the Fellowship we had become, side by side with each other. Fro stood in the middle with Rondol and I on his right and Pintoglas and Grinli on his left.

"I think an arrow into the eye of the large one would be appropriate right now," I said to the elf who held his bow at ready, an arrow cocked.

"I think an arrow in each of his eyes would be more appropriate," Pintoglas replied, and I knew he was completely serious. He was that fast with a bow.

There came the most awful sound I've ever heard. Bolehs laughed and by the gods above, it was a human sounding laugh, a high-pitched, gleeful chortle from the depths of hell. It made the hair on my head stand on end.

The monster made a move towards us. Pintoglas pulled back on his bow.

Everything froze.

None of us could move a muscle. We and the spiders stood there in that clearing facing each other like figures in a sculpture made by a mad artist.

From my right, a tall figure walked into the clearing. It was an old man. At least he had a long white beard and snowy white hair. He reminded me of the spirit in the *talimir's* vision, but he was thinner and taller and he was dressed in forest greens and browns. But what was most striking about him were the antlers that grew out of his forehead.

It was the Forest Lord, the Old Man of the Forest. Some say he's an immortal wizard who gave up the ways of men and disappeared into the forest. Others say he's a godling or even a god. Some say he's a spirit.

I say he was a welcome sight. I had no idea what he might do to us, but I trusted it would be better or at least more humane than what the spiders had in mind.

He turned and faced the spiders. "Now, now, you know better than to molest my friends, and *these* are my friends. I told you they would be coming, didn't I?"

A horrible parody of a human voice came from the monster spider. "Oh, were *these* the ones?" it asked innocently. "Sorry." Frankly, it didn't sound sorry at all.

"I told you to bring them to me."

"Well, we were going to...."

"Unwrapped."

Silence from the spiders.

"You were going to eat them, weren't you?"

The big spider shuffled its legs.

"You *should* be ashamed, Bolehs. We'll talk about this later. For now, begone." He made a gesture and the clearing was empty. No spiders anywhere. But we still couldn't move. Then he raised a hand, and we could.

"I'm sorry about that. They like to test my limits and see what they can get away with."

I put my sword into my scabbard. "I thought we'd seen our last sunrise."

"Well, I can guarantee you have one more sunrise in your future, but after that, I cannot say."

"That's...um...encouraging. But did you really know we were coming?"

"Not you specifically. Him." He pointed at Rondol. "I was sure he would bring others, I just didn't know who they'd be."

Rondol came forward. "It's you, isn't it? The old man who gave me the *talimir*."

"Yes, it was I. I was instructed by one greater than I to bring it to one who could act on the vision it contains, for there is a need in our land. I thought you were young enough and open enough to understand what it meant and act accordingly. You have justified my faith in you."

"I'm glad, but I'm not sure I *do* understand...not all of it, certainly.

Can you tell me more?"

"What you still need to know, you will discover on your own. But I can tell you this. The Ride is a gift of the gods of Light. It is a cosmic mystery that takes place on many worlds. It is different on each one, but it is always the Ride of the Lightbearers. The Ride always offers the magic of wonder and love that opens the heart. If that wonder is lost, the world may be lost."

I'm not one to pass up an opportunity, so I said to him, "Your power over wild things is legendary. Can *you* help us tame a dragon? Since this seems to be your quest?"

The Old Man of the Forest looked at me . "Not my quest. The land's quest." HIs eyes twinkled. "No one *tames* a dragon, Ranger, least of all me. You misunderstand who and what I am if you think I could do so. Whatever power I have comes from my partnership with the forest and all things in it. I have no power over anything. No good ever comes of that." He looked again at Rondol. "As I said, you will discover what you need to know, if you pay attention." He shrugged. "Or you will fail and be eaten."

With that vote of confidence, he disappeared.

I saw, though, that he had left us a gift. Leading out of the north end of the clearing was a straight, clear passage as if the whole forest has parted to give us a corridor in the direction we wished to go. Needless to say, we took the hint, and with our way thus eased, we were out of the Gloomwoods just as the sun sank below the westernmost peaks of the Bitterstone Mountains.

We made our camp in the foothills. The day's push through the forest and the battle with the spiders had left us exhausted, so we ate a quick meal and tumbled into our packs. Though very tired myself, I volunteered to take first watch, and Rondol said he would take the turn after mine.

So once again we met in the middle of the night. As before, we sat for at time together before I turned over to sleep. And as before, I had questions.

"I saw you the other night," I said to him, "talking to the spirit from the vision."

"Yes," he admitted. "He occasionally appears to me."

"I didn't know a being could come through a *talimir*."

"They can't. Not normally. That's why I suspect it's not a true *talimir*, or if it is, it has been crafted in a special way."

"What does he tell you?"

"Very little. We do not speak the same language, of course. He always says something I can't quite make out. And he laughs a lot, a deep, jolly laugh. His belly shakes when he does so. It reminds me of the bowl of pudding my mother used to make when I was a child and how it would shake in its bowl. That used to make me laugh, and this spirit makes me laugh, too."

He poked at the small fire we had built. "But though we do not speak in the same tongue, there is much that passes between us, as if I know what he is trying to say. His work is about inspiring wonder and generosity and opening people's hearts. That is the true magic, you know, the magic of love and kindness. If we learn that magic, the Unbodied One can never be a threat."

"And spirits cannot do this magic for us?"

"No. We must do it for ourselves. Oh, once we start, once we make the track for them to follow, then the spirits can add their magic to what we do. I had an image when this spirit was speaking to me of a man who reminded me of Sandovon the White or even the Old Man of the Forest. He was obviously someone of importance. I saw him moving through the darkened streets of a town throwing little bags of gold into the windows of houses, or if the windows were closed and shuttered, down their chimneys. He was not a spirit, but through his giving, he set a pattern that the spirits could follow and amplify. If I understood rightly, it was that pattern that allowed the spirit we saw to come into being."

He reached into his robe and drew out his pipe. It was already filled with sweetweed, and as soon as he brought it into the air, it lit itself and began to smoke. Nice trick, that.

"That's why I failed to conjure a spirit to do this job. The pattern doesn't exist yet in our world. It's up to us to create it. That is the spell I told you I was trying to weave when we spoke that night in the Moisty Mountains."

"Well, if all it takes is someone giving away gold, we could have found a rich merchant to do that and spared ourselves all this trouble. Why, Sandovon himself must have gold aplenty."

"No, it's not just the giving, though that's important. It's the wonderment. It has to have mystery and wonder and magic behind it, like the flying deer. But it can't be our usual kind of magic. Everyone's used to that. This has to be something different, something special and unexpected."

He puffed out a couple smoke rings and signed contentedly. "That's why I was so secretive in the city. I didn't want anyone to suspect I was on a quest or what it was about. If people knew what I was doing—even if the other wizards knew—it would spoil the surprise and the wonder of it. And that's also why it has to be a dragon, Ari. A dragon is the most magical, wonder-filled creature in our world. Imagine such a beast flying over a town, landing on rooftops while someone on its back—me, I suppose—delivers presents and dispenses magic. People would remember something like that. It would fire their imaginations."

"It would fire their houses. When dragons have flown over cities before, there has been burning and screaming and people being eaten. Not the effect I think you're looking for, though it would certainly be memorable."

"That's what Longrim's Ring would prevent, Ari. It would keep the dragon under control. And think of the wonder of it. A giant creature of destruction moving lightly about the world, bringing people joy and laughter instead of death and suffering."

"But even if you control it, it would crush any houses it landed on. Dragons are heavy, Rondol."

"Dragons are magical. They can be any weight they wish."

"I still think getting a fat merchant to give away gold would have done the trick. What could be more wondrous and memorable than that?"

And with that I climbed into my bedroll and went to sleep.

BOOK THE FOURTH
THE RIDE

The Bitterstone Mountains lie between the northernmost lands of the Kingdom and the ice and snow of the far north. They have the distinction of being the only mountains in the land that are not inhabited by dwarves. They say the stone is tainted. They say it "tastes bitter," which is where the mountains get their name. I wouldn't know about that since all stones taste pretty much alike to me—not that I go around tasting them all that much.

The Bitterstone Mountains are one of the more inhospitable places I've been, so I can well understand the dwarves—or anything else—not wanting to live in them. The mountains are wind-swept and barren and the stone is sharp and crumbly, making climbing treacherous. Grinly hated it and kept cursing the rocks around him as he stumbled and slid. Dwarves are usually more sure-footed in mountains than goats, but that was not the case here. No wonder his people never wished to live here, whatever it tasted like.

Fortunately, we did not have to climb very high before we came to a plateau with a pass that led deeper into the range between the high peaks. We were seeking a cavern complex, one that went down rather than up once you found the entrance. I was expecting some difficulty in accomplishing the latter, but at the end of a small draw leading out from the pass, the cavern entrance turned out to be quite visible. . It was hard not to notice it with the space in front of it littered as it was with bones, some even human.

"Well," said Grinli, "either a lot of people and other things climb up here to die or we've found the dragon's lair."

"It's the lair all right," said Pintoglas. "I can feel the Great Wyrm's magic in the rocks around here."

"And here," I said, reaching down and picking up something that looked like a thin, narrow piece of black, ribbed stone, "is a dragon's scale." I grinned at my companions. "The evidence mounts. I think this is the place."

"Do I use the magic ring now?" asked Fro, peering into the darkness of the cavern's entrance as if the dragon might be lying just inside with its claw conveniently sticking out.

"Not yet, my friend," said Rondol. "But soon, I'm sure." He kicked some bones aside and set his own pack down. "We have little time, I'm afraid. Tomorrow is Year's Turn Night. It's the most magical time. That is when the Ride must take place."

"Then we'd best go beard the beastie in its lair," said Grinli, hoisting his axe.

"Agreed," said the wizard. "What's the plan?"

"Well," I scratched my chin thoughtfully and grinned. "We go beard the beastie in its lair."

Rondol looked at me. "I'd expected something more subtle from a Ranger." He shrugged. "Well, why not. Nothing like the direct approach." And he picked up his pack and headed toward the cavern entrance, crunching across the bones.

I caught up with him. "The fact is, I know of no plan that will let us take the dragon unaware. Stealth will not work. It will sense us coming long before we reach it. Magical beings have a nasty way of doing that, so sneaking up on it is out of the question. All I can say is that the three of us engage the dragon with our weapons and keep it occupied while you and Fro get the ring onto its claw. It's not much of a plan, I know, but I can think of no better." Which it irked me to admit.

It also irked me that I was now missing Harold. The ghost's head-juggling trick might indeed have distracted the dragon, as Fro had suggested. A song and dance would have been at least as useful as a sword, a bow and an axe against a being who was for all practical purposes invulnerable and immortal. What could the dragon have done to Harold anyway? Dead is dead.

We pressed into the darkness of the cavern, and Rondol made a gesture with his hands. Balls of bright light appeared above each of our heads, clearly lighting our way. We could see every inch of the rock walls around us as they led deeper into the earth. We could also see the bones under our feet, a gruesome reminder of what lay ahead deeper into the earth.

It was not, however, hard going, and eventually the bones petered out. In fact, the deeper we descended the more the cavern's winding walls began to look hewn rather than naturally formed. I pointed this out to Grinli. "Yes," he said, "my people dug out these caverns long ago. How else would we have tasted the rock and found it bitter? You don't think we go around licking the sides of mountains, do you?"

Actually, that image had sprung to my mind, but I said to Grinli, "Oh, no, of course not. Who would do a thing like that?"

"Exactly. We discover a stone's taste by working with it, digging into it, trying to build with it."

I thought about this. I had been in a few dwarven cities. There was always a great hall which formed the central meeting place of the clan. Presumably that is where the dragon would be lairing. There was always a wide central processional way into the hall. I was sure the tunnel we were in would lead us to that. But there were also smaller side routes, even secret ones, which the nobles would use. I said so to Grinli.

"Aye," he said. "This is so."

"Then there *might* be a way to sneak up on this dragon, if we could find one of these smaller passages."

Grinli thought about it a bit. "'Tis possible," he said finally. "If the builders had gotten that far before they gave up. And if we could find them. And if..."

"Never mind the 'ifs.' It gives us more to work with than we had a moment ago." I dropped back to where the wizard was walking just in front of Fro. "Rondol, do you know any spells that reveal hidden passages?"

"Of course. That's second year knowledge, though most of us learn it the first year just to keep the higher level students from sneaking up on us and playing pranks. The Wizard's Court is riddled with secret passages."

I rubbed my hands together. "Then we may just have a way in that might surprise the dragon." I explained to him, and to Pintoglas and Fro who gathered close as well to listen to what Grinli and I had shared. "So, ahead of us will be secret ways into the central chamber. If we find them, we have a chance of sneaking up on the old wyrm.

"You said the dragon could sense us anyway," said Fro.

"Yes, here in the tunnels. But maybe if we are in a small passage, behind stone, it may not notice. It's worth trying."

"Indeed it is," said Pintoglas. "And if the wizard's spells fail to find such a passage, I'm sure my elven senses will do the trick."

I've never met an elf who was plagued with self-doubt.

We pressed on then with a renewed sense of possibility and purpose. Suicidal missions are all right if they're the only mission you have, but give a person a chance to survive, and you lighten his heart and strengthen his step considerably.

We moved deeper and deeper into the mountain. All around us there was silence. Nothing seemed to live here. Any small beastie that might have made these caves its home would long ago have been a snack for their prime tenant. Smart creatures give a dragon's lair a wide birth. Dumb creatures venture in and get eaten.

Guess which category we were in.

Rangers have an inbuilt sense of where they are in the world and when. Put us in a dark cavern and we can tell you what direction we're moving in and what time of day it is. Well, I was in a dark cavern and I knew we were moving north by northwest and it was an hour past midday. But none of us felt hungry, not even Fro which was a bit of wonder all in itself. *Halflings* and *meals* definitely go together in the same sentence. We all felt the need to keep pressing deeper into the earth, seeking that secret passage that would let us enter the dragon's lair in safety. Well, relative safety. Safer than walking in through the front door.

And we found it. Rondol's spell caused a portion of the cavern wall to glow a sickly green even as Pintoglas whispered loudly, "I can see the signs of a doorway here." If they'd been racing to see who found the secret passage first, I'd call it a tie.

Pintoglas and I ran our fingers over the rockface, looking for the means to open the doorway. I remembered a similar moment two days earlier when Harold had deposited us in front of a blank stone wall. But this time we found it. Actually, I found it first, which I could see nettled the elf. With a click and a groan, a part of the cavern wall moved inward, revealing a narrow passageway. Fortunately, it was high enough that even Fro didn't have to bend over, which would have been hard with the giant ring on his back.

"That reminds me of a question I have, Grinli," I said as we all made our way into the passage, the dwarf in the lead with me right behind him. "You're a short people. How come you always build such high roofs in your caverns? Not that I'm complaining."

"Dwarves are *not* short people," Grinli responded. "You are all abnormally tall people, especially that Halfling. But even with our stature, which is perfect, we like a lot of space around and above us. Dwarves are a spacious people." He snorted. "I don't see *your* kind surrounding yourselves with confining walls and ceilings."

"Point taken," I replied.

Stepping into the secret passage, we fell silent, for we knew we were getting closer to the central hall where, presumably, the dragon had made its home. It was the logical choice if only because it was probably the only space large enough for its bulk *and* the hoard of gold it was undoubtedly sitting on. No one knew exactly why dragons fancied gold and jewels and other treasure—they certainly couldn't spend it. I've often thought it was just to spite humans who loved the stuff. And I had to admit, it served as bait to lure in more than a few dinners.

The passage wound and twisted about and joined other, similar passages. Grinli seemed to know the way, though. Perhaps secret passages followed similar routes in all the dwarven cities, but more likely he, in the manner of his people, simply knew his way around under the earth.

Finally, he held up his hand for us to stop and indicated we should be quiet. With signs and gestures, he let me know the cavern we sought was just beyond the wall before us. I watched as he felt around over the stone with his fingers. There came a soft click of a latch being undone. I had Rondol extinguish the magical lights so they would not give us away in the dark of the chamber beyond. Grinli then pushed on the stone, and it slid aside quietly. I gave an inner sigh of relief. I'd feared the door would groan and creak when it opened like some old man trying to rise from his chair, but then, who makes a noisy secret entrance? It would defeat the purpose.

I indicated I should go first. Grinli stepped to one side, and I stuck my head through the opening. The cavern beyond, in typical dwarven style, was enormous, the ceiling rising out of sight into the darkness above me. And to my surprise, it was lit by torches burning on sconces around the wall, their light thrown back in glittering splendor by the huge piles of gold and jewels lying around the chamber. But then I supposed the dragon liked to see the gold gleam as much as people did.

What most caught my attention, though, was not the untold treasure lying before me but a rhythmic sound that filled the room. At first I wasn't sure what it was, and then I realized the dragon was snoring!

I couldn't believe our luck. If the old wyrm was asleep, then there was a chance we could accomplish our task and get away with our lives. Assuming Longrim's Ring actually worked.

I ducked back into the passage and huddled with the others. "The gods favor us," I whispered softly. "The dragon is asleep. If we move quietly, we may put the ring on the beast before it awakens." Then I turned and led the way into the chamber.

When Grinli saw the treasure, his eyes widened and his breath quickened, but he kept his tongue in his mouth and said nothing. I could see, though, that he was thinking deeply of all the wealth around him. Dwarves love their gold almost as much as dragons do.

We moved stealthily into the cavernous space. The dragon was indeed asleep, its great bulk rising high above us. Fortunately, it was not sleeping on top of a pile of gold. We could not have avoided making noise if we tried to climb such a pile to get to it. Instead, it lay on its side against a heap of jewels and finely wrought golden objects — I saw goblets, candleholders, chests, and other things I couldn't immediately identify. Best of all, it had one of its legs thrust out before it rather than curled beneath its body, the clawed foot temptingly near and available.

While Pintoglas and I kept watch, our weapons at the ready, Grinli, Rondol and Fro approached the great claw. It was easily larger than any of them. I could imagine it lifting a cow or a horse, or a man, up to the great jaws with no more trouble than I might lift a chickenleg to my mouth.

Rondol and Grinli helped Fro get out of his harness and put the Ring on the cavern floor. Grinli made as if to pick it up himself, but Fro put his hand on his shoulder and lightly pushed him aside. Believe me, it's not easy to push a dwarf. They stand on the earth as if rooted to it. But Fro did so and clearly indicating he was the Ringbearer, he picked up the great stone hoop and carried it over to the claw.

There, with Rondol and Grinli's help, he lifted it up and pushed it onto one of the dragon's talons. It fit perfectly, as if Longrim had somehow taken measurements before he made it. Then the three of them stepped back and came over to join us.

"What now?" I whispered.

Rondol shrugged. "I guess now we try it out."

He stepped forward, obviously ready to wake the dragon and give it his commands. But that was when I noticed the great black eye watching us. In its depths I saw cruel amusement.

"So," a great voice boomed through the cavern as the beast drew its head up and looked at us. "This is the fabled Ring of Longrim the Mage." He held up his claw and looked at the stone circle around the talon as if admiring it. "I've long heard of it and its power to control my kind. I've often wondered if it were real."

"Real enough, great dragon," Rondol said, and I had to credit him for not letting his voice quiver in the presence of so much power, under control or not. "And now you are under my command."

"Oh dear," the dragon said. "Really?" And then the beast laughed. If a mountain laughed before it buried you in an avalanche, it would sound like this dragon did as it shook with mirth.

It stretched out its leg, and as I watched, it flexed its claw. The ring shattered, the pieces falling at our feet.

So much for Longrim's magic ring.

"Aw," said the great beast. "The little ring broke. How sad." And it laughed some more.

We stood rooted to the spot, a stricken expression on Rondol's face.

"Run!" yelled Grinli, shattering the trance we were in, and as one we turned and headed for the entrance to the secret passage. The sound of gold falling and scattering about told me the dragon was rising to come after us.

Fro reached the entrance first, but rather than ducking in, he stood there waiting for the rest of us to reach safety first. I'm not sure what he meant to do. His fists, powerful as they were, would no more hurt the dragon than a catapult ball would.

"You cannot escape the lair of Fimfilomongous," the dragon roared. "You come hoping to enslave me, but you shall be my evening meal." It laughed again, and then I heard the hissing intake of breath as it prepared to breathe fire. I could already feel the searing heat hitting my back, and the dragon hadn't even let loose his flame yet. The secret passage seemed impossibly far away.

Then I saw Fro bend down and pick something large off the floor. It seemed to be a shield of some kind, but rather than holding it before him, he hurled it like a discus. Futile, I thought. It will just bounce off the dragon's hide.

But then I heard a snort behind us and a gasp. Glancing back, I saw that the shield had struck the dragon on the nose just as it was about to breath its fire. It couldn't have hurt, but it caused the dragon to suck in rather than out, swallowing his flame. Fimfilomongous began to cough, and clouds of smoke came out of his mouth and nostrils.

It gave us just the time we needed to make it into the passageway, Fro ducking in after us. Frantically Grinli slid the door closed.

Outside we could hear the dragon's voice. "Did you think to sneak up on me? I knew you were coming as soon as you left the Gloomwoods and entered the Bitterstone Mountains. I have watched you all the way." It laughed again. "Did you think that stone ring would really enslave me? Remember that Longrim was also called 'the Insane,' and for good reason. His ring was a fantasy, but it amused me to watch you try it out."

We heard loud scratching on the stone outside the entrance as the dragon raked its claws over it. We instinctively shrank back.

"And now, you think I cannot reach you where you are. Remember, I have all the time in the world. If you try to leave the passageway, I will know it and be there waiting for you. And if you stay, you will starve. That is a slow death. Come out. Face me and die quickly."

There was nothing else to do, so we retreated back into the passageway, and Rondol brought up the magic lights again so we could see each other. I'm sure my expression was as grim as the ones I saw on the faces around me.

"Thank you, Fro, for what you did. It was very brave, and it saved our lives," Rondol said to the Halfling.

"We are a Fellowship," Fro said simply.

"Yes, Fro, it was well done," said Pintoglas, "but our lives have only been spared temporarily, it seems. The Great Wyrm has us well and truly bottled up." He looked at Rondol. "I don't suppose you have any magic for situations like this."

Rondol shook his head. "Nothing the dragon couldn't counter if it felt me building a spell."

"Well," I said, "we might as well sit down and rest. Perhaps a plan will suggest itself to us." And following my own suggestion, I sat down and leaned my back against the stone wall.

"I thought it was too easy at the end there," I said after a time had passed. "I should have suspected the dragon wasn't really slumbering."

"He sounded like he was asleep," Fro responded. "My uncle Bilbun snores like that, only louder."

"It can't end like this," Rondol said quietly. "We have come so far in our quest. We cannot fail now."

"I'm open to suggestions, Wizard," Grinli said.

But Rondol had none to offer. We all fell into a gloomy silence. Fro even fell asleep, though thankfully he had not inherited his uncle's penchant for snoring. Grinli and Pintoglas soon followed his example. A warrior takes any chance he gets to have a nap.

"By all the gods of Light, I know where we went wrong...nay, where I went wrong," Rondol suddenly said.

"What are you saying, Wizard," I muttered, rousing myself, for I had been drifting into sleep myself.

"I've been thinking back over our quest. I remembered something the Forest Lord said."

"He said we would know what to do. He was wrong. We *don't* know what to do."

"He said we would know what to do if we paid attention, Ari. If I paid attention. But I have not been paying attention, at least not enough or in the right places. I have had clues, but I have ignored them."

"What clues, Rondol?" I was feeling a little stir of excitement. If the wizard indeed knew something that might change our situation, I wanted to hear it.

"Remember he said he had no power over anything?"

"Yes, but I took that for a bit of modesty. He obviously had power over the spiders and everything else in the forest, I would assume."

"But he said it was a power of partnership. He was in partnership with the forest, and it shared its power with him."

"So? I fail to see the point."

"The point is that I was wrong to seek power over the dragon. I tried to enslave it. That is not the way."

"Oh, I don't know. Enslaving a dragon seems like a pretty sane way to start any relationship with it."

"But it isn't, Ari. Don't you see? To do what we must do, we have to work as partners, the dragon and I. The pattern we want to create, the pattern of the Ride, it can't begin with enslavement. That is the way of the Unbodied One, not the spirits of Light."

I stared at him. I think my mouth even dropped open a bit. "You want a partnership with the dragon? Rondol, that's not possible. The only partnership Fimfilomongous wants with you is that of a diner with his meal."

"Then I must change his mind. And I know how to do it."

"You do? Is this some magic you have remembered?"

Rondol paused, then stood up. "Yes, as a matter of fact, it is. But not the kind you're thinking of. Its Fro's magic of the heart. It's what the

Ride is all about. It's about the magic of the Gift."

I stood up as well, feeling more than a little alarm. "Just what are you going to do, Wizard?"

He smiled at me. "First I'm going to insure that our companions sleep more deeply. And you as well, Ari."

I held up my hand in protest. "Oh no, you're not spelling me to sleep. I won't allow it."

He held back his hand. "I know now what I'm doing." He made a pass over the sleeping forms of the others, and I could hear their breathing deepen.

"They won't like you doing that," I said.

"Perhaps. But I don't want them interfering and possibly being hurt. That goes for you, too, Ari."

I took a deep breath. "Rondol, I *will* take part in what happens. You owe me that, Wizard. After all, you made me your questmaster."

He paused. "Very well. But whatever I say or do, do not interfere or question it. Our lives and the success of our mission depend on it."

The two of us made our way back to the entrance to the dragon's chamber and opened the door. Immediately, the dragon's great voice rang out. "Ah, so you've decided to take the quick and easy way out. How sane of you. How delicious for me! You always taste better fresh." And the beast laughed again.

With no hesitation, Rondol stepped out into the room.

"I am Rondol the Off-White," he proclaimed boldly, "junior assistant wizard to Sandovon the White."

"I know who you are, Wizard," the dragon said. "Your associations will not spare you. I have no fear of the Whites...and certainly not an Off-White."

"I am not asking to be spared. I come to offer myself to you as a gift."

"That is nice of you, but to what end? You can't be a gift if I already have you, and I do have you now, little Wizard." The dragon's tail flicked out and came within a foot or so of where we were standing as if to emphasize its point.

"You have my body at your mercy, 'tis true," Rondol said. "But not my spirit. Yet, in the power of my spirit, I choose to be a gift for you. You are a magical being. You know what power lies in a willing gift rather than a frightened victim."

The dragon thought for a moment. "Yes," it said, "this is true. You would be much more tasty this way. All right, I accept you as a gift."

"But if you are willing, I ask a boon."

"Ah, I thought so. Here it comes. You want to offer yourself to me if I spare your companions' lives. How very noble. But the answer is no. Even with the Halfling, the five of you are hardly enough to fill my empty spaces. Besides," it said, scratching its ear idly with a claw, "if I give you a boon, it becomes a transaction, not a gift."

"That is correct, Sir Dragon. I was not going to suggest any such transaction. I merely wanted to show you something before you ate me. It is a most curious and powerful magical artifact that the Forest Lord gave me. I thought you might be interested."

"A magical artifact? Well, that would be interesting, as you say. But I could just look at it after I eat you."

"You could, but it would do you no good. I must be alive and present for it to work. Again, I say, this is no bargain I am striking. It is, instead, a part of the gift I offer, giving you not just my body but a rare experience. I guarantee on my honor that it will not harm you."

The dragon laughed. "I would not be concerned about that. I am invulnerable, you know, even to magic."

"Then you have no reason not to enjoy the wonder of this artifact before taking me for your dinner."

"Hmmn, I must tell you I suspect something here, Wizard. You are being far too accommodating and reasonable, traits I rarely find in humans whom I'm about to eat, much less wizards. But why not? You have all given me the most amusement I've had in a long time. A little more would be pleasant. Show me this artifact and what it does."

Rondol reached into his robe and brought out the *talimir*. The dragon raised an eyeridge. "It's but a *talimir*, Wizard. I have others like it amongst my treasures here. It is hardly a 'curious artifact' as you called it."

"You have none like this one, Fimfilomongous, I assure you." With that, Rondol thrust it forward, and the sphere began to glow, and glow, and glow.....

****

I blinked my eyes, bringing myself back into the reality of the dragon's cavern. The experience had been just as real, just as wondrous as before.

If anything, it had been more so, as if the presence of the dragon's magic had made the *talimir* even more powerful. I could still feel the joy of the red-garbed spirit all around me.

Then I remembered where I was, and the joy drained away as I recognized the bulk of the dragon sitting before me.

Fimfilomongous had its great eyes closed. It just sat there motionless, and then it let out a huge sigh. It opened its eyes and looked down at us.

"That was a powerful experience indeed, Wizard. I have not felt such a presence since I was newly hatched. In those days, long before the elves and dwarves appeared in the world, much less the humans, the earth spirit walked freely upon the land. We would dance and fly with him. Our power was his gift to us. We served his life and rejoiced to do so. It was a time of meaning and purpose, a time of joy."

He sighed and a wisp of smoke came from his nostrils. "There came a time when the spirit withdrew and the land darkened. I fear we darkened with it. Since then, too much time has passed. I had forgotten. I am old. I had even forgotten how old I am. I'm not sure I appreciate you reminding me of happier days."

"Dragon, those days could come again. We can make it happen. I was wrong to come here with the ring to try to enslave you to my will. That is not the way the power works. It's not the way of the earth spirit. It is not the way of the Gift. I should have come to you seeking partnership, as I do now. You have seen the Ride and what it brings to a world. The gods have asked me to create this here. Will you join me in doing so? We can become Lightbearers to our world."

Fimfilomongous was quiet for a long time. Then he said, "I sit here on this treasure and wait for humans to come and take it from me. They give me entertainment and food, but only for a short while—and not much food at that! Not much entertainment either. Your kind dies so easily! But fewer and fewer come. The Forest Lord guards my lair, he says so I may be undisturbed, but I think it is really to protect men from coming here." The dragon sighed again. "My life has lost its lustre. I lie here and wait for things to kill and eat; I've become no better than a common animal. You offer me purpose, a way to serve the spirit of the land again, to remake our world and keep the Unbodied One away. You want this old dragon to become a Lightbearer, you say? All my kind were Lightbearers once. It would be a noble thing indeed to be so again. This is your true gift to me, and you knew it, didn't you? You are wise, young wizard. You deserve to be an all White."

The dragon rose and brought his face close to Rondol, who didn't flinch. "All right, I accept. I shall create the Ride with you."

I didn't realize I'd been holding my breath until I let it out upon hearing the dragon's words. Rondol had done it! We'd done it!

"Thank you, noble Fimfilomongous," the wizard said.

"And about us..." I ventured.

The dragon cast an amused glance my way. "As I said, even with the Halfling, you would hardly make a dent on my empty places. Besides, I can hardly eat my new partners, can I?"

Then he put back his head and laughed like the red-garbed spirit in the *talimir*. "Ho Ho Ho! Merry Christmas!"

Rondol turned to me, a smile transforming his face. "Yes, *that's* it! That's what the spirit keeps saying. 'Merry Christmas.' "

"What does it mean?"

He shrugged. "Haven't the faintest idea. Some kind of magical invocation, I'd guess." He started towards the secret passage. "Well, come on. Let's wake the others and let them know they won't be dinner. Besides, we have a lot to do to get ready for the Ride tomorrow night. Why, I've got sacks of little toys and goodies for the children somewhere here in my robe. We've got to get organized!"

And that's what we did. In the end, we all five rode the dragon's back, spreading magic and leaving little toys and candies for the children. The dragon even gave away some gold from his hoard. All the time we were yelling the strange invocation of the red-garbed spirit while the dragon laughed "Ho Ho Ho," throughout the night. It even wore a huge white and red hat on its head so that it wouldn't seem so frightening. After all, who can be scared of a dragon wearing a hat?

As Rondol had intended, we created the Ride of wonder, traveling here and there and back again.

In the years that followed, sometimes it was just one of us, sometimes more than one, who rode Fimfilomongous on the Ride. Fro, who developed a close friendship with the dragon, particularly took to the role, wearing a red and white hat himself and Ho-Ho-ing as enthusiastically as the old wyrm. As the pattern grew and deepened in the world, in time the spirits were able to join us and carry on when we became too old to fly. The wonder of the gift-giving dragon spread throughout the land,

and hearts were indeed opened and joy returned, even to the north. The Unbodied One was banished forever.

Through it all, none ever knew who we were that rode the dragon on Year's Turn Night. That was our secret, part of the mystery. But we knew. We had become Lightbearers.

We had become the Fellowship of the Ride.

THE END OF THE TALE

FRANKLIN'S
KEY

DAVID SPANGLER

CHAPTER ONE

"You're really going to have to take care of this." The woman's voice was sharp and insistent over the telephone.

"But why me, Mother? You know how I feel about going into the city. Besides, I really don't have the time." Jennifer could hear her voice moving towards a whine, and took a breath. She hated whiners and knew it would score no points with her mother, either. On the other hand, she simply did not want to do what her mother was asking. "I've got my book to edit before the end of the month, and preparations to make for my bit in the Renaissance Faire, and…"

"It will only take you a couple hours," the woman's voice smoothly interrupted.

"There's the preparation. You said I'll need to journey."

"Yes. I only have a part of the picture. You need to get the rest from your own sources as you know. You're the Priestess…"

"Mother! I'm not a priestess."

The older woman sighed, her voice indicating this was an old and fruitless argument. "All right, shamanness, sensitive, intuitive, whatever you want to call yourself. The name doesn't change the reality. The fact is it's your responsibility, one you have not been living up to lately."

Jennifer sighed. She knew there was no arguing with her mother when she felt the spirits were pushing her. And her mother did have a point. She was part of a lineage. However much she might wish otherwise, the mantle of leadership for that lineage had passed to her two years ago when she turned 27.

"All right, mother. You've made your point. I'll go. But who do I contact?"

Her mother snorted. "Really, dear, don't be dense. You'll have to see Smoke, of course."

Of course. There was no one else. And that, she admitted to herself, was the real reason for her reluctance to get involved. She had no desire to see Smoke again. *Where there's Smoke*, she thought wryly, *there's bound to be Fire*. I don't want to get burned again…or raise my mother's hopes. She wants grandchildren.

"Don't think I don't understand, Jennifer. First loves are always the most painful, especially when they end unneccessar…"

"Mother," Jennifer interrupted. "Leave it. I said I'd do it. OK?"

Having won her case and made a point, Jennifer's mother turned gracious. "Of course, Dear. You'll go in the morning? As I said in the letter, there's no time to waste."

"Yes, I'll go in the morning. Does Smoke know I'm coming? Does he know anything about this?"

"No. You'll need to call him.... well, no, I'll call him and let him know. After all, I received the original warning."

"Thank you, Mother," she said, adding mentally, *for small favors.*

"Call me and I'll let you know what we arrange."

"I will. And Mother, don't think I don't know what you're thinking, so don't get your hopes up. Another word for 'past' is 'finished.'"

"Why, Jennifer. I don't know what you mean. I know there's nothing now between you and Smoke. I wouldn't have you go to him on this matter if I thought otherwise. This is strictly business. If I thought anyone else could handle it besides the two of you, I wouldn't be so insistent."

Yeah, right, Jennifer thought. But out loud she said, "Thanks for the confidence, Mom. I'd better hang up now. Like I said, I have things to do to prepare. I'll talk to you in the morning before I leave."

"Fine. And have a good journey tonight. Say hello to Peekaru for me."

The receiver clicked in her ear as her mother hung up. "Damn," Jennifer muttered as she put her own phone back in its cradle. "Mother's acting like some oracle." *But then,* she thought, *that's the point, isn't it? She is the Oracle, the Sybil for the Lineage.*

She looked down at the letter she held in her hand. Walking over to the sofa that nestled in a bay window overlooking her front lawn, she smoothed the paper out where it had become crumpled. Her mother's handwriting was clear and strong, belying the ambiguity of the words themselves. Just like Mom. Clear and direct, always knowing what she wants. She should have been the Priestess, not me. But then, divination and tapping the usually vague patterns of unfolding events was a different skill and one her mother had in spades.

She reread the letter.

Jennifer,
I received this from the spirits yesterday morning.

Blackness upon the city
Blackness upon the land;
Danger.
Portals long closed
Opening to fire without flame.
Cold sun burns.
Many turn to ice.
Death to many, death in life;
Lost key dagger and scepter.
Lost in labyrinth of stone, not wood,
Hard soil, not earth.
Find or all is lost.

This is URGENT, Jennifer. You must go to the city immediately to investigate. Spirits very insistent. I have seen the cold sun burning in the city, turning all to ice. You must make a journey to see for yourself. Remember, you are the one now, my dear.
Call me.
M.

She lay the letter down on an end table next to the sofa. Resting her chin on the back of the sofa, she looked out the window. She couldn't see the city from here, off to the south and west, though on a dark night, she could see the glow in the sky from its lights. Beyond her lawn were trees, part of a state forest, so that she seemed to be in a little island of her own surrounded by woods. It gave her a sense of serenity and safety. Off to one side on her lawn was a large boulder. It had always been there, dropped by some glacier thousands of years earlier.

She knew that if she let herself go, a gift of Sight would open and she would see the boulder not just as a large stone but also as the physical nesting place of a being. This entity was the guardian of this house and land and had been since the house had first been built by one of her ancestors over a hundred years earlier. Fifteen feet in height, it looked like an ancient Native American warrior carved from granite, or at least it had the last time she had Looked. Spirit entities of its nature could change their shape.

She also knew if she Looked at the woods, she would see myriads of beings, some little more than flitting points of light but others as tall as the trees themselves, thin creatures seemingly made of wood and leaf, moving about, performing their tasks. But she did not wish to See in that way. It was distracting, dividing her consciousness between this world and others. She had worked hard over the years to be focused on one world at a time.

She decided a cup of tea would taste good right at this moment. Getting up, she walked across the living room and into the kitchen. As she put a kettle of water on the stove to heat, her eyes noted the time on the old-fashioned cuckoo clock on the wall. *Eight pm*, she thought. *If I'm going to do a journey, I had better do it soon. I still have the rest of that chapter to edit before I get to bed.*

She stepped outside her back door and walked a few steps into her herb garden. She hadn't just been making excuses to her mother. She really was busy right now. As often happened, her editor had been slow editing the latest manuscript in her popular children's series, *Canterberry's Tales*, but having finally sent her revisions and suggestions on to Jennifer, she now wanted the final version yesterday. And she was writing the play that she and her friends would perform as part of this year's Renaissance Faire in only three weeks.

She bent down and cut off a few sprigs of chamomile and mint, her nose tickling in pleasure at the aroma that rose up from the herbs. None of that, she knew, would mean anything to her mother once she put her Oracle's hat on. To her mother, the Lineage was everything. To Jennifer, it was an imposition she hadn't asked for.

She took the herbs back into the kitchen and stuffed them into a teapot she had made herself. It didn't look like much. Her skills lay with words rather than with potting, but she had woven some charm and energy into it so that it never failed to produce a spot-on cup of tea. The kettle was on the verge of whistling at her, but she decided the water was hot enough and poured it into the teapot over the leaves. Even without the whistle, there was a satisfying cloud of steam that rose up from the pot, carrying with it the strong smell of fresh mint. She put the lid on the teapot.

She carried the pot, a jar of honey, a spoon, and a mug she had also made herself back to the sofa in the bay window. The mug was in the shape of a woman's face peering out from a tangle of leaves, a Green Woman she had seen once years before while on a walk in the woods outside. The woman had had a long braid of dark brown hair. On the mug, Jennifer had looped this braid up and back and around to form the handle.

The letter lay on the table where she had put it, reminding her of unwanted responsibilities. She poured herself her tea and sat back. Even though it was eight o'clock in the evening, it was still quite light out. In the summer, the sun took a long time to set, though the days were beginning to get shorter. She could see a pair of deer venturing out from the forest.

She loved living in this place. It was like being out in the wilderness, even though twenty years ago the place had been incorporated into the plumbing and wiring grid of the local town. A three minute drive down the dirt road at the back of her property led her to pavement and the appearance of other houses, including a couple of farms. Five minutes away was a major highway that led through the suburbs and into the city. On a good day, she could be downtown in twenty-five or thirty minutes. But over the years, as traffic had built up, that number had gone up and up until at rush hour, which seemed to last most of the day now anyway, it was more like sixty minutes.

It was more than traffic that made her excursions into the city rare, though. She felt oppressed by the place, cut off from her natural affinity for the land, and surrounded by the energies of millions of people. It made her feel as if she had stepped into a vast, unknown ocean whose undercurrents could pull her under and drown her.

Now, because her mother was having visions, she had to venture into that ocean again in the morning.

Finishing her tea, she knew she couldn't put off the journey. She might not have wanted it, but her mother was right. She *was* the Priestess of the Lineage. *Damn you for dying when you did, Aunt Iris,* she thought, taking her tea things back to the kitchen.

The house had four bedrooms. One of them was hers, one was a guest room, the third she had made into her office and workspace. The fourth, though, she had turned into her ritual space.

There was another room that had been dedicated as a temple space when the house was first built. It was in the back and was partly sunken into the ground so one stepped down into it. It had no windows but a skylight opened to the heavens above. It had been used for that purpose by her mother in her work as the Oracle and by a great-grandmother who had also been the Priestess. Her mother's sister Iris had not been Priestess when she had grown up in this house. That dubious honor, to Jennifer's mind anyway, had not fallen on Iris until she had married and moved away.

Jennifer kept that room closed and locked, though as a nod to its history, she kept the key on her keychain as a kind of talisman. When she went into it, the power there felt too deep and demanding. She felt like the room opened into an abyss, and if she stepped into it, she would fall straight through the earth and out into the stars on the other side, becoming lost forever.

Yet, she could not avoid journeying altogether, the process by which she projected her spirit out to walk between the physical and non-physical worlds. She knew from experience that when the Call was on her, she could not resist. But she could go in her own way, from her own room. The power might be less, but it was all her own. She felt more in charge.

She could hear her mother's voice now in her head. "Being Priestess means not being in charge. It means surrendering to a higher power." Well, that might have been all right in the past, but if those higher powers wanted Jennifer Lynn Grant to be their Priestess, they were going to have to let her do it her way.

She opened the door to her ritual room and, leaving her shoes outside in the hall, stepped in. Unlike the older temple space, this room had windows on two walls, with heavy drapes she could close if she needed darkness. But Jennifer hated darkness. She always had, which was another reason she did not like the other room. Nor did she need it. If she had to, and sometimes she preferred to, she could journey quite successfully outdoors in the middle of the day with a bright noon sun overhead.

The room was bare except for a long, low couch with a pillow on it. A blanket with images of suns and moons lay folded at one end of the couch. Near the couch was a low table that held a bowl of water and a bowl of earth, two candles, an incense holder, and a small clock radio that was also a CD player. The last object was a small narrow vase with a fresh flower in it cut from her garden. The one ritual she followed faithfully was to select and cut a new flower each morning and put it in this vase, singing a little childhood rhyme her grandmother had taught her to start the day. She whispered it now as she entered. "Daystar Bright, Womb of Light, Guide my steps from Morn to Night. Stars Beyond both Night and Day, Guide my steps along the Way."

Perhaps because her grandmother, who had had no special powers whatsoever except an overwhelming presence of love (which was, she thought, the First Power, after all), had taught this rhyme to her, it had always brought her peace and comfort.

The curtains were pulled back as usual, letting the waning light of dusk come in like a sleepy old friend. She knelt by the table, lighting the two candles, murmuring in invocation as she did so, "Light from the One, Light from the Self, Light from the Allies, Light from the World." Then she put a fresh cone of sandalwood incense into the incense holder and lit it.

She set the alarm on her clock radio for forty-five minutes. After that period of time, a special CD would begin to play with drums sounding a recall code to bring her back from wherever she was journeying. Normally, a journey lasted from twenty to thirty minutes. As in a dream that seems to last for hours but is only two or three minutes long, time flowed differently on the inner realms anyway. Quite a lot could be accomplished in half an hour. She rarely had any difficulty coming back on her own. The tape was only a backup just in case. She believed in redundancy.

These things done, she lay down on the couch and pulled the blanket up over her. The evening was warm, but she knew from experience that journeying always chilled her.

She could feel the power building within her as she settled her mind and body and let herself relax. Even though she resisted doing it, journeying came easily to her. It was one reason she had been named Priestess in the first place. *Maybe a little too easily*, she thought. *That's been my problem.* But then the energy began to spiral within her, drawing her up and out. She closed her eyes, and she was gone.

CHAPTER TWO

Smoke was running. In the dim light, he couldn't see what was chasing him. He didn't know if it were man or beast or just a nameless fear. What he did know was that he couldn't let it catch him.

He was running down an alleyway, like a canyon between tall, dirty walls of stone and brick. He had glimpses of graffiti sprayed on the walls, but he couldn't make out the words or the signs. He had no idea where he was in the city, which was unusual. There was no place in the city where Smoke had not gone.

But this, he realized, was not the earthly city where he spent his waking hours. This was its counterpart, the spirit city that both mirrored and shaped the metropolis from which it emerged. It was different, though. It looked different, not the way he usually saw it in a dream or explored it on a spirit-walk. And it felt different, empty and desolate as if it had been stripped of life. Even his footfalls made no sound on the uneven pavement beneath his running feet.

Ahead was a wall. He knew the alley continued beyond it. Without hesitation, he leapt, his lithe body rising upward in a way he knew would not be possible in the physical world. He cleared the wall in a bound that would have broken every record for a high jump and landed running on the other side. He knew whatever was chasing him would have no problem with that wall either.

The alley ended. He emerged into a large empty square. All around it on three sides dark windows stared down from skyscrapers, like eyes that had been blinded lest they see what should not be seen. He recognized the skyscrapers from the physical city, but they were situated differently. There was no square like this in the Bodyworld.

He realized that he wasn't being chased anymore. As that realization hit him, lights came on in a building across the square from him. Unlike the skyscrapers, it was low, only two stories high, and was made of brick and wood. It looked old and slightly dilapidated. The light emanating from it was cold and piercing, a blue-whiteness that had none of the comfort or warmth that one usually associated with light. Yet, it was strangely alluring at the same time.

Smoke took a step forward into the square. As he did so, he thought, *I wasn't being chased. I was being herded here.*

There were no sounds, no people, no movement. Just blind windows, emptiness, and a building bursting with a sinister blue-white light. Something in him was drawn to that light. Something in him knew there was power there and lusted for that power. He began to walk across the square, moth to its flame. Wide doors at the base of the building opened to welcome him, and he could see within them the source of the light. It was like a miniature sun hovering and burning in the interior of the building, a sun that blazed with electric light but gave no heat. He squinted and raised his hand in front of his eyes.

Suddenly he saw movement to one side. Turning, he saw a figure with jagged, spiky limbs running towards him, the features on its strangely bulbous head showing alarm. *It's Zap*, he thought.

As the figure came closer, a tongue of lightning licked out from the open doors of the building and struck it. With a high-pitched wail, the figure fell to its knees. It seemed to stretch sideways, its head and limbs being impossibly pulled like toffee towards the blowing building.

Smoke's right hand came up without his thinking. Streamers of light shot from his fingers like webbing, surrounding the struggling figure and pulling it towards himself. The lightning from the building abruptly disappeared.

The webbing dissolved as Smoke lowered his hand. The figure, looking like a stick-man whose body and limbs had been drawn as jagged, zigzagging lines, got to its feet and ran towards him. It was shouting, its voice harsh with static like a badly tuned radio station. But Smoke was used to it and could just make out the words. "Retrieve the key," Zap was saying. "Retrieve the key."

Lightning flashed out from the building again and Zap was hurled across the square. Before Smoke could react this time, though, he saw a darkness descending on him from the sky. Looking up, he saw it was a giant, black hand. Before he could move, it had seized him and was drawing him up, shaking him at the same time. Shaking him...shaking him...

Shaking him.

Smoke opened his eyes. A face the color of rich dark chocolate or of dark, fertile earth was looking down at him, the black brows over the equally black eyes drawn forward in concern.

"MoBro?" Smoke stammered, trying to orient himself. Glancing around, he saw that he was in his flat, lying on his couch.

The big man stepped back. He was massive, six-seven in height, his body muscular and trim. He was dressed in a black T and black slacks. His shoes were black as well.

Smoke raised his hand up to him. "Help me up, MoBro. I've just had one unrighteous hell of a dream!" His hand was enveloped in MoBro's and he was pulled up gently. Smoke knew that if his friend had truly pulled hard, he would have gone flying across the room.

Smoke stumbled into the small bathroom and turned on the faucet. He plunged his hands under the cold water and splashed water on his face. He rubbed his wet hands though his hair. In the mirror, he saw an angular face looking back at him framed in shoulder-length sandy hair in which streaks of white were already appearing. His father's had gone completely white when he was in his early thirties, and it was looking like Smoke's hair was going in that same direction. The first white streaks had appeared when he was in high school. One of his friends at the time had said, "Hey, it looks like there's smoke in your hair," and his nickname—the only name he used now—was born.

Toweling off his face, he returned to his living room. Which was also his kitchen, his bedroom, his workspace and, when needed, his magical temple. MoBro, from past experience when Smoke came back from one of his dreams or journeys, was making coffee in the espresso machine, one of four modern appliances in his friend's living space. The others were his computer, a fully up-to-date sound system and a synthesizer-keyboard.

"Man, that's going to taste good!" he said, falling back down onto the sofa. "You're an angel, Bro MoBro!"

The big man turned and smiled. He signed with his hands, one eyebrow arching up.

"Yes, it was a bad one. Thanks for bringing me out of it. Worst I've had for quite awhile."

MoBro spread his hands open with a questioning look.

"Let me put some of your brew in me, and I'll tell you about it."

MoBro smiled and nodded. Smoke knew he could speak as well as anyone, but he rarely did. He was a devotee of silence and preferred signing to using his voice. The only consistent exception was in their band when occasionally he would sing. His voice was amazing, covering three octaves from bass to tenor. Perhaps its power came because he saved it for special moments. Smoke had never heard him singing for practice.

MoBro handed him a small glass of espresso, the liquid black and rich. He could feel just the aroma bringing wandering brain cells back to the here and now. He took a sip, inwardly wincing at the bitterness. Normally, a cup of coffee to him was half-coffee and half-soy milk, buttressed with three teaspoons of sugar. He loved it sweet and creamy. But coming down from a trip, he needed the shock of coffee unalloyed with anything else to get fully back in his body.

He nodded. "This is the right stuff, my friend! Thanks."

MoBro sank his frame carefully into a large, overstuffed chair that Smoke had purchased from a second-hand store just for when MoBro came to visit, which was pretty much every day. He waved the compliment aside, content to sit until Smoke was ready to tell him what had happened. Like many big men, MoBro was patient and gentle. Not surprising, Smoke knew. The black man was deeply connected with the elementals of the earth and even had a mountain spirit as one of his totem allies.

A cell phone rang. Smoke's hand automatically went to his pocket, but nothing was there. The phone rang again. Setting his espresso glass down, he thrust his hands in between the sofa cushions, rummaged around, and brought out the phone. He put it up to his ear and said, "Smoke."

"Smoke, this is Elizabeth." Even without the name, he immediately recognized the voice of Jennifer's mother, though it had been over a year since he had last had any contact with her.

"Elizabeth, what a surprise! How are you? How's Jennifer?" He glanced over to his right, where on a bookshelf two pictures were framed. One was the original art for the cover of the first CD his band, Liquid Stone, had produced. The second was a picture of Jennifer and himself, both smiling.

"I'm fine. You can ask Jennifer yourself when you see her tomorrow."

"I'm seeing Jennifer tomorrow? Is she coming in to my gig?" He felt a glow of pleasure. It had been over a year since he had seen her, too.

"No, on Lineage business. She's coming as Priestess."

"As Priestess?" Smoke was momentarily stunned. "How did that happen? I thought she wanted out of all that. That's one reason we broke up...." His mind whirled with memories.

"I know." There was a note of sadness in the woman's voice. "But though she kicks the traces, she still accepts the Call when it comes."

"Well that must be some business to bring her here! She hates the city. It blows her circuits. That's the other reason we broke up."

"I received something as Oracle. Let me read it to you." Smoke listened as Elizabeth read the prophecy she had received. When she came to the part about the "cold sun," he started. He remembered the image of the harsh, cold light emanating from the old building in the square. Elizabeth stopped. "I felt something from you just then, Smoke. You know something about this already, don't you?"

Smoke shook his head. "No, not really. It's just a dream I had."

"A dream? When? What was it? You must tell me!" Her voice took on some of the power he knew she carried within her. Elizabeth Grant, he remembered now, was a formidable woman when she wanted to be.

"Just now. This afternoon." He looked over at MoBro who continued to sit patiently, gazing at him. He related the dream in detail to both of his listeners. When he was finished, MoBro made the sign for trouble, and frowned. Elizabeth was not so silent.

"Something is going on, just as I saw and was told. Some kind of portal is opening in the city and something nasty is on the other side! You need to find it, Smoke, and do something about it. You and Jennifer."

"Well, it may not be so simple."

"Use your powers. I know you're not part of our lineage, but you're a priest just the same. I've seen you on the inner, Smoke. I know what you're capable of being and doing. And Jennifer, if she ever accepts it, is our most potent Priestess in centuries. Together you're very powerful!"

"I always thought so. But she had different ideas, I guess."

"She'll learn. Even if you're not fated to be a couple, you can still work together, and in this case, I think you must."

"So when is Jennifer coming tomorrow? I'm meeting my band to rehearse in the afternoon."

"Morning, say eight o'clock?"

"Make it nine, and it's a deal."

"There's some urgency to this, Smoke. Sooner started, sooner solved."

"I have things to do tonight. I may not get home till wee hours. Some sleep will make me better company tomorrow."

"All right. Nine it is. I'll let Jennifer know."

With all the abruptness that he remembered, Elizabeth Grant hung up. Smoke closed his cell phone and slipped it back into his pocket. "You've heard me talk about Jennifer," he said to MoBro, whose eyes were shining with interest. "She used to be my girlfriend." Smoke waved a hand towards the picture. MoBro nodded, signing understanding. "That was her mother, Elizabeth. Haven't talked with her in over a year since Jaylyn and I broke up." More memories surfaced for him suddenly, some sweet, some bitter.

MoBro raised an eyebrow. "Oh, that's my nickname for her," Smoke replied. "Her full name is Jennifer Lynn. Anyway, her mother's something of a prophetess. She gets messages about the future from a being she calls the Quatrain." He repeated what Elizabeth had told him to MoBro.

"Bad vibes around this," MoBro rumbled from the depths of his chair, closing his eyes.

Smoke looked at him in surprise. "They must be positively catastrophic to get you to speak," he said. "What are you feeling?"

The big man shrugged. "Just what I said. Is Jennifer the Priestess you mentioned?"

Smoke, still digesting the fact that his friend had actually said something, nodded. "Yeah. She and her mother are part of this very old group that calls itself the Lineage. They're a bit like Wiccans, but they've a tradition of their own, with their own way of doing things. Their ancestors were probably farmers who built up relationships with the guardian spirits of the land." He paused, remembering all that Jennifer had told him once and the things he had discerned on his own. Though he had not been part of the Lineage himself, Jennifer's mother and aunt, at that time the leaders of the group, had always made him feel he had been one of them. Sudden emotion rose up in him. *I miss those times,* he thought. *Maybe I'm not as much of a loner as I think I am.*

MoBro was watching him. Smoke cleared his throat and added, "They follow a being they call the Quatrain. I've felt its presence once or twice, very powerful. One woman is always the Priestess, the leader of the group. When she dies, the position is passed down to someone younger, not necessarily to a daughter, though the title does seem to run in certain families. Jennifer's aunt was the Priestess until a couple of years ago when she died, then the position passed to Jennifer. I think the Quatrain makes the choice." He frowned. "She didn't really want it. I think it scared her."

<Heavy responsibility>, MoBro signed, silent once more.

"Yeah it is. I don't fully understand it. But I think the Priestess is the focus for a power of guardianship over the land, similar to what I feel for the city."

<How did you meet?>

Smoke smiled, remembering. "I was having strange dreams in

which I'd find myself out of my body flying around the city or wandering underneath it in the sewers. They weren't frightening, but they were troubling. I always felt something was observing me, but I never could see what or who it might be. I was always alone. Then one night this man appeared in my dream. I was walking the empty streets of the city, and he stepped out of a bookstore I know down near Pioneer Square. It was the first time anyone had shown up in my dreams, and I was startled. He stared at me for a moment, then said, "I'll be seeing you." Then he disappeared.

MoBro whistled.

"Yeah. It was spooky. I woke right up. It was like four in the morning, but I couldn't get back to sleep. When it got light, I went down to Pioneer Square and found the bookstore. When I went inside, they had a flier stuck to their announcement board." He paused dramatically. "It showed a picture of the same man."

MoBro whistled again. <Who was he?> he asked.

"A teacher from England who specialized in dreams and shamanic journeying. The flier said he was giving a lecture at the bookstore the following week. Of course, then I had no idea what a shamanic journey was, but I knew I had to go to that lecture. How could I not, right?"

He looked at his empty coffee cup. "Time for another, I think."

He started to get up, but MoBro waved him back down. <You tell your story, I'll make the coffee>, he signed.

"Thank you," Smoke said gratefully. "You make better coffee anyway." He closed his eyes a moment, letting the memories drift back up from where he had stored them away. "I went to the lecture and listened to what he had to say. It was fairly introductory stuff about shamans and their work, but it was new to me. When he was done, I went up to talk with him. He was talking with two women who turned out to be Jennifer and her mother Elizabeth. When I came up, he turned to me and said, "I told you I'd be seeing you!" You could have knocked me over with a feather. Then he turned to the women and said, 'This young man has been doing shamanic journeys around the city, but he hasn't realized it yet. I happened to meet him on one of his journeys.'"

MoBro came back with the coffee. <You never told me this story>, he said.

"No, I guess not. Not sure why..."

<Brings back sad memories.>

"I guess that's it. Anyway, we went out for a late dinner. The man said he'd arranged to come here from England just to find me, as he'd known about me for some time from his own inner contacts. That was mind-blowing, I tell you! Of course, I wanted to learn everything this man knew, but he said he couldn't be my teacher because he lived too far away. He told me Elizabeth could train me, and she lived only a few miles from the city. So I began going to Elizabeth's house to learn how to be…well…whatever I am. A shaman of the city, I suppose. That's how I got to know Jennifer."

<Amazing story. What happened between you?>

"Oddly, I already felt I knew her. I'd read one of her fantasy novels the year before we met. Then when we did meet…well, it was like we'd known each other forever. One thing led to another, and we fell in love. Or at least I thought we had. She would come in to the city and stay with me here from time to time, and I'd stay out at their farm. We were both learning how to work on the inner planes, though Jennifer had a lot more experience than I did. She'd been doing it most of her life. That's where she gets a lot of inspiration for her stories." He sighed and put down the coffee cup. "I thought we had something going, and I'm sure she did, too, even though we knew that my work was with the spirit of the city and she…well, she never did feel too comfortable here. But we were sure we could work it out."

He stood up and began to pace, the memories driving him. "Then her aunt died and she became the new Priestess. It was like she shifted into overdrive. Her energy changed dramatically, as if she'd plugged directly into a power station. It frightened her. She had a hard time assimilating it. And the city became a harder place for her to be, she had become so much more perceptive. That's when we began to break up. I had my work here, she had hers in the country, and we couldn't seem to blend them together."

He sighed, remembering the arguments they had had at the end. "I really think we could have done it. There's no reason city and country energies can't blend. The problem I felt was that Jennifer would never fully accept what she was, so she wasn't able to fully integrate the energy she was receiving. She tried to push it away as much as she could, and in the end, that meant pushing me away, too."

MoBro leaned forward, his eyes intense. <Thank you for the story. But what do we do now with what her mother told you?>

"Frankly, I'm not sure." Smoke lay back on the sofa. He hadn't lied to Elizabeth when he'd said he had things to do this night. Although the band was playing tomorrow, they had rehearsed hard earlier in the day. He always believed in giving everyone the night off before a gig. And it wasn't a major gig anyway, just three nights at a rock bar downtown. Not much money, but a chance to observe the party scene and catch some vibes. *Another way to feel into the pulse and life of the city.*

Feeling into that life was what Smoke had had in mind. At least once a week, he would just take off and walk around the city at night, letting intuition guide his direction. Sometimes MoBro came with him. The past few days, though, he hadn't had the chance because of rehearsals. And he'd been feeling restless, as if some part of him had known something was brewing. Tonight he had planned on doing one of his walkabouts to see what he could discern.

In some ways, the city was Smoke's life, just as the forest seemed to be Jennifer's. He was a self-appointed guardian of its well being, at least in a magical sense. From some of his experiences, he more than suspected that the Powers That Be had approved his appointment. Like his namesake, he could drift anywhere, whereas some of the more formal Guardians, human and otherwise, were bound to certain inner structures. He preferred his freedom.

He thought about the dream, aware that MoBro was just looking at him, waiting for him to decide what to do. As he went over it in detail, something kept niggling at him, some detail.

He had it. He sat up. "Brother, I don't know where I've seen it, but I know I've seen that building in this world. It's a real building in the city. What say we give our feet a chance to lead us to it?" Without waiting for an answer, he pulled his jacket off the back of a kitchen chair. He felt the big man rise from the chair and come behind him. A large hand clamped him on the shoulder. Turning, he saw his friend smiling. His other hand swept out towards the door. The meaning was obvious: <After you, brother!>

CHAPTER THREE

As Smoke and MoBro went out from Smoke's flat, Jennifer was riding the spiral of energy into the Threshold, her name for an interim somewhere between the physical world and the more subtle non-physical worlds of energy and spirit. This place was totally non-descript. It could look like whatever she wished. At the moment, it looked like an alpine meadow on the side of the mountain that overlooked the city.

She stood there for a moment, then sat on a large boulder conveniently curved and molded to her shape. "Let Light bring me what I need, take me where I need to go, show me what I need to know," she said.

On her chest, a shimmering gold medallion appeared. It was about the size of an old half-dollar, hanging from her neck by a chain seemingly woven from tiny green vines. In its center was the figure of a tree carved from what appeared to be an emerald, and in the center of that was a star shaped from four small diamonds. The sign of the Quatrain.

She was not sure just what the Quatrain was. Legend within the Lineage held that it was a mighty being, a presence akin to an archangel perhaps, but one former Priestess had written that it was a collection of four beings each of whom represented one of the four elements of Earth, Air, Fire, and Water and one of the four Directions. Each of these four beings embodied a verse of some primal Song that had created the universe, hence the name the Lineage had given them. Another had written that it was a place, not a being or beings at all. Apparently different people experienced it in different ways. What was common to all the stories was that when the Quatrain appeared, music came with it, a haunting beautiful music unlike anything ever heard on earth.

Not that I would know, she thought. *I've never heard or seen anything of the mysterious Quatrain. I couldn't say from personal experience that it or they or whatever it is exists. Of course,* she admitted to herself, *I haven't particularly gotten with the Priestess program either. No wonder the Quatrain hasn't shown up.*

The medallion had come to her in a dream, passed on to her by her Aunt Iris after her aunt had died, a passing on of the power and responsibility of being the Priestess of the Lineage. And however faithful or faithless she had been to fulfilling the traditions of being the Priestess, it had been there around her neck every time she walked between the worlds. Obviously, whatever her feelings or misgivings might be, to the Quatrain she was the Priestess.

A sound in the sky made her look up. High up she could see a dot moving towards her. As she watched, it grew larger until she could make out the shape and color of a large parrot with bright yellow, red and blue feathers. It was Peekaru, her animal totem,

Well, specifically, he was the animal ally of whoever wore the medallion. She had other animal spirits that were her personal allies, specifically a large shaggy buffalo she called Buff. This animal had wondered out of her woods one day on her twenty-first birthday and up onto her porch where she had been sitting and reading a book. She had been so startled she had been unable to move as the large beast lowered its head and looked her in the eye in a very intelligent and disconcerting way. Then it had spoken to her. "Call on me when you need an ally." At which point the animal had turned around and calmly walked down the steps off her porch. As soon as its rear hooves touched the ground, it had disappeared.

She had been grateful for such a powerful inner ally, but she had been disturbed that she had not been able to tell that it had been a spirit being. To her eyes it had seemed perfectly real and physical. It had even smelled! That inability to distinguish the reality of one world from the reality of another had shaken her. She had not liked the feeling of being out of control and not sure of what was going on. It was one reason she had become reluctant to use her inner Sight. She appreciated the capacity to See; she just didn't like the Sight breaking in on her unexpectedly. So now she kept a tight leash on her abilities.

The rush of air in her face and the touch of wings brought her wandering thoughts back to the moment. Gracefully, Peekaru landed on her shoulder. He nuzzled his head affectionately into her neck and shoulder, a loving greeting, then he nipped her on the ear.

"Hey," she yelped, her hand pushing the parrot's head away. "That hurt!"

"Sorry," said the bird, not sounding sorry at all. His voice was deep and cultivated, sounding just like the actor, James Earl Jones. As usual, Jennifer felt a moment of disorientation hearing such a rich, resonant voice coming from a parrot. But what a spirit being looked like did not always indicate what it really was, and they could sound like anything they wanted. "I was just checking to see if you were real or merely a figment of my imagination."

"All right, so I haven't been coming here lately. I apologize. You know how I feel about all this Priestess stuff."

Peekaru squawked in her ear. "Then you should pass the Medallion on to someone else, Priestess."

"Don't think I haven't thought about it, old Droopy-Feathers." She chucked the bird playfully under the chin, then reached around to scratch the back of his head. Peekaru leaned into her touch, obviously enjoying the scratching. "But I'd miss your charming personality."

"And I'd miss yours as well, irresponsible as it can be."

"Don't start on me, too, Polly. I get enough guilt from my mother. Which, by the way is why I'm here. Something, probably the Quatrain, contacted her as the Oracle and delivered a warning. Apparently something big and dangerous is up in the city."

Looking up, Peekaru said, "In the city. Not our usual territory, is it?" The parrot squawked in annoyance and ruffled its feathers. "My colors turn dull when I go into the city. Psychic soot, you know. Still, some of us do what we must to serve the cause, whatever the sacrifice..." He squawked again.

Jennifer rolled her eyes. *I deserve it, I suppose, but this damned bird is enjoying it far too much.*

"I suppose you're here to find out what's going on, eh?" The parrot tilted its head and looked at her with one eye.

"Right the first time, Peekaru."

"Then you're going to take care of it, right?"

"That's right. What, you don't think I can?"

"Depends on what it is. But then, you're a mighty priestess, well versed in the ways of the inner..." He began nibbling at a feather in his right wing.

"OK, stuff a cracker in it, Polly. I'll come here more often. And I'm not handling it on my own. I'll have you and Buff and maybe Smoke..."

"Smoke? That nice young man with the brilliant aura that used to hang around you?"

"Peekaru," she said, "have you been talking to my mother lately?"

The bird looked at her, and she could swear he was grinning. "Oh no, not me. I keep away from Oracles!" He spread his wings and flew down from her shoulder. "Well, I guess we should get going."

"Fine. Let's do that." Jennifer made no attempt to keep the annoyance from her voice. Did nobody in either reality have anything to do these days but comment on her personal life? "Besides," she sniffed, "his aura wasn't all that brilliant."

As she watched, Peekaru swelled in size until he looked like one of the fabled Rocs that had carried Sinbad or one of the great eagles on whose back Gandalf had flown in *Lord of the Rings*. Climbing up on the boulder, she jumped lightly onto the parrot's broad back, wrapping her legs around its neck.

"Let's go, Ton-to!" she yelled.

The parrot swiveled its head, one very large eye looking back at her. "I have two requests first."

"Oh?"

"First, could you imagine some other meeting place besides this place in the mountains? A jungle would be nice. I am a parrot, you know. And second..." A huge talon raised up and hovered in front of her. "Stop calling me Polly or Tonto or anything else. I'm Peekaru!"

Confronted with claws the size of her forearm, Jennifer nodded her head. "Whatever you say, faithful animal ally."

"Fine. That's fine!" The parrot spread its wings. "Hang on, Priestess! To Infinity...and Beyond!" he squawked as he launched into the air. Jennifer sighed. Aunt Iris had been a great lover of movies.

High up into the sky they went, disappearing into a bank of clouds. When they emerged, the scenery had subtly changed. The land they passed over was recognizable to Jennifer as the land where she lived, but now it glowed with a soft radiance. The further they flew, the more it changed. Traces of towns and roads all disappeared until they were flying over a forest unbroken except by rivers and two large lakes. On a narrow strip of land between one lake and the large body of water that eventually led into the ocean, the city arose. From this height, the city looked pristine, its towers of steel and glass and stone all shining. It was, she knew, the city in its ideal state.

As they approached and began to descend, the scene shifted again. The city still glowed with energy, but at its base where the streets were, a dark mist was rising. She recognized this as a representation of the miasma of thoughts and feelings generated by a million or more people living in the metropolis before her. It was, as Peekaru had suggested, psychic smog, largely made up of pain and fear, longings and tensions arising from the struggles of the individuals below. The city could be an unfriendly, unloving, and hard place, and here was the inner result of that plain for her inner sight to see. And this city, she knew, had much less of this unlovely energy than many others.

Rather than descending into it, though, Peekaru lighted on the top of the tallest building. He swiveled his head about. "Tell me what the

Oracle said." Jennifer recited the words in her mother's letter. She knew that the parrot was not really listening to the words but was attuning to the energy behind them, trying to discern a thread between that energy of warning and the cause to which it was referring. She realized with a start that she could do the same thing. She was the Priestess who supposedly had the power, but she was letting Peekaru do all the work.

Holding the words from the Oracle in her mind, she sought the thread that wove them together, and then the spool from which that thread had come. The central idea, she realized, lay in the phrase "lost key dagger and scepter." "Lost in labyrinth of stone, not wood, hard soil, not earth," probably meant the city itself with its pavement and buildings and twisty streets. But what were the lost key, dagger and scepter? Scepter implied rulership. A dagger suggested a warrior or even death. What about the key? The means to open the "Portals long closed"?

Where in the city would a key, a dagger, and a scepter be hidden?

She shook her head. She was missing something. She could feel it. But she couldn't see what it might be. *Think,* she told herself. *If I were writing this in a novel, what kind of puzzle or clue would this be? What would I be trying to tell the reader without coming out and actually saying it?*

Peekaru squawked. "Hang on," he said. He launched himself into the air and began to spiral down. He moved away from the downtown region south towards a part of the city that she recognized as an older, more rundown section of town. Smoke's one-room flat, she remembered, was somewhere on the border between the two parts of town, old and new, poor and rich. *I'll be here in the flesh tomorrow.* The thought was not comforting.

She had assumed that the psychic smog would be denser and darker here, but realized that was just her prejudices showing. Indeed, some of the darkest patches she saw lay over and around some of the richest looking buildings in town. Stress comes in all places to all manner of people, she reminded herself.

Peekaru began to circle around a particular area. Looking down through the grayness, she was happy to see two very bright flames of light moving down one of the streets. Then she recognized the pattern of one of them. *That's Smoke! Is he looking for what we're looking for?* Watching him, she realized that he wasn't walking the worlds as she was. He was moving about in his physical form. *Impressive,* she thought. *Peekaru was right about him. And I wonder who that is with him. I've never seen an aura quite like that one. Perhaps I'll find out tomorrow.*

She sent both of them a silent blessing, a swift arrow of light that shot from her heart into the auras of Smoke and his friend. Their own light flared up briefly.

Abruptly, Peekaru stopped circling and rose up sharply. "What is it?" exclaimed Jennifer. "That was Smoke down there!"

"I know," the voice of the parrot filled the space around her. "But I found another thread. What we seek is down there, but only partly down there. It is also someplace else."

"Where?"

"Wherever we end up!"

With a loud squawk, the parrot sought the cloud bank above them. Once again he entered it, but this time, he stayed in it, the clouds fading away to become pure Light.

How long they were in this Light, Jennifer didn't know. Time was meaningless. It could have been years or only a second later when they emerged, to find themselves in the middle of a thunderstorm. Rain cascaded around them, and a lightning bolt crashed into the ground nearby, the answering bolt shooting back up into the sky as electrical potentials equalized themselves.

Off in the distance she could see the presence of a city, but it looked different than anything she was used to. It was much smaller, more like a town, but she could see it was overlighted by an angelic being of the kind that normally only resided over cities. And it was no ordinary angel but one that carried an unusual pattern in its aura. She could feel its power radiating out even from where she was at this distance.

"Peekaru, do you see that being?"

"Yes. Impressive, isn't it? It's one of the national angels, the ones that work with your country as a whole. This must be an important city."

"But what city is it? And why is it so small?"

"I don't know. But it is a place where brother loves brother."

"Huh?"

"I just repeat what I'm told."

Once again lightning crashed around them. Looking up, Jennifer could make out the beings playing with all the energy being released, frolicking in the midst of the storm.

Peekaru flew lower. "There," he said. "Over there. That's the other end of the thread."

She looked in the direction that Peekaru was turning to face. On a hill, she saw a man standing in the rain, moving about, his hands upraised. *Who is he? What's he doing? Doesn't he know that men on hills can get struck by lightning?*

"Uh oh," squawked the parrot. "Trouble. Shields up, Scotty!"

Jennifer looked up and saw partly hidden in the swirls of energy and clouds a silvery being looking down at her. She had an immediate impression of cunning and hunger. Then the being gestured, and a ball of energy flew in their direction.

By instinct, she grabbed the medallion at her chest. Light blazed out from her, surrounding her and Peekaru. She gestured back, and from her outstretched hands, another ball of light flew straight to intercept the one coming towards them. They collided, with a flash of lightning and an immense sound of thunder. Out of the corner of one eye, she had a glimpse of the man on the hill falling down. *Good,* she thought. *Stay down.*

Her arms thrust out again, and another ball of light shot out, rising into the clouds where it struck the entity in the process of drawing energy to itself for another strike at them. There was a discharge that lit up the sky and a screech like fingernails on a blackboard or a needle being dragged across an old phonograph record. *Ha!* she exulted. *Got you! Guess who's the fastest on the draw here!*

"Good shooting for a now and again Priestess, Priestess!" Peekaru shouted. Jennifer was about to reply when she felt herself slipping. She grabbed hold of the parrot's neck and tightened the grip of her legs, even as a rhythmic pounding surrounded her. She felt Peekaru fading away. "No!" she cried. "Not now!" She suddenly recognized the pounding for what it was. Her alarm had triggered the CD player. She was hearing the drumming rhythm that signaled the time had come to return to her body. "Not yet!" she howled into the wind and rain. "I haven't learned what I have to learn!' But she could not fight it. Had she had more experience, she might have been able to ignore the recall, but as it was, she couldn't. It was drilled into her as a safety, almost a post-hypnotic command.

Peekaru totally disappeared and she felt herself rushing back as if through a dark tunnel, surrounded by a fireball of energy. This is going to hurt, she thought. I didn't shed the energy properly. Then her body jerked with the force of the energy slamming into it like the tail of the comet that was her own spirit. Her eyes snapped open, as she spasmed on the couch. She groaned, and for a moment passed out.

When she opened her eyes again, the drumming was still pounding next to her head, and the room was spinning around. Her heart was beating faster than the drumbeat. She reached out an arm and fumbled her fingers over the radio, finally hitting the off button. The drumming stopped.

Finally, several minutes later she raised her head and realized the room had stopped moving. She sat up, her body aching and protesting and generally feeling like she'd gone fifteen rounds in a boxing ring. "Uh," she said, stretching her back and arms and legs. No wonder she didn't want to be the Priestess.

She thought for a moment about drinking another cup of tea, but realized she only had energy to get from here to her bathroom and then to her bed. Anything else could wait till morning. Including calling her mother.

And it did.

CHAPTER FOUR

Smoke and MoBro stalked a prey they could sense but not identify. They walked down one street and up another, the night's shadows growing deeper around them. At times they thought they felt something, a tremor of something not quite right or an apprehension of something about to happen. But when they pursued it, it vanished as if it had never been. Smoke was getting frustrated. Usually his intuition was very good, especially when it came to finding anything in the city. But now, he might as well be walking blind and deaf through a heavy mist.

In part he was hunting through his memory. He was trying to recapture the felt sense in his body of having seen the old building in his dreams. He knew if he could just remember not only what it looked like but what it felt like, he would be able to zoom in on it like a compass. So far, he had had no luck.

The next best thing was what he was doing now, examining every intersection they came to in case a store or building triggered his memory by association. His only clue was how the building had looked old and run-down. It was the kind of building he would expect to find in one of the poorer neighborhoods on the south side of town. That's where he and MoBro were now.

As they walked, he had drawn a cloak of invisibility around himself and his friend. Not that they were truly invisible. Anyone could see them if they looked. It was really an aura of being unremarkable, uninteresting, and not likely to be noticed. This was not for protection. Nothing human in the city frightened him, and when most people saw MoBro, they became polite very quickly. Instead, it was for speed. He wanted them to move quickly and without interruption.

As they reached the middle of yet another block, this time one of closed shops and a Vietnamese mom-and-pop grocery store, he felt a surge of energy and blessing light him up. Startled, he looked around, then looked up. The energy that had blessed them felt so familiar. He opened his Sight wide and deep. He had a momentary vision of a woman riding a giant parrot, her aura a wide, high flame of light. Then the bird began to accelerate upwards. "Jennifer," he said. "She must be looking too!" Beside him, MoBro, also looking up, nodded his agreement. Then the big man blew a kiss towards the retreating figures. Smoke, too, sent a blessing after them, but he wasn't sure they had felt it before they disappeared. Had they found something?

His inner and outer senses more alert than ever and boosted by the blessing he had just received, Smoke became aware of a tingling in the atmosphere, as if the air were charged. There was a trace here, a thread of energy, faint but here. He hurried forward, MoBro at his heels.

When he reached the intersection, he was startled to see a familiar figure. "Zap!" he called out. Zap was an energy elemental who acted as one of his primary inner allies. That he could see him meant the boundaries between the worlds was very thin here and Zap was projecting strongly. Or it meant that Zap was actually taking semi-embodiment in the physical world. He supposed either were possible.

He approached the little being, which at the moment stood roughly chest height with Smoke but only belt-buckle height with MoBro, who apparently could see him too. Smoke knew from past experience, though, that Zap could easily become skyscraper height if he needed or wished to or could be the size of flea if that suited his fancy.

"Zap, do you feel it, too?"

The elemental nodded and pointed down the street to their right, his white gloved hand glowing in the darkness.

"Great! Thank you. Are you coming with us?"

Again the elemental nodded. He reached down into the pavement and suddenly was sucked down out of sight, with only a couple electrical sparks floating in the air where he had stood. "He's traveling ahead of us through the electrical conduits under the street," Smoke explained to MoBro, who had a questioning look in his eyes. "He'll be our scout." Smoke paused and scratched his head. "You know, I'm never sure if he's fully a spirit being or partly a physical one. His energy seems to go between the worlds."

MoBro shrugged.

"Yeah, it probably doesn't matter. Well, whatever he is, let's follow him."

The two strode swiftly down the street. When they came to the next intersection, Smoke grabbed MoBro's arm. "There it is!" He pointed across the street. "That's the building I saw in my dream."

The building was one of several two-story structures that lined the block. Its main distinguishing feature was a pair of wide doors that at one time probably opened into a garage. Now they were bolted shut and seemed not to have been opened for a long time. Three windows, one to the left of the garage doors and two to the right, belonged to three different storefronts. Above all the stores and the garage doors were other windows, suggesting that the second story had been turned into apartments.

As they crossed the street, Smoke could see that the store to the left at the far end of the building was a pawn shop, its window filled with various items on display, all behind a combination of iron mesh and iron bars. The store in the middle, next to the garage doors, was that of a locksmith. The final store was empty. Faded lettering on the grimy window proclaimed that it had once been a bookstore. Now a small, discolored poster proclaimed that the space was for rent and listed a phone number. Between this empty shop and the locksmith was a door, presumably leading to the upstairs apartments.

"Well, well," Smoke said. "What was that line in Elizabeth's warning? 'Lost key dagger and scepter,' wasn't it?" MoBro nodded. "And here we have a store that deals in locks and keys." MoBro signed, pointing at the shop at the end. "Yes, and a pawn shop as well, a haven for lost things. A bit too much of a coincidence, I'd say." He smiled at MoBro, who grinned back affirmatively.

Smoke stepped up to the wall between the garage doors and the locksmith's window and put his hands on the worn brick surface. "Let's see what the building has to say."

One of his talents was an ability to listen to inanimate objects and to hear their stories. Not that they spoke in words, of course, but in images and impressions, feelings and memories, stored like ghosts in the energy and substance from which they were made. In trying to find this building, he could have listened to the pavement that lay everywhere under the city, but there would have been too much information. But now that he was here, it was like having found the specific book he needed that had been lost on the shelves of a vast library. Now he could open it and read.

He let his heart open to the ancient bricks and to the memories of the building itself, inviting them gently and lovingly to tell their stories. And as he listened, impressions began to flood into his mind. Like a skilled interrogator, he began directing and shaping the flow of memories, sorting them, bringing them up to the present time.

He felt a cunning, seeking, hungry mind. He felt elation and possessiveness, like a rat that has discovered something shiny and has brought it to its lair. He felt desire. An image of a thin figure hunched over a table, examining something in an ornate box, something small...

He adjusted his Sight, letting the memories speak to him from a different perspective. The man was still there, but around him was a nimbus of the cold light he had seen in his dream. But even brighter was the object that lay in the box, which seemed to blaze with fire. What was it? He pressed harder to see. He had an impression of a door opening... the garage doors? There was a lock, a key, and...

He was hurled back onto the pavement as a force struck him like an electrical shock. MoBro immediately jumped to his side, grabbing his outstretched hands that were tingling and burning as if on fire. As soon as his friend touched him, the pain left. He could see a thread of energy coursing out of his body, into MoBro, and then down into the earth where it disappeared. MoBro lifted him up. He could feel vitality pouring back into him from the big man.

"Wards," Smoke said. "I think I woke something up that didn't like me."

Abruptly, Zap was standing next to them, having apparently emerged from the pavement at their feet. His thin, jagged body was throwing off sparks at an alarming rate. Smoke could feel his voice in his mind. "Great danger here! Run away now!"

Light suddenly spilled out onto the street from a window over the garage. Smoke and MoBro immediately shrank back into the shadows against the building, though they both were careful not to touch the brick wall itself. Zap disappeared again down into the pavement. Grabbing Smoke's arm lightly, MoBro pulled him at a run down the street past the garage doors and the pawnshop and into a narrow alley between this building and the next.

Smoke touched the outer wall of the pawnshop. He felt a tingling in his fingers, and immediately pulled his hand back. "Interesting," he whispered to MoBro. "I think the whole building is warded." He focused his thoughts on his elemental ally. Immediately, Zap appeared before him. "Zap, these wards feel electrical in nature. Can you get into them and neutralize them, or at least get past them?"

Zap shook his head, frowning. "Too much danger. Not to you, yet, but to me." Smoke suddenly had an image of a vast electric-blue light, in which a mouth with shark-like teeth opened and swallowed Zap.

"Are you saying that there's another elemental in there, one like you only more powerful?"

"Yes. Much more."

"Much more?"

"It is one of the ancient ones, an ancestor, one of the First Ones."

Smoke looked at Zap, his mind whirling with the implications of what his elemental companion was telling him. "One of the First Ones...? You mean one of your ancestors?"

Zap nodded.

Smoke whistled in amazement. "In that case, I'm lucky the being didn't kill me just then."

"It's not fully here, in your world. Yet. But a key has been found. A door is being opened. When it finally opens, my ancestor will emerge, and all will be in jeopardy."

"A key? What kind of key? You mean, like a ritual of some kind?"

"No. A talisman of great power."

"And the dagger and scepter? What about them?"

The elemental shrugged in a very human way. "I don't know about them. They may be shielded beyond my view. They may not be here in this place."

MoBro, who had been listening to this exchange, touched Smoke on the shoulder. Smoke turned around so he could see his friend. <Who is doing this?> the big man signed.

Zap must have picked up his thought, for he said immediately, "A man who hungers. He hungers for power. He hungers for knowledge. He does not Walk as you do, but he can make portals. He can use keys."

"A magician?" Smoke asked. "He's using rituals and the talisman to invoke this being?"

"Yes. But he doesn't understand what he is calling forth. He thinks he is the master, but he is just the tool."

"When will he try to open this door you spoke of?"

"He will not just try. He will succeed. And it will be soon. He prepares for the full moon."

"The full moon….that's only two days away!"

Smoke turned back to MoBro. "Let's go home. I need to think about this, try to understand it more, figure out what we can do. From what Zap has said, the implications are enormous. I've never heard of one of the truly ancient ones, the First Ones, trying to enter the human world. Most of them don't even know we exist or if they do know, don't care. For one to show such personal interest…" He shuddered. "It's like an exterminator suddenly showing interest in an ant colony. It could be curiosity, but chances are it won't turn out well for the ants!"

MoBro signed: <We must walk carefully.>

"We need to move very carefully. Jennifer is coming in the morning. Before we do anything, I want to talk with her first. We'll need to pool our resources. Whatever her concerns may be about being a Priestess, I have a feeling this situation will take all our combined efforts to resolve."

As they silently moved away from the building and walked down the street, keeping to the shadows, a tall hunched figure standing in the darkness at the window over the pawnshop watched them, his eyes gleaming.

Fools, he thought. *Just as I was told! Meddlers would come to stop the Revelation, to stop me! And here they are. Little do they know I can feel them coming. Feel them try to break into my secrets and disrupt my great work! Just as I felt the other two flying high above, thinking they were safe just because they were in their fleshless bodies. But I am sure those two have been followed and dealt with! When my friends hunt, no one is safe!*

Facing the reality that someone might actually be trying to interfere with his plans, the tall man clenched his fists, grinding his teeth in anger. His rage spilled out of him. "You want to stop me," he shouted at the retreating figures, "but your efforts will be in vain! All in vain! You have no idea who you are dealing with! No idea how powerful I am! But when you come back, which you will, I will be ready for you. You will find out just who I am. Oh yes!" he muttered, "you will find out more than you bargained for!"

His laugh in the darkness was short and dry like a wind over a barren desert. And somewhere deeper in the building, a sharp, piercing blue-white light blinked out as if an eye had closed for the night.

CHAPTER FIVE

Jennifer eased her car into the morning commuter traffic on the freeway leading into the city, music playing from the portable CD plug-in on the seat next to her. At seven am, that traffic was already building up. The earlier people drove to work to avoid the peak traffic from seven-thirty until at least nine o'clock, the earlier the rush hour crunch began. It was a catch-22. *Although,* Jennifer thought with a grin, *if the trend continues, those who go in at eight will find the road empty as all the other commuters will have preceded them.* But she knew that would never happen. Traffic obeyed some kind of natural law that said nature abhors an empty freeway. If there was room to drive, there would be cars to fill it.

Still, the traffic was not as bad as she'd feared. She knew she would get to the city early and have an hour or so until it was time to see Smoke at nine. But that was alright. She had some thinking to do, and she knew a nice coffee shop not far from Smoke's apartment where she could do it. *Assuming it's still there and hasn't become a Starbucks in the year or so since I've been back here.*

What had been hard had been getting up at five am in order to leave her house by six. Thankfully, she'd had a dreamless sleep and felt better when she awakened. But her body still ached from the night before. *I hope I don't have many journeys like that one,* she thought ruefully, slowing down as a driver in a rush pulled abruptly in front of her. She made it a point never to get upset at anything any other driver did in an attempt to arrive at his or her destination a few seconds earlier. If she didn't, then she knew she would be a frazzled wreck when she arrived where she was going. Freeway driving was definitely not her favorite occupation. *Too bad I can't just fly in on Peekaru's back.*

The bright part of her morning so far had been the chance to call her mother before the sun had properly risen. It was petty, she knew, but getting her mother out of bed at five-thirty in the morning to find out when she had arranged for Jennifer to meet Smoke was a small compensation for her mother sending her on this errand in the first place. She felt delightfully wicked and justified at the same time about it. After all, she could still be under the covers herself! Besides, her mother could always go back to bed while she was here having to avoid reckless, impatient drivers.

To her pleasant surprise, it was only a quarter to eight when she turned down the street that ultimately would lead to Smoke's apartment but which first would bring her to her coffee shop. It was less pleasant and less of a surprise to see that the coffee shop was no longer there. Where the sign over the door had once said *The Cosmic Critters Coffee Corral*, it now said, as she had feared, *Starbucks*.

She almost didn't stop. Not that she had anything particular against Starbucks, except its imperial expansion; she actually liked their coffee. But the Corral had been funky and quirky and altogether idiosyncratic. Along with Smoke's apartment, it had been one of the few places in the city where she'd felt safe from unwanted energies, especially after the mantle of Priestess had dropped on her and she'd become so much more sensitive to the vibrations around her. She'd spent hours in the Corral writing while Smoke had been off with his band. Seeing it gone was like discovering an old and beloved friend had died.

Still, she had over an hour to kill, and she didn't know any other place nearby, so she stopped and parked. She unplugged her CD player and put it in the glove compartment out of sight. Then she got out, locked the car, and went into the coffee shop. Her spirit lifted the moment she saw a large, overstuffed, very comfortable looking, and, most importantly, empty chair. She marked it with her purse and her jacket and went to get her not-so-secret vice, a caramel macchiato.

As she sat in the big cozy chair sipping her drink, a sense of relaxation came over her in spite of the fact that she was in the middle of a city with its vibrations and energies so jarring to her sensitivities. She thought back to the journey that had ended so painfully yesterday and to the prophecy which her mother had shared.. She was still puzzling over that enigmatic line about the key, the dagger, and the scepter, Nor was she sure what the "cold sun" was. Like so many oracular statements, this one was obscure. *Is there an Oracle's Code somewhere*, she wondered, that says, *"Thou shalt not speak plainly!"* How come Mother never gets a message like, *"Go to 59 South Phillips Street at precisely 10:05 in the morning where you will find the Bad Guy summoning demons to take over the world. Bring with you the following items to banish the demons and save the day."*

She turned her thoughts to the journey itself. Obviously, Peekaru had seen something that she hadn't, a "thread" he had called it. It had been, she was sure, an energy link between where they had been in the city and that other place, that other city. But just where was that other city? It hadn't looked like any place she knew of, not that she was an expert on cities. But it hadn't felt right. It had felt different. And why had it had a national angel overlighting it? That would make it very important, as she understood these things.

And what about the man? Had he been important, or just a bystander while she and whatever that thing had been had hurled lightning bolts at each other?

And what about brothers loving brothers? Had there been two men, two brothers on that hill in the rain, and she'd only seen one of them? If so, who would they be?

Too many questions. If she were one of the characters in her novels, she would already have figured out what was going on. Probably a voice would have spoken in her mind, giving her the clue...

Think when, not where...

A voice just like that, she thought, sitting up and looking around. *Say, who's writing this story anyway?* OK, some part of her subconscious or perhaps one of her Priestess allies had just given her a clue, and right on cue, too!

But what did it mean? She wondered how her mother kept from going mad if these were the kind of messages she regularly got.

Think when, not where, eh? Did Peekaru take her someplace else in time? It was certainly possible. Or at least back into the memory of the world? But again, when? And where?

She stared out the window at the passers-by. Everyone seemed in a hurry. She looked at her watch. Eight-thirty. She would have to go soon, too.

So what did she have to bring to Smoke? Not much. A riddle about a lost key, dagger, and scepter. A strange city somewhere in time in the middle of a rain storm. Two brothers who love each other. An attack by something like a lightning elemental. A man dancing on a hill in the rain.

What was the thread that linked them? She knew there was something she was missing. She needed another voice in her head.

Right pieces, wrong puzzle.

She sat up again. *Hey, thanks,* she thought. *Not to sound ungrateful, whoever-you-are, but you wouldn't have something more clear than that would you? Like a name or something?*

Ah, poor Jennifer. Just like poor Richard.

"Who's Richard?" she exclaimed out loud. A man sipping a latte and reading the paper at a nearby table looked up at her. She smiled at him sheepishly. "Just thinking out loud," she said. The man smiled back, then returned to his paper.

Peekaru, she thought intensely. *Is that you? Stop being the trickster and give me a hand here.* She opened her Sight as much as she felt safe to do in a public place in a city. Sure enough, the parrot was standing on the arm of her chair.

You mean a hand like this? The bird raised up one of its talons. *Hey, how are you this morning, Priestess? That was some flight we took yesterday, eh?*

Peekaru, she said, directing her thought at the figure of the parrot. *I'll give you a cracker if you tell me where we went.*

I don't eat crackers. Remember? I'm not a Polly. I just look like this when I'm with you.

Be serious! This is important. I'm trying to figure this out.

The parrot pulled out a loose feather which drifted down a few inches towards the floor, then disappeared. *And I am helping you, Priestess. I'm like the helpful voices you put into your characters' heads when you write your stories.*

You're giving me more riddles. Give me some straight answers, for heaven's sakes!

The parrot spread its wings and preened itself. *Do the voices you write in your characters' heads ever give them straight answers?*

She thought a moment. The bird had a point. *Um, no... It's no fun that way for the reader.*

Ta-Da!

But we're not in a novel, Peekaru. This is the real world!

According to whom? And don't I deserve some fun? That was a rough flight! But listen, just think about what I've said. Think of everything I've said. Think when, not where. Right pieces, wrong puzzle.

The bird looked at her expectantly.

OK, she thought, *but who's Richard....*

Her mouth fell open for a moment, then she closed it. *"Think of everything I've said" the parrot said. All right. It wasn't just Richard. Peekaru said "Poor Richard." Poor Richard. But why is Richard poor, or who is poor Richard...*

Her mouth fell open again.

Aha, said Peekaru. *Are we having fun yet?*

She drained the remainder of her coffee and got up. *Come on. We've got an appointment with Smoke.*

She hurried out the door and climbed into her car. *Poor Richard,* she said to herself as she started the ignition. *Of course. Now it all fits. I really was trying to fit the pieces to the wrong puzzle. Or I hadn't just understood what the puzzle was.*

She drove the four blocks down to where Smoke's apartment was, aware that her spirit ally was sitting on the seat next to her. She had shut her Sight down when she left Starbucks, but she could still feel the parrot's presence. "You're talking about Ben Franklin, aren't you? He wrote Poor Richard's Almanac. And the city where brothers loved each other? That was Philadelphia, the city of brotherly love. It all fits. The national angel was there because that's where the Congressional Congress met during the Revolutionary War. That's where the Constitutional Convention was held that formed our country. It was even our first capital."

By Jove, I think she's got it, the parrot's voice intoned in her mind.

"And that man on the hill," she said, as she turned into a parking place right in front of Smoke's apartment building - there were perks to being a Priestess! "he was Benjamin Franklin." She smiled, pleased with herself. Then she frowned as she turned off the car.

"But why? What connection does he have with Mom's prophecy? What's his role in all this? Bah! More mysteries!"

She climbed out of the car, aware that Peekaru had vanished back to wherever he lived when he wasn't being a parrot. *Hey,* she said, calling after him, *we're not finished yet!*

But there was no answer.

She faced the door to the apartment building. There was a row of names and buttons to press attached to the wall of the building next to the door. She went up and started to push the button labeled "S", then turned around and went back to her car.

Climbing in, she pulled down the mirror that was in her sun visor and looked herself over. Well, not too bad, she thought. She took a small brush out of her purse and gave her hair a good brushing. Satisfied, she climbed back out of the car, locked the door, and with her hand, brushed and straightened the blouse and skirt she was wearing. *Not that I care,* she thought, as she walked back up to the door and pushed the "S" button. *But it never hurts to be presentable. It's not for Smoke. Who knows whom I might meet going up the stairs?*

This time she felt a smirk coming from wherever Peekaru had gone.

CHAPTER SIX

Smoke stood in the hallway outside the door to his apartment, listening to Jennifer's footsteps as she climbed the stairs. As he watched, his face carefully impassive, she appeared around the corner from the top of the stairs. His heart stopped for a moment. It was as if no time had passed since he had last seen her, except... He looked again. Except that she was more beautiful than ever.

He smiled, and stepped towards her. He immediately sensed that her inner shields were up. Though she was smiling, too, prickliness followed her as she walked towards him.

They met and embraced, a brief embrace of two old friends, nothing more. They both could feel tension rising in the hallway.

"JayLynn, it's great to see you. You look fine!" Taking her by the arm, he led her back into his apartment.

"You, too, Smoke. And my name's just Jennifer now." But she smiled at him to take any sting out of her words as she pushed away the use of any pet names they had had for each other and the feelings they might raise.

"Yeah, sure, Jennifer," he said, closing the door. MoBro was in the kitchen area, working the espresso machine. He turned and walked towards her, his grin bright white on his dark face.

"Jennifer, this is my good friend, MoBro. He's one of us. We met while walking the inner roads between the worlds. He was in Los Angeles at the time. He caught a bus and came up here looking for me. Came right to this apartment and knocked on the door." Jennifer looked at the black man with new respect. "That's impressive," she said.

"I'll say. I couldn't have done that if I'd gone to Los Angeles to find *him!*"

MoBro smiled, bowed, then straightened up and extended his hand. As she took it, her hand disappearing in his, Smoke added, "He doesn't speak. He can, but he doesn't..."

"Unless the occasion is right, which this is," MoBro said. "It is an honor, Priestess. My heart welcomes you."

"And mine yours, Mo... er..."

"MoBro," he said. "It's short for More Brother."

"Because if he likes you, and maybe even if he doesn't, he'll be more a brother to you than any brother you've already got," laughed Smoke. "And he's already said more words to you than he has all year so far to me!"

"Because I am called to a place of silence, beautiful Jennifer, where words are precious jewels of power to be used most sparingly."

"That is very sweet of you, MoBro. Then I honor even more the words you have shared with me." She felt wholly charmed by this large, black man who radiated such a deep and interesting power. She knew his was the aura she had seen last night on the street with Smoke as she and Peekaru had flown overhead in their spirit forms.

"This calls for a celebration!" exclaimed Smoke. "Jennifer's here. MoBro is speaking. What other wonders lie before us?" He bounded over to the kitchen counter. "Espresso, anyone?"

Jennifer laughed, too, feeling more at ease than she had expected. It was hard to feel nervous in MoBro's presence. "Maybe later, Smoke. I just had a Starbucks on the way."

"Ah, then I'll wait, too. MoBro?" The big man shook his head.

"Then, let's sit and visit and do what we've come together to do, whatever that may be. Then later we can have lunch before MoBro and I need to go to rehearsal."

Jennifer sat down on the sofa, intuiting that the big overstuffed chair probably was MoBro's. He's quite a presence, she thought. Smoke threw himself down on a futon chair, and MoBro settled into his chair as Jennifer had expected.

She looked at Smoke. "You have a rehearsal?"

"Yes, my band, Liquid Stone. We're doing a gig tonight. Would you like to come? You'd be very welcome. MoBro is our drummer."

For a moment, Jennifer was tempted. Then she stiffened her resolve. She did not want to reawaken old feelings. It was better to keep this contact to a minimum. "I'm sorry," she said. "I know it will be lovely, but I have other things I have to do tonight."

"I understand," said Smoke. *She's still afraid,* he thought. *Afraid of her power. Afraid of me. Afraid of what might happen between us. Just plain damn afraid. Oh well...* His voice became businesslike. "So, here we are, just as your mother planned, to deal with a prophecy she received. I should let you know MoBro and I have already done some investigating."

"I know. I saw you last night when I was walking the worlds. Or I should say, flying. My ally is a parrot, and he had me sitting between his wings."

"Then it was you! I thought so. We saw you with our Sight. You sent us a blessing. It was very helpful, thank you. But where were you going? We saw you circling, then you took off as if you were heading right to the moon! I sent a blessing back to you, but you had gone."

"Peekaru, my ally, had found a thread of energy that he felt was part of whatever we were looking for. We were following it."

"And?"

Jennifer then related what had happened to them, the flight through time, arriving in a rain storm near Philadelphia—though she hadn't know it was Philadelphia at the time—seeing the man on the hill that she now suspected was Benjamin Franklin, being attacked, and her fall back into her body. She finished by relating her conversation with Peekaru in the coffee shop and the conclusions to which she had come.

"But what I don't understand is what Benjamin Franklin has to do with any of this," she concluded. "We seem to have journeyed into still more mystery."

Smoke sat still, letting his thoughts arrange themselves. As Jennifer had been speaking, his mind had been whirling, pieces beginning to fall into place. He leaned forward. "I think I can supply some missing pieces. I'm not sure why this is happening, but I think I know better *how* it is happening. And believe me, your mother was right. There is great danger here."

Smoke then related his dream of the previous afternoon and the adventure he and MoBro had had going to the building in his dream. He told her what his ally, Zap, had said about the talisman and even more disturbingly, about the greater elemental whom Zap had called one of his ancestors.

When he was done, Jennifer said, "Maybe I'll take that coffee now."

"Right," said Smoke, starting to get up from the futon. But MoBro, moving with a grace and speed that surprised Jennifer, pushed him back down and strode into the kitchen area.

"Wow," said Jennifer, her thoughts racing. "One of the First Ones. I thought they never had any business with humanity or human affairs." The First Ones were beings that had helped form the earth from stellar dust and cosmic gases. They lived and operated on a scale that normally did not bring them into contact with human beings; a person's life span was the equivalent of a second or less in time for them. "This magician must be very powerful to have made contact."

"Oh, contact isn't as rare as all that. I know two people who have contact with the First Ones."

"Really? Two? I'm amazed. Who are they?"

Smoke indicated the big man making coffee and lowered his voice. "MoBro is one. He's made contact with an Old One of the Earth. As a result, the Spirit of the mountain out there became one of his allies."

Jennifer looked out the window and saw in the distance the peak that overshadowed the city. "That's impressive! And who's the other?"

Smoke smiled. "Don't you know? It's you, Jennifer."

"Me?" She was so surprised her voice squeaked.

Smoke laughed. "Sure. The Quatrain. It's got to be one of the First Ones. Wouldn't you say?"

Jennifer suddenly felt a wave of embarrassment sweep over her. She should have known that and might have known that perhaps if she had been more diligent in her role as Priestess. As it was, the only contact she had with the Quatrain was through the medallion she wore when Walking between the worlds. "I...I don't know. I've never really contacted the Quatrain, at least not that I know of."

Now it was Smoke's turn to be surprised. "But how can that be? You're its Priestess."

"Well, technically. But I don't practice at it much. I do it when I have to, like now, but frankly, I'd rather forget it."

Smoke didn't respond. He just looked at her. Was that pity in his eyes, she wondered, anger beginning to rise. But at that moment, MoBro stepped between them, handing each of them a cup of espresso. He stood there for a moment, then stepped back. He signed to Smoke, but he kept his eyes on Jennifer.

"He's asking you…"

"I know what he's asking me," she said sharply. "I read sign, too." She looked at MoBro, who was sitting down in his chair again. "I don't know why I stay the Priestess. I could give it up. There is a procedure, but it takes about a year to do and there's also a cost. Many, if not all, of the doors between the inner worlds and me would be closed. I don't think I'm ready for that."

She looked down at her hands. "It's not that I don't like what I do or what I am. I've always been able to see into the inner worlds. When I was ten years old I discovered how to leave my body and journey into them. That's always been cool. And when Aunt Iris presented me with the medallion of the Priestess, I thought that was cool, too. I didn't realize all that came with it." She remembered well that moment of feeling the awesome power that had descended upon her, the crushing sense of responsibility and of belonging to someone else. It had been the most frightening moment of her life.

"I remember that," said Smoke. "You were pretty pissed."

"I was unprepared for all that it meant. Anyway, maybe I'll give it up one day. I certainly should give it up if I can't manage the responsibilities. I don't think I was cut out for leadership. My mom, now, that's another story!"

"What would happen if you just quit," asked Smoke.

"That would not be good. If I just severed the power threads between the Quatrain and me, there would be a backlash. It could kill me. One former Priestess did that. She just walked away from it, didn't go through the procedure for transferring the power. I don't know why. She just wanted out." She took a final sip of coffee and put her cup down on the table next to the sofa. "Two days later she had a stroke. Spent the rest of her life paralyzed and unable to speak."

Both Smoke and MoBro looked shocked.

"Oh, it wasn't punishment. It was just that when she refused the link with the Quatrain, the energy that had entered into her had no place to go. It circulates, you see. So it exploded within her body. Poof! She could easily have died." She shrugged. "Might have been better if she had."

"But," she continued, "talking about me isn't going to get us to the solution of our problem. You said you had pieces to add. I've heard your story, and I have to say the idea of a meddling First One frightens me, but I don't get how it solves my puzzles."

Smoke smiled. "Your mother's prophecy mentioned a key, and Zap said that the magician was using a physical key as a talisman. This key is the way he's contacting the First One, which, by the way, may not be as powerful as we're assuming. Zap said he was an ancestor and thus may appear more powerful to him than he might to us. But there were many First Ones and not all of them were the super-powerful Elementals that shaped the earth."

MoBro signed: <It's probably powerful enough.>

"Yes, I'm not saying we shouldn't be cautious." He looked at Jennifer. "Your journey was important. Peekaru was right in where he took you. I think the talisman we're looking for is Benjamin Franklin's key."

"Franklin's key? Why?"

"Because it fits. Surely you remember the story. In June of 1752, Franklin went to a hill outside Philadelphia and flew a kite in the middle of a thunderstorm. The kite was essentially a long lightning rod, to which he attached a key. When lightning struck the kite, the electricity ran down the string and electrified the key, which gave Franklin a shock. In that way, he proved that lightning and electricity were the same thing and that it was a force of nature."

Jennifer slapped her forehead in mock admonishment. "Of course! I'd forgotten. So Benjamin Franklin's key is the key in the prophecy."

"I'm sure of it." Smoke got up and began to pace, his eyes alight with excitement. "You know me, Jennifer. Technology is what I'm attuned to, just like you're attuned to nature. Cities are my forests. You talk to nature spirits, I talk to techno-spirits. And in the past hundred years or so, a whole new kind of elemental being has been appearing, mostly in cities. These are beings of electricity. Think of it, electricity is everywhere, all around us all the time. In a way, we have entered their world, drawing them into ours. My ally Zap is one of these beings."

Smoke paused for a moment, collecting his thoughts. "Franklin was the person who started all this. He was a serious inventor and scientist who was fascinated by electricity. One might call him the first electrical engineer. He invented the lightning rod, for example, which made him famous all over America and Europe. He was the one who opened the portal for humanity's engagement with the realm of the electro-elementals."

"And it was his key that opened that door, both literally and figuratively."

"Yes. That moment on the hillside in the rain was the historical turning point when humanity entered the age of electricity. No wonder that specific key became such a powerful talisman, a link between both the human and the elemental kingdom of electromagnetism. I don't know if even Franklin knew what he had created or started. But he was a pretty canny fellow, on more levels than one, so I suspect he did know. The real mystery is how this guy here acquired Franklin's key. But that doesn't matter, I suppose. The fact we need to deal with is that he has it."

Now Jennifer got to her feet, equally excited. MoBro watched the two of them, amusement in his eyes. "OK, I'm sure, too, that's the key, like you say. But what about the dagger and the scepter? Where are they? How do they figure in this?"

Smoke laughed. "They don't. There are no dagger and scepter."

Jennifer looked at him. "What? What do you mean? The prophecy specifically talks about them."

"Come on, Jennifer. You know oracle-speak. It's never clear, always ambiguous, and sometimes misleading. You have to read it carefully. Its purpose is not to inform but to trigger intuition, which is always more powerful than simple information. The line went, 'Lost key dagger and scepter.' It's really saying that the lost key is both a dagger and a scepter, a weapon and a talisman of power."

Jennifer saw it in an instant. "Of course! I know that's right! I feel such a fool. I should have seen it!"

"Well, if it's any consolation, I didn't see it either until Zap told me there was only one talisman involved. He didn't know anything about a dagger or a scepter. If there had been such instruments involved, I'm sure he would have known it. He's pretty accurate about such things because he can feel the currents of power and energy as only an electrical elemental can."

MoBro clapped his hands softly, and both of the others turned to look at him. He signed: <Tomorrow's full moon begins at six in the morning. We must stop this magician before then.>

Jennifer and Smoke both sat down, this time side by side on the couch. "You're right," said Smoke. "Both Zap and the prophecy warned us about what will happen if this elemental gains full access to this world. It could easily use the entire electrical grid of this country as its body. For that matter, it could use all electrical energy anywhere as its body. We would be at its mercy in more ways than one."

Jennifer looked at the two men. "So, gentlemen, what are we going to do to stop this?"

MoBro got up from his chair, a determined look on his face. He looked at them and mimed eating.

"Of course," said Jennifer. "Your basic first step in saving the world. Lunch!"

CHAPTER SEVEN

"These could be hotter," Jennifer complained, munching on a raw jalapeno pepper from the bowl in front of her. MoBro and Smoke stared at her in undisguised admiration and horror respectively.

"It's the power of the Quatrain that's letting you do that, isn't it?" asked Smoke.

Jennifer smiled and offered him one. He vigorously shook his head. "No, mama," he said. "I'm Smoke, not fire." MoBro grinned.

They were sitting in a small Mexican restaurant a block away from Smoke's apartment. Stacked around them were dishes dirty with the remains of their lunch.

Jennifer pointed a half-eaten pepper at them. "Your ally Zap said that this man was being used. Maybe some part of him knows that and wants out. Maybe we could go and talk with him, convince him to stop whatever he's doing."

Smoke shook his head. "The impression Zap gave me was of someone who was obsessed and convinced of his power. I doubt he would listen."

"But he might," Jennifer insisted. "I'd be willing to try."

MoBro signed: <It's worth a shot. The worst that could happen is that he would refuse. We'd be in the same place we are now.>

"Except he'd know we were on to him. We'd lose any element of surprise we now have," Smoke admonished. "Besides, we really know nothing about this guy. He could be crazy. It fact, he's got to be crazy to be doing what he's doing. Talking to him could be dangerous."

"We could all three go," she said. "Besides who's going to try anything with Man Mountain here." She patted MoBro's hand. "I should call you ManMo, instead!"

MoBro grinned at her, but then frowned and pointed to his watch.

"I know," Smoke said. To Jennifer's querying look, he said, "It's a complication. We have a gig tonight, like I told you, and we're meeting the rest of our band to rehearse this afternoon."

Jennifer stared at him incredulously. "You're not thinking of playing in a band tonight with all that's going on, are you?"

"If I can. It's bad magic not to honor your agreements. Besides, I think I'd rather face an angry First One than our mates if we don't show up." MoBro signed agreement, adding: <They're crazy dudes!>

"Not as crazy as the thing we're up against! Let's get our priorities straight here. Honestly! And people call me irresponsible as a priestess."

Smoke looked down at the remains of rice and refried beans on his plate. His voice was soft as he answered. "Responsibility is a whole thing, Jennifer. I can't divide it up. Not and remain responsible." He looked at her. "Can you understand that? I have a responsibility to this problem we're facing, yes. But I also have a responsibility to my band and to the people who will come to hear us, and to many other things as well. Once I have committed, I can't pick and choose and say I'll do this one but not that one."

"For god's sake, Smoke, there are *priorities*."

"Yes, there are. And if I need to, I'll talk with my band and we'll cancel tonight. But I will not simply not show up, nor assume I won't be there. They are depending on me and on MoBro. If I break one chain of dependence, one thread of responsibility, then all the others may begin to unravel. I'll become a leaky vessel, Jennifer. I could begin to lose my power."

"Yes, I understand, but…"

"No, Jennifer. I don't think you do understand. It looks like I'm a loner, I know. And I am. I like to act outside of structures, to drift about like the smoke I'm named for. But I'm also part of a community, Jennifer, the community of all those with whom I've made commitments…and that's a much wider community than it looks. My magic, my power, is not just my own. It's held for me in my community as well. If I begin breaking the bonds, even in a small way in the name of a greater good, I will end up alone. Then where will my power be?"

Jennifer didn't respond. His words, delivered softly and without emotion, struck her as if he had slapped her. She was part of a community, too, her Lineage. But she had been pushing it away, denying the responsibilities it placed on her, refusing the full commitment. *But I don't want it,* part of her wailed. *It will consume me, and I'll be lost. It's better to be alone.* MoBro enveloped her hand in his, warmth flowing from kind eyes. She immediately felt herself calm down, sinking down into peacefulness. How does he do that, she wondered.

Smoke shook his head, shifting the conversation. "I think the solution is to get hold of Franklin's key. Without the talisman, this guy won't be able to open the portal."

"And how do we do that?" Jennifer asked quietly. "He's not just going to hand it over to us." She swatted at a fly that was buzzing over her plate and missed.

"Well, I was thinking of a little breaking and entering. Unfortunately, that's harder to do in the daytime. We may have to wait until late tonight to do it."

"I still think we should go talk to the man. That's a lot less dangerous, it seems to me, than breaking and entering. It's certainly less likely to get the police involved."

"The police don't worry me. His wards do. We ran into them last night. But now that I know they're there, I can do something about them."

MoBro pointed to himself. <I can take care of them>, he signed.

Smoke nodded. "Yes, with your connections, I bet you can."

"What about confronting all this on the inner?" Jennifer asked. "Between the three of us, we could conjure some powerful mojo, I'd say."

"I'd like to leave that as a last resort. This elemental attacked you when you journeyed into the past. You felt what it can do, and I'm betting you encountered only a fraction of its power. I'll tangle with it if I have to, but it's nothing like your usual natural elemental. Its power is different. And if we end up fighting it here, this isn't your territory, Jennifer. You're very powerful, but cities constrict you. You could be more vulnerable. No, if we can, I'd rather we solve this on this level. Which brings us back to getting the key."

"Or talking with the man," Jennifer insisted

Smoke looked at her. "You seem to feel pretty strong about talking with him. Is this guidance you're getting or something?"

"No. Just call it a woman's approach."

"Good enough. I accept that. But I think MoBro and I should do it."

Jennifer bristled. "Why? You don't think I can handle the responsibility?"

Smoke didn't rise to the bait. "I just have a feeling we shouldn't put all our eggs in one basket. I would feel safer knowing we had backup. And, as you said, MoBro can look pretty intimidating, even if he wouldn't hurt a fly."

MoBro's hand flashed out with amazing speed, his fingers forming a closed fist. He opened it, and the fly was sitting on his palm. It immediately flew away. He grinned a sly grin at Jennifer.

"Ah...All right," she said, staring at where the fly went. "You two talk with him."

They left the restaurant and climbed into Jennifer's car. Five minutes later they were cruising down the street where their target lay. True to form, a car pulled out of a parking space just in front of the locksmith's shop. But as Jennifer headed towards it, Smoke laid a hand on her arm.

"I'd rather you drove past and dropped us off in the next block. Then we'll walk back."

"Cloak and dagger stuff?" she said.

"I guess. I just feel better about it. Then you can park somewhere out of direct sight of the building but where you can watch the door. Hopefully we won't be long."

"When's your rehearsal start?" she asked.

"In two hours. But if we're going to be late, I'll call the band and let them know."

She stopped the car in the middle of the next block past the pawn shop. Smoke and MoBro climbed out. Smoke leaned back through the window. "One other thing. I don't recommend trying to probe the place with any of your Priestess powers. You're not used to working here in the city, and it has some strong protective powers I'm not familiar with."

"Sure. If anything goes wrong, I'll just bat my eyelashes and use my feminine wiles. Give me some credit, Smoke!"

He grinned. "All the time, JayLynn. See you in a bit!"

"Good luck. And it's Jennifer!"

She pulled away from the curb, and MoBro and Smoke watched her go. <Prickly, isn't she,> the large man signed.

"Ha," Smoke replied, "you don't know the half of it!"

They headed back down the street in the direction from which they had come. They walked past the pawnshop and the garage doors and then past the locksmith, stopping in front of the unlabeled door. There was a mail slot in the door, and a button next to it on the wall of the building.

"I have a plan," Smoke said. "It's a bit far out, but it's direct and I think it makes some sense. At least it might get him to talk about Franklin's key." MoBro nodded in acquiescence.

Smoke pushed the button. They could hear a buzzing inside and higher up. They waited, but there was no answer. Smoke pushed the button again. Still no response. MoBro signed: <Not here?> Smoke shrugged and pushed the button a third time. He had just assumed the man would be at home.

"Are you looking for me?" The voice came from their left. Turning, they saw a tall, slightly hunched man standing in the door to the locksmith's shop. "The button rings in here, too, so I can hear it when I'm working."

Smoke smiled at the man and walked up to him, MoBro walking slightly behind him. "I think so. Are you the man who lives upstairs?"

"Yes." The tall man looked at them curiously. "And you are?"

"Collectors," Smoke said. The man had a long, lean face with bushy eyebrows shading his dark eyes. The eyebrows raised like caterpillars arching their backs.

"Collectors? How odd," said the man, ushering them inside his shop.

"Yes, we were told you had a rare artifact. A key."

"Really?" A twinge of a smile played at the edges of the man's lips. "Well, I am a locksmith, so if I had anything rare, it probably would be a key. What key is it?"

Smoke had decided to be direct. There was not enough time, he felt, to be coy. Better to bring everything into the open. "Benjamin Franklin's key, the one he used with his kite to prove lightning was electricity."

"Oh my!" the man said, as if surprised, but there was no surprise in his eyes. "That would be rare indeed! And worth a great deal. Why do you think I have such a thing? As you can see from my surroundings, I'm hardly a wealthy man."

"There were rumors. You know how it is. Someone finds something or buys something and the word gets out. Whispers travel the grapevine."

"And those rumors led you here?" The man's lips twitched again. Perhaps, Smoke thought, it's a nervous tic.

"Yes, as a matter of fact. Were we misinformed?"

This time the man smiled fully, showing perfect teeth. But there was no warmth in the smile. "I'm amazed, gentlemen. Truly amazed. No, you were not misinformed. I do have Franklin's key, but I have taken great pains to keep it a secret. Very great pains."

Uh oh, Smoke thought. I'm getting a bad vibe from this. "Well, in the collecting world, even the best secrets have a way of getting out."

"I guess they do." The man laughed, a dry, whispery kind of laugh. "And because of that, here you are. Fellow collectors. I suppose you would like to see it? But of course you would. How could you resist? It's why you're here, isn't it?"

"Uh, yes, it is. We would love to see it." But all Smoke's alarms were going now. Somehow, he realized, this man had been expecting them. He suddenly felt like a mouse that a cat had decided to play with.

"Well, then, follow me." The man turned and went to a door in the back of the shop behind his desk. "I'm sure I can trust you gentlemen," he said, as he opened the door. "You seem like trustworthy sorts." He disappeared down a dark passage.

"Oh, we are," said Smoke, following him, with MoBro on his heels. The hallway was so narrow that they had to walk single file. He realized it was heading in the direction of the garage.

"Mind your step," the man called back. "I'm afraid the light bulb burned out in here, and I just haven't had it replaced." Then a door opened ahead of them, and a weak light shone through. They emerged into a small room that was empty except for a table against one wall. On the table was a plain box. The locksmith approached it reverently. Smoke could feel the power in the room. The key's here, he thought.

The man paused by the table and turned back to face them. "In this box, as you probably have guessed, is the most famous key in the world. In fact, you might say this key opened the door that led to the world we know today."

He reached down and opened the box. It was lined with velvet. From it, he took out a plain brass key about the length of his finger. He held it up so they could see it. Smoke could feel the power radiating from it. No doubt about it, this was Franklin's key. It was also one hell of a magical talisman, more powerful than any other he had ever seen.

"I didn't buy this, you know," the man said, looking at the key fondly. "I found it in the attic of my great-uncle when he died in Philadelphia, oh, five years ago or so. I wouldn't have known what it was, but there was a note in this box. The note was from William Franklin, old Benjamin's son, the one he disowned because he took the side of the British during the Revolution. It was addressed to one of my ancestors, an early researcher into the mysteries of electricity. William gave him the key as a gift."

He looked at Smoke and MoBro, his smile widening. Smoke thought of the image of the shark that Zap had shown him the night before. "That's why I was so amazed you had heard about it. It's been forgotten in my family for generations. No one but I even knows it exists. Until now..."

Before Smoke or MoBro could react, a bolt of blue-white energy lashed out from the key, hitting both of them in the chest. For a second they were each surrounded by an aura of energy, their bodies spasming. Then they collapsed unconscious to the floor.

The man put the key back into the box. Then he stood over their prone forms. "Predictable fools," he sneered. "Collectors!" He laughed. "Tomorrow, they can discover what my partner does to collectors."

CHAPTER EIGHT

Jennifer fidgeted in the car, wishing she'd brought a book or some knitting or something. How long had it been? She glanced at her watch. About an hour since Smoke and MoBro had gone met the locksmith and gone into his shop. *They must really be having a conversation,* she thought.

She leaned back, her eyes on the door that they had entered, the fingers of her left hand tapping a rhythm on the side of the car just outside the driver's window. She could feel the tension in her body. *What was taking them so long?*

When she had dropped Smoke and MoBro off, she had gone up another block, made a u-turn and come back. There had been a parking space waiting for her just across the street from where she had let the men off, giving her a good view of the building they had entered in the middle of the next block up. Then she had sat and waited.

And was still waiting.

"I'll give them fifteen more minutes, then I'm going over there," she said to the steering wheel. It made no response.

Smoke, she know, could talk to inanimate things. But she couldn't. At least she had never tried. She was too much a nature girl. She used mechanical things when she had to, like the car in which she was sitting, but she was never entirely comfortable with them. But at the moment, she would have given anything to do what Smoke could do. Then she could ask things to tell her what was going on in that building.

She sat up. What kind of Priestess was she, sitting here, fretting, twiddling her thumbs, getting upset? She had skills, too. She could calm herself down, for one thing. She could center herself in her own power. Unless she did that, she wasn't any good to anyone, not to herself, not to Smoke or MoBro, and certainly not to her community, the Lineage, which was depending on her in this situation. And maybe she could talk to things. It was worth a try. Smoke had said not to probe the building directly, and she wasn't going to, but perhaps she could tune in and get information in other ways.

She focused her attention on her breath, not trying to breathe in any particular way, just falling into an awareness of the rhythm of her breath, letting her chest rise and fall in a natural way. As she felt herself relaxing and calming down, she then focused her attention on the energy centers in her body. Located along the axis of her spine, these centers coordinated the flow of subtle energies in and around her. Then she let her attention go another level deeper to a place of wholeness and peace from which even the energy centers emerged. Here she tapped her power at the center of her being.

She knew if she went any deeper, she might initiate the spiraling energy that would take her out of her body. But she didn't want to do that. So she held herself where she was. *I'm afraid to take this next step,* she thought. *I think it's going to hurt. I know it's going to hurt. But it's time I faced it to see what's on the other side.*

Gingerly, she reduced her shields and opened herself up to the energy of the city around her. Immediately she could feel the jangled, sharp energies of the stressful psychic smog that rose from the city. She could feel the presence of thousands of people, their thoughts and feelings bearing down on her, pressing upon her, shooting through her. She felt the helplessness, the hopelessness, the searching, the hungers, the yearnings, the suffering of people in the city. It did hurt!

She wrapped herself in her shields again, shuddering. How did Smoke do it? How did any sensitive person live in the miasma of the city?

By not being so damned sensitive! she told herself. She opened her shields up again. *There's more here than just this pain. Millions of people love cities. They delight in them. Cities are centers of culture and art, of creativity and life. All that energy is here, too, not just the suffering. And I will find it!*

The pain crashed in upon her, like a slimy, dirty flood. She steeled herself. *I will not surrender to this,* she thought fiercely. *I will resist and break through!*

DON'T!

The thought crashed through her, a psychic shout that vibrated throughout her. *What?* she thought,

Don't resist. Accept it. Let it pass through you. Surrender!

What? No! I'll be lost!

You're lost now.

She felt something huge, warm, and shaggy nudging against her, a warm breath on her ear. She opened her eyes, but nothing was there.

Buff?

Yes. Draw on my strength. Trust me. I won't let you be lost. Just let go.

She had a mental image of the huge bison shielding her from a storm. *Thanks! But if I let go, this stuff will overwhelm me.*

No! It is your fear that overwhelms you. It is your resistance that brings pain.

That's true, she suddenly realized. It's just my fear. And with that thought, she let go. She let the pain of the city sweep through her, unresisting. For a moment it was like she was drowning. *Help!* She felt Buff's strength. But then she felt something else, something...pure and bright and light, something holding her and lifting her...

And she was out the other side, in a clear space. Her Sight opened up and she could See the city before her, gleaming with vitality and radiance. *No wonder Smoke loves it,* she thought in wonder. *I could never see this before.*

Then she realized she wasn't Seeing it now, at least not through her own inner vision. She was seeing it through other eyes, even she was being embraced in a loving presence. *Where am I? Who are you?* she asked.

If I were in a forest, you'd know me. If I were on a mountain or over a sea, you'd know me.

You...you're an angel aren't you. But not the angel of a forest or a mountain. You're the Spirit of the City.

And you are a Priestess of the world, of which both forests and cities are a part.

Jennifer gulped mentally. She'd never thought of herself in those terms. More responsibility, part of her cried.

No, said the sweet voice within her. *Not more. The same. Always the same. To see the One in all things. To love with the One in all things. To serve the One in all things.*

Jennifer mentally bowed her head, but said nothing.

Yes, you have your domain in which you are most skilled, but you need not be limited to it. Joy is everywhere. Life is everywhere. There need be no boundaries to your celebration of life.

I understand.

Look at my world.

Jennifer looked. She saw herself held in the hand of a vast shining presence, whose flowing energy embraced all the city. Below her, she saw the shining lights of thousands and thousands of auras, the people living and working in the city. And she saw beings she had never seen before, spirits of the streets and skyscrapers, the underground and the parks, the machinery and the electronics. She saw them all.

I serve all of them, the Spirit of the City said. *I serve human and non-human alike in their strivings to shape a world of blessing. There is pain and fear, but there is growth and courage and vision, too. There is darkness, but there is light as well.*

I see it, she said.

Then you see into yourself. Have compassion.

Light passed before her eyes, like a cloud covering the city. Then she was back in her car. She took a deep breath, conscious of tears rolling down her cheeks. *Wow,* she thought.

Then she was aware that a strange being sat on the seat next to her, its face contorted in worry. Its body was stick-thin and jagged, while its head looked like nothing so much as a large light bulb. It looked like an old cartoon figure in an advertising poster she'd seen for an electrical company. What was it called? Reddy Kilowatt, or something like that?

"You're Zap, aren't you?" she said. "You're Smoke's ally?"

The little being nodded. Then it pointed a white gloved hand and finger towards the building down and across the street. "They're in trouble," it said. "Bad trouble, and I can't help them!"

"What kind of trouble?" Jennifer asked, her heart beginning to race.

"I'm not sure. I can't get inside to see. The ancestor blocks me."

"If you got into the building, could you see?"

"I think so."

She thought. Then she reached into her glove compartment and drew out her portable CD player. She turned it over and undid the lid to the battery slot. Taking out one of the batteries, she looked at Zap. "Can you get into this?"

Zap nodded, grinning.

"Good. Then I'll carry you in and you can do your stuff."

"Shocking!" the little being said with delight.

Oh no, she thought, it's picked up Smoke's humor.

The elemental turned into a swirl of energy and flowed into the battery on her palm, a trail of sparks following it. She felt a mild tickle in her hand. Then she put the battery in her purse, the CD back into the glove compartment, got out and locked the door. Straightening her skirt and making sure her inner shields were in place, she strode across the street.

Never send men to do a Priestess's job, she thought.

CHAPTER NINE

A little bell tinkled as Jennifer walked into the locksmith's shop. No one was in sight, but a voice called from somewhere in the back, "I'll be right out." She took advantage of being alone to take the battery out of her purse. She saw a tiny blue thread of light snake out of it and into a nearby electrical outlet.

Good luck, Zap, she thought, putting the battery back in her purse.

A door opened and a tall, slightly hunched man came in. "Yes," he said smiling. "What can I do for you?"

She smiled back. "I have a key I'd like copied. It's my car key. I locked myself out of my car yesterday and swore I'd have a spare made today. I was driving by, saw your shop, and remembered."

"I see. Well, it's always good to have duplicates. Can you show me the key?"

She took out her key ring and laid it on the counter. "It's that one," she said, pointing it out among the four other keys that were there. "Would you mind taking it off for me? Last time I tried, I broke my fingernail." She smiled sweetly at him.

"Certainly. No problem." He reached for the key ring and picked it up, but suddenly dropped it as if he'd been burned. A look of astonishment crossed his face.

"What is it?" she asked, equally startled.

"Oh, I'm sorry. Just clumsy." This time he picked up the key ring and lifted out the car key. Deftly he took it off. As he did so, he held up another key. "What is this one? It's quite unusual."

Damn! Jennifer thought. *It's the key to the temple in my house. I forgot it was on the key chain. He must feel the energy around it.* "Oh, it's just a key to an old storeroom in my house. Actually my family's house. Why? Is it special?" She tried to keep her voice nonchalant.

He looked intensely at her for a moment, then smiled again. "It's just old. I have an interest in old keys that fit unusual locks."

"I see. Well, that's what that old lock on the door is, all right. Very unusual and large. I've been thinking of replacing it with something more modern. If I do, I'll bring it in and let you see it."

"I'd be most interested, thank you. It must protect a special room, eh?"

She shrugged. "Not unless there's treasure mixed up with all my dad's boxes and papers!" She laughed. "Like I said, it's just an old storeroom."

"Of course." He turned to his workbench and began grinding a duplicate key. As he did so, Jennifer was tempted to probe a bit with her inner senses to see what she could discover, but she remembered Smoke's warning about the wards. With Zap on the loose, she didn't want to do anything that might arouse suspicions. She was afraid her temple key had already done that.

She spied a blue flash down at the base of the wall near the electrical outlet. Taking the battery out of her purse, she held it in her hand. She felt the tickle of energy as Zap flowed back into it. *Welcome back,* Zap, she thought with a deep breath of relief.

The locksmith turned around, holding up two keys. "There you are," he said. "One original and one spare. That will be five dollars even." He handed her one key, then picked up her key ring and put the original key back on it. As he did, she saw his fingers caress the temple key.

"Thank you," she said, taking the key ring from his fingers. "And if I ever replace that lock, I'll bring it in to you."

"I'd be grateful. And I do house calls. I could replace it for you."

I bet you could, she thought. "I'll keep that in mind," she said aloud, and walked out the door, the little bell tingling behind her.

She walked across the street, down the block, and got into her car. There she pulled the battery out of her purse and held it in her palm. *Maybe I should rub it like a bottle,* she thought, but then Zap flowed out and took shape beside her.

"Well?"

"I was able to get in, thanks to you. I found them! They're asleep or unconscious in a cage."

"A cage?"

"Yes, filled with electricity. And there is funny music playing."

"You mean, like jazz or rock or something like that?"

"I don't know. Human music doesn't sound right to me. This was more like my music, but not quite."

"Hmm. I wonder what that's about? Where are they?"

"In a big room, very large, the room behind those big doors."

"The garage."

"Yes."

I could call the police, she thought. *But just what would I tell them? My friends have been kidnapped and are being held prisoner in a locksmith shop? I could say there are drugs being stored in there or it's a meth lab or whatever they call it.* But she suspected Smoke would prefer to keep the authorities out of it, if possible. Not only did he like his anonymity, but there would be the danger of innocent people getting hurt by the elemental forces involved. Besides, finding Smoke and MoBro locked in a cage would certainly raise questions neither might wish to answer. *It's better for we who work with the inner worlds to solve our own problems if we can.*

Which brought her back to Smoke's original plan: breaking and entering and taking the key. And now rescuing Smoke and MoBro besides. *The only problem is that breaking and entering are not among my skill sets. What was that movie where people had new skills downloaded into their brains so they could immediately use them? Oh, yeah,* The Matrix. *Dreadful movie! Turning people into batteries. Awful.*

But that, she realized, might be exactly what the First One had in mind.

She looked down at herself. One thing was for sure. She needed different clothes for breaking and entering than the skirt and blouse she was wearing. At the least, she needed a pair of pants. She certainly didn't have time to drive home, change and drive back. She needed an alternative.

She reached down and started the car. She knew where she could find one nearby. Smoke and she were close to the same size. She'd go to his apartment and see what she could find there.

As she pulled away from the curb, she realized that Zap was still sitting patiently beside her on the seat. "Am I seeing you with my regular eyes or with my inner Sight or both," she asked the little elemental.

"With both, I think."

"Can anyone see and hear you?"

"No, only if they already have the Sight…and if I want them to," it added smugly.

It regarded her gravely as she drove. "You have decided what to do?"

"Yes. I'm going to break in to that building, rescue Smoke and MoBro, and take the key. That should prevent the magician from invoking your ancestor."

"No, it won't."

"What? Why not?" She turned the corner onto Smoke's street.

"Because he is not invoking my ancestor."

She slid into a parking place just vacated by another car in front of Smoke's apartment house. She turned off the ignition and looked at Zap. "What do you mean? There's someone else doing the invocation?"

Zap nodded, his light bulb head flickering. "Yes."

She waited. When nothing more seemed to be forthcoming, she asked, "Well, who, for heaven's sakes?"

"You."

She was thankful she was parked. Otherwise, she might have run into something in her surprise. "*Me?* What do you mean?"

"I don't mean you personally. I mean all you humans. You are invoking us all the time with your use of our energies. Your whole world invokes us and draws our world close to yours. Some of us welcome it. It opens new opportunities for us to grow and learn. Others of us, though, do not and are angry. They feel you are confining us and making us your slaves."

She thought about this. It made sense. More and more, human civilization was becoming electrified. More and more humans lived in an increasingly electronic world. It was one of the things she disliked about modern society. *Of course we're invoking them. We're mixing our world and energies with theirs.*

"I take it your ancestor is one of those who is not pleased."

Zap nodded again. "It is one of the angry ones, yes. It wants to separate the worlds again and keep them apart. It wishes to destroy your civilization. But there is more."

"More? Besides destroying civilization, there's more? I'm not sure I like the sound of that."

"It wants to correct what it sees as a mistake."

"Mistake? What mistake?"

"Humanity." Zap's voice became agitated. "Not all the First Ones agree humanity was a good idea. Your evolution is so different. Don't forget, from the elementals' point of view, you're dangerous, too. Look at the world!"

"You've got a point," said Jennifer. In her own wanderings and explorations, she had occasionally met nature spirits and elementals who were angry and upset with human beings for their polluting ways. Sometimes these entities were downright hostile and malicious. The idea of a malicious, hostile First One, though, chilled her heart. "But what about Franklin's key? It must play some role in all this. The prophecy said it was important, that we had to find it or all would be lost."

"The key was a bridge between your world and ours, between my ancestor and the man who summoned him…or was summoned by him. But the key has already been turned most of the way. Even if the key is taken, enough energy, enough momentum has built up to push the door open."

You're saying it's hopeless? Isn't there anything we can do to stop this First One from entering our world?"

"I don't know. I know that my ally cannot. He is too close to the world you humans create. Some of his power comes from the very elemental sources that my ancestor controls."

"What about MoBro?"

"He is...different. I have never encountered a human like him. Perhaps."

"And me? Can I make a difference?"

Zap looked at her strangely. "You are not of my kingdom, yet we are linked in a strange way. And you represent the powerful forces of life in this world. Yes, I think you could make a difference."

Her heart warmed a bit and she began to feel more confident. But Zap hadn't finished speaking. "Unfortunately, you are not as linked to your power as you could be. You're disconnected, so perhaps you could not make a difference after all."

"What is this?" she said, rolling her eyes to the heavens. "Everyone dump on Jennifer day?" She opened the car door. "Boy, you sure have a way of making a girl feel good about herself!"

"Sorry," said Zap, who promptly disappeared.

Jennifer stomped up to the door to the apartment building. Of course it was locked, and she had no key. She looked around. Reaching into herself, she drew on a bit of power and focused it on the door lock, willing it to open.

Nothing happened.

Oh, great!

She did it again, and once more nothing happened.

Come on, I'm a Priestess. I can always find parking places. Surely I can magic a door open.

A third try proved equally unsuccessful. But then a white, gloved finger appeared in front of her, a spark of electricity shooting from it into the door. The lock buzzed open. She sighed. "Thanks, Zap," she said.

She bounded up the stairs to Smoke's floor and walked up to his door. *Now, if only he has the same habits he'd had a couple of years ago when we were dating....*

She tried the door knob, and the door opened. Ah, she thought, some things never change. Smoke never locked his door. He just created a "don't-notice-me-I'm-not-here" aura around it so no one ever tried to open it, unless they knew his secret, of course.

She entered the apartment, feeling a curious tingling on her skin as she did so. *Mmm,* she thought, *I guess he's added some new protections just in case, but they didn't seem to bother me.*

Rummaging through his closet and drawers—he's neater and more organized than he used to be—she found a pair of dark jeans she could get into and a dark long-sleeve flannel shirt that fit her. *A bit hot for a summer evening,* she thought, putting the shirt on, *but it'll have to do.*

It was strange being in Smoke's flat by herself, surrounded by his things, his feel, his smell, his presence. Memories crowded in on her like passengers rushing onto a waiting subway. Walking to the kitchen area to make herself a cup of tea and a sandwich, sadness welled up. Her throat caught at the thoughts of what-might-have-been and what-if. She pushed them all away from her. *I can't afford such distractions. Time enough to sort things out when this is over, if there's anything at all to sort out.*

Of course, if I fail, relationships may become a moot question in the face of an elemental First One out to erase the mistake of humanity.

And Zap had implied that she would fail, or at least that nothing could really be done to stop the First One from entering. The key had already been turned, the elemental had said.

But there's a difference between a door opening smoothly and one that has to be battered open, she thought. That difference in energy might be an edge in their favor. She still felt the key had a part to play.

And what about her own part? Zap had felt some hope for her but not much. You're disconnected, he had said. That really was her problem, she admitted. She was disconnected, running away from connections, hiding out in her woods, refusing commitments.

Doesn't mean it has to stay that way. I have some time left. I can't do anything until after dark, and that's at least eight hours from now. I can work on my connections, seek out the Quatrain, do what a Priestess should do. I can prepare. It may be too late, but I'm not giving up hope yet.

The alternative was to accept failure. As she thought about it, she realized that she feared being a failure more than she feared losing herself in the immensity of the Quatrain. She'd never failed at anything to which she'd put her mind, and she knew if she started now, the consequences could be more than she could imagine.

She ate her sandwich and drank her tea, thinking through what she needed to do. When she was finished, she cleaned up the kitchen, then went about gathering some tools of her trade. She found two candles, filled a bowl with water and another bowl with some earth from one of Smoke's potted plants—*how nice he has green growing things here*—and rummaged around until she found some incense.

She took all these things to a table in his living room and made herself a small altar. When all was arranged and the incense and candles were burning, she sat down to enter her inner place. Then she remembered one other thing. *There's going to be some angry musicians tonight,* she thought. So she got up and locked his door, just in case. Satisfied, she turned off her phone, sat back down and composed herself.

As she sank into her inner self, she had a final thought. *How comfortable it feels here. It's just like being at home.*

CHAPTER TEN

The light of a practically full moon shone down brightly from a clear sky as she parked her car on the street a couple of blocks away from her target. The time was a little after two in the morning. *Just about three hours until the moon is officially full,* she thought. *All the time in the world!*

She got out, feeling both nervous and confident about the task ahead. She was nervous because, well, because she was breaking and entering, something she had never done before. She wasn't sure just what might await her. *If it's death,* she thought, *I'm well prepared.*

She was confident, though, because her meditations had gone well. At least no further problems had arisen, and while she did not feel she had been able to reach the Quatrain—*it might take a long time to repair that disconnection,* she thought sadly—she had gathered her inner allies and had felt into the spirit of the community of the Lineage, which had welcomed her gladly. It was the best she could do.

She had even taken a short nap and eaten a light dinner. She hadn't been hungry, but she knew she would need the energy. She even had brought some Power Bars she had found in Smoke's pantry.

She had also called her mother and told her most of what was going on. Her mother had been concerned, but practical as ever, had given her blessings on Jennifer's less than legal operations tonight and had promised to alert all the men and women of the Lineage who would be sending energy and support her way. Her mother also promised that if she hadn't heard from her by the next morning, she was calling the police, whether or not Smoke might like it.

She was wearing a long overcoat she'd found in Smoke's closet in order to hide the rope and crowbar she was carrying at her side, figuring that to display those things openly would attract more attention than the overcoat would. But as it turned out, no one was around.

She turned down the street running at right angles to the block with the target building. Halfway down was an alleyway for garbage trucks to rumble through, picking up the trash left behind the buildings. And there, too, she saw what she hoped would be there: a fire escape.

It was basically no more than a ladder that descended from the roof, passing by a window on the second floor, and ending about three feet or so above her. There was an extension that was designed to slide down the rest of the way to the ground.

Standing under it, she laid down the crowbar and the coiled rope. Then she pulled a dark woolen cap out of a pocket and put it on her head. It wasn't a ski mask or anything, but she hoped it would help make her less visible. She had never quite mastered Smoke's ability to turn himself unnoticeable, but then she had little use for such a skill out where she lived.

Stretching her hands up, she leaped to catch the bottom rung of the fire escape ladder. Her fingers missed it. She tried again and missed it again. She looked around for something to stand on, but the alley was bare.

She lifted the crowbar in both hands, the hook side upwards and jumped again. She jumped, and the crowbar struck the bottom of the ladder with a clang, but didn't hook it. Exasperated, she ducked into what few shadows there were, clutching the crowbar to her, hoping no one had heard the noise. *How do cat burglars do it,* she wondered.

When no one appeared to investigate what to her had seemed like a clanging of cymbals, she crept out under the ladder again. This time she put the crowbar down and picked up the rope. Holding one end of it, she threw the rest of the coil up at the ladder. It hit and fell back, not passing over the bottom rung. Rolling her eyes, she tried again, and this time it went through. Holding the two ends of the rope that now was looped over the bottom rung, she pulled on the fire escape ladder.

At first it resisted. Age, rust and neglect had done their work. But finally with a groan and clanking that she was sure would waken the dead, the ladder descended to where she could climb it. *Good grief,* she thought. *Why don't I just call him up and tell him I'm scaling his roof tonight?* But in spite of the noise, no lights went on anywhere and no one seemed interested in investigating. She suspected that her allies might be helping her out by keeping all the neighbors asleep tonight. At least she could hope.

She pulled the rope through and coiled it up again, wrapping it over her shoulder. Then, awkwardly holding the crowbar in one hand, she began climbing the ladder. She went as slowly and quietly as she could past the window, which had thick curtains pulled across it. When she reached the top, she slid the crowbar ahead of her onto the roof. She did the same with the coil of rope. Finally, she hoisted herself up, where she lay for a moment on the roof, looking up at the moon and wishing she were up there and not where she was.

She realized she felt no electrical shocks from being on the roof. Were the wards down or were they not as active here on top? She wished she could ask Zap.

Thinking of Zap, she reached into an overcoat pocket to assure herself the little battery was still there. She and Zap had decided that what had worked once today would probably work again.

Rolling over on her stomach, she came up into a crouch, looking around. There were ventilation pipes sticking up here and there, but unless she shed a hundred and thirty-four of her hundred and thirty-five pounds and lost five and a half feet off her five foot nine height, she sure wasn't going down any of them.

However, in the middle of the roof over where she knew the garage was, was a skylight.

Thank the Quatrain, she thought. *That looks perfect.*

Concerned about being seen, she crouch-walked over to the edge of the window. Lying down flat on the roof, she pulled herself towards it just enough that her eyes could peer down over the rim.

Looking down, she realized she was staring at a film of grime over the window. Years of grime, she groused to herself. Sliding back and sitting up, she saw the whole skylight was a mass of soot and grease, bird droppings and other things. There might as well have been curtains drawn over it as far as seeing anything down below went.

Well, she thought, *no one's going to see any sky through this thing and damn little light, either.*

She crawled around the sides of the skylight, feeling the edges, looking for some lock or catch that would open it up. But she found nothing. Or if it were there, it was so caked and buried in grime that she couldn't recognize it for what it was. For all practical purposes, the window was cemented to the roof.

But she had to find a way at least to see through it. As far as she could tell, it was her only hope for getting into this place.

Sighing, she took off the overcoat, transferring the battery into a pocket in her jeans. Spitting on one of the panes of the skylight, she began to furiously rub the sleeve of the overcoat on it. The fabric turned black immediately. *Oh well, I can always buy him another one later.*

After several minutes of hard scrubbing, she had cleared a small space that seemed less obscure than every other part of the window. Peering through it, she thought she could make out shadows down below, but it was dark in the garage. Still, she felt she was making progress.

Spitting some more, she applied even more pressure. Suddenly, there was a "pop", and the pane broke out of the molding to fall to the floor beneath. There was no mistaking the tinkling, cracking sound of breaking glass.

That tears it, she thought, ducking back down and lying prone on the roof. *Here come the wards, here come the electrical shocks, here come the burglar alarms, here come the police.*

But none of that happened. Silence returned and was not disturbed in any way except by her own rapid breathing, which she immediately sought to calm down.

Finally, she pushed and pulled herself forward until she could look over the edge again. Now she could see, and what she saw made her heart leap. Standing in the dark outlines of a cage, she could see Smoke looking up at her, his eyes wide with what she hoped was admiration but probably was incredulity. She couldn't see MoBro, but he was so black that he wasn't visible in the darkness anyway.

She also heard as if from a distance something faint that sounded like cats being tortured and their screams set to music, all heard over a radio station that wasn't properly in tune. *What in the world is that?*

She stuck her hand through the window and waved briefly. Smoke waved back, but it looked more like he was waving her back, telling her to get away and get out. *Fat chance of that,* she thought. *I'm the Marines.*

An idea struck her. Reaching into her pocket, she pulled out the little battery. "Zap,' she whispered to it, "I'm sending you down to Smoke. Do what you can do to help us." The battery tingled in her fingers with acknowledgement.

Reaching her hand through the opening, she tossed the battery down. Her aim was good. It would have hit Smoke on the head, but something stopped it. It bounced up and fell to the floor. *There's mesh around that cage,* she thought. She watched, but there was no streak of blue Zap-light flowing out of the battery. In fact, she couldn't even see the battery. *Something's gone wrong,* she thought.

She reached her hand, wrapped in the cloth of the overcoat, under the window pane next to the hole where the missing one had been. She pushed upward as hard as she could from such an awkward angle. She thought she felt some movement. She brought her hand out. Using the sharp edge of the crowbar, she worked away at the molding and grime around the pane, loosening it up, then she put her wrapped hand under it again and pushed up. The pane popped loose. She pulled it out. Now there were two triangles of emptiness where before there had just been one.

She reached under the skylight on the inside and felt around. This time, she was immediately rewarded. There was a catch, latched shut on the inside. Using the crowbar carefully, she was able to loosen it and then to open it. *All right!* she thought. *Now we're cooking!*

Working on the outside, she used the crowbar to hack way at the accumulated grime that was holding the skylight down. Finally, sweating from her work—the flannel shirt was definitely not helping—she pushed on the skylight and it opened up, swinging upwards with an awful squeal on old, rusty hinges. She had done it.

Throughout all this effort, Smoke had stood watching her, the awful music playing faintly in the background. From time to time, he tried signing to her, but once she realized he was telling her to run away, she ignored him. *He's going to be by god rescued by me whether he likes it or not! I'll show him who's responsible!* Finally, he gave up and sat down.

She took the rope and ran over to the nearest ventilation pipe. Tying one end of the rope around it, she ran back to the skylight. She threw the other end down to the floor two stories beneath. She would shinny down, free the men, grab the key, and then they'd all shinny back up again. Easy as getting a parking place.

That's the ticket, she thought. *Think "parking place." Easy as getting a parking place.*

Looking down one last time before taking the plunge over the edge, she could see Smoke moving about in an agitated way. He seemed to be yelling at her, but she couldn't make out his words. Strange, she thought. *Well, I'll find out what he's saying soon. Probably something typically masculine like "Be Careful!" Well, of course, I'll be careful.*

She swung her feet over the edge of the half-open skylight, ducked her head and body under the glass, gripped the rope, and began to climb down. Piece of cake, she thought, as she went carefully hand over hand.

Then the lights came on, so bright and hurtful to her eyes that she almost lost her grip on the rope. She shut her eyes tight and began to shinny down the rope even faster. Suddenly, she was assaulted by sounds, the "music" she had heard so faintly before now loud and painful in her ears. She was slipping faster down the rope, feeling its rough fiber burning into the skin of her hands.

The final blow was a bolt of electrical force striking her from somewhere, turning her world blue-white. She screamed, felt herself let go of the rope as her body jerked and spasmed. She felt herself falling.

And then there was darkness.

CHAPTER ELEVEN

Jennifer opened her eyes, her hands burning, her head bursting, the world spinning. The only good thing was there was light and she could see Smoke's face over her. She realized her head was in his lap. *Good place to be,* she thought. She closed her eyes. The awful screeching noise was still there, but not as loud.

"Jennifer! Can you hear me? What are you feeling?"

She opened one eye again, then the other. "Has the world ended yet?" she croaked.

"No." Smoke's voice was filled with relief. If she was joking, he reasoned, she couldn't be too bad.

"Feels like it!" She moaned and tried to sit up. Putting her hands on the floor beneath her, though, brought up a gasp.

"Bad rope burn," Smoke said. "Don't touch anything." He raised her up into a sitting position. She brought her hands up in front of her. They were raw and bleeding. She moaned.

"I haven't had a chance to do anything for them," he explained. "You've only just been thrown in here with us."

"How long was I unconscious?"

"Not long. No more than five minutes, I'd say. When you fell, Tremenos immediately dragged you to the cage and tossed you in to us."

"Tremenos?"

"Herman Tremenos, the world's greatest adept and magician. Or so he likes to tell us."

"What happened?"

"He knew you were coming. Bragged about it to us. He had a trap all set for you. I tried to warn you."

"I could see you shouting, but I couldn't hear anything."

He reached over and thumped the side of the cage. It was, she saw, a clear, transparent plastic, surrounded by a tightly woven metal mesh. "This cage is nearly soundproof and energy proof. It's a modified Faraday Cage, which keeps electromagnetic energies from going in or out. We're basically inside a giant magnetic field."

"Can you journey?"

"Hardly. Hear that noise? Just try going inward with that squawking at you all the time. Besides, there are subtle energy fields at work here too that press against us. It's a multi-level cage, complements of the First One. Who, by the way, is the one who zapped you on your way down."

"Not enough to kill me."

"No, I gather than comes later."

She grinned up at him. "Not now. He's made a huge mistake."

"Oh?"

"Yeah. Now that we're together, he hasn't got a chance!"

Smoke laughed. Then he looked at her searchingly. "Do you mean that?"

"Of course." She started to squeeze his arm, then winced with the pain.

Smoke, a silly grin on his face, turned his head. She saw MoBro sitting against the side of the cage, looking as peaceful as ever. *Didn't anything rile this man?* "Do you think you can do it?" Smoke asked his friend.

MoBro signed, <I think so>, and slid over next to Smoke and Jennifer. Smoke said to her, "When we saw your hands, MoBro told me he thought he could heal them. We just hadn't had a chance before you came to."

MoBro took her right hand gently and held it between his own. He seemed to disappear inside himself. She could feel peace radiating from him, even with the awful noise surrounding them. A soothing coolness spread over her hand, different from anything she had felt before. She knew what it was like to be healed. Usually she felt heat from the healing energies. But not now, not this time. She closed her eyes and just floated on the cool river that seemed to be flowing through her. Not only did her hand feel better, but all her aches and pains were subsiding.

Finally, MoBro laid her right hand down and picked up her left one. The process repeated itself. When he was done, he sat back, a satisfied smile on his face. She looked at her hands. Fresh, pink new skin covered her palms. There were no scars, no evidence at all that they had ever been injured.

"That's...that's remarkable." She looked at the big man. "Thank you." MoBro nodded. <You're welcome,> he signed.

"What I don't understand is how you could do that with all this screeching going on."

Smoke picked up her hands to look at them. "Remember, I told you that he followed a discipline of silence. It's not just that he keeps silent. It's that he is silence in some strange and wonderful way."

Jennifer saw movement outside the cage. Getting to her feet, she saw the tall, hunched locksmith walking over to them. He pulled what looked like a cell phone from his pocket and held it up to his mouth and ear. When he spoke, his voice emerged from a speaker at the top of the cage some two feet above their heads.

"Ah, welcome to our new guest. I thought you might be back, my dear. Did your new key work all right?" He looked up at the ruined skylight. "Obviously you didn't need it for that lock!" He chuckled. "Which reminds me. When this is over, I really do want to see that old key of yours. Something tells me it opens some very interesting doors itself." A look of avarice and hunger crossed his face momentarily. "But that pleasure shall have to wait until our current business is concluded."

"There are laws against kidnapping," Jennifer snapped.

"There are laws against breaking and entering, too," the man, Herman Tremenos, replied.

"But my friends didn't break in. You took them prisoner."

"Well, in a manner of speaking. I think they were planning to rob me of a very valuable artifact. Let's just say, I took preventive measures. I'm sure the police will understand...if there are any police after today." He looked at his watch. "Very soon, now, too. We are nearing the world's last hour, at least in its current form."

"Tremenos," said Smoke. "You don't know what you're doing. You think you'll survive the coming of the First One? Stop kidding yourself. You're just food like the rest of us. You've just been a tool in its plans.

Don't go through with it, for your own sake."

"For my own sake? How charitable of you, granting me the right to act selfishly, appealing to my own good. But my good is well in hand. You think I don't know what I'm dealing with? I know all too well, and I welcome it."

He came up to the cage, peering in at them. "I know you think I'm insane. Maybe I am. But the fact is that I am more like my partner than I am like you."

"You're a living being, like us," Jennifer protested.

"Living, yes. Like you, no. Humans are all messy beings. They ooze and slurp and slush with fluids, they go this way and that way, they want this, they want that. They are all incoherent, without pattern, without cohesion. They are hot and wet, like the steamy oceans they come from. Electricity is cold and dry. It moves cleanly. It is stark and brilliant like the stars; it is pure, like the depths of space. It is orderly. It is what I yearn for, what I am!"

He paced back and forth. "This is the part in the story when the villains gloat, isn't it? When they explain their motives, reveal their plans? But this is no story, and I am no villain. When I found Benjamin Franklin's key, I had been a student of magic for years. I had studied the elemental kingdoms, finally realizing that only the realm of the electricals held what I needed, gave me what I wanted. And when I found Franklin's key, the key that had bound their realm to ours in the first place, forcing them into engagement with warm and slimy life, I knew I had something they wanted. Something that would return their realm to them. If this key had bound them, it could free them."

His foot kicked something that rolled across the floor and struck the side of the cage. Looking down, he walked over to it and picked it up. It was the small battery from Jennifer's CD player. "Interesting," he said. "I wonder how this got in here? No matter. It is a sign." He held it up before them. "You see. This is what I mean. This is a symbol of bondage, a cage to hold electricals and make them serve us. The whole human civilization has become like this battery, a cage to bind electricals. In just a little over an hour, I will shatter that cage and be their liberator. And they will thank me. Oh yes, they will thank me!"

"They will kill *you*, you fool!" Smoke challenged.

The man laughed. "You think I fear that? That was my bargain! They will make me one of them. Oh, I will have rulership over this world.

That's what a mad villain is supposed to say, isn't it? But it will be as an electrical, not as a human." He put the battery into his pocket. "Now I must go to prepare the final stage. Enjoy your last hour of life!" Grinning, he walked out of the room.

"That man's crazy," Smoke said. "No way he's going to become an elemental."

MoBro spoke. "He might be right. It's not impossible."

As always when his friend spoke, Smoke felt like something strange and miraculous had happened. "All right," he replied. "It's not impossible. But....but...Hell, how he must hate his humanity."

He turned to Jennifer. "What did he mean when he talked about some special key you had?"

"It's the key to the temple attached to my house. I forgot it was on my keychain and he felt its energy when he duplicated a key for me."

"He duplicated a key for you?"

"Part of my super plan to rescue you." She told him about the events of the afternoon, how she had smuggled Zap into the building inside the battery from her CD player, how Zap had found them and told her where they were, how she had gone to his apartment and borrowed his clothes.

"I thought those looked familiar," Smoke said. Then he added, "Tremenos told us you'd be coming."

"How did he know?"

"Because of that key. He doubted an ordinary person would have a talisman that powerful. Having you show up a couple hours after he captured us made him suspicious. I don't think he knew for sure you were coming back or were connected to us, but he was prepared just in case. I'll give him that, he's very careful and well-prepared. And his own magical abilities have been augmented by the First One. He could see you clairvoyantly as you went about trying to get into this place."

"Well, I never claimed to be a good second-story woman."

At that moment, Tremenos returned, wheeling in a metal table in. On it was something large covered in a cloth. "The final element," he said, raising the cell phone to his lips. He positioned the table under the remains of the skylight. "The cloth is only for dramatic purposes," he said. "Something to provide a "Ta-Da!" moment for our amusement. You can probably guess what's under it."

"Franklin's key," said Smoke.

"The very one! Very astute of you, as befits the doomed hero. Shall I tell you what's about to happen? In about fifteen minutes, the ritual will commence. Of course, very little will happen here. No lighting of candles, no incantations, nothing like that. But on the inner, where the two realms meet, much will be happening. You'll feel the power, I'm sure…or maybe not, inside the cage."

He walked over to the side of the room. There Jennifer could see another wheeled table. This one had a black box on it from which electrical wires snaked out and down into outlets in the walls. He wheeled the table over beside the first one.

"Then, my wondering guests, I shall take out Franklin's key with an appropriate flourish, dedicate it to my partner, and place it into this box here. This is specially designed to transmit current out into the electrical grid, out into the world."

"The First One is going to enter our world through Franklin's Key," said Smoke.

"In a manner of speaking. The key has symbolic value as much as anything. The key that once bound becoming the key that releases. Poetic, don't you think? It's like the red carpet that one spreads before the feet of a king for him to walk on from the palace to his chariot. He could walk across the ground anyway, but this way gives him more power, more pleasure."

He looked at his watch. "Ah, look at the time. How it flies when we're not noticing. If you have any last words for each other, I suggest this be the time to say them. My partner is arriving." He threw the phone to the floor and stepped on it, smashing it to pieces. Then he withdrew from a pocket of his jacket a pair of safety glasses with dark lenses.

"I can feel it," Jennifer whispered. It was like seeing a vast storm appearing over a mountain, the black clouds beginning to bear down on her. Only she wasn't seeing it. She was feeling it.

"I do, too, "said Smoke. He took her hand. "There must be something we can do."

"I'm sure there is, but I can't think what it is just now!"

"Then I suggest you hurry. I'm just smoke; you're the Priestess!"

But time had run out. Streaming through the skylight, smashing and melting what was left of the glass and frame after Jennifer's depredations, came a flash of actinic light, like fire from a cold sun. It filled the room, causing them to shut their eyes to keep from being blinded, Even then, the brilliance was painful enough that they had to turn away.

They could hear a roaring sound even through the soundproofing of the cage. Stealing quick glimpses, it was like seeing a tornado of lightning swirling through the room, with Tremenos standing at its calm center.

Then the sound and light diminished. Jennifer, Smoke, and MoBro all opened their eyes cautiously. The whirling had stopped, but filling the room was a large presence. It was shapeless, formless, but they could feel its cold sentiency aware of everything that was happening. They could feel the pressure of a mind that was cold , logical and brilliant...and totally inhuman. Standing in the midst of this presence was Tremenos, his goggles now removed, surrounded by a nimbus of glowing blue-flame, his face ecstatic. He glanced in their direction, smiled, and with a graceful bow and a flourish, he removed the cloth from the box on the table.

Tremenos reached into the plain box that had been thus revealed and withdrew a large brass key. Franklin's key, now glowing with magical force and power. He raised it up to the presence before him, and they could see tendrils of power flowing from the First One, caressing the key in an almost human way, causing it to glow even more.

Once more, Tremenos turned to them, raising the key mockingly above his head. Jennifer felt her hopes lowering in equal measure. He turned to place the key in the transformer box.

"This would be a good time to do something before it's too late," Smoke shouted.

"I think we've passed 'too late!'" Jennifer said.

Suddenly something burned her leg like a branding iron, and the pain of it made her jump.

Which was when hell broke loose.

CHAPTER TWELVE

Everything happened at once.

As Tremenos raised the Franklin key to place it in the black box, he was suddenly surrounded with blue-white sparks as a miniature lightning bolt lanced out of his pocket and struck him. His hands convulsed, and the key went flying across the room as he fell to his knees.

At that moment, MoBro came up behind Smoke and Jennifer and grabbed both of them in his arms, hugging them to his chest. They were immediately plunged into the most blissful silence and peace. Leaning close to her ear, MoBro whispered to Jennifer, "You can save us. Remember, electricity is part of nature, and you are a priestess of nature."

I AM a priestess of nature, she thought. Thinking this, she impulsively thrust her hand into her pocket to touch the key to the temple room in her home. It was burning hot, the source of the pain in her leg. But as she touched it, the heat and the pain went away, and with them, the world around her as well.

Jennifer found herself in her home, standing before the door to the Priestess's room. The door was closed and locked. She held the key in her hand. On the other side of that door she could feel the power of the Lineage, the power of the Quatrain. It was a power that had been around her all her life, one she had tapped into unconsciously as her own talents and power grew. It was a power that had descended on her when she became Priestess, frightening her with its demands, its responsibilities, its awesomeness. It had been as if she had been paddling a canoe all her life on a placid lake and then suddenly found herself adrift in the middle of the ocean, great waves towering above her.

She had retreated. She knew it. Fear had constricted her, and shame had followed, feelings she had denied by calling them personal freedom and choice.

She looked down at herself. She was wearing the medallion of the Priestess. The door was before her, beckoning her, inviting her. All she had to do was put the key in the lock, turn it, and step in.

And surrender my life forever.

But if I don't, there will be no life for anyone. I really have no choice.

"You always have choice," a familiar voice said. She turned. Aunt Iris was standing beside her. "You must have choice. You cannot be human without it."

"But a Priestess has no choice. She obeys the Quatrain."

"Is that what you think? Then you are wrong. The Quatrain lives for choice, for freedom, for the sovereignty of each person."

"But, I have to surrender..."

"To what? All choice is a surrender, a surrender to what you choose, to what you care for, to what you love, to what you will serve and defend."

Her Aunt looked at her with loving eyes. "You're not afraid to surrender, my silly girl. You're afraid of the power. You're afraid you'll make a mistake. You're afraid of making the wrong choice, that you'll surrender to the wrong thing. I know. I felt it, too. Every person feels it sometime."

"But what can I do?"

"Trust. It's what makes a person a Priestess or a Priest. You have to trust."

"The Quatrain?"

"No, my dear. Yourself."

Her Aunt disappeared.

"Aunt Iris! Don't go..." But she knew she was alone. Alone to make a choice. Alone to trust herself...or not.

Jennifer put the key in the lock and turned it.

The door opened.

There was no room on the other side. There was a boundless plain stretching towards infinity. On one side of it was a vast city filled with millions of people spread out as far as she could see. On the other side was an equally vast forest, filled with millions of animals and plants, stones and mountains, lakes and rivers. She didn't know how she could see them all at once, but somehow she did. She was standing on a road that passed between these two, stretching off to infinity as far as she could tell. Ahead of her, it was crossed by another road joining the city and the forest.

In front of the crossroads formed where these two roads came together stood her mother and her aunt and all the other members, living and dead, of her Lineage. Beyond the crossroads, she could see Buff standing and Peekaru was flying overhead. Other spirit beings were there as well. This is my community, she thought. *All of it is my community. As Smoke said, it's where my power lies. It holds my power for me. It holds power for all of us.*

Above the crossroads, something appeared to her view. Something alive. Something majestic. Something powerful. *The Quatrain,* she thought. *I can see it.*

As she watched, the Being gestured, and from the forest a great tree arose. It gestured again, and from the city a disk of shining gold spun up into the air. The disk and the tree came together and merged to become a giant copy of her medallion.

Then the being gestured a third time, and from the crossroads itself four diamond shapes emerged, one from each road, taking the shape of a star—or of the crossroads. It burned itself into the center of the tree in the disk.

Jennifer nodded, *And now I know what this medallion means.*

Smiling, she stepped through the door. *I surrender,* she thought. *I choose you all.*

Light surrounded her, and instead of becoming lost, she was discovered.

****

Smoke looked around. One moment he had been standing in the cage, watching a First One about to seize and transform the world. Now he was in his apartment. Wondering, he looked around. Everything here was precious to him. It was part of his world, a good world.

Following an impulse, he went out into the hallway and up the stairs to the very top. In the highest hallway, there was an emergency escape with a ladder that led to the roof. He often used it when he wanted to look out over the city or just sit under the stars and moon at night.

He opened the door and went out, climbing up the ladder and stepping onto the roof. Walking to the edge, he looked out over his city.

Except it wasn't his city.

Or not just his city. Spread out before him were all the cities of the world, in all the ages of the world. From the mud huts of ancient Ur to the skyscrapers of New York, they all were there. And above them floated an angel, the most magnificent he had ever seen. It looked at him. "You know me."

"Yes."

"Who am I?"

"You are the Spirit of my city."

"What else?"

"You are the Spirit of all cities, of all the ways human beings strive to create civilization for themselves."

"And you are?"

"A servant of the City."

"Of what City?"

"Of all Cities, of the City that is within all cities, of the City that lies like a dream and yearning at the heart of all cities. I am your servant."

"No. You are my brother." The angel disappeared.

For Smoke, it seemed that all the cities in the world drew together and become one vast, universal City, a womb in which human consciousness and much else besides could grow and gestate and be reborn again and again in a search for perfection. And as he watched, that City rushed into him, into his heart, filling him with its presence.

Light surrounded him, and he was known.

****

MoBro looked about himself and smiled with deep and unalloyed pleasure. He knew where he was. He was home.

He was in the heart of the mountain, in the hall of the Mountain King, the realm of the Mountain Spirit. He was in the depths of the earth, embraced by stone, one with the deep silence at the heart of things. He was at the heart of the planet, where molten rock spun and a great magnetic field was born to wrap around the planet like wings shining in space.

He was in the Mountain that stood at the center of the universe, the axis around which all things revolved.

Light surrounded him, and he was home.

****

Jennifer emerged from the light. On her chest, her medallion glowed, but no brighter than her heart. She looked about and saw she stood at a crossroads. Paths between the infinite worlds of creation radiated from this place. She could look down them and see the cosmos unfolding in infinite diversity and wonder. But four great roads formed the cross. To her right were all the realms of humanity, to her left all the realms of nature and the non-human worlds. Behind her were the infinite worlds of spirit. And before her was...the Promise, the unknown realm constantly emerging, constantly being discovered, constantly being revealed.

And where she stood was where they met. Here was where they come together, not to become one but to become partners, co-creators, fellow discoverers and shapers of the Promise. Here was the place of Choice and Trust from which new worlds emerged.

This was the place of the Quatrain, the Spirit of the unfolding, fostering heart of the cosmos itself, the First One of First Ones, First

Servant of the One. She felt its presence in her heart.

To one side, she saw Smoke, the Universal City burning in his heart. Behind him, the First One that was the spirit of unfolding Humanity itself held him in its fire.

On the other side, she saw MoBro, the Universal Mountain from which all planets are formed solid in his soul. Behind him, the First One that was the spirit of the Earth held him in its depth and Silence.

With her power, she reached out to them and drew them to her side, knowing each of them as a part of Nature, part of who she was. Then she stepped forward into time and space, into the Promise…

…and all three of them were standing in the cage. Around them, white noise screeched, seeking to block their passage into spirit. Around them, energies wove a barrier against them, an imprisonment for their minds and spirits as well as their bodies.

Beyond them a human screamed in frustration as a small electrical elemental shocked him again and again, and a glowing key spun across the room.

Before them, a glowing, formless, electric presence pulsed in the room, hungry, angry, and insane, temporarily helpless as it was caught in the middle of a transition between the worlds.

They looked at each other and nodded.

MoBro stretched out his hands and spoke, and his voice was like the voice of all the mountains, as irresistible as glaciers that flowed down them, as deep as their roots in the heart of the world. It was as if Silence itself spoke and yet remained Silent.

"STOP!" he said, and everything stopped.

The noise stopped.

The energies of the cage stopped.

The little elemental stopped his zapping and retreated into his battery.

The man stopped his screaming and fell to the floor.

The electric presence stopped its turbulence.

Silence reigned.

Smoke reached out and touched the cage. Its energy flowed into him, and it shattered, falling away.

There was a moment of silence. Then two voices, one human, one not, screamed in unison. "No!" The inhuman voice lashed out in all directions, its energy a wave of anger and hatred beating against the walls of the room. The smell of burned and smoldering wood filled the room, and here and there small flames began to appear.

A figure rose up from the floor, its face and hands burned, its clothes smoking. Like a demon from some nether pit of hell, it stood there before them, ignoring the electric hell that swirled and pulsed behind it. It raised an object in its hands. Jennifer saw it was Franklin's key.

"No! I must prevail!" Tremenos's voice was like a banshee, hardly human. He thrust out the key, and bolts of electrical energy shot from it towards the humans...

...and were stopped by a wall of light streaming from the temple key Jennifer still held in her hand. "No one prevails against a Priestess and her community, Tremenos," she declared. "My key against your key, little wizard!"

The man screamed as the energy from the Franklin key was caught, held, and then rebounded against him. Electrical light engulfed him, and he collapsed. The Franklin key spun away from him, its glow vanished.

The First One roared with rage, lightning flashing at them. It moved towards them to engulf them in its fire, but drew back as a large, brightly colored form darted down at it from somewhere, its talons slashing and beak rending, and a large, shaggy buffalo moved protectively between it and the humans. It was joined by something that made Jennifer think of the Hulk carved from granite. "Peekaru!" she shouted. "Buff!" The other being, she realized, had to be MoBro's mountain spirit.

"Tally Ho!" yelled the much-more-than-life sized parrot in its incongruous voice as it made another pass at the elemental.

Her flank protected, power moved through Jennifer. Knowing that Smoke and MoBro were being similarly Called and used, she saw herself walking out from her forest and into the city. But the city was not strange or alien. It was just another forest, another place where life was. She felt herself in a place where Life was everything, filled with potential and waiting for that potential to be released.

She looked at the raging elemental before her and saw in it not an enemy but a part of nature caught as she had been in a fear of surrender, a fear of change, a fear of the future. Drawing on her power, she reached out to it and embraced it. It slashed at her with bolts of lightning, but none of them injured her. There was pain, but it passed as soon as she felt it. She drew this being into the power of the crossroads, into meeting and engagement with the diversity of life, with the Light of the Promise. It flowed into this immensity and disappeared, like a drop of ink dispersing throughout the ocean.

Smoke, likewise, found himself stepping forward on a wave of power, stepping into the streets of his city. Before him, trapped in a building that was no part of its realm, was a fiery electric elemental. Seeing its distress, he reached out in all directions, calling to him the life of the city. And from all around, beings of energy and light, electricity and magnetism, machinery and skyscrapers and plumbing and wires, and all the things that allow a city to live on all its levels streamed to his call. Like bees around a beekeeper, they swarmed over him and around him, and his heart received them all in love. And from him they moved to the one who was in distress, who thrashed about neither here nor there, caught between the realms, and they surrounded it. They flowed around it, holding it, creating a barrier between it and the world of form, letting its energy flow into theirs, sweeping it to the far ends of the earth, where it disappeared.

MoBro stepped out of the heart of the earth, carrying great strands of magnetism with which he embraced the raging being before him, drawing it close to him. And as he held this being to himself, he let himself sink into the earth, deep into the silences at the core of the world. There it could no longer rage. It dissolved into Stillness and disappeared.

And when they were done, they were themselves again, alone in a room lit only by moonlight and the memory of vast and loving presences. A haze from smoldering wood swirled around them. The building was beginning to burn, though not yet so much that they were in danger.

"Gaaaa," said Smoke, bending over, his body shaking with the release of power. "That was....awesome. I'd rather not do that every day!"

"Not yet anyway, "said Jennifer, equally spent. Only MoBro seemed relatively unaffected, though in the moonlight he seemed pale, as if the dark chocolate of his skin had been mixed with milk.

Looking around, they saw Tremenos's body crumpled on the floor. Bending over him, MoBro felt for a pulse, then looked at Jennifer and shook his head.

"What's this?" said Smoke, bending over a dark lump. Reaching down, he picked it up. It was hot to the touch, but not unbearably so. It was a half-melted piece of brass, with the upper half in the shape of a loop with a stem.

It was the remains of the Franklin key.

"Well, there goes a bit of Americana," said Jennifer, walking over and looking at it. "Too bad."

"All for the better, I think. This was one piece of our history that was dangerous. No more though. It's dead." Jennifer knew it was true. There was no energy in it or radiating from it at all. It was just a lump of brass. "Nevertheless," Smoke added, "I think I'll keep it just in case."

"Good idea," Jennifer said.

In the distance, they could hear the wail of sirens. "Someone's called the fire department."

"Our cue to leave."

But just then a trail of blue fire emerged from the pocket of Tremenos's jacket. It spiraled up, quickly becoming Zap. The little elemental was grinning broadly. "Zap zapped, right?" he asked.

Jennifer clapped her hands. "Zap, you are the hero of the day. I shall write a book about you! I was afraid we had lost you!"

"No, I lay hiding in the battery until it was time to zap."

"You were magnificent!" said Smoke.

"I was charged!" said Zap, grinning and spinning about, celebratory sparks flying in all directions.

MoBro beamed at the little elemental, then reached down and pulled the battery from the dead man's pocket. He gave it to Smoke. <A souvenir,> he signed. Zap immediately flowed into it. "No, my new home," he called back.

The sirens were definitely closer.

"So do we climb up my rope?" asked Jennifer.

"No, we know where the door is," said Smoke.

"What? Just stroll out? That's it? No dramatic exit?"

"Can you shinny up that rope right now?" Smoke demanded skeptically.

She looked up, then shook her head ruefully. "Well…no. Not tonight. I've had enough!" "Me, too."

"But I do have my car up the block."

MoBro clapped them both on the shoulders. "Then let's go," he said softly, pushing them towards the exit as flames began to catch in earnest along the walls around them.

A few minutes later, they were in the car and heading down the street, fire engines passing them going in the other direction. As Jennifer drove, Smoke leaned over and said, "It's a long way back to your home.

You can spend today at my place. Tonight, too."

She looked over at him, one eyebrow going up. "Is that a proposition?"

"If you'd like. It worked for Persephone and Hades. You know, two people from two realms getting together."

"Only if we change the myth and let Hades spend time in Persephone's realm as well."

"I think he can handle that," Smoke replied with a grin. And in the light of the new day, two sets of fingers found each other and entwined.

David Spangler

STARHEART

Slowly, taking care that each step was carefully placed so as not to make a sound, Dom, Prince of the Blood and Heir to the White Throne of Ramakan, advanced upon his foe. Somewhere else in the forest, he knew Lord Sukai, his Quiver Brother, and the Elven Rangers of Vellian, were moving into position with equal stealth, ready to deliver their blow upon the dreaded Umagh. Ahead of him, he could see the green, elephantine skin of an Umagh guard just beyond the forest's edge.

Crouching by a thick *thaline* bush with its blood-red berries, he readied his sword. When the signal came, he would rush forward and kill the guard with a blow to the base of his neck, knowing that Sukai and his forty Rangers would be doing the same thing all around the perimeter of the Umagh fortress where the Elven Queen Mishta and her human ward, the Princess Serradel, were being held prisoner. He could feel excitement coursing through his body.

The shrill whistle seemed to come from everywhere. Without pause, Dom leaped from his cover, swinging his broadsword as the Umagh stood, bewildered by the sudden noise. His stroke was good, as befitted a student of the High Weaponmaster, Lord Strober, and he felt his blade sink deep into the muscle and bone of the guard's thick neck. Dark green blood gushed out, and the Umagh collapsed without a sound at his feet where it proceeded to vanish as if it had never been.

Startled, Dom stepped back. Looking around, he realized that everything around him, the trees, the boulders, even the ground, was fading away into darkness. He wondered if some foul magic was at work, though as far as he knew no wizard was present at the fortress. He raised his blade but dizziness overcame him. He felt a moment of vertigo as his world dissolved into blankness and then back into light.

"Time to go, boys," a woman's voice said cheerily as Dom blinked his eyes.

"You'll have to finish your adventure later."

Dominic Stewart shook his head to clear it. The transition from Avatar to Real Self was usually much smoother. Being dumped so abruptly out of *alarte* left him feeling disoriented and woozy. Looking up at his mother standing in the door to the stateroom he shared with Sukai, he suspected she had done it on purpose. She had made no secret of the fact she thought the two boys spent too much time in *alarte* playing imaginal games. But what else was there to do in the three weeks it took to travel from Earth to Titan Station?

Across the room, he could see his best friend, Sukai, holding his head in his hands, his head-crest drooping. The Vellian took a deep breath. "You did not have to use the emergency cut-off, Second Mother," he said reproachfully. "The return to this reality did not need to be so.... sudden."

"Oh, I'm sorry, boys. Is that what I did?" Dom's mother said innocently. "Well, you know me and remotes. I always seem to press the wrong button!" She waved at the thin *alarte* rod standing upright on a tripod in the middle of the room, lights twinkling up and down its length. "I apologize, Sukai, but you and my son need to get yourselves ready. We have just arrived at Titan Station."

"Which means," interrupted Dom, "if the captain immediately sends the rendezvous signal back to earth, Sukai's parents should arrive in the scout ship in about an hour and twenty-five minutes from now."

Sukai looked up at him with a frown. "How do you know this, Earth Brother?"

Dom grinned. "It's simple, and if you really were a Vulcan instead of just looking like one with your pointy ears, you'd understand. At Saturn's current distance from our planet," he paused, doing rapid calculations in his head, "it takes an hour and twenty minutes or so for radio waves to travel home. Assuming they left immediately upon receiving the signal, the scout ship with your parents should show up a couple of minutes later." He smiled at his mother.

"All right, showoff," she said, smiling back. "All basic information the son of two astrophysicists-turned-ambassadors should know. I suppose spending time in *alarte* isn't rotting your eighteen-year old brain." She turned to Sukai. "And the *Filimal* is here, too!"

The lanky Vellian teenager looked up, his head crest suddenly rising up in excitement, and smiled. "The *Filimal*! At last! Now we will not have to live like *ferraki*!" His crest fell in embarrassment. "I'm sorry! I meant no disrespect..."

"It's all right, Sukai," Dom's mother said. "No offense taken." She laughed. "I've never been on one of your Tarnships but believe me, I know how close-quartered our own vessels are. The *Abraham Lincoln* is one of the largest of our fleet but it's still cramped even to me. For you, well...I don't know about the *ferraki*, but our expression is 'like sardines in a can.'"

"Close enough, Mother," Dom said, remembering pictures Sukai had shown him of clusters of tiny rodent-like creatures all jammed into narrow underground burrows. "So when do we board the *Filimal*? Or do we go over to Titan Station first?"

"You have a choice. When they arrive, your father and mother will go directly to Titan Station, Sukai. There is a diplomatic reception there celebrating our mission as the first humans to travel to Vella. Lots of boring speeches and toasts, I have no doubt, all being broadcast back to Earth. "

"Cool! A party," Dom said. "His tone suggested that it would be anything but."

"Well, a modest one, anyway. But while we're involved a shuttle from the *Filimal* will come here to the *Abe* to pick up the various supplies and materials that are going with us. It will return to the Tarnship as soon as it's loaded and then pick us up at the Station after the celebrations are over. You two can hop a ride with it and go directly to *Filimal* if you want. No need for you to go to Titan Station unless you want to join the reception."

Sukai stood up, the crest on his head, still erect with excitement, nearly brushing the top of the seventy-four inch high stateroom ceiling. An adult Vellian, Dom knew, would have had to stoop in order to stand anywhere in the *Abraham Lincoln*. "Oh, we must go with the shuttle," Sukai said, his eyes alight. "I cannot wait to show you the Tarnship!"

Plus it will get you out of this cramped human ship quicker, Dom thought, but he didn't say it. The fact that Sukai could have traveled almost instantaneously in a Vellian ship from Earth to Saturn but instead had made the three-week journey in the *Abraham Lincoln* just to be with him said volumes about their friendship. It made Dom love his alien brother all the more.

"But seeing Titan Station would be exciting, too, Sukai. It's the only Station that our two peoples designed and built together. It's very different from Ganymede Station which we visited on that field trip, and much bigger!"

Sukai grinned. "Well, we needed to have a place where we could stand upright when meeting you short people." Because the Tarnships could carry much more cargo and building materials than human skip-ships, there'd been no need to stint on space when Titan Station had been built; further, Vellian engineers seemed to approach everything from an artistic perspective. The result was that the furthest human outpost in the solar system was extravagant—some even said flamboyant and outrageous—in its design and construction.

"It would be fun to see the result," Dom urged.

Sukai shook his head. "No. We would have more fun going to the *Filimal*." The Vellian's head crest bent sideways in what Dom knew meant stubborn determination. "I have no desire to listen to speeches, no offense, Second Mother."

"None taken, Sukai," Margaret said. "I don't much like them myself, and I have to give one!" She laughed. "So have you decided then? Are you taking the shuttle to the Tarnship?"

Dom looked at Sukai, who nodded vigorously. "All right, you Vulcan space elf, we'll do it your way." Sukai grinned and clapped his hands together, his head crest standing upright in excitement and pleasure.

"Well, then, that's settled," Dom's mother said. "So get your gear together and report to the shuttle bay." She gave both boys a hug. "I'll see you on the *Filimal*." She turned and went out the door.

Sukai gripped Dom's arm, though carefully. Dom knew that with his strength, the Vellian could have snapped the bone easily. It was one of things Sukai had been carefully taught by his parents: *humans are fragile*. "Dom, I didn't want to say anything in front of your mother. I know she's not happy when you spend time in *alarte* with me. But my family has a private *alarte* room on board the *Filimal* that makes this," he picked up the sparkling wand on its tripod, "seem like...well, like the toy that it is."

"So while our parents are listening to boring speeches..."

"We'll be having the best adventures ever!"

****

Margaret Graham Stewart hurried down the narrow corridor towards the section where the crew quarters were. She had little time before she had to be ready to join her husband in transferring over to Titan Station. Still, now that the Tarnship had arrived, it was important that she have one last attunement with Maria and Catheryn. What they were going to attempt, if discovered, would create more than a mere diplomatic incident. It could precipitate a crisis that would severely alter or even sever the relationship between humanity and the Vellians. *But if we're successful,* she reminded herself, *it could mean humanity will have the knowledge at last to gain the stars.*

She came to an unmarked door. She knocked, and the door was immediately opened. The room she entered was small, but then all rooms aboard the Lincoln were small. Skip-ships, by the nature of the technology that allowed them to momentarily achieve faster-than-light travel for short distances, put a premium on mass and thus on space. Crews learned to make do with cramped quarters, much like living and working on a Terran submarine. In this room, one wall held a digital frame, currently showing an alpine meadow with towering, snow-covered peaks beyond, giving a sense of spaciousness to the small living area. One wall held bunk beds, while the other two walls were filled with shelves which, aside from a few personal items, mostly contained a variety of potted plants. In the center were a small table and three chairs.

Maria White Feather, a young woman her own son's age, sat in one of the chairs, smiling as Margaret entered. Dr. Catheryn Raveneye, Maria's mother, stood by the door that she had just opened. Well-known for her research in low-gravity biology while living at Lunar Colony, she had been selected to manage the hydroponic farms on Titan Station. Since the assignment was for a minimum of two years, she had been given permission by the Station co-commander, Jeremiah Dark, to bring her daughter, who was in any event following in her mother's scientific footsteps. In fact, the potted plants all represented experiments she'd been conducting over the three-week voyage under her mother's supervision.

Margaret knew, however, that it was other qualifications than their scientific expertise that had led Jeremiah to bring these two women to Titan Station at this time.

"Margaret!" Catheryn said, closing and locking the door behind her. Relief was evident in her voice. "We weren't sure you'd be able to make it. We were preparing to go on without you."

Margaret smiled. "I needed to be with you, Catheryn, but none of us have much more than an hour before the shuttle departs for Titan."

"Then we should start." Catheryn Raveneye said, pulling out and sitting down in one of the two available chairs.

As Margaret took her place at the table, the younger woman reached across and touched her hand. "I'm going to miss you, Margaret. Who knows when we'll see you again?"

"I'll miss you, too, Maria, and you, Catheryn." She sighed. "I don't know when either. The ambassadorship is scheduled to last a Terran year, and then the project will be evaluated to see if it is working out for us to be on Vella. If so, we may well stay indefinitely. If not, then Adrian and I will be home again by next Christmas. Of course, if we're successful in what we're planning here..." She shrugged.

"The future will take care of itself, Margaret, if we do our work properly now. The Path only demands we take the next step."

"Of course, Catheryn." Margaret squeezed both women's hands.

Maria opened a drawer set into the table and pulled out a circular object made of wood, string, and feathers and laid it on the table between the three of them. It looked like a traditional Native American dream catcher, about seven inches in diameter. At its center was a small cradle of silver supported by an intricate web of threads.

"The Hoop," said Maria. "Symbol of the interconnectedness of all life throughout the universe."

Catheryn then reached into a pocket and drew out a small silk bag. Inside was a jade box. Opening it, she withdrew a pale blue crystal with a star-shape shining within it. "The Star-Stone," she said. "Would you like to do the honors, Margaret? After all, this rightfully belongs to you."

"I appreciate that, Catheryn. One last time, then, before I journey to the stars themselves, and it passes to you. I know you will keep it safe." She held the stone up. "This is the symbol of the Light at the center of the community of life, the Light that binds us together." She laid it in the cradle at the center of the Hoop, and it immediately began to glow with a soft radiance.

The three women placed their fingers on the rim of the Hoop. Catheryn began to chant softly, almost in a whisper. Margaret closed her eyes and felt herself sinking into a warm darkness, the words, barely heard but deeply familiar, triggering a hypnotic trance. The chant stopped. Then Catheryn said, "I am the Anchor."

"I am the Link," replied her daughter.

"I am the Scout," Margaret intoned. And suddenly the dark opened up, and she found herself in a familiar alpine valley, a snow-capped mountain rising above her. Across from her stood Catheryn and Maria, but now the Hoop encircled them while the pale stone was a shining sphere floating between them. This was what they called their "Base Camp," a foothold they had created in a different layer of reality, one close to but not quite part of the physical universe that was home to their bodies.

Margaret looked around, marveling as always at how tangible and real this place seemed even though she knew it was essentially a construct of their three minds impressed through thought and memory upon the fluid and malleable substance of this realm that they called Metaspace. She wondered if this was what Dominic experienced when he and Sukai entered what the Vellians called *alarte*. In fact, it might be the same level of reality, one that the Vellians could enter and control technologically while human beings—and only a very few humans at that—did so through a shift in consciousness and mental manipulation. It was why she worried when Dom played his adventure games in this alternate reality. She was concerned that if as her son he had a latent ability to enter this astral space, it might be awakened prematurely by using the Vellian *alarte* technology.

But this was not the time or place for such worries. There was work to be done and not much time to do it, at least not on the physical level. Time seemed not to have much meaning here in the realm where she was standing.

"Come," she said to the others, her thoughts impressing themselves upon their minds, and held out her hands. They formed a circle. At their center, the sphere expanded to encompass them while the meadow and peak disappeared. They were floating in space surrounded by stars. Off to one side was Titan, the only moon in the solar system with a significant atmosphere, and beyond it hovered the glowing, ringed presence of Saturn. Nearby was the Terran Skip Ship *Abraham Lincoln*, looking like a giant lollipop. The candy ball at the end was the massive Skip engine while the "stick" was the ship itself where, in a small room near the center, their bodies now sat in trance.

Beyond it was the Vellian Tarnship *Filimal*, looking like at first glance like a confection spun out of sugar and lace, with spires and towers interwoven with graceful spirals, all radiating in four directions from a central sphere that resembled a pearl aglow with inner fires. It looked more like a flying city made by artisans and sculptors than a battleship, but nevertheless it was one of the most powerful flagships in the Vellian fleet.

And somewhere in-between in design, with the curving, elfin look of Vellian construction blended cunningly with the angular and blocky human elements, was Titan Station.

The two ships and the space station were fuzzy to look at and surrounded with a misty haze. In this realm, Margaret knew, she wasn't seeing their true physical forms but a kind of reflection made up of their energy emanations. In spite of the mistiness, the shapes were clear enough to distinguish, but at the same time, other information was available that wasn't visible with physical eyes.

"You see?" Catheryn said, indicating the *Filimal*. "That's not the emanation of a technological artifact. You can see the difference with the *Abraham Lincoln*. The Tarnship is radiating across a wider spectrum. Looking at it, I think it may not be a ship at all but a living entity."

"Which might explain why the Tarnships never enter the inner solar system," Maria replied, her thoughts conveying an undertone of excitement. "If this ship is alive, the solar radiation closer in may be uncomfortable, even deadly for it."

"There's so little that we know," Margaret said. "The Vellians themselves have never allowed a human on any one of their ships until now, not even on the small scouts that visit Earth, nor have they offered any explanation why Tarnships never come closer than the orbit of Saturn. We have so little data, we have to be careful not to jump to conclusions."

"But Margaret, I'm a biologist. Trust me when I say I recognize here the energy signatures of life."

Margaret paused, trying to assemble her thoughts. "I absolutely trust you, Catheryn. If you say this ship is alive in some way, I believe you. At the same time, I sense something more...something I can't quite name. I'd almost say the ship seems more like an idea than an entity, an artifact of consciousness if that makes any sense. We already know the Vellians have technology that can operate across several levels of consciousness and reality. Think about their *alarte* devices which can create alternate realities malleable to the thoughts of the operators. Perhaps their Tarnships operate similarly."

"Are you saying the Tarnship is *imaginary*?" asked Maria.

"I...I don't know. I once heard *jin* Portak say that Tarn means the 'star-thought.' I thought he was being poetic, but maybe he was being literal..."

"A 'star-thought-ship?'" Catheryn's thoughts conveyed the wonderment she was feeling. "But what does that mean? The *Filimal* seems perfectly real on the physical level. You and Adrian are going to be traveling in her, for heaven's sake!"

"I know…I know….still….there's something there I don't understand. I feel that I should recognize it, but…I can't."

Maria's thought cut in strongly, filled with conviction. "Well, you will, Margaret. I know you will! That's why we're here, what we've all prepared for, especially you…"

"Of course, Maria." She projected a feeling of calm and confidence to the younger woman. "This *is* the opportunity we've waited for…" *for nearly a hundred years*, she added silently to herself, *ever since my great-grandfather disappeared, leaving behind the star-stone and the beginning of the Qiva…*

"Yes, a chance for one of us to gain entry to a Tarnship," Catheryn said, "and discover the information we need if we're to stop being mere wards of the Vellians. If a Tarnship is a mental construct as you say, Margaret, then hopefully you'll be able to detect that from within and let us know just what's going on."

"I'll be waiting here in Metaspace for your transmission, Margaret," said Maria, who all three knew was the best among them at shamanic travel into this ethereal realm.

"And I'll be Maria's anchor in Titan Station. Anything she receives from you I'll learn from her telepathically and record immediately," Catheryn said. "Between the three of us, we have a chance of discovering the secrets the Vellians have been hiding."

"Well, then, let's have our final attunement together and make our links, then I have to get my body back in gear for the reception." Margaret paused, frowning. "Remember, we've never had success at gaining information psychically from a Vellian scout ship when they've come to Earth. They've always been shielded to our probing, and some have had defenses. The *Filimal* is much, much larger than any scout ship. If it is a living being or even a mental creation of some kind, it may well have much greater protections. So be careful, especially you, Maria. Out of your body, you will be the most vulnerable."

"No, Margaret. Not me. *You're* the one who will be in the belly of the beast."

****

Dom Stewart looked at the screen giving a forward view from the shuttle. There was the Tarnship *Filimal* resting in space before him. His mind hurt trying to take in the beauty and strangeness of it. No human, he was sure, could have built—or even imagined—such a thing. It awed him that he was soon to be on this ship, journeying into interstellar space to a whole new alien world.

He knew from discussions he'd had with his parents that great hope was attached to this enterprise, that it would mark a turning point in humanity's relationship with the often standoffish and condescending Vellians. They would be the first humans ever to visit the mysterious Vellian home world; for that matter, they were the first ever allowed on a Tarnship. Which meant, he suddenly realized with mixed shock and elation, that by coming over on what was essentially a baggage shuttle, he, Dominic Stewart, would be the first human to set foot on a Tarnship. He, a teenager, was boldly going where no person had gone before! Very cool!

Dom looked around and saw Sukai talking to two Vellian crewmen. He felt a wave of affection for his alien brother. Ten years ago the newly appointed Vellian ambassadors to Earth, *jin* Portak and *jina* Sardel had chosen his parents to be their liaisons with the various human governments. It had been a huge surprise for the diplomatic community, for Adrian and Margaret Stewart had both been astrophysicists, not diplomats. But his parents had been part of the design team that worked to build Titan Station and Sukai's mother and father had been their opposite numbers for the Vellians. They had developed a deep friendship which had translated into diplomatic positions when that time came. As a result, they had lived closely together on Earth, and he and Sukai had been raised practically as brothers.

Sukai must have felt Dom's attention, for he suddenly turned and grinned at him, his top crest standing up in excitement. His friend made his way over to him, two glass flutes in his hand, each filled with a green effervescent liquid. He handed one to Dom, who sipped its contents cautiously. Sukai had been known to give him the most foul tasting stuff in the guise of introducing him to Vellian "delicacies." In this case, though, the drink was delicious, sweet and slightly tangy. "Wow," he exclaimed. "For once, this is good! What is it?"

Sukai laughed. "Only the very best Portallian wine, made from our own vineyards. Our family is famous for it." He lowered his voice conspiratorially. "Sometimes I think it's how Father became the ambassador to your world. He threatened to stop production unless the appointment was his."

"Really?"

Sukai shrugged, a very human gesture that Dom knew he had learned while living on Earth. Another Vellian would have been more likely to bob his head up and down while his head crest bent backward to express the same emotion. "I don't know," he said, grinning. "Knowing Father, though, I wouldn't be surprised. He can be very adamant about getting his way."

"Like getting my Dad and Mom appointed co-ambassadors to your world?"

Sukai laughed. "That was my idea. I couldn't think how else to show you my home."

"So now you're influencing interstellar relationships?"

"Sure! Why not?"

It was Dom's turn to laugh and shrug his shoulders. Even after knowing each other for nearly ten years, he still never quite knew when his friend was kidding. But when it came to getting his way, Dom had no doubt Sukai had inherited his father's persistence. So his boast could be true. He tilted the glass back and took a long swallow of the wine.

"Hey," said Sukai, "you're supposed to sip and appreciate it, you oaf, not gulp it like a *borlak* guzzling water!"

"Will it get me drunk?" He hiccupped delightedly.

"No, not unless you have Vellian blood."

"So it'll get you drunk! That I want to see! A drunken, Vulcan elf!" Vellians were notoriously unaffected by any kind of Terran alcohol.

"Then you'll have to wait a long time, my primate human friend. I was raised on this stuff. I'm immune." He lifted his chin in a show of proud dignity, but the effect was spoiled when he hiccupped, too. Then he sneezed and coughed. Dom slapped him on his back. "Raised on it, eh?"

Sukai sneezed again. "It just... went up... my nose, you dolt," he stammered. "Stop....stop beating me on the back!"

Dom laughed. "Sure, O Proud Scion of a Thousand Generations of Greatness, Prince of Princes, Wine Lord of..."

"Oh, shut up," Sukai grinned and pushed his friend away. They both laughed.

Dom looked back at the window. The Tarnship was much closer, its beauty and strangeness ever more overwhelming the nearer they got. As they approached, he thought he could see a fire burning in the core of the pearl-like sphere at the center of the ship.

"Beautiful, isn't it?" Sukai said. "The pride of the fleet, my father says. It was designed over three of your centuries ago by the great *Tarnshem jina* Surella."

"A woman?" He knew enough Vellian to know that a *jina* was a female noble.

"Yes. They are often the best ship-designers. They have a sensitivity to Tarn that males often lack."

"Is that what *Tarnshem* means, a ship-designer?"

Sukai looked at him. "Not really. I'm not sure how to explain it in English."

"But you said she designed the *Filimal*. So wouldn't she be a ship-designer?"

"Well," Sukai grinned, "since you put it that way, yes. But look," he said, changing the subject as he turned Dom around to face a screen showing a rear view from the shuttle. Behind them was the *Abraham Lincoln*, a lollipop on a stick that could hardly match the grace and elegance of the Tarnship. But seeing it gave Dom a feeling of pride. For a moment he felt his eyes go moist. He wondered when he would see an Earth ship again. Or Earth itself, for that matter.

He raised his glass and took another swallow of the Portallian wine. Once again it made him hiccup, and he used the moment to wipe his eyes. But he could see his friend watching him, and he guessed that Sukai wasn't being fooled. "It's a good ship, Dom," Sukai said. "You should be proud of it and of what your race has achieved. Had we not arrived in your solar system eighty years ago, I'm sure that old *Abe* there would be considered a wonder and a monument to your species' ingenuity and technical prowess."

"Still, it's not a Tarnship. It won't give us the stars." He made a motion like flinging a stone across a pond. "Not when all it can do is skip a short distance at light speed before falling back into normal space." The pride he had felt suddenly melted away and a strange depression came over him. He wondered if it was a reaction to the alien wine.

"Hey, perk up. Look at it this way. You told me once it took your Pioneer II spacecraft six and a half years to get to Saturn from Earth back when you were just starting to explore your solar system. We made it in only three weeks on the Lincoln." He grinned. "Believe me, I know! Three *long* weeks having to watch my head when I stood up!"

"You could have come with your parents today and made the trip in an instant."

Sukai playfully punched him. "And leave you on your own without guidance from a superior species? Hardly!"

Dom knew his friend was only kidding him, but instead it made him feel more depressed and even a little angry. "So why couldn't we all have traveled on the scout ship with your parents? Why have you kept humans off your ships? For that matter, why don't your precious Tarnships come to Earth instead of making us come all the way out here to meet them? Do we have the plague or something? For that matter, why don't you share your technology with us so we can go to the stars with you?"

It all blurted out, and Dom felt both surprised and embarrassed. But Sukai seemed to understand and took no offense. "Hey, I don't know, Earth Brother," he said. "You think my father discusses interstellar politics with me? Besides, you are going to the stars with me. You're coming to my home!"

Dom saw his friend's head crest begin to droop and was immediately sorry to spoil the mood. "Brother, I'm sorry. I think your wine is getting to me. But you're the one who said he could influence interstellar relationships. I figured you'd know the answers." He gave a weak smile.

"Not me. My powers, while undoubtedly great as befits a future *jin*, don't extend quite that far. Say, look, the reception has started." He pointed to a smaller monitor set into the wall to their right. Sure enough, it showed a picture being broadcast from Titan Station of the departure ceremonies. Dom knew that millions, if not billions, of people would be watching this back on Earth and on the Lunar and Martian colonies, as well as on Ganymede Station.

Dom's father, wearing an elaborate ambassadorial sash, was standing at a podium speaking, while his mother, similarly attired, stood in back of him. Next to her was the Station co-commander, Jeremiah Dark, a friend of his parents whom Dom had met several times on Earth when he was growing up. Then, standing behind and towering over these two were the elaborately robed Vellian co-ambassadors to Earth, *jin* Portak and his wife *jina* Sardel, their head-crests held at a dignified angle, and the Vellian Station co-commander, *par* Limmix. And behind them, its star-adorned top barely visible over the heads of the Vellians, stood a well-decorated and brightly lit Christmas tree. Dom wondered where it had come from.

The sound was low, but as he watched, he could hear his father say "Today we celebrate how far humanity has come in the ninety years since First Contact with our allies, the Vellian. This magnificent Titan Station around me is evidence of this, but a much stronger proof stands before you. Representing all of you and the progress we have made, my wife and I are now going to the stars, to Vella. Like the tree behind me, this is a symbol of hope and new promise for both our peoples, Vellian and Human."

"Hey," Sukai said, nudging him in the ribs, "If you wanted to hear speeches, we could have gone to the Station instead."

Dom took a last glance at his father and mother, suddenly wishing he could hear more and feeling his pride and love for them pushing out the remnants of his sudden depression. He turned to his friend, "Well, I would have liked to hear about the plans to colonize Titan..."

"Ah, you scientist types! Listen, you can watch the replays later. But for now, when we get on board, I'll take you to my parent's quarters. As I said, they have a private *alarte* room. It will be outstanding!"

"You have an adventure in mind?"

"Well, we still have an Elven Queen and Princess to rescue..."

The screens around them momentarily went dark as the shuttle entered the airlock to the *Filimal*'s large shuttle bay and transmissions shut down. Dom could feel his excitement rising. "That's right! Damsels must be saved and the evil Umagh taught a lesson! Gather your Rangers, then, and lead on, Quiver Brother!"

****

Dom, Prince of the Blood and Heir to the White Throne of Ramakan, stood in the Elven Queen's cell deep in the Umagh fortress. The Queen herself was imprisoned in what appeared to be a giant diamond. At his side stood the Queen's human ward, the Princess Serradel, whom he had earlier freed from her chains in another part of the dungeon. It had been a long fight into the citadel and down into the dungeons, and his sword dripped with green Umagh blood. Somewhere in the fighting, he had become separated from his Quiver Brother, the Lord Sukai. He hoped he was all right.

"So, what do I do now?" he mused out loud. "This magical field that imprisons the Queen is resistant to my best blows."

"It's the product of foul magics," the Princess said. She held an Umagh cutlass at her side, as bloody as his own. He had to admit her fighting prowess was every bit the equal of his own, not at all what he was expecting of a princess. "I know of only one blade that can pierce it and free my Queen: the Star-Sword."

"The Star-Sword? Where might we find this weapon?"

She shrugged helplessly. "I know not. I only know of it from legends the Queen told me as a child."

Dom sighed. "Perhaps that's all it is, a legend for children."

At that moment, a stone fell lose from a wall of the cell. As they watched warily, their swords held at ready, a secret door opened. A human lad stepped out dressed in a black tunic and trousers. He looked to be no more than sixteen or so, and he held no weapon. Dom thought he looked vaguely familiar.

"Be at peace," he said. "I'm a friend."

"I know this lad," exclaimed the Princess, rushing forward to embrace him. "He has often served my Queen in adventures dire and clandestine!"

The youth hugged her back. "It's good to see you free, Princess. Obviously, you are a hero, good sir," he said to Dom, bowing in his direction. "But now we must free our Queen."

"Do...do you know how?" Dom asked. "Do you know magics?"

The boy nodded. "Some. But for this you need the Star-Sword, and I know where it is."

"You do?" exclaimed the Princess. "Then it's not a legend?"

"It might as well be," the boy said, "for it is fiendishly difficult and dangerous to obtain. Only the most fearless of men...or women...might attempt it."

Dom, a veteran of many of these *alarte* adventures Sukai had dreamed up, knew this was his cue. "I will attempt it. If you can lead us to it, I shall obtain it!" Adventure protocol demanded confidence and a good boast now and then.

"Fair enough," said the lad. "Follow me, then." He ducked back through the secret door. Dom and the Princess followed him into a dimly lit corridor, one dripping with moisture and narrower and more cramped than even the corridors in the *Abraham Lincoln*, if that were possible, Dom thought. As they began to descend deeper into the earth, the door behind them closed. Again, he wondered where Sukai had gotten to. *I suppose he'll show up at the right time,* he thought.

They descended deeper into the earth for many minutes, the corridor winding and turning like a snake as it went. At one point Dom called out to the boy who was leading them, "What is your name?"

"You can just call me 'Friend,'" came the reply. In front of him, the Princess turned her head and whispered, "That is how I know him as well, but I've heard others speak of him as the Webmaster." *Well,* thought Dom, *that's as good a name as any for someone who seemed to be a spy.*

Eventually, they came into a brightly lit chamber. It was not large but at its center was a glowing pool of lava. Dom could feel the heat radiating from it and had to squint against the sudden light. Then he realized that most of the light wasn't coming from the lava but from a sword standing upright at the center of the pool, unharmed by being partly plunged into molten stone. The sword blade itself glowed with a silvery light, but embedded in the hilt was what appeared to be a gem with a small, blue-white star shining within it.

"The Star-Sword," breathed the Princess in awe.

"Aye, how do we get it? It's in the middle of a pool of lava!"

"It's as I said, Hero. Only the most fearless will dare the task."

Dom gulped, sweat already beading on his skin from the heat. This was a little too real. It was light-years beyond any virtual reality simulation he'd tried on Earth, and he tried the best, including the new iWorld. It was, as Sukai had predicted, also much more realistic than what the *alarte* rod had produced. If he stepped onto the lava, which he could now see was covered with a thin crust, and fell through, would he truly die? He'd read of people who had died of heart attacks just from imaginary wounds suffered in ordinary virtual reality, and he suspected that the reality the Vellians called *alarte* was more than just virtual. As he contemplated the pool of lava and the shining sword in the middle, he began to feel fear growing in the pit of his stomach.

"Well?" asked the boy. "Are you the one?"

"You must decide quickly," said the Princess. "I fear it will not be long before the dreaded Umagh Legion arrives to reinforce the garrison here. Your attack cannot have gone unnoticed."

Dom sighed. *Hey,* he thought, *it's for moments like these that I play these games.* He stepped forward. "What must I do?"

"It's simple. You must cross the pool and pull out the sword."

"Yeah, simple. And if the crust breaks? It looks very thin. Are you sure there's no other way, a magical bridge or something?"

"There is no other way, Hero. You must be light of heart as well as of foot."

Dom took a deep breath. *Light of heart.* The way these games worked, this was a clue. But what did it mean? He stepped forward. It was like approaching a blast furnace.

"Keep your eye on the goal, not on the danger," said the Princess. "And remember..." *More clues,* he thought.

Step by step, sweating more all the time, he approached the lip of the pool. Part way there he had to drop his sword which was becoming too hot to handle. Light of heart? Eye on goal? Remember? What did these mean? Perhaps just what they said.

At the lip of the pool, he lifted his eyes away from the lava at his feet and focused on the star-gem on the hilt of the sword. *I see you,* he thought. *You are my goal.*

<And I see you, my child.> The voice resonated in his head. Startled, he stepped back. Who said that? Then he realized it was a magical sword, after all, so it must have been the sword speaking. Cool!

He stepped up to the lip of the pool again, his eyes on the star-gem. Before he stepped out onto the lava, though, he began to remember happy, joyous moments in his life. Be light of heart, the boy had said. He thought of his love for his mother and father and his love for Sukai. He could feel joy swelling within him, and it felt like some other presence was being joyous with him.

He stepped onto the lava.

The joy grew stronger. He felt happier than he'd ever felt before.

He took another step, then another. The heat was painful but not so much that he couldn't bear it. He stepped again, his heart singing.

And then he was at the sword. He reached out and clasped his hands around it and pulled, feeling like Arthur when he'd pulled the sword from the stone. *I'm going to be King Dom,* he thought, then laughed inwardly at the pun he'd made.

The sword refused to budge.

He pulled again, and still nothing happened. He could feel the fear beginning to return. Wasn't he worthy? Had he been found wanting? Was he now going to plunge into the lava and die? He felt the heat more intensely and cried out with the pain of it. Ominously, he heard the crust beginning to crack.

No! he thought. I shall succeed. He pushed the fear away and focused on the gem-star, which seemed to have grown brighter. He pulled again, straining as much as he dared lest he push himself through the crust, but with no success.

Then he remembered.

This was *alarte* and the adventure had been created by Sukai, a Vellian. Vellians did everything in pairs. Relationship was vital to them. It's why they hadn't offered an ambassadorship only to his father or his mother but to both of them. It's why Sukai's parents were co-ambassadors as well.

Sweating, his hands still around the hilt of the Star-Sword, he looked back to where the Princess stood. "Princess," he croaked, his mouth dry from the heat. "I can't do this on my own. I need your help."

With no hesitation, she strode forward light as a feather across the lava, her eyes filled with joy. Standing beside him, she gripped the hilt with him and together they pulled.

The sword came free. Shouting with joy, they held it upright together where it shone with a blinding light, the gem in the hilt pulsing warm like a living thing within their grasp. Beneath their feet the lava suddenly turned to cold stone, and Dom heard the strange voice in his head: <**You are the one.**>

****

Jin Portak stood next to *par* Simen, the captain of the *Filimal*, observing the routine of preparing the ship for its journey. All was order and efficiency on the bridge as the crew went about their work. Behind him, in an enclosed spherical chamber, the eight *Tarnshem* rested in their meditative couches, ready to form the connection to the *Tarnfal*, the Starmind, that would lift them into Tarn-space. *Soon*, he thought, not for the first time, *we will cease to exist except as memories in the thoughts of stars, only to be remembered at our destination.* Not that anyone on board would experience any difference from their normal state. *But it's just an illusion carved in alarte until we can be joined with the physical universe again. But what if we are forgotten? What would become of us then?*

There had been stories of Tarnships disappearing, never to be seen again. And he himself had seen recordings of a ship caught in The Smearing, a loss of integrity in space and time that left a vessel and all within it like a phantom, not quite existing in any realm and slowly dissipating into unreality. But he had traveled Tarn-Space many times, and there had never been a problem. And while only two *Tarnshem* were really needed to make the journey, *Filimal* had four times that number, a redundancy that should more than ensure their safe passage.

Par Simen, standing next to him observing his Bridge crew, said softly, "Are the humans settled?" Glancing at him, *jin* Portak could see the other's head-crest vibrating ever-so-slightly, the only indication that he felt any agitation over the situation. There were many who objected to this mission of bringing humans on board a Tarnship, much less taking them to Vella. *Jin* Portak knew that his Captain was one of them, though his commitment to duty and his position would never allow him to say so openly.

"Yes. All is well. My wife and two *Tarnshem* are with them. And the boy has been in *alarte* with my son." Then, though he knew he didn't have to say it, he added as an after-thought, "It is what the *Jintel* has decreed. I am merely serving their commands." Which was not entirely true. The ruling body of Vella had certainly given their permission to allow human ambassadors to come to the homeworld, but he had been lobbying behind the scenes for some time for this to happen.

"Do you believe they are ready? They are Tarn blind."

"The *Jintel* believe they are ready." And that was all that needed to be said. Pir Simen nodded his head slightly in acknowledgment, though his head-crest still trembled slightly.

"All systems are balanced and secure, Captain," said one of the crew. *par* Simen grunted, his head-crest steadying and rising slightly. He turned to *jin* Portak. "We leave at your word, my Lord," he said.

Jin Portak smiled to himself, remembering an ancient Terran television show that his son Sukai enjoyed. "Make it so," he said in honor of that imaginary human starship captain and turned to face the eight *Tarnshem* in their bubble. Beside him, *par* Simen made a gesture with his hand. *Jin* Portak watched as a misty iridescence rose up around the skin of the bubble, hiding the *Tarnshem* from view. At the same time, he felt a slight tremor in the floor beneath his feet as the *Filimal* began to move in normal space away from Titan Station. More and brighter colors began to swirl around the bubble before him. The transition had begun, and though he knew it was only his imagination, that there were no physical sensations involved, he fancied he could feel his flesh and bones begin to dissolve.

One of the Bridge crew monitoring the local underspace called out, "I'm detecting *Montauk*."

"Single or swarm?" *par* Simen asked, his voice showing no concern. Even his head-crest remained calm. *Montauk* were an underspace phenomenon that sometimes appeared when a ship was entering Tarn-space. No one quite knew what they were. Theories ran from ripples in the quantum flux to semi-sentient entities composed of dark energy. The Captain knew they could be dangerous to an unprotected ship, but the *Filimal* was far from being that.

"I don't know," the crewman admitted. "It's the size of a swarm but it has characteristics of a single entity."

Both *par* Simen and *jin* Portak went to stand behind the crewman so they could see for themselves in the monitor. "Hmmn," said the Captain. "That is strange. If it's a single, it's one of the largest I've seen." He turned to another crewman. "Defense, heighten the shields. We'll take no chances. And prepare the Lance. If need be, we'll use Tarnfire on it."

"Is it wise to do that while transiting into Tarn-space?" *jin* Portak asked.

"Yes, if need be. It should disperse the *Montauk* with no ill effect for us. Of course, once we're in Tarn-space, we're perfectly safe."

The Defense officer said, "Shields heightened."

As they watched, the black blob on the underspace monitor stopped and veered away. "There, you see," said the Captain. "Problem solved."

But then the Defense officer spoke up again. "Shields are dropping, Captain."

"What?" *par* Simen crossed over to the Defense station to read the monitor there, his head-crest rising in puzzlement. "It says there's an energy drain leeching away our shields. But how? And from where."

The Defense officer frantically made various adjustments on the controls in front of him but with no effect. His own head-crest rose in alarm. "Shields gone!"

"*Montauk* striking," came the voice of the crewman monitoring underspace. The ship suddenly gave a lurch. *Jin* Portak looked back and saw the jagged streaks of black criss-crossing the bubble enclosing the

Tarnshem like lightning bolts. "The transition field is destabilizing," he called out, horrified at what he was seeing. "Sound the alarm and send a message to *par* Limmix on Titan Station. Ask for help!" *Though if what I fear is happening is true, he thought, there won't be any help for any of us.*

****

In a much larger room than they'd shared on the *Abraham Lincoln*, Catheryn Raveneye and her daughter, Maria White Feather, prepared themselves for their mission, the secret reason both of them had come to Titan Station. While Catheryn sat relaxed in a chair, a tablet close to hand on which she could both write and draw in response to what her daughter communicated telepathically to her, Maria herself lay on a bed and composed herself, preparing to enter Metaspace. Before her on the wall where she could see it was the digital frame that had been in their room on the *Abe*, and as before, it showed the scene of the mountain-ringed alpine meadow to reinforce her mental image of their "Base Camp." In one hand she held the Hoop with the star-stone at its center.

Holding that image firmly in mind, she recited the words that allowed her to sink into a self-induced trance. A moment later, she found herself looking out onto that same meadow, the transition smooth and easy from long years of practice. "I'm at Base Camp," she thought back to her mother. "Can you hear my thoughts?"

There was a moment, then the reply came, firm and strong: "Yes." She and her mother had practiced this form of communication since she'd been a little girl, an essential part of her training as a member of the Qiva. "Good," she replied. "I hear you clearly, too. I'm stepping into space now."

"May the Force be with you," came the response, tinged with humor. Her mother knew that Maria was a huge fan of the legendary *Star Wars*, a classic of pre-Contact fiction.

Maria smiled to herself. Then she stepped into the shining sphere that was the presence of the Star-Stone in this place, and as before, she found herself floating in space, surrounded by stars. Beneath her was Titan Station's reflection in this realm and in front of her, though some distance away, was the glowing entity that was the Tarnship *Filimal*.

She drifted forward, propelled by her intent, drawing near to the Tarnship. In what felt to her to be halfway between the *Filimal* and Titan

Station, though in fact distance had little meaning in Metaspace, she stopped. She held the image of Margaret Graham Stewart clearly in her mind. *Whenever you're ready, Margaret,* she thought to herself, *I am.*

****

On board the *Filimal*, the woman in question was sitting with her husband in the company of *jina* Sardel, now out of her co-ambassador's robes and wearing a very Earth-like tunic and trousers. With them were two other Vellians who wore hooded robes like priests. At the moment, the hoods were thrown back on their shoulders, revealing Vellian faces that were more angular and Elf-like than Margaret was used to seeing. They had been introduced as *Tarnshem*, but no explanation had been offered as to what that meant. She wondered if they were security agents.

"I can imagine that the two of you are tired after all the celebrations," said *jina* Sardel. "I know I am."

Adrian smiled. "I'm sure it will hit me later, but right now I'm feeling like a child on Christmas Eve. It's very exciting to be on board one of your ships at last. Will it be possible to take a tour?"

"Why, yes," *jina* Sardel replied. "I think my husband has a tour planned for tomorrow after breakfast."

When they had disembarked from the shuttle, the two Vellians had escorted them directly to their quarters, seeing very little other than corridors. However, where they were staying was a multi-room suite. It was spacious and beautifully appointed, more like what he would expect to find in a high-class, luxury hotel on Earth than on a starship. It was certainly a very far cry from the Spartan and cramped spaces on the *Abraham Lincoln*. They'd hardly had a chance to get settled, though, when their friend *jina* Sardel had arrived.

"Well, *I'm* feeling tired, even if you're not, my dear," said Margaret yawning. "If you'll all excuse me, I think I'll turn in to bed. I want to be fresh for that tour!" In fact, she felt wide-awake and as excited as her husband. She was ready to make connection with Maria and Catheryn, but she couldn't do it in the company of the Vellians. Going to bed would be the perfect excuse to lie down and journey into Metaspace.

Jina Sardel frowned, her head-crest bending over in apology. "I'm very sorry, Margaret, but you'll need to stay here until we enter Tarn-space. It would not be safe for you otherwise."

Margaret frowned in return. "Not safe? What do you mean, Sardy?" Inwardly, she felt a stab of fear that perhaps their plan had been discovered.

One of the *Tarnshem* stepped forward. "Let us simply say that the transition will put unusual stresses upon your minds and bodies. It could be dangerous."

"So what do we need to do," asked Adrian. "Do we need to be in special acceleration couches or something like that?" He looked around at the comfortable furniture in the lounge. None of it looked like it was designed for anything other than providing luxurious comfort.

The *Tarnshem* smiled. "No. We...my companion and I...will be with you through the process. We have the ability to see that no harm comes to you."

"But what about Dominic? He's not here," said Margaret.

"No, he's with my son," said *jina* Sardel. "The two have been making up adventures in *alarte*. But you need not worry about him. His time in the *alarte* chamber has prepared him for Tarn-space. He will not be harmed."

"But Sardy, what has playing fantasy games in virtual reality have to do with interstellar travel?"

"Oh, it's not the fantasy games, Margaret. *Alarte* is much more than virtual reality. It's a place where he can be seen and remembered by the *Tarnheim*...what you might call the 'Starheart.' But you have not been seen and thus cannot be remembered when we arrive."

"I don't understand," Adrian said.

Jina Sardel laid her hand on Adrian's knee. "I know, my friends. There is much you don't understand and which we could not explain. But you will understand in time."

"That is why we are here," said the first *Tarnshem*. "We are the eyes and ears of the *Tarnheim*. We will see you and know you and the *Tarnheim* will remember."

"I couldn't be seen and remembered asleep in bed?" she asked, still hoping to find some way to be by herself.

Jina Sardel chuckled. "Not unless Adrian allowed the *Tarnshem* to be in the bed with you. He needs to have physical contact."

The second *Tarnshem* leaned forward and whispered into the other's ear. The first one nodded. "It seems that the transition has begun." Both of them pulled their hoods over their heads so that their faces disappeared into shadow. Then, the first one held out his hands. "Please," he said, "take hold of my hands, Co-Ambassador Margaret Stewart." His companion did the same with her husband.

I have a bad feeling about this, she thought, but she took the Vellian's hands as he indicated. Immediately, she felt herself being pulled into a familiar warm darkness. *Omigosh,* she thought, *he's pulling me into trance. I can't let him know I'm familiar with the process.* So she pretended to struggle and resist the feeling. "Please, Co-Ambassador, don't struggle against me," the *Tarnshem* said gently. Just let yourself relax and all will be well."

She suddenly felt as if she were being embraced and held by a very large presence, as if she were a child again and her mother had just picked her up. *What is happening,* she wondered. As if in response, an unfamiliar voice said in her mind, <**Don't worry. I see you, my child.**> Without knowing how, she knew that it did not come from the Vellian who was holding her hands. It was the most beautiful voice she had ever heard, and it filled her with peace.

It was at that moment that the alarm sounded and ceiling panels began flashing with a strident, blue light which, she knew, was the color of emergency for a Vellian. The *Tarnshem* let go of her hands and stood up, allowing his hood to fall back. She could see his head-crest waving in alarm.

She started to stand up, but fell back as a wave of dizziness washed over her.

"Stay here! " cried *jina* Sardel. Then she and the two *Tarnshems* turned and ran from the room.

Margaret looked over at her husband who looked as stunned as she felt. He seemed to also be having trouble getting to his feet. "Adrian!" she said, fighting the dizziness and trying to stand, filled with an urgent conviction that she had to find her son. "Damn what Sardy said! I must get to Dominic!"

****

Dom and Sukai were sitting in Sukai's room in one part of his family's suite, sipping cups of hot chocolate, a drink unknown on Vella but one to which Sukai had become very attached. "And then," said Dom, "the Princess and I took the Star-Sword and freed the Queen!" Dom thought he would never forget that moment. Games just didn't get any better than that.

"Bummer! I missed out on all the fun. I got myself lost in some maze in the fortress. I couldn't find my way out until you freed the Queen. Then it seemed like the maze just disappeared." He took a sip of chocolate, his head crest bending in puzzlement. "You know what's so strange about all this?"

"What?"

"I never programmed that sequence. You should have been able to free the Queen with a necklace the Princess wore. There was no Star-Sword in the game, at least none that I put in. That's the funny thing about *alarte*. Sometimes it goes in unexpected directions, as if it had a mind of its own."

"Well, I'm glad it did. I'll never forget that moment when we drew the Star-Sword together."

"Hummpf. Well, I'm glad you had your heroic moment. Say, what did you think of the ending? That I did program in as a surprise for you."

Dom laughed, remembering that moment at the top of the fortress tower with overwhelming numbers of Umagh warriors climbing the stairs behind them when Santa Claus and his sleigh swooped down out of the sky with his flying reindeer, and carried the Queen, the Princess, Sukai, and himself to safety. Well, it *was* Christmas Eve back on Earth!

"I thought it was...." He was interrupted by a shrill whistle that pierced his ears and a bright blue light that began flashing from ceiling panels.

"What the hell," exclaimed Dom, springing to his feet.

"Something's wrong," said Sukai, standing up as well. "That's the emergency alarm. Don't worry. We'll be safe here."

"Is there something we should be doing? Donning space suits or something?" He remembered the emergency drills on board the *Abraham Lincoln*.

Sukai laughed. "Oh no, nothing can harm a Tarnship. I don't know what's happening, but I'm sure it will soon be taken care of."

But Dom did not feel reassured. A feeling was growing in him that he needed to be with his parents. He stood up. "Thank you for your offer, Sukai, but I feel I need to be with Mom and Dad."

"But Dom, they're perfectly safe, too, I'm sure."

"Please, Sukai. Tell me how to get to our suite from here."

Sukai stood up as well. "All right, if you insist. I should stay here in case my father needs me, but I'll show you the way. It's easy."

He led Dom out of his room and through a series of other rooms that made up his family's suite. They passed through a doorway into a short hallway that led to an intersection where Dom could see two corridors branching right and left. The one going to the right was painted in emerald green with gold designs on the walls. The one on the left was plain white and unadorned.

"Here," Sukai said. "Take that green and gold corridor off to the right. You will pass one corridor and come to a second branching to the left. Its walls will be colored purple and gold. Just follow it and it will lead you to your family's suite. See? It's easy."

"All right," Dom said, gripping his friend's arm. "Thanks! I'll see you when this is over, whatever this is." He left Sukai who turned and went back into his family's rooms. He ran to the right down the green corridor, filled with a sudden sense of urgency.

Dom turned and headed down the green corridor. He had only gone a few meters, though, when the world seemed to fall away from him. It was like running in low gravity, but instead of his body being weightless, if was as if his soul was floating away, losing touch with reality.

Then reality returned, and Dom stumbled and fell to the floor. Dizzy, he tried to get to his feet. The floor fell away again, or was he falling through it? He couldn't tell. Reality seemed to pull in all directions, and his body seemed to stretch to keep up. Pain lanced through him, and his mind exploded in light. He cried out.

Then he was back in the corridor, lying trembling on the floor. What was happening? The blue light was still flashing from the ceiling and the shrill whistling still filled the air, but everything seemed different somehow. He felt like he had been thrown against the walls of infinity and had bounced back.

He rolled against the wall of the corridor. The pain was gone, but he was shaking. He wanted to stay where he was, but he knew he had to get to his family's rooms. There his mother and father would be waiting for him. There would be safety.

He pulled himself up and started down the corridor again. He felt as if he had been running forever, and it was all he could do to put one foot in front of the other. But ahead he could see the purple and gold corridor that branched to the left, the one that would take him to where his family was waiting. He was so close.

Suddenly, the whistling stopped and the blue light stopped flashing. The silence was eerie after all the noise and all the more disturbing because of this. He was running, but nothing seemed to change, as if he was suspended in space. All around him the walls of the corridor became ghostly and semi-transparent. Beyond them he could see the unwinking stars in the depths of space, but he knew that was impossible. The corridor he was in was deep inside the Tarnship with layers of other rooms and corridors between him and the outer hull.

From somewhere he could hear his mother's voice urgently calling him. *No, I'm not hearing it with my ears,* he thought. *Mom's speaking in my mind. How can that be?* He looked ahead along the rapidly vanishing corridor, and he thought he saw her in the distance, reaching out to him. He tried to run harder, but everything seemed to be drifting away, his body becoming impossibly long and thin.

With a final act of will he reached out to his mother who also seemed to be morphing and twisting in the chaos that was replacing reality. He felt something in him shift, and for a moment, normality returned. He felt his feet touch the solid surface of the corridor, pitching him forward so that once more he stumbled and nearly fell. Around him the blue light again flashed and the whistle was painful in his ears. Ahead of him, he could see his mother start down the corridor toward him, and his father was just emerging from their suite behind her. They were shouting something, but he couldn't make out what they were saying. His ears were ringing and his mind spinning from whatever had just happened.

He got his balance and ran on, and now he could hear his parents calling his name. But everything shifted again, and it was as if they were figures in a nightmare, running, shouting, but not getting anywhere. Then the silence descended again. He felt his body twisting, as if he were a string of putty being pulled by some unseen giant.

Ahead of him, he could see his mother, and he reached out to her with all his will, attempting to reach her. But then he saw it wasn't his mother, or rather it was his mother turning into another face and form. It was a young woman who looked vaguely familiar, clad in a white tunic and white trousers. *She can't be here,* he thought. *My parents and I are the only humans on the Tarnship. How could this strange woman be on board?*

Then he realized she was not on the ship. Impossibly, she seemed to be floating in space. *How could this be? Who is she?* His head was hurting like it would split open.

<**Be at peace. I have you.**> The strange voice filled his mind. Before he could wonder who had spoken, he was hurtling forward as if propelled by a giant hand pushing on his back. The last thing he saw before he passed out into darkness was the young woman, her mouth opened in surprise and shock, raising her hands as if to catch him…or push him away.

****

Maria White Feather floated in Metaspace, observing the Tarnship as it began to slowly move away from Titan Station, and wondering when Margaret was going to make contact. It could not be long now before the great ship faded into Tarn-space. If Margaret was going to send her any information, it would have to be soon.

As she watched, she saw a glow begin to emanate from the central pearl-like sphere. *Could this be it,* she wondered. *Is the transition starting? Where was Margaret? Had she been discovered?*

Filled with questions, all she could do was watch. Then out of the corner of her eye, she caught movement from another direction. It seemed like a dark ripple moving through Metaspace, something she had never seen before. What was it? As she tried to see it more clearly, the Tarnship, as if in response, began to glow more brightly. *Shields,* she thought. *They've detected whatever this is.*

But then the glow around the ship began to dim until it faded away entirely. The ripple seemed to pounce, launching itself at the Tarnship. Even here in Metaspace, the great ship seemed to shudder. At first, it was as if nothing had happened. But then Maria could see the glow around the central sphere become erratic, expanding and contracting in random ways. As she watched, it looked as if the ship was fading in and out of existence, each time becoming more insubstantial. Then it seemed to stretch and deform as if it were a large piece of taffy that was being pulled in many directions. It wasn't coming apart. It was more like it was being smeared across the space in front of her.

Horrified, she sent out a distress call to Margaret, and for a moment she thought she might have made contact. There was the familiar feeling of Margaret's mind, though it was colored by feelings of anxiety and alarm. Then she lost it. *Did Margaret die,* she wondered. *But no, I'd know if that happened.*

At that moment, she felt herself in contact with another mind entirely, one filled with confusion and fear. She recognized it as Dominic, Margaret's son. He was not part of the Qiva, but she had seen him occasionally on the *Abraham Lincoln,* almost always in the company of the Vellian co-ambassadors' son.

Then, to her surprise, an unfamiliar voice resounded in her mind: <**I have him. I have you.**> A powerful force shot through her like a giant arm, reaching out for and grabbing this mental contact. She had no idea where this had come from, and the power of it left her breathless. Before she could think any more about it, she saw a figure flying towards her from the *Filimal.* Shocked, she put up her arms to brace herself...and all went black.

****

In the command center of Titan Station, Co-Commander Jeremiah Dark stood on a raised platform gripping a hand rail and stared uncomprehendingly at the view screen that dominated the wall before him. Beside him, he could hear the sharp hiss as *par* Limmix, the Station Co-Commander, reacted in shock and horror at what was happening. On the screen, they could see the *Filimal* stretching and twisting, becoming ghostly and unreal.

A moment earlier, the Tarnship had been moving majestically away, preparing for transition into Tarn-space and the voyage to Vella. Then something seemed to happen, though Dark had been unable to make it out. There'd been a garbled transmission from the *Filimal,* filled with static, but two words had stood out: *Help us!*

"Impossible! It's impossible!" *par* Limmix exclaimed, staring at the view screen.

"What's happening, *par* Limmix?"

"Smearing! The ship has failed transition and is being spread out over time and space between this dimension and Tarn-space. But I don't know how it could have happened...."

"Is this Station in danger?"

"No...I...I don't think so. I'm not a dimensional engineer, Jeremiah. I don't know what long range effects smearing may have on the local space around it."

"All right. We need to get your people and ours figuring this out. I want our shields reinforced just in case, and I want rescue craft sent to look for survivors."

"No, you can't do that!" *par* Limmix exclaimed. "They would be destroyed."

"What do you mean?"

"I said I don't know about long-range effects, but I do know that a smeared ship is caught in a bubble of temporal and spacial distortion. Any other ship that approaches it too closely will be caught in the bubble and destroyed."

"I take it this has happened before, then?"

"Yes," the Vellian answered, his voice betraying his reluctance. "But it is very rare, and it has not happened in my lifetime, which would be two hundred of your years."

"Are the people in the *Filimal* dead?"

"I don't know. I don't think so. They are frozen in a moment of time. But eventually the bubble will degrade and when it does, the ship and all within it will cease to exist."

Margaret, Adrian, and Dominic's faces flashed through his mind with a shock. "When will that happen?"

"It is random. It could happen within hours or days of your time."

Dark sighed. "So is there *anything* we can do, Limmi?"

Par Limmix shook his head, the Vellian equivalent of a shrug, while his head-crest waved about in extreme agitation. "The only one who could help is a *Tarnshem*, and even then, it would be risky and doubtful. To my knowledge, a smeared ship has only been recovered once and it took three *Tarnshem*s to do it. One of them died in the process."

"A *Tarnshem*? What or who is that? I'm not familiar with the term."

Par Limmix paused. "A *Tarnshem* is a..a Tarn specialist, what you might call an interdimensional physicist."

From the way *par* Limmix's head-crest bobbed, Dark suspected his co-commander wasn't being entirely truthful with him, but he decided not to press the issue. He had more important things to worry about than semantics. He knew there were things *par* Limmix—and all other Vellians—routinely kept secret, but now was not the time to probe. Instead he said, "Can we get one of these...specialists here?"

"I will send an emergency message to Vella immediately. I'm sure my superiors will send help right away. But Jeremiah, even using Tarn-space, Vella is two days away. They may arrive too late."

"All right, Limmi. I know you'll do everything you can. After all, the lives of both our co-ambassadors are at stake...and who knows what else?"

Par Limmix reached out and touched Dark's arm. "This is a sensitive issue, my friend. There are many in my government who objected to bringing humans to Vella. They may well use this accident to prevent any further progress in that direction between our peoples."

Dark frowned. "That's not our problem right now. Our job is to save the lives of our people if we can. Politics can take care of itself later."

Par Limmix nodded. "As you say, my friend. I'll go make my call."

As the Vellian walked away, Dark's personal communicator buzzed. The signal told him it was on his private line. He drew the small device off his belt and activated it. "Yes?"

"Jeremiah. This is Catheryn. You need to come to our quarters immediately. We have an emergency."

"Catheryn, I've got an emergency up here, too, a big one. Can't it wait?"

"I'm afraid not. And I guarantee you, my emergency is bigger than yours!"

****

Catheryn Raveneye held a cold compress against her daughter's head where she lay on her bunk. Maria moaned. "Mother, forgive the expression, but I have the mother of all headaches right now."

"You're lucky that's all you have. You came back with quite a jolt. A shock like that could have stopped your heart."

Maria tried to sit up, but her mother pushed her down again. "Dominic?" she asked.

Catheryn shrugged, looking at the young man stretched out unconscious on the other bed. "He's out cold, but he's here and alive. I don't know how. What happened out there?" But Maria's eyelids fluttered, and she lapsed back into unconsciousness herself. However, her breathing was steady and her pulse was strong, so Catheryn knew her daughter would be all right. She just needed to recover herself.

Only moments earlier, Catheryn had been sitting in her chair, telepathically tuning in to her daughter and receiving Maria's impressions of what was happening to the Tarnship. There'd been a bolt of pain in her head, and she'd lost contact. A moment later, her daughter had convulsed on the bed, shocked back into consciousness. At the same time, there'd been a crash, and Dominic's body had fallen, apparently from midair, onto the floor. The question was, how had he teleported himself from the *Filimal* to Titan Station?

She was gratified to see that his breathing had stabilized, too. Checking his pulse again, she found that it was slower and steadier than it had been. Whatever had happened, it looked like Dominic Stewart would recover. *Or,* she thought grimly, *at least his body will. I have no idea what may have happened to his mind.*

There was a knock at the door. Getting up, she opened it a crack and saw that it was Jeremiah Dark. She let him in and closed the door behind him. "So, what's the emergency?" he asked. Then his eye caught sight of Maria lying on the bed closest to the door.

"Is she all right," he asked, rushing to her side and looking down at her. "What happened?"

"She's fine, Jeremiah. She's just in a healing sleep right now. She was slammed back into her body and suffered a shock, but she's OK."

Dark looked at her puzzled. "So what's the emergency that I had to see right away?"

She pointed to the other bed which was partially in shadow. "There," she said.

Dark went over to the bed and looked down at the figure. At first he wasn't sure who he was looking at or why, then the face of the young man registered. "My god!" he exclaimed. "What's Dominic Stewart doing here? His parents told me he was on the Tarnship."

"He was. But now he's here, and I don't know how."

"Does Maria know?"

Catheryn shook her head. "I don't think so, but she wasn't conscious long enough to tell me much."

"Catheryn, the *Filimal* has suffered some kind of catastrophic accident. *par* Limmix called it a transition failure. Apparently she's caught between our dimension and that of Tarn-space, and who knows what else."

She whistled. "You were right! You do have a big emergency on your hands." Then as the impact of what he'd said hit her, her hands flew up to her mouth. "Oh no! Margaret?"

"I don't know. Limmi says everyone on board is frozen in time, not dead but not quite alive, either. But the whole ship will gradually fade until it and everyone on board ceases to exist."

"My god! How long do we have?"

"Hours, maybe a day at the most. I'm sorry, Catheryn. She and Adrian were my friends, too." He looked down. "At least Dominic is alive and safe, God knows how."

Catheryn laid a hand on the boy's forehead. His skin felt normal. "It seems to me that what happened to the *Filimal* and Dom appearing here are related."

"I don't know. When it comes to Tarnships and Tarn-space, we have so little information. That was why you and Margaret and Maria were investigating." He looked at Dominic and shrugged. "Maybe when something like this happens to a Tarnship, people are ejected, like when a hull is breached. A Vellian scout can practically teleport itself from Earth to here. Maybe whatever Tarn is, it involves teleportation. Maybe Stewart here got himself caught in some kind of energetic backlash or explosion that teleported him here." He reached for his communicator. "I need to talk to Limmi. This is Vellian technology. I need his advice."

Catheryn caught his hand. "Before you call him, you need to think this through. It's probably not random that Dominic showed up here with us. I think the psychic link we had with Margaret on the Tarnship drew him here. Do we want anyone else to suspect this? *par* Limmix will undoubtedly have many questions. Can we answer them? Do we want to risk having our operation uncovered?"

Dark frowned, considering. "That's a good point, Catheryn." Then he frowned even more deeply. "Could the link you three created have interfered with the transition into Tarn-space? Could our operation have caused what happened to the *Filimal*?"

"I don't see how. We were merely observing," she said, but inwardly she wondered, *were you doing something else, Margaret? What else were you up to?*

"We know that observation can have an effect on quantum phenomena. Maybe the same is true with whatever phenomenon Tarn is? We've long suspected that part of Vellian technology was mental in nature or involved some phenomena of consciousness. Maybe Margaret's probing or Maria's link with her upset some kind of psychic balance. You're the expert in these fields, Catheryn. Is it possible?"

"Jeremiah, I just don't know. But if there's any chance at all that we might have precipitated what happened…." The horror of the thought was plain on her face.

"Then *par* Limmix cannot find out. It's bad enough that a Tarnship has been destroyed, killing the four co-ambassadors. This alone may give ammunition to the factions that don't want Vellians to have anything to do with humans. But if it were suspected, much less proved, that we had caused that destruction through our spying…well, that would be an unthinkable provocation. It would set our relationships back by decades; it might even cause them to break the alliance…or worse." There was no military man that Dark knew, including himself, who did not at times worry about what a war with the Vellians would mean. Earth would have little chance against their advanced technology.

He made a decision. "Catheryn, I really have to get back to Command. I'm going to have to leave this in your hands. For the moment, this is purely a Qiva affair. When Maria or Dominic comes to, find out what happened. Keep me informed."

She squeezed his hand. "I will, Jeremiah. I will."

****

Slowly consciousness returned and with it memory of his nightmare run through the corridors of the Tarnship, trying to reach his mother. He could feel he was lying on his back on a bed. Had he succeeded? Was he now lying in his parents' rooms?

He opened his eyes. He could see he was in a dimly-lit room, and while from what he could see it was roomy, it most definitely was not as spacious as any of the rooms in his parents' suite on the *Filimal*. *Where am I?* He wanted to rise up and look around, but for the moment he didn't feel enough strength even to lift his head.

"He's awake, Mother," a calm voice said from nearby. He turned his head in that direction and saw a young woman who looked his age, concern in her eyes as she looked at him. *Blues eyes,* he thought, *like the sky on Earth.* He felt her hand on his wrist and realized she was taking his pulse. She looked up at someone standing on the other side of him. "His pulse is normal."

"Excellent!" came another, older woman's voice. He wanted to turn his head to see who it was, but something about the young woman's face held his attention. She was lovely, yes, but...."I know you," he blurted out, his voice a croak. "You...you're the woman floating in space..."

"Floating in space...?" Catheryn asked.

The young woman smiled, not taking her eyes off him. Some deep hormonal part of Dom's mind hoped she'd never take her eyes off him. "He's remembering, Mother. He saw me in Metaspace."

"He saw you? How? Oh, never mind. That's just a small mystery compared to how he got here, and he *is* Margaret's son, after all. He may well have inherited the Graham abilities." He heard her soft footsteps move away from the bed. "Where am I," he croaked again.

"You're on Titan Station, Dominic," Maria answered. "You're in the room my mother and I share. I'm Maria White Feather."

"Titan Station? How... I was running on the *Filimal*...trying to reach Mom..." He suddenly felt it was urgent that he get up, but his body wouldn't respond. Panic flashed through him. "I...I can't move. Am I paralyzed?"

The older woman appeared beside her daughter who stepped back to give her mother room. The woman was carrying a drinking cup. "Dom, you're not paralyzed or harmed in any way, as far as we can tell. You've just had a terrific shock, and your body is recovering." She put a hand under his head and raised it up. "I'd like you to drink some of this. I think you'll find it helps." She brought the cup up to his lips and helped him take a few swallows. Whatever it was, it had a tangy aroma and taste that he found pleasant.

"What is it?" he said, his voice sounding a little more normal.

"It's just a mild stimulant, something to help restore your strength." She put the cup down on a table beside the bed. "Dominic, do you know who I am?"

He did. "You're my mother's friend, Catheryn. Right?"

"That's right. Catheryn Raveneye. We were on the *Abraham Lincoln* with you."

Dom remembered. He had seen her around, sometimes visiting with his mother. He now remembered as well seeing Maria. At the time his attention had mainly been on Sukai, but now an idle thought said that it might have been nice if he'd been more aware of the other people on the ship. Especially Maria.

Maria stepped next to her mother and to Dom's delight, took one his hands in hers. "Dominic...er, Dom, isn't it...what happened? You saw me in space. What else do you remember?"

"I...I'm not sure. Most of it. Sukai ...he's the son of the Vellian co-ambassadors..."

"We know," Maria assured him.

"Well, Sukai and I had been playing an adventure game in his family's *alarte* chamber..." He suddenly remembered very vividly the moment he had pulled the Star-Sword from the pool of molten lava. "I rescued a princess...and a queen...but I needed a Star-Sword to do it... strange..."

"What's strange," asked Maria.

"The sword...or the star in the sword...or someone... said, 'You are the one.' But it was just a game, right? Yet right now, it seems so real..."

He saw a startled expression cross over the older woman's face and she glanced at her daughter. Maria seemed to pay no attention. Instead, she asked, "And after you'd rescued them, what happened?"

"Sukai and I were sitting in his rooms, drinking chocolate. He loves chocolate. Then...then....everything turned blue. I mean, emergency lights came on. For Vellians, blue is the color of emergency, not red. Isn't that funny? Anyway...anyway..." he was finding it hard to focus. His mind seemed to want to drift away.

"Here, Dom," said Catheryn, "drink some more of this." She helped him take more swallows of the brew she'd made for him.

"You were telling us what happened, Dom," said Maria after her mother put the cup down. "Blue emergency lights?"

"Yes, and a whistle. Hurt my ears. Sukai said something was wrong and wanted me to stay with him in his rooms. But I knew I needed to find my parents. It was as if I could hear my Mom calling me. So I set off down the corridors to our suite. But it was so hard to run! Everything kept fading in and out. It was like a nightmare! But I saw my mother and I tried to reach her. Then...then...it wasn't my mother at all, it was you..." He looked at Maria. "I saw you in her place."

"He was seeing your link with Margaret," Catheryn said. "Fascinating."

"I wasn't floating in space, Dom?"

"Not at first. But then...you were. How could you be in space, Maria?

You weren't wearing a spacesuit or anything!"

"I wasn't really in space, Dom, or rather, my body wasn't. My body was here. What you saw was a projection of myself into what we call Metaspace. It's like another dimension."

"Like *alarte*," he blurted out. "Maybe you were in *alarte*."

"I don't know what that is, Dom."

"It's like virtual reality, only it isn't. It's something else, a place where the mind can create its own surroundings. It's where we play our games, Sukai and me. He said it's a place all the Vellians know about and visit."

Maria looked at her mother. "If this is so, it might explain a lot about the Vellians." Then she turned back to Dom. "You may be right. Maybe Metaspace is a kind of *alarte* or vice versa. They sound very similar. But the same or not, I was in space but not in my body. And you saw me, which means that you were in Metaspace or *alarte*, too."

"No, I wasn't. I was running down the corridor...and then...it disappeared. And I was flying through space towards you..."

"So somehow you went from the physical world into a non-physical dimension," said Catheryn. "Dom, do you know what has happened to the *Filimal*?"

Panic shot through him. He tried to rise up, and this time his body responded. Both women helped him sit up. "Mom! Dad! What's happened? Are they alive?"

Catheryn took his hands. He felt calm flowing into him from her. This was something his mother often did, too, when he became distressed. "As far as we know, but we don't know much." Then she told him what Jeremiah Dark had shared with her.

He was stunned. "How did this happen?"

Catheryn sighed. "That's what we're asking ourselves, too. More importantly, how did you start out there and end up here?"

Dom felt lost. There were too many mysteries here. He didn't know what to say or what to do. "Can they be rescued? My parents? And Sukai...and his parents?"

Catheryn said, "We don't know how. And help from Vella may arrive too late."

"But I was saved somehow. Maybe there's something we—you—can do to save others, too. You seem to have special powers. Can't you reach into this Metaspace and bring the others out, as well?"

"I wish we could," Maria said, sitting at the foot of his bed. "I really, really wish we could. But we don't have those kind of powers. As Mother said, we don't even know how you came to be here. Some power was at work, but what? Or whose?" she shrugged, tears forming in her eyes.

Dom lay his head back on a cushion. Somehow he felt like he should do something, that he could do something…but what? How? Probably he'd played too many adventure games where the hero comes up with a life-saving plan right at the last possible moment. But right now, he felt a long way from being a hero.

Catheryn pulled up a chair and sat down next to the bed. "Dom," she said. "You said something earlier that interests me. You mentioned a Star-Sword. Could you say more about this?"

"Why? It was just a stupid fantasy game."

"Humor me. I'd really like to know."

Maria chimed in. "I'd like to know, too, Dom."

So he told them about the adventure he and Sukai had played and how he'd come to gain the Star-Sword and free the Elven Queen. When he was finished, Catheryn said, "It sounds like you were both very brave and very smart," while Maria smiled and nodded.

"Sure," he said, "in a game. But that's all it was." He felt embarrassed. It had felt wonderful at the time, but it was just a fantasy game. It wouldn't save his Mom and Dad or Sukai and his parents. Then he remembered something else. "There was one interesting thing about it, though."

"What was that," Maria asked.

"Sukai creates these games. He's like a programmer, I guess. But he said he hadn't included the whole Star-Sword sequence. He was surprised at what happened. That hadn't been part of the game he designed at all. He said the *alarte* must have made it up, whatever that means."

Catheryn was silent for a moment, then she took Dom's hand again. "Dom, has your mother ever told you anything about your *great*-grandfather, Webster Graham?"

"My great-grandfather? No. I don't think so."

"Well, he had an adventure, too. A real-life one. In it, he had to find a Star-Sword, too."

"Really? No way!"

"And he *did* find it, Dom." She got up and went to a bureau where she pulled out a small silk bag. She brought it back to the bed and sat down. From the bag she withdrew a small jade box. "*This* was embedded in its hilt." She opened the box. Lying within it, Dom saw a pale blue crystal with a star-shape within it. "We call it the Star-Stone. Your great-grandfather gave it to your grandfather who in turn passed it on to your mother. It is a talisman of considerable power."

Dom looked at the stone in shock. It was exactly the same as the gem in the hilt of the Star-Sword, except that it wasn't shining. "It's the same...! But how?"

"That's what I'd like to know, Dom. There's something going on here that, frankly, I don't understand. There are too many synchronicities. Your adventure with a Star-Sword that from your description is identical to one your great-grandfather found. What's happened to the *Filimal*. You being sent here in some magical way, and I use the word sent deliberately. There's no other explanation for it I can see." She looked around as if the room itself might be able to answer her questions. "Some other power is taking a hand in our lives here. But as for who or what it is, I haven't a clue."

She closed the jade box. "There's one other part to the story that not even Maria knows. I know it only because Margaret told me when she passed the Star-Stone on to me for safe-keeping while she went to Vella."

"What's that, Mother?"

"When Webster Graham gave the Star-Stone to his son, he said, 'In the future, at a time of danger, one of my descendents will need this if he is to meet his destiny. Keep it safe until then.'" She looked at Dom. "I think you may be that one."

Dom was having a hard time following what she was saying. It was too much all at once. "What do you mean? Why would you say that?"

"Because you were told you are the one."

"But that was just a fantasy game. It was all make-believe."

"I think not, Dominic. You said your friend Sukai didn't create that part of the game. He was as surprised about it as you. So who did create it? I don't think it was make-believe. I think it was a test. And you passed."

"But...but who was testing me?"

"Ah, now, that is the question. That's why I say that an unknown power is taking a hand in our affairs right now."

"But Mother, even if Dom is the one Webster Graham spoke about, what can he do about the people in the *Filimal*? That's where the danger is, for all of us. He's here now, not over there. And how can the Star-Stone help? All it does is boost our ability to enter Metaspace."

"That's all it does for *us*. Who knows what it can do for Dom, if he's the one." She opened up the jade box again. "Let's find out."

Maria reached forward, hand outstretched to touch her mother's arm. "Mother, are you sure?"

Catheryn paused. "I appreciate your doubts, Maria. But we're at a dead end. We're surrounded with mysteries with no way to resolve them. Our friends will die if we don't do something, yet what can we do? How do we save a starship that's slowly dissolving into a dimension we know nothing about? The only path forward I can see is based on a coincidence I cannot ignore."

"What do you feel, Dom? Are you willing?" Maria asked.

"I don't know anything about this 'one' business, but if there's anything I can do to help, I'm game. What do I need to do?"

"Take the Star-Stone, Dominic. Just hold it in your hand."

Dom took a deep breath and reached out to take the gem from its box. He closed his fist around it and waited for something to happen. There was silence in the room.

"Now what?" he asked.

Catheryn frowned. "I don't know. I thought maybe if the stone made contact with you, something would happen."

"I have an idea," said Maria. "Dom, use your imagination and put yourself back to that moment in the game when you pulled the Star-Sword from the lava. Metaspace is responsive to thought and feeling, to what we call the *felt-sense*. See if you can remember the felt-sense you had in your body and mind when you drew the sword. That may activate the Star-Stone."

Dom thought it was a crazy suggestion, but he did what she asked. He cast his mind back to that moment in the game when he had stood in the center of the lava with the Princess and had drawn the Star-Sword. He remembered how he had felt, the power, the sense of joy and triumph, the feeling of exaltation, even the relief that he wouldn't now fall into the lava.

He looked down at the stone in his hand. The star shape within the gem sparkled, but nothing else happened. *This is stupid*, he thought. *It's just a stone.*

"Nothing," he said.

"Yes, nothing," said Catheryn, disappointment in her voice. "I was so sure...."

Dom looked from one woman to the other, from older to younger. They both looked downcast. But what could he do? He wasn't a hero. He didn't have special powers. Never mind what some stupid game had said, he wasn't "the One," whoever or whatever that was.

Catheryn reached to take the stone back from him, and as she did, he remembered something. "Wait," he said. He thought again about that moment in the lava pool, the pulling of the sword, the feel of the Princess's hands upon his.... *The Princess's hands.*

He looked at Maria. Now that he thought about it, she even looked a bit like the Princess. At this point, he didn't even question the coincidence. He just knew he had to go with it. He said, "Maria, would you hold the stone with me?"

"Me? Why, yes..." Her mother got up and moved back, and Maria took her place on the chair by the side of the bed. She reached over and grasped Dom's hand, and he moved the Star-Stone so that it touched both their palms simultaneously.

The gem exploded with light, blinding both of them. When they could see again, they were somewhere else.

****

Co-Commander Jeremiah Dark was back in his chair in the Station Command center. Through the view screen, he could see the distorted shape of the *Filimal*. It looked more "smeared" now to him than it had when he had left to go to Margaret's room. It no longer was the graceful, airy craft it had been. Now it resembled nothing so much as a bloated, spiky sea urchin, its spines stretching out in four directions around a venomous, glaring eye. He shuddered.

He looked around at the various crewmen, both human and Vellian, attending to their tasks, various monitors and information stations occupying their attention as they tried to figure out what to do with the unfolding disaster before them. While his Co-Commander *par* Limmix had a command chair next to his, the Vellian also had his own command center in which no human was permitted, not even Dark.

This was part of the agreement made when the Vellians had helped the humans build this station. To break that agreement was to invite a shut-down of the Station itself, something the Vellians were quite capable of doing. Dark knew that "V-Com," as it was called by the humans, held advanced technology to deal with the Tarnships that the Vellians had no wish to share with humanity. He hoped that *par* Limmix was using that technology now to discover some answer to their problem.

Not knowing what else to do, he began thinking about Dominic. That was one more mystery to deal with. He knew that at some point he would have to tell *par* Limmix about the Stewart boy's appearance on board. It could hold vital information that could help the situation. But it was risky. *Par* Limmix was smart, very smart. He would investigate the phenomenon very thoroughly, and that could well lead to uncovering the Qiva operation. If so, what was happening to the *Filimal* would pale beside the political explosion that would ensue.

As if Dark's thoughts had summoned him, *par* Limmix appeared and sat down in the co-Commander's chair next to him. His head-crest drooped with bad news and agitation.

"What's the matter," Dark asked.

"The situation is worse than we believed, my friend. As you know, our monitors are more sensitive that yours. What they are telling us is very disturbing."

"Well, come on, Limmi. Just seeing what your crest is doing is alarming enough for me! Give me the bad news."

The Vellian sighed. "It's unprecedented. Whatever is happening to the *Filimal* has created a shock wave of dimensional distortion that's slowly spreading out. It grows weaker as it expands, but…."

"But what, Limmi?"

"It will be strong enough to destroy Titan Station when it reaches us."

Surprisingly, Dark felt an icy calm descend upon him. "When will it reach us, Limmi?"

"I can't say exactly. The wave front is moving irregularly. But it should strike in less than an hour."

Dark turned and stared out at the distant Tarnship, gripped in its own death-agony. *Well,* he thought, *if we go, that will solve the problem of Dominic Stewart. No one will ever know.*

****

Dominic and Maria stood in a cavern. The rock walls around them glistened with reflected heat from the lava pool at the center. In its center, as before, was a sword, shining with its own internal light. He looked down where his hand still clasped Maria's. The Star-Stone was gone. Squinting as he looked, he realized that it was back where he had first seen it, embedded in the hilt of the sword.

"We're back in the game world," he said. To his delight, Maria pressed closer to him for comfort as she looked around at her surroundings. He could feel her body trembling a bit, but whether it was from fear or from the transition into this realm, he didn't know.

"It feels so real," she whispered, sweat already beginning to bead on her forehead.

"It is real," said a familiar voice from behind them. "And it's not the game world."

Looking around, he saw the same lad that had led him and the Princess to the Star-Sword in the first place. "You!" he exclaimed. "You're responsible for this, aren't you? Who are you?"

"Like I said, a friend."

"No," said Dom, struck with a sudden hunch. "You're my great-grandfather, aren't you?"

The boy smiled. "Got it in one. Not bad, great-grandson."

"But you're just a kid!"

The boy chuckled. "Sweet sixteen. But I'm older than I look. This is how old I was when I first drew the Star-Sword."

"You came to this cavern?"

"Well, no. But you're not equipped to go where I went, not yet anyway. You have some training ahead of you to do that. But fortunately, having drawn it, I can bring the Star-Sword where I want. In a way, it's part of me now, as it will be for you if you're successful."

"But where are you now," asked Maria, getting over the double shock of the transition and meeting the legendary Webster Graham. "The story is that you disappeared, leaving only the Star-Stone behind. Where did you go?"

"Ah, welcome, my dear. It's good to see you! I'm glad my great-grandson figured it out and brought you along." He bowed to her. "As for where I went and where I am, well, I'm afraid that's a longer story than we have time for. You see, things haven't gone exactly as planned—do they ever?—so unless we move quickly, you're all going to die. That would be a pity. It's taken me many years to set all this up. I'd hate to have to start over."

"Die! What do you mean?"

"There's a transdimensional shock wave heading towards the space station you're on. If it hits, the Station won't survive. Unfortunately, neither will you."

"But…"

"There's no time for buts, my boy. If you succeed, you'll understand. If you don't, it won't matter."

"I need to cross the lava and draw the sword again, right?"

"Got it in one again. Guess my granddaughter raised you right! But it's not lava. That's just what it looks like, the way your mind conceives it in this place."

"So what is it?"

"Life. Information. Knowledge. It's everything a star is and knows. The Sword is merely a symbol of your ability to have a relationship to it. Think of it as a library card giving you access to the largest library in the universe. You don't have to hold all the knowledge. That's more than any human mind or heart can encompass, at least at our present state of evolution. But you can hold the connection. And if you do, you will become a starshaman. That's what I am."

"A starshaman?"

"That's my term for it. The Vellians call it *Tarnshem*, one who holds the heart of a star within himself. Or herself in your case, Maria. Other races have their own terms for it, and there are many other races in the universe."

"Me? But I'm not the One. I'm not here to draw the Star-Sword."

"Yes, Maria, you are," said Dom. "Remember what I told you about the game. I couldn't pull the sword without the help of the Princess. And the Star-Stone didn't work if just I held it. It needed both of us."

"That's right, Maria. I really should have told my son to keep the stone for the Two, but I think that would have confused him!" He smiled. "I think you have thirty minutes left, now. Are we done talking?"

"All right." He turned to Maria. "We need to cross the lava pool, which we can do by keeping our hearts light and our eyes on the goal, not on the danger," he said, quoting the clues he'd been given in the game. "Then we draw the Star-Sword together." He looked to his great-grandfather. "Is this right?"

The boy nodded. "That's how the game put it. The reality is this. Joy is the language of the stars. For them to see you and know you and draw you into their life, you must come to them with joy. And you want to focus on your own sovereignty, your own identity. You have to hold the heart of the star but you have to hold your own heart as well."

"How do we do this," Maria asked. "Please. I wasn't in the game!"

"By being joyous about yourself," the boy said. He paused. "And now we're down to twenty-five minutes."

The two of them immediately turned and approached the lava pit. "Are you ready?" he asked her as they stood on the lip of the pit. "Are you thinking of joyous things?"

She smiled up at him. "Yes. And Dom....you're one of them." She squeezed his hand, and his heart leapt. In that moment, he realized that having her there made his heart lift, too. "Ditto," he replied. "You make me joyous, too."

Together they stepped onto the lava.

****

Catheryn started dumbfounded at the empty chair and bed where a moment before her daughter and Margaret's son had been. There had been a burst of light as the Star-Stone flared up when the two of them touched it. Then they had gone, where she had no clue. *Surely not back to the Filimal,* she thought.

She reached for her communicator. Jeremiah had to know about this, whatever else was going on. She called him on their private number, and a moment later he answered.

"Yes?" His tone was formal and clipped, so she knew he wasn't alone. Most likely *par* Limmix, his Co-Commander, was with him. He would not be able to enter into any personal discussion.

"Commander," she said, returning the formality in case the Vellian could overhear. "I need to report that the item we were concerned with has disappeared and another item with it."

"Are you sure," he asked. "Could there be a mistake in inventory?"

"No. They have vanished. Has anything happened or changed at your end?"

Dark didn't answer immediately. She heard voices but couldn't make out what they were saying. Then he was speaking softly and urgently to her. "I excused myself to wander around the Command Center to look at monitors. I don't think Limmi can hear me as I move; frankly, I don't think he's interested. Our emergency here just turned worse."

"What happened?"

"Apparently a shock wave is approaching the Station from the *Filimal*. We probably won't survive the encounter."

She drew a breath. "This time *your* emergency is definitely bigger than mine! Are you sure?"

"Yes. I'm sorry. Did you mean that Dominic and Maria have disappeared?"

"They held the Star-Stone and vanished. Where, I have no idea. But I hope it was to get help. There's some other power involved in all this, Jeremiah. I'm sure of it."

"Well, let's hope you're right. We have twenty minutes at most before we're smeared like the *Filimal*. Wherever they've gone and whatever they're doing, I hope they're not dawdling!"

****

This time it was nothing like the game. There was no heat, no sensation of burning, no blinding light. Instead, there was.... He struggled to find a word for it. *Immensity,* he thought. *That's what it is. Immensity.* He was stepping into the mind of a star, the sun of his solar system. *It's like stepping into the largest room in the world.* But that wasn't quite it. *It's a room connected to other similar rooms.* The sun was in touch with other stars, part of an incomprehensibly vast community of life and consciousness. *It's Tarn!* he thought.

The sheer spaciousness and fullness of it surrounded him, pulled at him. He felt his mind, his whole identity would dissolve in its immensity as surely as his body would dissolve in lava.

How can I occupy an infinite mansion of infinite rooms?

<You don't have to be a big room. You just have to be a room.> It was the same voice he'd heard on the Tarnship. He realized now it was the voice of the star that was his world's sun. "What do you mean?" There was no reply.

Be a room? It was getting increasingly harder to stand in the power of this place. He knew he had to do something soon or he would be lost. But *"be a room?" What did this mean?*

He felt overwhelmed. *I'm going to die here,* he thought, and fear coursed through him. His sense of joy wavered, and he felt the immensity of the starmind pressing in on him, threatening to crush him. *No! I don't want to die!*

<**Why not?**> the star voice asked.

Because...because my life is precious to me. It's my life....

And then he knew. Life wasn't measured by size. He might be small compared to a star, but his mind, his heart, his whole life was just as valuable to creation. As his great-grandfather had told Maria, he had to be joyous about himself. He didn't have to become a bigger room. He already was a room, the right size room for who and what he was as a human being. If he honored the room he was, then the mansion would honor him as well. He just had to be part of the mansion. He had to connect.

But how do I connect with a mansion where all the rooms are stars?

<**By being a star,**> the voice said. And in his mind, he realized he was a star, a human star. He radiated ideas, feelings, actions, visions, dreams, all the things that added to the rich texture of human life. He had the power to generate joy, to generate love, to generate friendship, to radiate compassion and understanding. Like a star, he could bring light to others if he chose.

In that moment, he felt his Starheart begin to open.

He realized that he was standing next to the Star-Sword, and Maria was beside him, the glow in her eyes showing that her Starheart was opening, too. He placed his hand upon the hilt and Maria did the same, their hands together gripping the sword. They pulled.

Nothing happened.

It worked in the game, Dom thought. *Why isn't it working here? Because this isn't like the game. We're not really pulling a sword. What are we doing, then?*

"Dom," said Maria. "Your grandfather said that to hold a star's heart, we had to hold our own. I understood that. But I think there's more to it. We can't fully see our own selves, and we can't hold or honor what we can't see. We need another to see what we cannot and hold it for us. It takes another to see our Starheart in ways we can't and call it forth. We have to pull the Star-Sword out for each other."

As she said it, he knew it was true. He opened his mind and heart to her and looked deeply into her as she did the same to him. And in that moment, he saw her. He saw all her strengths, all her weaknesses, all her virtues, and all her faults. He saw it all and he held it and honored it without judgment, without fear, but with love as if it were his own. And he could feel her doing the same for him.

Their Starhearts opened.

"I *see* you," he said.

"I *see* you," she replied.

The Star-Sword came free, and they were lifted into Tarn, the life and thought of the stars.

****

Catheryn Raveneye made her way up to the Command Center. If she was going to die, she wanted to do it in the company of her friend and fellow Qiva member. Once or twice, a crewman thought to stop her or question where she was going, but when they saw the determination in her eyes and bearing, they thought better of it. If Co-Commander Dark didn't want her in Command, they reasoned, he could deal with her.

As it turned out, he very much wanted her in Command. *Par* Limmix had left to be with his people in V-Com, and Dark had been feeling alone, even though he was surrounded by an increasingly somber command crew.

"Are you all right," he asked Catheryn as she came up and stood by his chair.

"I've been better. This isn't how I'd planned to spend....what is this, Christmas Eve still or Christmas Day?" She wrapped her arm around his.

"I suppose it depends on what part of Earth you're setting your clock by."

They stood silently for a moment, then he asked, "Dominic and Maria...they never came back?"

"No. I can only hope now that wherever they are, they are safe."

Dark nodded. His communicator beeped. Taking it out, he saw it was a text message from his co-commander. It said: **SHOCK WAVE STOPPED, REVERSING. STATION SAFE.** *Filimal* **CHANGING. STAYING HERE TO MONITOR.**

"Well, I'll be damned," he said. "And just in the nick!"

"What's happened, Jeremiah. Tell me!"

He laughed and gave her a hug. "Our minutes were numbered, but the number's just gotten larger. In fact, it's disappeared!"

"What?"

"The shock wave has stopped. We're safe!" He laughed again as the tension drained from his body. "Maybe the kids got help after all."

They waited, then, in silence, staring at the *Filimal* through the viewscreen. "Limmi said the Tarnship was changing, but he didn't say how. I can't see any difference, but he has more powerful instruments than I do here."

"Jeremiah!" Catheryn gripped his arm. "Look there. By the pearl at the center. What are those bright specks?"

"Magnify," Dark ordered. "Let's see what's happening." The view on the monitor swept in towards the Tarnship as if they were traveling towards it at high speed. In a moment the *Filimal* was swelling in size and filling the screen.

"Oh my God," said Catheryn. "Are you seeing what I'm seeing?"

The monitor showed two people, a man and a woman, floating unprotected in space, surrounded by a silvery radiance. In their hands, they held rods of light that they were plunging into the central sphere of the Tarnship. As they did, the sphere began to glow with a steady light. Before their astonished eyes, the *Filimal* began to unsmear. There was no other word for it. Slowly but with increasing speed, it began to resume its original shape.

"Catheryn, are those...."

"Yes. That's Maria and Dominic!"

****

Maria was using her new-found power to disperse and drive off the last of the dark thing that they'd found apparently feasting on the energies of the Tarnship. It was, their new star-born knowledge told them, a blob of sentient energy formed by a dimensional distortion, like an eddy in a river that had achieved a semblance of life and become able to move independently in the water. It had become bloated and swollen, expanding towards Titan Station. They had both seen that if it reached the Station, the latter would be destroyed.

As it turned out, it was easy to disperse as they wielded swords forged of star energy. So Maria took on the task of removing it while he focused on restoring life and consciousness to the Tarnship.

Now Dom floated over the *Filimal*. His star-brother, Earth's own Sun, thought of him as protected, and he was. Vacuum could not harm him. From his star-heart, he projected a rod of living power into the starmind in the central sphere of the Tarnship, which he now knew was a part of the life of the star that shone in the Vellian's home system. *A piece of star-thought in every Tarnship,* he thought. *That's how they travel.*

It was perfectly clear to him. Tarn-space was the thought-life of the stars, and *Tarnshems* were men and women who had awakened their own Starheart as he had and thus could commune with that life. When a Tarnship traveled, the *Tarnshems* would awaken the starmind within the ship, and it would see and remember everything, every atom, every molecule, every person, within the ship. The ship became a thought held in the mind of a star, a thought passed from star to star until they reached the star of their destination. This presence would then *remember* them, turning the thought from an idea back into physical reality.

The Vellians traveled by "conversation power," measuring interstellar distance not by light-years but by star- relationships.

"Come, my friend," he said to the starmind within the *Filimal*. "It's time to live and remember again." For that's all that smearing was, a starmind that had forgotten, releasing the bonds that held the Tarnship together, it's memory of the ship becoming fainter and fainter until finally it faded away altogether and the starmind returned to the star that was its source. As he drew near the sphere where the starmind was held, a beam of energy like a rod of light shot out from his own Starheart, stimulating the starmind back to consciousness, back to memory and life. Slowly the *Filimal* began to come back together and take on more solidity. Resuming its normal shape. And inside, all aboard were restored as well as the ship's starmind remembered them. Including, Dom knew, his own parents who fortunately had been seen and known by *Filimal* before the accident occurred. Otherwise, they would have been lost forever.

"It was deliberate, you know." Dom looked over his shoulder and saw his great-grandfather floating in space beside him, still looking like a sixteen year old.

"What do you mean?"

"The stars did this. It was a conspiracy. Of course, it hit a few unexpected bumps."

"The stars caused the *Filimal* to smear? Why"

He smiled affectionately. "To make you appear, Starshaman."

"Me? How did the stars know about me?"

"I told them. My body is a long way away, but I'm still able to keep track of my kin now and again. The stars help me."

"You knew I was the One?"

"Actually, one half of the Two." He winked, and gestured at Maria who was floating over to add her energy to that of his in re-stimulating the *Filimal* starmind. "But no, I didn't know. I hoped. So I arranged a test to find out."

"You changed Sukai's fantasy game."

"Bingo! It was easy to do. *Alarte* is like a hallway leading to Tarn-space, just as what Maria calls Metaspace is an anteroom to *alarte*. It's all connected, you see. Your games take place in a mindspace; it was easy to manipulate."

"You wanted to see if I would do what you did."

"Yes. And you passed. That's when I—and my starbrother, the Sun—knew that you were the one, the descendent I'd known would be born one day. It was time to create a crisis to stimulate your awakening."

"You caused the *Filimal* to smear?"

"Me? No. The stars simply asked the Tarnship starmind to feign a bit of amnesia, so to speak, forgetting you all. What we hadn't counted on was that thing Maria has so expeditiously cleaned up. It took advantage of the situation to attack and feed. That drove the ship's starmind into unconsciousness from shock."

As if on cue, a small cloud of darkness drifted between them. A bolt of light shot out from Dom's great-grandfather and disintegrated it. He smiled and then looked back at Dom.

"We almost lost you on the *Filimal* then, but fortunately, using the link Maria had created with your mother and hers, the Being that is our sun was able to hold you and teleport you to Titan Station. But had you not been able to open your Starheart, everything would have been lost. It would have been a terrible setback."

"You took a risk."

"Stars often take risks. They don't see things from a human point of view, you know. They think in terms of millions and billions of years. Makes a difference. But they have one great objective. To enable all life to become star-conscious, able to enter into the realm of star-thought."

"Into Tarn."

"That's what the Vellians call it, yes. You know, they didn't come to earth on their own, the Vellians. They were assigned to come here by their own star at the request of our own." He smiled. "I had a little bit to do with that."

Dom snorted. "They haven't been all that helpful. Their Tarnships never come to Earth and they never allowed any of us on board any of their ships."

"For your protection and theirs. Being on a Tarn ship can be very dangerous for an unprepared mind, one that has yet to experience star-consciousness or has an inkling of its own Starheart. The Vellians call it being 'Tarn-blind.' As for coming to Earth, Tarnships exert a strong presence. They can stir things up that are better left unstirred. Things like what Maria has been removing. Unfortunately, there's a lot of them around Earth. There often are around primitive planets. So it was better to stay away."

"They could have shared something with us, even if only the smallest part of their technology."

"Prime Directive, great-grandson. Don't mess with the evolution of primitives."

"But they could have told us about Tarn instead of keeping it such a mystery!"

"No. Same reason. Besides, each species has to develop its own star-consciousness, attuned to its own parent sun. Tarn for humans is not quite the same as Tarn for Vellians." He sighed. "I found my Starheart out of danger and necessity, and after I did, I tried to develop a way of spreading the knowledge and skills among others. I started an association that I called the Qiva, but the job proved too much. Humankind really wasn't ready."

"Is that why you disappeared?"

"No. That was....something else. But it is why I asked the stars to send guardians for Earth. They sent the Vellians."

"Guardians? From what?"

"You'll find out one day, great-grandson, just as I did. Don't be eager for the experience. The stars are our allies, but there are other powers at work in the depths of space that are not so...friendly."

****

"And then he said goodbye."

"That was it? That's all he said," asked his mother.

"He said it was enough for now."

"He didn't say where he was or what he was doing..." his mother continued.

"Or what had happened to him?" asked his father.

Dom shook his head. They were all assembled in the large lounge of *jin* Portak and *jina* Sardel's suite on the *Filimal*. Around him sat his mother and father, Sukai and his mother and father, the two Co-Commanders of Titan Station, Catheryn Raveneye, and, next to him, Maria White Feather. He and Maria had been regaling them with the story of what had happened and how they had come to be as they were.

"This is an astounding story," said Jeremiah Dark. "Frankly, I would have a hard time believing it if the two of you weren't living proof."

"And it's good I didn't know about this Qiva of yours, otherwise there could have been trouble," said *jin* Portak. "Now, though, I can see the stars' purposes behind it. Still, it was an amazing coincidence that it worked out as it did. It seems that having you here, Co-Commander Dark, was vital to the enterprise."

"It was no coincidence," said Dom. "Great-grandfather said he had arranged it."

"Really?" said Catheryn. "I always wondered how it had worked out. I thought you had done it, Adrian."

"I thought *I'd* done it on the merit of being an outstanding commander," Dark said, and everyone laughed.

"I'm sure that's true, too," said Adrian. "But once it happened, we all felt it was a chance to, well, do what we did."

"A little spying," said *jin* Portak, frowning.

Adrian smiled. "We called it information-gathering."

"So what now?" asked Maria. "You've heard our story. Does it change anything? Are Margaret and Adrian still going to Vella?"

There was a silence. Then, *jin* Portak said simply. "No. We're not going to Vella."

"No?" said Adrian. "But Dom explained...."

Jin Portak held up his hand for silence. "You do not understand. Dom and Maria are now *Tarnshem*. You have awakened your Starhearts.

What two can learn, others can learn, too. I think that is our work, now, with the help of your Qiva."

"Of course," Margaret said.

"We shall have to report this to the *Jintal*, our governing council, of course," *jin* Portak continued. "I guarantee this will change everything." He reached over and took his wife's hand. "In the meantime, I take it upon myself to give us a new destination. I think I have my wife's agreement." *Jina* Sardel smiled and nodded. He paused.

"Where are we going, then, Father," Sukai asked.

"I believe it's time this Tarnship went to Earth!"

THE END